DOC ARDAN

The Abominable Snowman
and Other Tales from the Archives of the *Société Secrète des Aventuriers*

IN THE SAME SERIES

Doc Ardan: The City of Gold and Lepers
*Doc Ardan: The Troglodytes of Mount Everest * The Giants of Black Lake*

also translated and adapted by J.-M. & R. Lofficier:
* *by Marc Agapit*: Despair (*screenplay*)
* *by G.-J. Arnaud*: The Ice Company
* *by Arnould Galopin*: Doctor Omega; The Man in Grey
* *by Jean de La Hire*: The Nyctalope Steps In; Night of the Nyctalope
* *by Maurice Leblanc*: Arsène Lupin vs. Sherlock Holmes: 1. The Hollow Needle; 2. The Blonde Phantom; Arsène Lupin vs. Countess Cagliostro; Arsène Lupin: The Island of the Thirty Coffins; Arsène Lupin: 813
* *by Gaston Leroux*: The Phantom of the Opera; Rouletabille and the Mystery of the Yellow Room

The Abominable Snowman
and Other Tales from the Archives of the Société Secrète des Aventuriers

by
Guy d'Armen
adapted and retold in English by
Jean-Marc & Randy Lofficier

With additional stories by
Jason Scott Aiken, Christopher Paul Carey, Matthew Dennion, Win Scott Eckert, Peter Gabbani, Travis Hiltz, Vincent Jounieaux, Rick Lai, Jean-Marc Lofficier and **John Peel**

A Black Coat Press Book

Acknowledgements: Guy Costes, Win Scott Eckert, Rick Lai.

English adaptation, introduction & bibliography Copyright © 2016 by Jean-Marc & Randy Lofficier.
Individual stories Copyright © 2016 by their respective authors.
Cover illustration Copyright © 2016 by Vincent Laik.

Visit our website at www.blackcoatpress.com

ISBN 978-1-61227-564-2. First Printing. November 2016. Published by Black Coat Press, an imprint of Hollywood Comics.com, LLC, P.O. Box 17270, Encino, CA 91416. All rights reserved. Except for review purposes, no part of this book may be reproduced or transmitted in any form or by any means, electronic or mechanical, including photocopying, recording or by any information storage and retrieval system, without permission in writing from the publisher. The stories and characters depicted in this novel are entirely fictional. Printed in the United States of America.

TABLE OF CONTENTS

Before the Bronze Age 7
Additional Bibliography 17
Guy d'Armen: *From the Archives of the Société Secrète des Aventuriers* 33
   1. The Abominable Snowman... 33
   2. The Giant Bat.. 40
   3. The Vampire of the Hamada...................................... 46
   4. The Lair of the Javanese Witch-Doctor 52
Rick Lai: *The Midas Menace* 59
John Peel: *The Biggest Guns* 71
Jean-Marc Lofficier: *The Star Prince* 91
Vincent Jounieaux: *The Dreadful Conspiracy* 93
Jason Scott Aiken: *Ardan at the Pole* 121
Travis Hiltz: *Family Reunion* 137
Christopher Paul Carey & Win Scott Eckert: *Iron and Bronze* 164
Matthew Dennion: *A Scientist First and Foremost*............. 190
Peter Gabbani: *Small Dreams of a Floating City* 201
Win Scott Eckert: *The Eye of Oran* 214
Win Scott Eckert: *Les Lèvres Rouges* 236
Win Scott Eckert: *The Vanishing Devil* 261
Credits 282

Doc Ardan by Fernando Calvi

Before the Bronze Age

As readers of our two previous volumes, *The City of Gold and Lepers* and *The Trogolodytes of Mount Everest/The Giants of Black Lake*,[1] already know, there is virtually no biographical information about the writer who signed indifferently "Guy d'Armen," "Francis Annemary," and "Jacques Diamant" (as well as employing other *noms-de-plume,* but these three are the most frequent) a number of adventure novels and what turned out to be a huge number of short stories for a numner of pulp magazines such as *L'Intrépide* and *Sciences et Voyages* published in France by the Offenstadt Brothers between 1899 and 1939.

Curiously, the character of "Francis Hardant" (in French "Ardan" and "Hardant" are phonetically indistinguishable) appears only in *City of Gold and Lepers* and a few short stories, and even there, his first name seems to vary a great deal. But d'Armen's characters are all exactly the same: they are about 25, doctors or scientists of some kind, polymaths, explorers, adventurers, tall, blond, strong, brave and resourceful. They all have overbearing millionaire fathers driving them hard and absent mothers, and share the same colorful, megalomaniacal gallery of foes.

One might legitimately wonder why, instead of switching the names of his heroes, d'Armen did not reuse the same protagonist each time. Was it because the Offenstadts discouraged him from turning his stories into a single "series," fearing that readers might not follow it, or was it because of the necessity dictated by the morals of the times to marry off the hero to the heroine at the end of each novel? We will never know for certain.

---

[1] Black Coat Press ISBNs 978-1-932983-03-6 and 978-1-61227-483-6.

One of the things we did when we decided to translate *City of Gold and Lepers* for an American audience was to harmonize d'Armen's works and use the name of "Francis Ardan" throughout, and skip the marriage at the end, while tightening a few other narrative loose threads. D'Armen wrote quickly, not rereading himself before going to press, was obligated to meet a certain quota of words per chapter (or story) and chapters per novels, and occasionally contradicted himself or digressed somewhat.

But beyond this simple work of editing, we could not help notice—as was the case when we pulled Doctor Omega out of French literary limbo—that young Doctor Ardan was altogether similar to another well-known character of American pulp fiction, in this case the ever popular Clark Savage, Jr., a.k.a. Doc Savage. Hence the notion that Francis Ardan's globe-trotting exploits, which all take place in the 1920s, are, in reality, the secret exploits of a young Doc Savage, whose first recorded adventure, *The Man of Bronze*, takes place in 1931.

How does that notion withstand the scrutiny of further examination? As it happens, very well, as we shall now demonstrate in the following exercise in fictional biography, for which we are indebted to Rick Lai and Win Scott Eckert, the two most prominent experts on the life of Doc Savage.

According to all biographies, Clark "Doc" Savage Jr. was born on November 12, 1901, on the schooner *Orion* in a cove off the northern tip of Andros Island, Bahamas.

Doc's father was Clark F. (for Francis) Savage Sr., an American industrialist, explorer and amateur archeologist. Some biographers have claimed that he, too, was a doctor, and a descendent from a proud British lineage from Yorkshire; others that he was a native-born American descended from Richard Henry Savage, who had served as a Rough Rider under Theodore Roosevelt and had fought Indians in the southwestern United States.

There is also some controversy about the identity of Doc's mother. While some biographers believe her to be Arronaxe Larsen, a descendent of Wolf Larsen, Ned Land and Armand Chauvelin, investigations conducted in France by the undersigned have revealed that she might instead be Jacqueline Ardan, the granddaughter of space pioneer Michel Ardan, heir of the proud lineage of Chevalier Ardent de Rougecogne, whose exploits were chronicled by the historian François Craenhals.

Under French Law, a child may be registered by and in the name of his mother if he/she was born out of wedlock or if the marriage was not registered with the French authorities. A French birth certificate listing the baby as "Francis Clarke [sic!] Michel Ardan" born of father [left blank] and Jacqueline Gwendoline Estelle Ardan was recently located in the archives of the Mairie d'Asnières, near Paris.

The final fate of Jacqueline Ardan is still controversial. According to some, she was killed in Siberia in the summer of 1908; others claimed she drowned in 1902.

In the early 1900s, a group of wealthy members of the notorious Gun Club, led by Hareton Ironcastle,[2] became concerned about the threat posed by the Black Coats and other crime syndicates. Clark Savage Sr.—who sometimes went by the alias of "Francis Ardan Sr." to preserve his anonymity—was a member of this group. He proposed to train his son's mind and body from an early age to give him great strength, endurance, a mastery of the martial arts and vast scientific knowledge in order to fight this threat. The Gun Club agreed to fund this training.

Ardan Sr. began recruiting scientists to oversee his son's training. Unfortunately, in 1903, one of the men he hired was

---

[2] See J.-H. Rosny's *Hareton Ironcastle's Amazing Adventure* [L'Etonnant Voyage de Hareton Ironcastle] (1922) included in *The Mysterious Force*, Black Coat Press, ISBN 978-1-935558-37-8.

Dr. Howey, the leader of the gang of the Secret Raiders [3] and a high-ranking member of the Black Coats, also known as Dr. Erich Heinz Malbodius. However, his plan is to kidnap young Francis and extort a fortune from his father failed. The consequence of that failure made the Kaiser's Secret Service aware of the potential of the Ardan boy.[4]

Over the next decade, young Francis studied various disciplines with Sherlock Holmes, Arsène Lupin, Richard Wentworth, Dr. Thorndyke, Craig Kennedy, Kent Allard, Sexton Blake, Harry Houdini, and Tarzan.

In 1911, Ardan Sr. found a legendary Mayan "city of gold" in Central America and thus vastly increased his personal fortune.

In 1917, Francis enrolled at John Hopkins University as a medical student, but left soon after to fight in World War I. Upon his arrival in France, a friend of his father, the famous French explorer Léo Saint-Clair, a.k.a. The Nyctalope, introduced Francis to the *Société Secrète des Aventuriers*.[5]

---

[3] See Arthur Bernède & Louis Feuillade's *THE RETURN OF JUDEX*, Black Coat Press, ISBN 978-1-61227-159-0.
[4] See Rick Lai's "*The Midas Menace*" included in this volume.
[5] The *Société Secrète des Aventuriers* [Secret Society of Adventurers] is an exclusive French explorers club founded in 1657 by Hercule-Savinien Cyrano de Bergerac. Its prestigious roster of members has included at one time or another (in alphabetical order) Michel Ardan, Nestor Burma, Chantecoq, Robert Darvel, Sâr Dubnotal, Jérôme Fandor, Camille Flammarion, Rodolphe de Gerolstein, Antoine Gerpré, Hareton Ironcastle, Jean Kariven, Armand & Robert Lavarède, M. Lecoq, Dr. Abel Lenoir, Aurore Lescure, Arsène Lupin, Jacques Massé, Pierre de Mésange, Bob Morane, the Duc de Multipliandre, Cigale Mystère, Dr. Omega, Frédéric-Jean Orth, Rocambole, Joseph Rouletabille, Lord John Roxton, several Sainte-Claires/Saint-Clairs including Léo Saint-Clair, Hector Servadac, Jean-Pierre Severin, Jacques de Trémeuse, Jean-Louis de Venasque, Teddy Verano and others.

Ardan then joined the Lafayette Escadrille and flew many missions, especially against the notorious Rittmeister Hans Von Hammer. In March 1918, with the help of Lord John Roxton, another friend of his father and a member of the London branch of the Gun Club, and his aunt, Pamela May Thibault (who had married his uncle Alex),[6] Francis managed to destroy a super-gun the Germans were using to threaten Paris.[7]

Alas, Francis was captured by the Germans and sent to the hellish internment camp of Loki where he met his future companions, Ham Brooks, Monk Mayfair, Renny Renwick, Johnny Littlejohn, and Long Tom Roberts. Thanks to their help, he managed to escape in July.[8]

On November 11, 1918, an Armistice was signed and the Great War was over.

According to some biographers, c. 1919-20, Francis went on an expedition with his father and Hareton Ironcastle to Maple White Land in Brazil. Others have claimed that during the same period, Francis, discovering evidence that his paternal grandfather, Stormalong Savage, was marooned on Skull Island, mounted an expedition with his father to rescue their lost relative.

Between 1919 and 1926, Francis managed to earn not one, but two medical degrees, the first from John Hopkins in the U.S., and the second from the Faculté de Médecine of Paris, where he was mentored by Dr. Jules de Grandin. This feat was achieved through the mechanism obtaining "equivalencies" between the two universities, as well as by Francis' re-

---

[6] Alex appeared in Kenneth Robeson's *Brand of the Werewolf*; Pamela May Thibault, his wife, was also the aunt of Jean Thibault, the great French-Canadian secret agent codenamed "IXE-13" as well, on her mother's side, Douglas Renfrew of the Royal Northwest Mountain Police. They were the parents of Francis's cousin, Patricia, born in 1914.
[7] See John Peel's "*The Biggest Guns*" included in this volume.
[8] See Philip José Farmer's *Escape from Loki*.

markable talent which enabled him to achieve in one year what took other students two, sometimes three, years.

During one his vacations in Southern France, Francis happened to release the legendary Rose Bruyère a.k.a. the Sleeping Beauty, who went on to become the celebrated French heroine known as the Phantom Angel and a later joined the *Société Secrète des Aventuriers*.[9]

During that period, Francis was often encouraged by his father and by Dr. de Grandin to take breaks and go on exploring journeys to remote locations. Some of his adventures were dutifully reported to, and consigned in, the Archives of the *Société Secrète des Aventuriers*, which have just started to be released to the world.

One of the most perilous missions undertaken at that time took place in the Summer of 1921 when Francis and his father were exploring the remotest regions of Upper Siam (now Thailand). There, they encountered a race of artificially-created green-skinned men, the "Jade Men", who lived a recluse existence in the mysterious underground city of Inramonda, ruled by His Eternal Wisdom, the Jade Lord. With the assistance of British Archeologist Archibald MacSlaine and his daughter Margaret, the two Ardans managed to defeat the immortal villain and destroy Inramonda, but not before more treasure came flowing into the family coffers.[10]

Towards the end of 1925, as Francis was about to present his graduate thesis at the Sorbonne, he teamed up with Dr. de Grandin to defeat a sinister plan by the Oriental mastermind known as the Yellow Shadow. During this adventure, his path crossed that of the French avenging crime-fighter known as Judex. Judex's methods to rehabilitate criminals, as well as the colony set up for the same purpose on a Pacific island by fellow member of the *Société Secrète des Aventuriers*, Sâr

---

[9] See Randy Lofficier's "*The Reluctant Princess*" included in *The Trogolodytes of Mount Everest/The Giants of Black Lake*, q.v.

[10] See *The Fall of Inramonda*, to be translated.

Dubnotal, provided the inspiration for Francis' Crime College which he was to implement in 1928.[11]

The following year, 1926, Francis took a few graduate courses in Wien in the Spring then completed his medical studies from both John Hopkins and the Faculté, thus earning the title of "doctor." In the Summer, he embarked on a cruise around the world with his father, but instead was kidnapped by Captain Mendax, a science pirate who planned on ransoming him for $100 million. Mendax had built a super-powered flying craft, *The Astaroth*, and operated from a secret base at the top of Mount Everest. Francis escaped with the aid of Milarepa, a Tibetan princess, and eventually returned to destroy Mendax's base. The pirate was captured and executed by the British.[12]

A few months later, Francis retuned to Central Asia and, in an underground city, renewed his acquaintance with the Comte de Bertheville, a.k.a. Kyzyl Kaya, the "Red Wizard", a 250-year-old alchemist whom he had previously encountered in Mendax's Citadel. Using scientific secrets from pre-cataclysmic races, Kyzyl Kaya had created giant spiders and other colossal creatures and planned to conquer the world. Francis escaped and soon teamed up with Suleyma, a young Mongolian woman who had fled from an arranged marriage. They were eventually recaptured and turned into giants, but ultimately managed to defeat the Comte.[13]

In the Spring of 1927, Francis spent sometime in the UK [14] before launching himself into a new Tibetan adventure. This time, he met the diabolical Dr. Natas, master of the "City of Gold and Lepers", who also entertained plans for world domination. With the able help of Louise Ducharme, Francis was

---

[11] See Vincent Jounieaux's "*The Dreadful Conspiracy*" included in this volume.
[12] See *The Troglodytes of Mount Everest*, q.v.
[13] See *The Giants of Black Lake*, q.v.
[14] See Philip José Farmer & Win Scott Eckert's *The Evil in Pemberley House*.

able to defeat the evil mastermind and destroy his stronghold.[15]

The following year, in January 1928, at the behest of Ironcastle, Francis traveled to the Arctic and rescued fellow member of the *Société Secrète des Aventuriers* Jean-Louis de Vénasque from a strange and advanced race of reptilian humanoids. That journey, in turn, provided the inspiration to build for himself what he would call later his "Fortress of Solitude".[16]

Later that year, while working on a scientific degree at the Collège de France, Francis was asked to investigate mysterious hurricanes that perturbed maritime traffic in the French Pacific. He was able to expose and defeat the science pirate Krakatax, master of Hurricane Island. During that adventure, Francis rescued the youngest daughter of American billionaire William Dorgan, Mabel Dorgan. He was ably assisted by an operative from the Continental Detective Agency who went by the alias of "John Flash."[17]

Towards the end of 1929, Francis and Ironcastle teamed up again to thwart a scheme hatched by Queen Antinea and the villainous Harry Killer to use extraterrestrial vegetal life forms to take over the world.[18]

As the Archives of the *Société Secrète* for the years 1929 and 1930 are being released, more heretofore unknown adventures of Doctor Francis Ardan are coming to light. In addition to various exploits undertaken during his exploring journeys across the globe, we now know that Doc Ardan found a Lost

---

[15] See *The City of Gold and Lepers*, q.v.
[16] See Jason Scott Aiken's "*Ardan at the Pole*" included in this volume, and Charles Derennes' *The People of the Pole*, Black Coat Press, ISBN 978-1-934543-39-9.
[17] See *The Hurricane Master*, to be translated.
[18] See Christopher Paul Carey & Win Scott Eckert's "*Iron and Bronze*" included in this volume. Travis Hiltz' story "*Family Reunion*" tales place simultaneously.

City in Patagonia[19] and that, together with the South American adventuress Dolores Metaxas, he used the Ultra-Z rays technology he had just discovered to prevent the tyrant Demonio from taking over Venezuela.[20]

No doubt other similar exploits will be revealed in the course of time, based on the partial list of files reproduced here.

Jean-Marc Lofficier

---

[19] See *The Secret of Frigidopolis*, to be translated.
[20] See *The Ultra-Z Rays*, to be translated.

Doc Ardan by Michelle Bigot

Additional Bibliography

Previous bibliographers had not been able to systematically index the contents of magazines such as *L'Intrépide*. The major novels and a few short stories had been listed, but the vast majority of Guy d'Armen's literary output had gone unnoticed. The list below references all the stories (and *NOVELS* in *CAPS*) published in *L'Intrépide* for the years 1927 to 1935. Stories translated are marked in **bold**. Additional information will be published in future volumes if and when it becomes available.

J.-M. L.

1927 (incomplete listing): *L'Intrépide* Nos. 854-905
* 898-930 : *LE PIRATE AUX YEUX BRIDÉS* [The Pirate with Slanted Eyes] (33 chapters) (Francis Annemary) (illustrated novel)
* 899-917: *LES ONDES MYSTERIEUSES* [The Mysterious Waves] (15 chapters) (Guy d'Armen)

1928: *L'Intrépide* Nos. 906-958
[Nos. 906 to 908 missing]
* 909: *Saurien contre Pachyderme* [Saurian vs Pachyderm] (Guy d'Armen) (Explorer's Tale)
* 911: *Le Démon des îles Soulou* [The Demon of Sulu Islands] (Jacques Diamant) (Explorer's Tale)
* 912: *Homme ou singe* [Man or Ape?] (Guy d'Armen) (Explorer's Tale)
* 913: *En Visitant les tombeaux des Rois de Golconde* [Visiting the Tombs of the King of Golconda] (Guy d'Armen) (Explorer's Tale)
* 914: *Le Moulin à prières* [The Prayer Wheel] (Guy d'Armen) (Explorer's Tale)

* 917: *Scènes de Cannibalisme aux îles Solomon* [The Cannibals of the Solomon Islands] (Guy d'Armen) (Explorer's Tale)
* 919: *Le Python du Sahara* [The Python of Sahara] (Guy d'Armen) (Explorer's Tale)
* 920: *Au Flanc du cratère du diable* [On the Flanks of Devil's Crater] (Guy d'Armen) (Explorer's Tale)
* 921: *Le Sac de cailloux* [A Bag of Pebbles] (Guy d'Armen) (Explorer's Tale)
* 922: *Cernés par les éléphants* [Surrounded by Elephants] (Guy d'Armen) (Explorer's Tale)
* 924: *L'Aventure du Professeur Mendax* [An Adventure of Professor Mendax] (Guy d'Armen) (Explorer's Tale)
* 925: *Une Désagréable surprise* [A Disagreeable Surprise] (Guy d'Armen) (Explorer's Tale)
* 929: *La Prisonnière du Hoggar* [A Woman Trapped in the Hoggar] (Guy d'Armen) (Explorer's Tale)
* 931: *Sur les Pentes du Rovenzori* [On the Slopes of the Rovenzori] (Guy d'Armen) (Explorer's Tale)
* 934: *En Dérive sur un Iceberg* [Stranded on an Iceberg] (Guy d'Armen) (Explorer's Tale)
* 935: *La Panthère qui parle* [The Talking Panther] (Guy d'Armen) (Explorer's Tale)
* 936: *La Traversée de l'Atlantique en tonneau* [Crossing the Atlantic in a Barrel] (Guy d'Armen) (Explorer's Tale)
* 940: *Les Sacrifices humains du Ghonduana* [The Human Sacrifices of Gondwana] (Guy d'Armen) (Explorer's Tale)
* 949: *Nuit d'épouvante* [Night of Terror] (Guy d'Armen) (Explorer's Tale)
* 951: *Au Fond de la vallée de l'agonie* [At the Bottom of the Valley of Agony] (Guy d'Armen) (Explorer's Tale)
* 955: *Dans la Vallée supérieure de l'Amazonie* [In the Upper Vallrey of the Amazon] (Guy d'Armen) (Explorer's Tale)
* 956: *Minutes d'épouvante* [Minutes of Terror] (Guy d'Armen) (Explorer's Tale)
* 957: *Quinze heures d'angoisse* [Fifteen Hours of Terror] (Guy d'Armen) (Explorer's Tale)

* 958: *L'Aventure de Jacques Longueteau* [Jacques Longueteau's Adventure] (Guy d'Armen) (Explorer's Tale)

* *Sciences et Voyages*, Nos. 453-479 : *LA CITE DE L'OR ET DE LA LEPRE* [The City of Gold and Lepers] (Guy d'Armen)

1929 (incomplete listing): *L'Intrépide* Nos. 959-1010
* 961-985: *LES TROGLODYTES DU MONT EVEREST* [The Troglodytes of Mount Everest] (25 chapters) (Guy d'Armen)
* 974-1031: *LE MOUSSE DE* LA MÉDUSE [The Cabin Boy of the *Medusa*] (58 chapters) (Francis Annemary) (illustrated historical novel)
* 988: *L'Effroyable Aventure de Nam-Bou* [Nam-Bou's Terrifying Adventure]

1930: *L'Intrépide* Nos. 1011-1062
* 1012: *Aux prises avec une panthère* [Tackling a Panther] (Guy d'Armen) (Explorer's Tale)
* 1013: *L'Attaque du barrage* [The Attack of the Dam] (Guy d'Armen) (Explorer's Tale)
* 1015: *Dans la tourmente polaire* [Inside a Polar Storm] (Guy d'Armen) (Explorer's Tale)
* 1016: *Au cœur de la Sibérie* [In the Heart of Siberia] (Guy d'Armen) (Explorer's Tale)
* 1016-1049: *L'ONDE INFERNALE* [The Deadly Wave] (34 Chapters) (Guy d'Armen) (illustrated novel)
* 1016: *Les Compagnons du tigre* [The Companions of the Tiger] (Guy d'Armen) (Explorer's Tale)
* 1017: *L'Antre du sorcier javanais* [The Lair of the Javanese Witch-doctor] (Guy d'Armen) (Explorer's Tale)
* 1018: *Les Boucaneurs de têtes* [The Head-Shrinkers] (Guy d'Armen) (Explorer's Tale)
* 1018: *Supplice d'antan chez les Bhils* [A Torture from the Bhils] (Jacques Diamant) (Explorer's Tale)

* 1021: *Une Heure dans un tombeau* [An Hour Inside a Tomb] (Guy d'Armen) (Explorer's Tale)
* 1021: *Une Ascension en ballon libre* [A Climb in a Balloon] (Guy d'Armen) (Explorer's Tale)
* 1023: *Au Fond d'un tonneau* [The Bottom of the Barrel] (Guy d'Armen) (Explorer's Tale)
* 1024: *Dans les fourrés de la savane* [In the Bushes of the Savana] (Guy d'Armen) (Explorer's Tale)
* 1025: *Au-dessus du gouffre* [Above the Abyss] (Francis Annemary) (Explorer's Tale)
* 1026: *Dans les Crevasses du Chimborazo* [Inside the Cracks of the Chimborazo] (Francis Annemary) (Explorer's Tale)
* 1027: *Le Mystère du cirque du dragon* [The Mystery of the Dragon Circus] (Guy d'Armen) (Explorer's Tale)
* 1028: *Le Cirque de la faim* [The Circus of Starvation] (Guy d'Armen) (Explorer's Tale)
* 1029: *Sur les rives du Gange* [On the Banks of the Ganges] (Francis Annemary) (Explorer's Tale)
* 1030: *Le Voleur de chevaux* [The Horse Thief] (Jacques Diamant) (Explorer's Tale)
* 1032-1081: *LE SECRET DE L'ARAIGNÉE DE FER* [The Secret of the Iron Spider] (50 chapters) (Jacques Diamant) (illustrated historical novel)
* 1032: *Sur les hauts plateaux de l'Angola* [On the High Plains of Angola] (Jacques Diamant) (Explorer's Tale)
* 1033: *L'Antre des Çabann* [The Lair of the Çabann] (Guy d'Armen) (Explorer's Tale)
* 1035: *L'Orang-Outang de Bornéo* [The Orangutan of Borneo] (Jacques Diamant) (Explorer's Tale)
* 1039: *Au large des Îles Marquises* [In the Waters of the Marquesas Islands] (Francis Annemary) (Explorer's Tale)
* 1041: *Dans le Haut Oubanghi* [In Upper Ubangi] (Francis Annemary) (Explorer's Tale)
* 1042: *Un Terrible duel avec un ours* [Dreadful Fight with a Bear] (Francis Annemary) (Explorer's Tale)
* 1043: *Le Mystère de la fosse aux tigres* [The Mystery of the Tiger Pit] (Francis Annemary) (Explorer's Tale)

* 1044: *La Catastrophe du Kraal* [The Kraal Catastrophe] (Francis Annemary) (Explorer's Tale)
* 1045: *La Sieste interrompue* [An Interrupted Nap] (Francis Annemary) (Explorer's Tale)
* 1046: *Aux prises avec les boeufs sauvages* [Tackling the Wild Oxen] (Francis Annemary) (Explorer's Tale)
* 1046: *En sous-marin* [Inside a Submarine] (Jacques Diamant) (Explorer's Tale)
* 1047: *Sur les bords de l'Ogoué* [On the Banks of the Ogoue] (Francis Annemary) (Explorer's Tale)
* 1048: *Une Chasse à la baleine* [On a Whale Hunt] (Francis Annemary) (Explorer's Tale)
* 1049: *Un Effroyable combat* [A Frightful Battle] (Guy d'Armen) (Explorer's Tale)
* 1050: *Un Singulier mécanicien* [A Strange Mechanic] (Francis Annemary) (Explorer's Tale)
* **1051: *L'Homme des neiges* [The Abominable Snowman] (Guy d'Armen) (Explorer's Tale)**
* 1053: *Le Mystère du puits de Tamellah* [The Mystery of the Well of Tamellah] (Guy d'Armen) (Explorer's Tale)
* 1054: *Le Monstre du Lagon* [The Lagoon Monster] (Jacques Diamant) (Explorer's Tale)
* 1055: *A Bride abattue* [The Wild Ride] (Guy d'Armen) (Explorer's Tale)
* 1056: *Trois heures au fond d'une fosse* [Three Hours at the Bottom of a Pit] (Guy d'Armen) (Explorer's Tale)
* 1057: *Dans la vallée du Mouroussou* [In the Mouroussou Valley] (Guy d'Armen) (Explorer's Tale)
* 1059: *Une Aventure dans le Népaul* [A Nepalese Adventure] (Guy d'Armen) (Explorer's Tale)
* 1060: *Le Tireur aux balles d'or* [The Shooter with Golden Bullets] (Francis Annemary) (Explorer's Tale)
* 1061: *Douze heures d'angoisse* [Twelve Hours of Terror] (Guy d'Armen) (Explorer's Tale)
* 1062: *Une Chasse au Gaur* [A Gaur Hunt] (Francis Annemary) (Explorer's Tale)

1931: *L'Intrépide* Nos. 1063-1114
* **1065-1089: *LES GÉANTS DU LAC NOIR* [The Giants of Black Lake] (25 chapters) (Guy d'Armen)**
* 1066: *L'Indésirable passager* [The Undesirable Passenger] (Francis Annemary) (Explorer's Tale)
* 1067: *Dans les souterrains de T'aoudeni* [In the Underground Tunnels of T'aoudeni] (Francis Annemary) (Explorer's Tale)
* 1068: *Dans les roselières du lac Bangouelo* [In the Marshes of Lake Bangouelo] (Francis Annemary) (Explorer's Tale)
* 1069: *Le Temple des Supplices* [The Temple of Tortures] (Francis Annemary) (Explorer's Tale)
* 1073: *La Caverne des Aigles* [The Eagles' Cave] (Francis Annemary) (Explorer's Tale)
* 1075: *Dans les Ruines de Tekout* [In the Ruins of Tekut] (Francis Annemary) (Explorer's Tale)
* 1076: *Trois heures d'angoisses* [Three Hours of Terror] (Francis Annemary) (Explorer's Tale)
* 1077: *Le Sonneur de cloches* [The Bell Ringer] (Francis Annemary) (Explorer's Tale)
* 1079: *Sous la tente tartare* [Inside a Tartar's Tent] (Francis Annemary) (Explorer's Tale)
* 1080: *L'Aventure de Robert Fourcade* [Robert Fourcade's Adventure] (Francis Annemary) (Explorer's Tale)
* 1081: *La Capture d'un fauve* [Capturing a Wild Beast] (Francis Annemary) (Explorer's Tale)
* 1082: *La Course à la mort* [Death Race] (Francis Annemary) (Explorer's Tale)
* 1083: *Une Singulière révélation* [A Strange Revelation] (Francis Annemary) (Explorer's Tale)
* 1083: *Les Loups Aveugles* [The Blind Wolves] (Jacques Diamant) (Explorer's Tale)
* 1084: *Le Prisonnier de Samory* [Samory's Prisoner] (Jacques Diamant) (Explorer's Tale)
* 1084: *Aux prises avec les ours du Cachemire* [Tackling the Bears of Kashmir] (Francis Annemary) (Explorer's Tale)

* 1085: *Curieux combat au cœur de l'Afrique centrale* [Strange Fight in the Heart of Central Africa] (Jacques Diamant) (Explorer's Tale)
* 1086: *Le Serpent dans le Stradivarius* [The Snake in the Stradivarius] (Francis Annemary) (Explorer's Tale)
* 1087: *Poursuivi par un solitaire* [Hunted by a Lone Elephant] (Francis Annemary) (Explorer's Tale)
* 1087: *Une Chasse au Kong-Min* [A Hunt in Kong-Min] (Jacques Diamant) (Explorer's Tale)
* 1088: *Sur les Rives du Brahmapoutre* [On the Banks of the Brahmaputra] (Francis Annemary) (Explorer's Tale)
* 1089-1113: *LE SEMEUR DE CYCLONES* [The Hurricane Master] (25 chapters) (Francis Annemary/Guy d'Armen)
* 1089: *Combats dans la jungle* [Jungle Fights] (Jacques Diamant) (Explorer's Tale)
* 1091: *Sur le Zambeze* [On the Zambeze River] (Guy d'Armen) (Explorer's Tale)
* 1092: *Une Aventure au Bengale* [A Bengali Adventure] (Guy d'Armen) (Explorer's Tale)
* 1093: *Le Gardien du temple* [The Guardian of the Temple](Guy d'Armen) (Explorer's Tale)
* 1094: *Dans le Haut-Laos* [In Upper Laos] (Guy d'Armen) (Explorer's Tale)
* 1095: *Prisonnier des Cercopithèques* [Prisoners of the Cercopitheques] (Guy d'Armen) (Explorer's Tale)
* 1097: *Dans la Haute Amazonie* [In the Upper Amazon] (Guy d'Armen) (Explorer's Tale)
* 1098: *En tournant dans l'Ouganda* [A Turn in Uganda] (Guy d'Armen) (Explorer's Tale)
* 1099: *Minutes d'angoisse* [Minutes of Terror] (Guy d'Armen) (Explorer's Tale)
* 1100: *Une Panne sur le Niger* [Breakdown on the Niger] (Guy d'Armen) (Explorer's Tale)
* 1101: *Sur le Plateau du Matto-Grosso* [On the Plains of the Mato Grosso] (Francis Annemary) (Explorer's Tale)
* 1103: *Dans la passe de Khyber* [In the Khyber Pass] (Francis Annemary) (Explorer's Tale)

* 1104: *Dans le Temple de Kampa Dzong* [In the Temple of Kampa Dzong] (Francis Annemary) (Explorer's Tale)
* 1105: *Bataille dans un camion* [Truck Fight] (Francis Annemary) (Explorer's Tale)
* 1107: *L'Effroyable combat* [The Frightful Battle] (Francis Annemary) (Explorer's Tale)
* 1108: *La Lettre* [The Letter] (Jacques Diamant) (Explorer's Tale)
* 1109: *Pendant un Vol à voile* [During a Flight] (Jacques Diamant) (Explorer's Tale)
* 1110: *La Tragédie de Berberah* [The Tragedy of Berberah] (Francis Annemary) (Explorer's Tale)
* 1100: *Une Aventure en Tartarie* [A Tartar Adventure] (Jacques Diamant) (Explorer's Tale)
* 1111: *La Tragique aventure de Marion* [Marion's Tragic Adventure] (Francis Annemary) (Explorer's Tale)
* 1113-1137: *LES RAYONS ULTRA-Z* [The Ultra-Z Rays] (25 chapters) (Guy d'Armen)
* 1114: *L'Attaque du Bordj* [The Attack of the Bordj] (Jacques Diamant) (Explorer's Tale)

1932: *L'Intrépide* Nos. 1115-1166
* 1115: *Le Cirque des Ourann* [The Circus of the Ourann] (Francis Annemary) (Explorer's Tale)
* 1117: *L'Attaque dans la Montagne* [The Mountain Attack] (Jacques Diamant) (Explorer's Tale)
* 1117: *A coups de harpon* [A Harpoon Fight] (Francis Annemary) (Explorer's Tale)
* 1118: *Dans les Montagnes du Kouen-Lun* [In the Mountains of Kwen Lun] (Francis Annemary) (Explorer's Tale)
* 1119: *Le Dernier voyage de Cook* [Cook's Last Voyage] (Francis Annemary) (Historical)
* 1120: *Dans la Jungle de Birmanie* [In the Burmese Jungle] (Jacques Diamant) (Explorer's Tale)
* 1121: *Dans les rapides du Niger* [On the Niger's Rapids] (Francis Annemary) (Explorer's Tale)

* 1122: *Sur les Berges du Congo* [On the Banks of the Congo] (Jacques Diamant) (Explorer's Tale)
* 1123: *Le Voyage du Capitaine Speke vers les Sources du Nil* [The Journey of Captain Speke Towards the Source of the Nile] (Francis Annemary) (Historical)
* **1123: *Le Vampire de la Caverne* [The Giant Bat] (Jacques Diamant) (Explorer's Tale)**
* 1124: *Le Voyage du Hollandais Schouten* [The Voyage of Dutchman Schouten] (Jacques Diamant) (Historical)
* 1125: *Les Contrebandiers du Mekong* [The Mekong Smugglers] (Francis Annemary) (Explorer's Tale)
* 1126: *Dans les Nilgheiries* [In the Blue Mountains] (Francis Annemary) (Explorer's Tale)
* 1126: *Trois légionnaires* [Three from the Legion] (Jacques Diamant) (Explorer's Tale)
* 1127: *Au-dessus du gouffre* [Above the Abyss] (Jacques Diamant) (Explorer's Tale)
* 1128: Sauvé d'un tigre par un guépard [Saved from a Tiger by a Leopard] (Jacques Diamant) (Explorer's Tale)
* 1129: *La Mort des six pirates* [The Death of Six Pirates] (Jacques Diamant) (Explorer's Tale)
* 1130: *Duel sauvage* [Savage Duel] (Francis Annemary) (Explorer's Tale)
* 1131: *L'Effroyable nuit* [The Frightful Night] (Francis Annemary) (Explorer's Tale)
* 1132: *Le Dernier Voyage de Soleillet* [Soleillet's Last Journey] (Francis Annemary) (Historical)
* 1133: *Le Voleur de Fourrures* [The Fur Thief] (Francis Annemary) (Explorer's Tale)
* 1134: *Dans le désert de Gobi* [In the Gobi Desert] (Francis Annemary) (Explorer's Tale)
* 1136: *Le Lanceur de bombes* [The Bomb Thrower] (Jacques Diamant) (Explorer's Tale)
* 1136: *Au Pays des Bhils Hospitaliers* [In the Land of the Bhils Hospitallers] (Francis Annemary) (Explorer's Tale)
* 1137: *Chasse Tragique* [Tragic Hunt] (Jacques Diamant) (Explorer's Tale)

* 1138: *La Capture d'un boa vivant* [The Capture of a Living Boa] (Guy d'Armen) (Explorer's Tale)
* 1138: *Un Explorateur poitevin* [An Explorer from Poitou] (Francis Annemary) (Historical)
* 1139: *L'Aventure de Jim Crampton* [Jim Crampton's Adventure] (Guy d'Armen)
* 1139: *En traversant le fleuve rouge* [Crossing the Red River] (Jacques Diamant) (Explorer's Tale)
* 1140: *La mort du sorcier noir* [The Death of the Black Witch-Doctor] (Guy d'Armen) (Explorer's Tale)
* 1141: *Entre un gorille et un caïman* [Between a Gorilla and a Cayman] (Guy d'Armen) (Explorer's Tale)
* 1141: *Le Tragique voyage du Major Laing* [Major Laing's Tragic Journey] (Francis Annemary) (Explorer's Tale)
* 1142: *Le Terrible voyage de Barentz* [Barentz' Dreadful Journey] (Jacques Diamant) (Historical)
* 1142: *Dans la forêt hindoue* [In the Indian Forest] (Guy d'Armen) (Explorer's Tale)
* 1143: *Le Mystérieux Inconnu de Cawnpore* [The Mysterious Stranger of Cawnpore] (Guy d'Armen) (Explorer's Tale)
* 1143: *Terrible angoisse* [Frightful Terror] (Jacques Diamant) (Explorer's Tale)
* 1144: *Dans les ténèbres de l'Afrique Equatoriale* [In Darkest Equatorial Africa] (Guy d'Armen) (Explorer's Tale)
* 1144: *Au Pays Moï* [In the Land of Moy] (Guy d'Armen) (Explorer's Tale)
* 1145: *Une Nuit Mouvementée* [An Event-Filled Night] (Guy d'Armen) (Explorer's Tale)
* 1145: *Un Explorateur chasseur* [A Hunter Explorer] (Francis Annemary) (Historical)
* 1146: *Au sein de la jungle* [In the Heart of the Jungle] (Jacques Diamant) (Explorer's Tale)
* 1146: *L'Aventure du Baleinier* [A Whaler's Adventure] (Guy d'Armen) (Explorer's Tale)
* 1147: *La Mystérieuse cachette* [The Mysterious Hiding Place] (Guy d'Armen) (Explorer's Tale)

* 1148: *Dans les solitudes des grandes dunes* [In the Loneliness of the Great Dunes] (Guy d'Armen) (Explorer's Tale)
* 1149: *L'Aventure de Kummer* [Kummer's Adventure] (Guy d'Armen) (Historical)
* 1152: *Un Marin à Tombouctou* [A Sailor in Tumbuktu] (Guy d'Armen) (Historical)
* 1152: *Sur la Voie Ferrée* [On the Railroad] (Jacques Diamant) (Explorer's Tale)
* 1153: *Le Voyage de Partadieu et de Caillé au Bondou* [Partadieu & Caillé's Journey to Bundu] (Guy d'Armen) (Historical)
* 1154: *Sur le Haut Yang Tse Kiang* [On the Banks of the Upper Yang Tse Kiang] (Guy d'Armen) (Explorer's Tale)
* 1154: *Sur les pentes de l'Himalaya* [On the Slopes of the Himalaya] (Francis Annemary) (Explorer's Tale)
* 1156: *Aux prises avec un Killer* [Tackling a Killer Whale] (Guy d'Armen) (Explorer's Tale)
* 1158: *Trois Explorateurs Anglais en Afrique Centrale* [Three British Explorers in Central Africa] (Guy d'Armen) (Historical)
* 1159: *Aux prises avec un guépard* [Tackling a Leopard] (Guy d'Armen) (Explorer's Tale)
*1160: *La Vengeance de l'Hindou* [The Hindu's Revenge] (Guy d'Armen) (Explorer's Tale)
* 1161: *Le Lieutenant Mage à Segou-Sikoro* [Lt. Mage at Segu-Sikoro] (Guy d'Armen) (Historical)
* 1162: *Prisonniers du désert* [Trapped in the Desert] (Guy d'Armen) (Explorer's Tale)
* 1162: *Le Voilier en panne* [Stranded on a Sailboat] (Francis Annemary) (Explorer's Tale)
*1164: *Naufrageurs* [The Ship Wreckers] (Guy d'Armen) (Explorer's Tale)
* 1165-1189: *LE SECRET DE FRIGIDOPOLIS* [The Secret of Frigidopolis] (25 chapters) (Guy d'Armen)
* 1165: *Les Cannibales de Bornéo* [The Cannibals of Borneo] (Francis Annemary) (Explorer's Tale)

* 1166: *Dans la Forêt de Goa* [In the Forest of Goa] (Guy d'Armen) (Explorer's Tale)

1933: *L'Intrépide* Nos. 1167-1219
* 1168: *Le Temple Souterrain* [The Underground Temple] (Guy d'Armen) (Explorer's Tale)
* 1169: *Dans le Se-Tchouen* [In the Se-Chouen] (Jacques Diamant) (Explorer's Tale)
* 1170: *Le Fort de glace* [The Ice Fort] (Guy d'Armen) (Explorer's Tale)
* 1171: *Ruse de pirate* [A Pirate's Ruse] (Jacques Diamant) (Explorer's Tale)
* 1173: *Sur la Route des Grands Lacs* [On the Road to the Great Lakes] (Jacques Diamant) (Explorer's Tale)
* 1175: *Mendana aux Marquises* [Mendana at the Marquesas] (Francis Annemary) (Explorer's Tale)
* 1176: *Le Voyage de Du Tisné* [Du Tisné's Journey] (Jacques Diamant) (Historical)
* 1177: *Le Voyage de Mungo Park* [Mungo Park's Journey] (Jacques Diamant) (Historical)
* 1177: *La Mystérieuse Prisonnière* [The Mysterious Woman Prisoner] (Francis Annemary) (Explorer's Tale)
* 1179: *Sur le Chari* [On the Chari River] (Francis Annemary) (Explorer's Tale)
* 1180: *Un Jugement chez les Niams-Niams* [A Judgment Amongst the Niams-Niams] (Jacques Diamant) (Explorer's Tale)
* 1182: *John Bruce sur le Nil* [John Bruce on the Nile] (Francis Annemary) (Historical)
* 1183: *Une Singulière aventure* [A Singular Adventure] (Francis Annemary) (Explorer's Tale)
* 1184: *Descente en parachute* [A Parachute Descent] (Jacques Diamant) (Explorer's Tale)
* 1185: *Une Chasse involontaire* [An Involuntary Hunt] (Jacques Diamant) (Explorer's Tale)
* 1186: *Une Prise de film en forêt* [Filmmaking in the Jungle] (Jacques Diamant) (Explorer's Tale)

* 1186: *Voyage de Pinteado au Bénin en 1553* [Pinteado's Journey to Benin in 1553] (Francis Annemary) (Historical)
* 1187: *Nuit mouvementée* [An Event-Filled Night] (Francis Annemary) (Explorer's Tale)
* 1188: *L'Effroyable poursuite* [The Deadly Pursuit] (Francis Annemary) (Explorer's Tale)
* 1188: *Le Roi des cannibales* [The King of Cannibals] (Jacques Diamant) (Explorer's Tale)
* 1190: *Dans le Désert de Gobi* [In the Gobi Desert] (Jacques Diamant) (Explorer's Tale)
* 1191: *L'Aventure du Sorcier Koossa* [The Adventure of the Koossa Witch-Doctor] (Guy d'Armen) (Explorer's Tale)
* 1192: *Assiégés par des lions* [Besieged by Lions] (Jacques Diamant) (Explorer's Tale)
* 1192: *L'Homme du Volcan* [The Man from the Volcano] (Francis Annemary) (Explorer's Tale)
* 1193: *Un Voyage au Spitzberg en 1743* [A Journey to Spitzberg in 1743] (Jacques Diamant) (Historical)
* 1193: *A Bride abattue dans le désert* [Wild Ride in the Desert] (Guy d'Armen) (Explorer's Tale)
* 1195: *La Vengeance du Targui* [The Targui's Revenge] (Guy d'Armen) (Explorer's Tale)
* 1196: *Les Deux gardiens de phare* [The Two Lighthouse Keepers] (Jacques Diamant) (Explorer's Tale)
* 1197: *Duel sur une baleine morte* [Duel on a Dead Whale] (Guy d'Armen) (Explorer's Tale)
* 1198: *Une Exploration à Madagascar en 1607* [An Exploration of Madagascar in 1607] (Jacques Diamant) (Historical)
* 1199: *Une Evasion de Juchereau de Saint-Denis* [An Escape by Juchereau de Saint-Denis] (Guy d'Armen) (Historical)
* 1200: *Le Plongeon du Lt. Bartex* [Lt. Bartex's Dive] (Francis Annemary) (Explorer's Tale)
* 1202: *Dans le Bahr-el-ghazal* [In Bahr-el-Gazal] (Guy d'Armen) (Explorer's Tale)
* 1202: *Une Aventure au Kanem* [An Adventure in Kanem] (Jacques Diamant) (Explorer's Tale)

* 1203: *Un Voyage à Mexico en 1795* [A Journey to Mexico in 1795] (Jacques Diamant) (Historical)
* 1204: *La Termitière* [The Termite Mound] (Guy d'Armen) (Explorer's Tale)
* 1204: *Le Revenant du Haut Yukon* [A Revenant in Upper Yukon] (Francis Annemary) (Explorer's Tale)
* 1206: *Emilio l'alcoolique* [Emilio the Drunk] (Guy d'Armen) (Explorer's Tale)
* 1207: *L'Aventure de Robert Lenoncier* [Robert Lenoncier's Adventure] (Guy d'Armen) (Explorer's Tale)
* 1209: *Cerné par des Buffles* [Cornered by Buffalos] (Guy d'Armen) (Explorer's Tale)
* 1212: *L'Enlisé* [Trapped in Quicksand] (Guy d'Armen) (Explorer's Tale)
* 1213: *Le Médecin noir* [The Black Doctor] (Guy d'Armen) (Explorer's Tale)
* 1214: *Le Voyage de Cornelius Houteman* [Cornelius Houteman's Journey] (Francis Annemary) (Historical)
* 1215: *Le Sauvetage* [The Rescue] (Guy d'Armen) (Explorer's Tale)
* 1217: *La Fête du Ram-Lila* [The Feast of Ram-Lila] (Guy d'Armen) (Explorer's Tale)
* 1219: *Au-dessus du précipice* [Above the Abyss] (Guy d'Armen) (Explorer's Tale)

1934 (incomplete listing): *L'Intrépide* Nos. 1220-1271
* 1235-1259: *LE MYSTÈRE DES PERLES NOIRES* [The Mystery of the Black Pearls] (25 chapters) (Francis Annemary)
* 1236-1304: *GOULVEN LE GALÉRIEN* [The Cabin Boy of the *Medusa*] (69 chapters) (Francis Annemary) (illustrated historical novel)
* 1268: *Le Secret de Bora-Bora* [The Secret of Bora-Bora] (Francis Annemary) (Explorer's Tale)

1935: *L'Intrépide* Nos. 1272-1323
* **1272: *Le Vampire de la Hamada* [The Vampire of the Hamada] (Jacques Diamant) (Explorer's Tale)**
* 1274: *Une Aventure en Tasmanie* [A Tasmanian Adventure] (Francis Annemary) (Explorer's Tale)
* 1274: *Dans la vallée de la Betsiboksa* [In the Betsiboka Valley] (Jacques Diamant) (Explorer's Tale)
* 1276: *L'Enlèvement du Mousse* [The Cabin-Boy's Kidnapping] (Francis Annemary) (Explorer's Tale)
* 1276: *Aux prises avec le poisson-diable* [Tackling the Devil Fish] (Jacques Diamant) (Explorer's Tale)
* 1277: *En Afrique Equatoriale* [In Equatorial Africa] (Francis Annemary) (Explorer's Tale)
* 1279 *L'Armoire* [The Cupboard] (Francis Annemary) (Explorer's Tale)
* 1280: *Distraction de Mandarin* [A Mandarin's Distraction] (Jacques Diamant) (Explorer's Tale)
* 1280: *Dans les Marais Africains* [In the African Swamps] (Francis Annemary) (Explorer's Tale)
* 1281: *Aux prises avec un lion* [Tackling a Lion] (Francis Annemary) (Explorer's Tale)
* 1281: Le Voyage d'un volontaire canadien [The Journey of a Canadian Volunteer] (Jacques Diamant) (Historical)
* 1284: *Dans Khiva la mystérieuse* [Inside Mysterious Khiva] (Jacques Diamant) (Explorer's Tale)
* 1284: *Une Pêche mouvementée* [An Event-Filled Fishing Party] (Francis Annemary) (Explorer's Tale)
* 1285: *Le Voyageur attardé* [The Delayed Traveler] (Francis Annemary) (Explorer's Tale)
* 1286: *Au-dessus de l'abîme* [Above the Abyss] (Jacques Diamant) (Explorer's Tale)
* 1288-1312: *LA FIN D'INRAMONDA* [The Fall of Inramonda] (25 chapters) (Jacques Diamant)
* 1290: *Vengeance d'Indien* [A Hindu's Revenge] (Francis Annemary) (Explorer's Tale)
* 1291: *Le Voleur* [The Thief] (Francis Annemary) (Explorer's Tale)

* 1294: *Massacre et vengeance* [Massacre and Revenge] (Guy d'Armen) (Explorer's Tale)
* 1295: *Dans les Jardins du Cachemire* [In the Gardens of Kashmir] (Guy d'Armen) (Explorer's Tale)
* 1295: *Voyage du* Hunter *aux Iles Viti* [The Journey of the *Hunter* to the Viti Islands] (Francis Annemary) (Historical)
* 1298: *La Dernière Aventure de Magellan* [Magellan's Last Adventure] (Jacques Diamant) (Historical)
* 1300: *Une Aventure à Marrakech* [An Adventure in Marrakesh] (Francis Annemary) (Explorer's Tale)
* 1304: *Singulier réveil* [Strange Awakening] (Francis Annemary) (Explorer's Tale)
* 1305: *Chasse à courre* [The Hunting Party] (Guy d'Armen) (Explorer's Tale)
* 1307: *Un Passage encombrant* [A Bothersome Passenger] (Francis Annemary) (Explorer's Tale)
* 1310: *Chez les Dincas* [Amongst the Dincas] (Guy d'Armen) (Explorer's Tale)
* 1312: *Dans la Brousse* [In the Brush] (Guy d'Armen) (Explorer's Tale)
* 1313: *L'Inondation* [The Flood] (Francis Annemary) (Explorer's Tale)
* 1315: Un Bandit [A Bandit] (Francis Annemary) (Explorer's Tale)
* 1317-1318: *L'Indienne reconnaissante* [A Grateful Hindu Woman] (Guy d'Armen) (Explorer's Tale)
* 1317: *Une Chasse inattendue* [An Unexpected Hunt] (Jacques Diamant) (Explorer's Tale)
* 1320: *L'Arbre providentiel* [A Providential Tree] (Francis Annemary) (Explorer's Tale)
* 1321-1322: *Dans les Montagnes rocheuses* [In the Rocky Mountains] (Jacques Diamant) (Explorer's Tale)
* 1322: *Dans la Jungle Hindoue* [In the Indian Jungle] (Francis Annemary) (Explorer's Tale)

Guy d'Armen: *From the Archives of the Société Secrète des Aventuriers*

These are tales told by Doc Ardan to other members of the *Société Secrète des Aventuriers* and consigned in its Archives, which have just started to be released.

1. The Abominable Snowman

That evening, we had been discussing the various legends surrounding the intermediate stages of man from the apes to *Homo Sapiens*.

"So, you essentially believe that we're all descended from the apes?" asked Léo Saint-Clair, one of the oldest regulars of the *Société Secrète des Aventuriers*.

"Whether you like it or not, the intermediate stages of man between them and us existed," I retorted. "I think you'll change your mind when I tell you about my own experience with the subject."

Everyone present immediately demanded the story. I didn't need to be asked twice and began:

"You may remember that three years ago, I was traveling around in Tibet. Unfortunately, I was not able to reach Lhasa as I'd hoped. To be honest, you can't say you know the Roof of the World if you haven't seen the Potala, which is the Dalai Lama's palace. Nevertheless, I managed to get to within twenty miles of the Holy City.

"My team was made up of a dozen men. Eight of them were from the Sikkim Valley and the two others were Tibetan monks.

"Perhaps you're surprised that Tibetan monks were so willing to help me enter a country which is off-limits to Europeans? I should add, so that you better understand, that monks abound in every village in Tibet, and are always looking for any occasion to earn a bit of money. Usually they live on handouts that they receive from the peasants; and they're always ready to pressure them when their generosity is lacking. In short, they're veritable leeches who will never disappear from that strange country!

"The two monks were Kampa-Dzongkha and Tsong-Kaba, names that were understandable to Western ears. And, to be fair, the two men were very helpful to me, as they were both quite intelligent. Also, their influence as religious figures did much to expedite my mission. However, this came at a high price, and more than once, the two of them held me to ransom. Since I was completely at their mercy, and there were no other options, I had no choice but to pay.

"To cut to the chase, in the dead of winter we arrived on the Tibetan high plateau, approximately 5600 meters above sea level. I don't know if you ever climbed that high, but you must realize that, at such an altitude, the least amount of effort is exhausting. When I walked, my lungs burned due to the lack of oxygen.

"My companions were much better trained for such an activity than I. Because they mostly lived in areas with similar altitudes, they were hardened to its effects.

"This first stage of our trip had taken ten days. Therefore, I decided that we should rest for awhile before continuing on our way. I wasn't particularly sorry, as I hoped we'd have a sunny day so that I could experience the amazing view which the two monks had told me about.

"We had to wait for several days, because at that time of year, the mountain peaks are usually hidden in heavy cloud. However, one morning, the ice shards seemed to burst into flame in the rays of the rising sun. I could barely tear my eyes away from the beauty of that spectacular vision, which also seemed to me a good omen for the success of our endeavor. I think I would have spent the entire day, sitting there entranced, if Tsong-Kaba hadn't suddenly come running towards me in abject terror.

"I leapt up at the sound of his cries and asked, 'What's happened, Tsong-Kaba?'

"He answered, 'We are doomed, sir! There is a *Mi-Go*—an abominable snowman here!'

" 'An abominable snowman?' I repeated, 'What on Earth is that?'

" 'They are demons who have been chased from the lowlands by the Tibetans,' he replied. 'They had no choice but to take refuge in the regions that were all but inaccessible, where the snow is permanent and people rarely venture.'

" 'What do these creatures look like?'

" 'They're over seven feet tall and covered in hair. They possess inhuman strength, and it is said that they can break a man in half as if he is a piece of kindling!'

"I must admit that Tsong-Kaba's words gave me pause. But I thought that this was probably just one of those legends that exist in every culture. I questioned my companions further. One man said a relative of his was eaten by an abominable snowman, while another said that shepherds had disappeared without a trace, which he blamed on the revenge of an abominable snowman, in short, it was impossible to determine what was fact and what was fiction in their stories.

"I decided that I must see this abominable snowman described by Tsong-Kaba for myself. I took my rifle, and despite the pleas of my comrades, I set out to find the strange creature.

"It was not the least bit difficult to follow the beast's tracks. They resembled those all plantigrades usually left on the snow. I think if I hadn't been told that the plateau was usually uninhabited, I would have assumed the footprints were merely those of other men. The snow does not show the same details of footprints as one would find in damp ground.

"Now and again, for a bit of courage as well as to combat my fatigue, I would take a small sip of rum from my flask.

"All around me was total solitude, which had the effect of making me feel anxious and unnerved, finally becoming almost unbearable.

"I was soon overtaken by a disturbing thought. I struggled to remember everything I had read about Tibet. I don't know if you've ever experienced, while being in an extremely diminished physical state, desperately making an effort to remember something? I can tell you that, for me, it was so physically painful that I soon had a blinding headache.

"Suddenly, I cried out.

"A hundred meters ahead of me, I saw a tall creature, covered in black hair. I remembered that I had read in one of Rockbill's works that the wild men of Tibet were nothing more than bears. I tried to determine to which species the being in front of me belonged. Man? It didn't seem to me to resemble a man as much as an orangutan. Ape? Perhaps. Although the creature was holding a club that he might have picked up in the nearby forest.

"The idea of shooting the thing never even entered my head; my thoughts were totally dominated by scientific interests. I needed answers at any cost.

"And, the abominable snowman seemed as interested in me as I was in him. He watched me closely, but without appearing to be frightened by my presence. I called out:

" 'What are you doing here?'

"You realize that I didn't expect him to understand me; I just wanted to see if he had a language like men.

"But the strange creature made no sound at all. That convinced me that the snowman was nothing more than an ape, and of an inferior intelligence.

"A fortuitous circumstance revealed to me another fact about the animal. I removed my rifle from my right shoulder and realized that the snowman made the exact same gesture. Apes have the ability to mimic, but no other creature is known to possess the same aptitude. I performed a certain number of gestures and the snowman repeated each of them. I felt I had sufficiently documented what I had seen and wanted to return to camp, but the snowman began to follow me and slavishly mimicked each of my movements.

"I cogitated, all the while increasing my speed. I realized that if the accursed beast followed me as far as the camp, my companions would take it as a sign that our expedition was doomed to failure. I decided my only recourse was to chase the creature away, and waved my rifle at it, but he only echoed my movement with his club. Looking back, this might seem comical, but I assure you that it wasn't the least bit amusing at the time.

"I finally shot at the poor beast, hitting it in the shoulder. Wounded, it fell to the show-covered ground.

"He got up almost immediately, with a raucous cry. I saw his face was twisted in anger and decided that I needed to flee as quickly as possible.

"Even though I ran at top speed, I took time to occasionally glance behind me. Despite his wound, the snowman was catching up to me rapidly. He was not only in better shape than I, he also knew the terrain far better.

"Gentlemen, I don't know if any one of you has ever been pursued by a giant ape in Borneo or elsewhere, but I can tell you what it feels like to have an animal who is almost a man, running on two legs, breathing down your neck; it's out and out terrifying! I know that, for me, despite the penetrating cold, I was quickly in the grip of the cold sweat of fear.

"And yet, I needed this fantastic pursuit to be over before I arrived at my camp, as I've already said. That is why I decided that the only thing to do was to stop, turn around and fire a second round.

"Unfortunately, to my horror, I discovered that the trigger of my rifle was hopelessly broken. I found myself standing, unarmed, face-to-face with my enemy.

"Unarmed? That wasn't entirely true, as I could still use my rifle like a club. Although it was clearly less impressive than the one held by the abominable snowman!

"The latter approached me, brandishing his weapon. I didn't hesitate as I took my rifle by the barrel and used the stock to bash him on the head. There was a dull thump and a trickle of blood appeared. The beast again fell and the snow around him was stained with his blood.

"As he fell, the creature managed to grab hold of my right arm. I cried out as his fist tightened; sure that I was about to die.

"I tried to break free from the monster's grip, but it was impossible, and I lost consciousness from the horrible pain in my arm.

"When I reopened my eyes, I realized that I was inside one of our tents. Tsong-Kaba and Kampa-Dzong were both by my side. They explained that they heard me cry out and immediately came running to assist me. Tsong-Kaba had plunged his knife into the beast's neck and had freed me.

"I asked him if he hadn't been afraid to approach the demon that closely. He replied that when he had seen the blood flowing from the creature's skull, he had realized that it was vulnerable.

"And that, gentlemen, is how the two monks acquired the certainty that the abominable snowman was nothing more than an ape—albeit one still unknown to science."

2. The Giant Bat

"In those days," began Ardan, "I was sailing around the Sunda Islands. I was in my early 20ies, and was quite naturally excited by the region, which I consider to be one of the most spectacular in the world. That explains why I sought to spend two weeks on Bali and Lombok, which made up two links in the chain of that archipelago.

"I didn't tire of wandering in the forest that was as magnificent as all of those in the Malaysian Archipelago. Naturally I hunted, since I had guns that I had brought with me from France.

"One beautiful day, I was chasing some wild pigeons, when I found myself in the midst of luxuriant vegetation that was so dense that I had difficulty in finding my way out. It was while I was cutting through the vines and brush that surrounded me that I saw a strangely shaped rock, from which I startled a multitude of brilliantly colored birds that deafened me with their shrieking. These birds were in all different sizes, and for a few minutes I watched them flying above my head. I felt I had disturbed their tranquility and realized I must be the first human they'd seen in a long time.

"I thought I would search in the clefts of the rock to see if I couldn't find some of their eggs, as I was fiercely hungry and hadn't thought to bring along any food, thinking I would return to the hut that a kindly Malaysian had offered me, with the typical hospitality of those generous and friendly people.

"I climbed the rock by hanging onto the vines, and discovered I was in front of a long, narrow crevasse, from which a few more bird escaped.

I lit my electric torch and began my exploration, which soon seemed as if it would be quite fruitful. Indeed, I found a large quantity of eggs of all sizes, and naturally chose the largest.

"This continued until I slipped on the stone, which had been polished smooth over the years by the water. I felt as if the current was carrying me faster and faster, and the terrifying thought that I'd never be able to climb up the slippery walls of the crevasse overtook me.

"A brutal shock announced that I'd struck a wall. It seemed to me that I heard the loud fluttering of wings all around me. I imagined that I'd disturbed the slumber of a flock of bats, but I realized my mistake as soon as I was once again able to light my torch, which had gone out when I'd fallen in the water.

"What I saw was a giant vampire bat, whose folded wings seemed almost demonic. I shuddered, because I'd lost my rifle when I'd fallen and I realized I had no way of defending myself, other than with a kriss, which is a Malaysian ceremonial knife. On top of that, I had been badly bruised and that slowed down my ability to react and maneuver.

"Several minutes went by with the vampire remaining quiet, which left me hoping I'd be able to escape without a fight.

"But that hope was soon dashed when the horrible beast suddenly became took on such an aggressive air that I quickly realized this would be no easy battle. The creature attacked me with such ferocity that I was only able to fend it off by kicking at it furiously. The vampire immediately unfurled its massive wings as it fought back. It easily avoided the light that I tried shining in its eyes to blind it, and it flew around the cave making a hideous and terrifying noise.

"I knew that if my lamp went out, I was doomed. Indeed, I had noticed that its light was becoming paler, and in total blackness the vampire would have all the advantage.

"My fears soon proved to be well-founded, and several minutes later I was in complete and terrifying obscurity. I backed up to the end of the cavern and stood with my back to the wall so I wouldn't risk being turned around in the dark. It was the only tactic I could imagine which stood any chance of helping me escape.

"The vampire returned to the charge and I felt a painful bite on my arm. I shook it off with a violent movement and stabbed blindly with my knife. My hand felt only emptiness and I heard the creature beating its wings farther away from me.

"I was overtaken by a terrible fury, and began striking haphazardly in the feeble hope that I would somehow be able to wound the beast, who must have clearly seen all my efforts, thanks to its ability to see in the dark.

"Exhausted, I was soon forced to stop. I suddenly felt something run across my face and felt a sharp pain as something bit me; it was a red ant. I had a flashing vision of the terrible fate that awaited me, and it was even more terrifying than that of the vampire bat.

"The ants were everywhere on the archipelago, and they were three or four times as large as their European brethren. Their powerful mandibles could rip through the skin and they could devour even the strongest man if he could not escape them.

"Mad with fear, I again tried to climb the steep walls to flee this new danger. But I slipped once more and had to resolve myself to tolerate the horrible bites of the red ants, which had started to crawl around on my body.

"Terrified, I reflected on my pitiful situation. No one would expect me to be in this fissure, since even I had not seen any trail through the vines at the base of the rock. So, it appeared as if I was fated to be devoured by the ants or annihilated by the vampire.

"The latter must have been nearby, waiting for signs of fatigue before once again renewing its attack. That thought caused me to try lighting my torch again, something that was impossible, as the battery had obviously run out.

"Then I remembered that I had, in my pocket, a wick and a lighter. I took them out and lit the wick.

"In its feeble light I was able to see that the vampire was in a far corner of the cave. He had again folded his wings and sat like a demon, watching for the best moment to torture his human victim.

"I just wanted it to be over, so I launched myself at him, but he took off with a rapidity that I would never have suspected of him. I had nothing to show for my effort.

"I saw him suspended upside down from the cavern's ceiling, as if he was taunting me, knowing I was unable to reach him.

"I then gathered up the pebbles that were around my feet and threw them at him, forcing him to fly off anew.

"Meanwhile, the ants continued to bite me and I was becoming mad with rage. I started shouting, as if my shouts could be heard outside. I thought I heard a shout in return, but thought this was due to the fever that was now burning within me,

"Soon, the vampire attacked me again, and this time bit my thigh painfully. The pain was so bad that I passed out.

"When I awoke, I was horribly weak. I could barely move and felt extremely cold. My head was spinning and I thought I heard a voice nearby, a voice that seemed amplified by the cavern's echo.

"Suddenly, it seemed as if a blinding light had invaded the cave and I heard an explosion followed by a harsh cry.

"Then I saw before me a tall Malaysian who walked on the glistening rocks in his bare feet, not seeming to be the least bit perturbed by their slippery surface, which had caused me to fall.

"I was incapable of articulating a single word, but close to me I heard him say in Malaysian:

" 'The demon is dead! You're safe!'

"In my stupor, I understood that the vampire was dead. And, indeed, the native lifted the body of the hideous beast and threw it into a corner.

"He took a rope that had been wrapped around his waist and tied it around me. Then, he climbed up the slope and I felt myself pulled along behind him. I was too weak to handle the effort and fainted again. When I awoke, I found myself inside the hut of the Malaysian who had saved me,

"He was busy rubbing my body with an unguent, which had the effect of soothing the pain from my multiple ant bites.

"He gave a potion that seemed to give me back some of my strength. Then I noticed that he had brought the vampire's body back, too, and I was able to get a better idea of its size, which was impressive. Its wingspan looked like it was at least four meters long!

"The Malaysian at last told me how he had found me:

" 'I was fishing nearby,' he said. 'The sea was calm and I saw the swallows flying towards the rock, then suddenly turning and flying off with cries of alarm.

" 'I know those birds well, because I collect their nests to sell to the Chinese, who like them, as you know. I realized that there was something wrong in the area. That's why I headed for the fissure that you used to get to the cavern. There's a legend around here that there's an evil genie who lives in that fissure, but I'm not superstitious. I decided I would look inside from the entrance and see what was what.

" 'That's when I heard you calling out. I had already found your hat, that you'd lost when you went inside. That made me think there was someone who might have been attacked by the bats, but I never thought that there was a vampire, especially not one of this size.

" 'As I descended into the cavern, I found your rifle, which was what allowed me to kill the beast. ' "

Someone asked Ardan if there were many people attacked by vampire bats in the Sunda Islands.

"A fair number have had encounters with the beasts," he continued, "but I doubt there are many who have been confronted by one of that size. The one that bit me was exceptionally large. I'm lucky that the Malaysian showed up when he did, because that horrible monster would have sucked me dry. But there is something even stranger in this affair, and that is that I became an object of great curiosity in the region, where they believed that a demon lived in that cave. They couldn't understand how I had survived the monster's bite. I tried to explain that I'd been saved by one of their countrymen, but they insisted that I must have been under the protection of the gods."

3. The Vampire of the Hamada

Doctor Francis Ardan was excited. Earlier that morning, he had bought himself a camel in the southern Algerian village of El-Guerbi. His new means of transportation would allow him to quickly reach the hamada (rocky plateau) where he hoped to study a set of significant ruins.

The young man had already developed a certain reputation during his multiple voyages to Africa, and had several reports that had been well-received at the *Société Secrète des Aventuriers* and the *Académie des Inscriptions et Belle-Lettres*.[21]

Brave and endowed with remarkable energy, his father had given him an eclectic education with an emphasis on

---

[21] The *Académie des Inscriptions et Belles-Lettres* is concerned with the study of the monuments, the documents, the languages, and the cultures of the civilizations of antiquity, the Middle Ages, and the classical period, as well as those of non-European civilizations.

physical perfection. He had excelled at all of his studies, and had a doctorate in medicine as well as in archaeology.

Ardan set out early and stopped once, only briefly, to eat and rest his animal before continuing on his way. He reached the hamada several hours later. The ground was covered in flat, shiny black stones.

Caravans had left paths, called *medjebels*, by removing all the stones in a width of eight or ten meters, then piling them to the right and left of the road. Thus, Ardan was able to take one of the *medjebels*, which led him straight to a *wadi*, or dry riverbed, where he decided to camp for the night.

The young explorer hadn't chosen this location by chance. He had noticed that near the *wadi* there was a well where several date palms grew, as well as bushes, the leaves of which his camel seemed to particularly enjoy. He had also been stuck by the peculiarities of the hamada's rocks. Their color reminded him of jet, and the ground of the area was comprised of red clay and covered in cracks.

After tying his camel to the trunk of a palm tree, Ardan began to look around the area. That was when he noticed an astonishing mirage. It caused him to see some of the plants as trees and he had the impression that a Chamba[22] horseman was watching him. By precaution, he grabbed his rifle and waited. But, since the rider didn't move, the young man decided he would approach him instead.

He smiled at his own foolishness when he realized that the "horseman" was nothing more than a large, black asparagus plant, or *el-ebsioui*. Because the plant was growing next to a rock, the mirage had so deformed and enlarged the two objects that they had appeared as something entirely different,

"Now it's time for me to settle in for the night," Ardan told himself. "I should be sheltered from a sudden storm if I keep to the *wadi*."

He found a crevasse near the well and simply covered himself with a blanket and went to sleep.

---

[22] The people of the area

But, two hours later a strong wind blowing down the *wadi* awakened the sleeping explorer. He saw that the moon was ringed by a halo and noticed that the temperature had fallen dramatically. Still, he was so tired that he was about to fall back asleep when he saw something so unexpected that he was immediately wide awake.

Ten steps from where he was sheltered, he saw someone dressed in a white robe holding a cup up towards the moon. He stood there, immobile, as if paying homage to a respected deity.

What could the strange individual be doing? At first sight, it seemed clear that he was one of the Chambas, as he was dressed in their fashion. But it was odd that he was alone, as the Chambaa horsemen traveled in groups.

Deeply intrigued, Ardan waited breathlessly.

He saw the mysterious man bring the cup to his lips and drink in large gulps. Then, the stranger moved towards the well, coming so close to the young explorer that he could have reached up and touched him.

When he passed, Ardan realized with horror that the man's face was covered in bleeding wounds. He saw him climb over wall of the well, that was built from palm trunks, and disappear!

"My word!" Francis exclaimed to himself, "that was the most extraordinary thing. Even though this has nothing to do with archeology, I need to find out if that stranger went into some sort of hidden passage."

He quickly arose and looked around him he shivered when he saw a small, dark puddle on one of the stones. Kneeling down he touched it with a finger. There was no doubt about it: it was blood!

"That man might be severely wounded," thought Ardan, "perhaps he was drinking some type of elixir before. At any rate, I need to find out."

He approached the well and leaned over the edge. He was able to see a pale light reflecting on the water below.

He grabbed his electric torch and a heavy rope, which he attached to a solid palm trunk. Then he carefully climbed over the edge of the well and lowered himself towards the water, slowing his progress by using his feet as brakes against the walls.

Ardan stopped suddenly. He found himself in front of an opening from which came the light of a lantern. He waited, silently, until the light disappeared. Then he began his reconnaissance. He moved slowly, trying to make as little noise as possible. He followed a roughly-hewn, horizontal tunnel, which was high enough that he could walk without too much discomfort. So as to not take a chance on being surprised because of using too bright a light, he had veiled his torch with his handkerchief.

In this way, he eventually arrived at a short staircase comprised of four steps. His attention was drawn to a small, dirt-spotted basin standing on one of the steps. He picked it up to examine it. It took all of his strength to stifle a cry of horror; the basin was filled with blood!

Nearby, the young explorer saw a cup that resembled the one used earlier by the mysterious man, and at its bottom was also a small amount of blood.

This seemed to prove that the moon worshipper had been drinking blood! But where had that blood come from? Indeed, there were no birds or animals on the hamada, other than those used by the caravans, that could account for it. The many tracks that crossed the plateau testified to the number of camels that had crossed its rocky surface. It was possible that one of them had been stolen.

"I need to be sure," the young man told himself.

He checked his revolver, verified that his knife was still in place beneath his burnoose, then moved forward again. He climbed the few steps and entered a small chamber of less than three meters on each side.

Just then, he felt a shiver run down his back. In front of him was a vision that he knew he would never forget: a man was curled up in the corner, his face drained of blood and a cutlass driven deep into his throat. He had been bled like a pig!

There was the answer. A bandit, perhaps a dangerous madman, was drinking human blood!

Overwhelmed by horror, Ardan took the handkerchief from his torch so he could better explore the chamber. He noticed that there was a low door in the left hand corner. But just as he made this discovery, he heard a string of curses in Arabic that he understood clearly, given his fluency in the language.

But, before he had the time to turn and flee, there was a loud bang. The man he'd heard swearing had shot the long barreled rifle he carried. Furious at having missed his target, he continued his foul imprecations, all the while advancing on the young explorer.

Luckily, Ardan had thrown himself to the side, after discovering that the firing pin on his revolver was jammed. He hurriedly pulled out his knife.

The man kicked at the lantern, which was on the floor, but at the same time, the young man was able to hit him in the face with his own electric torch, hurting him badly.

"Murderer!" yelled Ardan, as he barely managed to avoid being smashed in the face by the Chamba's rifle, which he was now using like a club.

Francis threw himself at his attacker, holding his right arm straight out in front of him. There was a cry of pain and the man crumpled to the ground, bleeding from a severe wound to the abdomen. Within minutes he was dead.

The explorer used the lamp to examine the man more closely. He saw that he suffered from a skin condition that gave his face the repulsive appearance he had noticed earlier. But the key to the mystery was provided by a piece of paper that Ardan found in a metal box.

The paper came from an Arab sorcerer. This was easy for him to decipher thanks to certain symbols on the seal, particularly one of a scorpion. The supposed sorcerer said that he'd studied the stars under which Mohammed Kantera had been born, and he had deduced that the only possibility of a cure was for him to not be exposed to the sun's rays. He advised the sick man to live underground and to procure blood for his treatment at night.

From that, the explanation for Mohammed Kantera's behavior became clear: he was following the sorcerer's prescription to the letter.

Ardan, who was to spend a fair amount of time on the hamada, resolved to investigate amongst the passing caravans. And, a month later, he encountered some travelers who told them that one of their brethren had disappeared in the wadi valley. The description they provided perfectly matched the body that the young man had found in the cavern.

But the mystery didn't end there. One night, soon after he had questioned the caravan, the explorer saw a shape go to the well and disappear inside a few seconds later. He approached the well himself, and a few minutes later the stranger reappeared. In the interval, Ardan had prepared a rope, which he used as a lasso to capture the figure. But the man refused to speak.

Francis tied him up and interrogated him, but the native remained silent.

His exploration was reaching its end, so the young man loaded his prisoner onto the camel and took him to El-Guerbi, where the man was immediately identified by the police. He was an sorcerer named Moniav-Ali, who admitted that he had gone to the well to demand payment from the rich Chamba who he had been treating.

The investigation revealed that the sorcerer had committed many crimes and he was found guilty and executed soon after. And that, at last, was the end of the vampire of the hamada.

4. The Lair of the Javanese Witch-Doctor

After leaving Risnak at dawn, Doctor Francis Ardan headed towards the center of the nearby forest to prospect for tin, which he estimated to be particularly rich in the area. He had brought his servant, Malais Kandaliah, who was not only devoted to him, but had a profound knowledge of the Javanese forest.

Ardan had arrived on the island a month ago after having earned a degree at the Ecole Nationale de Médecine. His life-long love of adventure had led him to offer his services to a Franco-Dutch-American mining consortium, in which his father had shares, that was looking for tin in Java. The young man had immediately succeeded in finding a rich vein of the metal that justified setting up a mining operation. His goal was to locate a second vein, which he hoped to find quickly.

Unfortunately, an unpleasant surprise awaited him. When he arrived at the location where he had been working for the past week, all of the markers he'd set out had disappeared.

His first thought was to wonder who else might be interested in exploiting the tin mines. He thought that perhaps a rival consortium had managed to bribe some of the locals to remove his markers. But he quickly rejected that hypothesis, as there were none but the one for which he already worked.

Suddenly, Kandaliah yelled in surprise, and at the same time an arrow flew into a nearby tree trunk. Attached to the arrow was a piece if papyrus covered with writing.

"What does it say?" asked Ardan, who, while speaking some Malay, was not yet able to read it.

"What does it say?" repeated his Malaysian servant as he shook his head, "Terrible things! It accuses you of being a horrible white man who has come here to steal the riches from our sacred lands. There are threats if you don't immediately abandon your search."

"Is it signed?"

"Yes, by Baja!"

"Baja? Isn't that the name of a snake?"

"Yes. It's a reptile about a meter long, with red-spotted, yellow skin. Its bite can kill a man in less than five minutes."

After a few minutes of silence, Kandaliah added, "I think it was written by a snake charmer. There are a lot of witch doctors on the island."

"Are you afraid of these witch doctors?" asked the young explorer.

"Not in the least," replied his companion. "I lived with the Dutch long enough to have learned that these so-called witch doctors are parasites who exploit the fears of the Malaysians."

"Good! Then we're going to calmly get on with our work and put in new markers. We'll deal with anyone who tries to stop us when the time comes."

Ardan once again took the measurements he needed, made a few more surveys and planted his markers. He had barely completed his task when another arrow whistled past and planted itself in a eucalyptus tree exactly 20 centimeters above his head.

The young doctor immediately threw himself to the ground. Hidden by the tall grass, he looked at the surrounding jungle and didn't take long to notice a native trying to hide behind a thatch of bamboo.

He called to Kandaliah in a low voice, and the two men carefully crawled towards the hiding man. From time to time they checked to make sure he was still there, but didn't want to risk shooting at him.

Soon, they arrived at a small clearing surrounded by enormous cactus plants that at first sight seemed to form an impenetrable barrier. But after a few minutes of careful examination, they noticed passages that had probably been made by animals. The ground in the clearing was covered by tall grass that hid everything around them from view.

"Strange vegetation," murmured Ardan, "these flexible stems wind around our legs like vines, but they aren't actually vines. I wonder what they're hiding. Say! Look over there!"

He pointed to a dome that just barely showed through the grass.

A few minutes later, they had reached a large hut, with walls made of some type of yellow clay. The roof was made of artfully woven reeds.

"Something tells me that the villain who shot at us has taken refuge here," said Ardan. "What do you think?"

"We can always introduce ourselves as simple travelers seeking refuge for the night to whoever lives here," answered Kandaliah. "Then we'll see what happens."

It was wise advice, and Ardan immediately agreed with his companion. The two men resolutely approached the hut.

Once they were past the last of the tall grass, they found themselves in front of a partially opened door. Inside stood a tall, elderly man. His emaciated face was testimony to the ascetic life he led. It was clear that the two men were in the presence of a witch doctor.

The man was in the midst of boiling plants in an earthenware cauldron that was balanced on a brazier made of two large stones with a wood fire blazing between them. When he noticed the two travelers, he interrupted his task and walked to the door, which he opened wide. He bowed and held his right hand on his heart and said,

"Peace be with you. My home is yours."

"Thank you, O Wise Elder," replied Ardan. "We are tired travelers who have lost our way. We gratefully accept your generous hospitality."

The elderly man directed his visitors towards two wooden chairs. Francis examined their host with curiosity. His face looked like heavily creased, old parchment, topped off with a long, white beard. His eyes, in deeply sunken orbits, burned like hot coals.

By George, he thought, *I don't think it's a good idea to let down our guard around a man like this.*

He surreptitiously patted his pocket to reassure himself that his pistol was still in place, feeling that it was, he felt strangely reassured.

During their conversation, the hermit offered to prepare a meal for his two guests. But picking up on an almost imperceptible sign from Kandaliah, Ardan refused, saying that they had provisions of their own in their packs. The old man didn't insist, instead questioning the two travelers further about the purpose of their journey.

"We were hunting jaguars," explained the young man.

"And we're you planning to kill the wild beasts with rocks?" asked the witch doctor. "Do you not even have a bow?"

"We don't," admitted Kandaliah, "but we do have traps that we've dug on the trails the beasts use. There are stakes at the bottom to impale them when they fall into the hole."

The hermit had a satisfied smile and a knowing look burned in his eyes. Ardan had the uncomfortable feeling that the wily old man had been making sure that the two travelers were unarmed.

The witch doctor went back to making his strange potion and murmured unintelligible words over the cauldron.

Suddenly, he smiled amiably as he had when they arrived, and asked his guests if they would like to take a well-earned rest. The two friends agreed, and the old man brought them straw mattresses that he laid on the floor.

Ardan and Kandaliah stretched out, while the witch doctor again bowed to them and wished them a good night. Then, he left the hut on the pretext of going to check on some of his own traps.

"He's clearly planning something," whispered Ardan. "I think we had a bit of luck in coming here, because I'm certain that he's our man."

"In any case," answered Kandaliah, "we need to be on our guard and..."

He stopped as a whistling sound was heard in the room.

The young man had just enough time to turn on his flashlight. In its beam they saw a five foot long boa constrictor; its head high and its eyes evil. There was no room for error, as the witch doctor had left his pet serpent behind to kill the two travelers to whom he'd shown his generous hospitality! Ardan saw the snake preparing to attack, when a shot rang out; Kandaliah had fired on the reptile!

The serpent was decapitated, but its body continued to thrash wildly.

"He's dead, Kandaliah," said Ardan. "Thank you, I was..."

A horrifying vision appeared before them. Three meters away, in the same direction as the boa, a rattlesnake was preparing to strike! His neck was engorged with venom and bore the hideous death's head for which the beasts were known.

This was an enemy even more redoubtable than the last, as it wouldn't take minutes for his victim to die, but mere seconds.

It was Ardan's turn to fire, but his shot missed the monster. Luckily, the young man had the presence of mind to jump to the side, causing the beast to miss. When the furious beast made a turn to try again, the explorer was able to shoot him through the neck, then he jumped on the wounded serpent and crushed its head under his boot.

"Let's get out of here!" he yelled as he ran for the door.

It was locked! However the door of a forest hut couldn't long resist the blows of two strong, young men. It wasn't long before the adventurers were breathing the fresh forest air. They heard a savage cry at the same time that a bullet pierced the shadows.

But Kandaliah had seen the man in time, and while the bullet missed its target, the shooter was not so lucky.

Another raucous cry split the night. Ardan and Kandaliah rushed in the direction from which it had come. They quickly discovered that they had just killed the old witch doctor,

"So, the old thug locked us in," said Ardan, "expecting that his snakes would get rid of us."

"And," added Kandaliah, "I'm sure that if we'd agreed to eat whatever he offered to us, we'd have been dead before the serpents got their chance."

The two friends returned to the village of Risnak. The natives, who had lived in terror of the old man, came to thank them when they learned of his death, and that moment on, they didn't have the least problem with their work.

This new story, penned by Rick Lai especially for this volume, is a prologue of sort to a vaster work, entitled The Stahlman Initiative, *which will tie together the origins of Doc and The Avenger. Rick focuses here on Ardan's father and his long-term plans to oppose evil by any and all means, which is going to force him to cross paths with some very dangerous individuals...*

Rick Lai: *The Midas Menace*

New York State, 1902

It is generally believed that no caves exist in Long Island, New York. Nevertheless, there was an old gypsum mine located there. Abandoned in the 1880s, it had secretly been purchased in 1899 by a very unusual organization. Inside it was an enormous cave, the vastness of which was largely unknown. For the last three years, it had been the site of meetings illuminated by torchlight. One such gathering was transpiring now.

Nearly sixtyfigures were assembled reverentially around a 12-feet high metal platform. A metal pole of the same length arose from the top of the structure. Extending vertically from it was a rod, five feet long, from which dangled a hangman's noose. Adjacent to this gallows was a huge, two-armed prospector's scale. Next to it was a wheelbarrow, covered by a golden cloth.

The celebrants wore golden robes with pistols holstered in belts tied around their waists. Their faces were hidden by hoods of the same gleaming hue. Two other similarly clad individuals stood on the platform. The taller of the two wore a crown on his hood. The robe and hood of his companion were black rather than gold. The masked man wearing the crown raved in front of the scales.

"I am the reincarnation of King Midas, and you are my Minions! We lust for gold! We live for gold! We live for gold! We kill for gold!"

"We kill for gold!" echoed his followers.

"I am merely a king. I serve a greater power."

Midas knelt before the figure dressed in black.

"Our Lord and Master is the Dark Tyrant, the Keeper of our Treasure," he continued. "All hail the Dark Tyrant! All hail the Treasure!"

"Hail the Dark Tyrant! Hail the Treasure!"

"Has anyone ever heard the Tyrant speak?" whispered one of the Minions to another.

"Never," answered the other in hushed tones. "Not a single word."

The Dark Tyrant gestured for Midas to rise.

'My Minions," resumed Midas, "we are the disciples of the Dark Tyrant. If we do not receive our proper tribute, we demand payment in blood! The Minions of Midas have asked two plutocrats for donations. One of these men, Aloysius Doran, has agreed to our terms in exchange for the lives of his daughter and grandchildren. His cash contribution has been converted into gold. Let me reveal the ransom"

The man wearing the crown then removed the cloth concealing the contents of the wheelbarrow. A pile of gold bars was exposed. He placed them one by one in the nearest circular tray hanging from the two-armed scale. Once the last ingot was placed, he proudly proclaimed the value of the extortion payment.

"Five million dollars! There shall be no blood for gold!"

"There shall be no blood for gold!" repeated the Minions.

"We also sent Grace Dunbar Gibson an ultimatum for 15 million in tribute. She refused! There shall be blood for gold!"

"There shall be blood for gold!'

"Our wrath shall fall upon Grace Dunbar Gibson! Bring forth the prisoner!"

Prodded by a Minion armed with a rifle, a tall brunette mounted the steps leading up to the platform. Attired in an elegant pink blouse and a red skirt, Grace stared defiantly at the Dark Tyrant and Midas. She walked towards the trap door beneath the noose.

"See how haughtily she strolls," observed Midas. "They call her the Gold Queen. Do you know her story, my Minions? She was originally an Englishwoman of humble origins. She was hired by Neil Gibson, the mining magnate, to be the governess to his two children. After driving the first Mrs. Gibson to commit suicide, this home wrecker married her employer. But her domestic bliss was short-lived. It lasted only a year, because her husband came to our attention. For years, the press christened Neil Gibson the Gold King because of his mining empire. How stupid these reporters are! There is only one Gold King, and his name is Midas! Three months ago, we insisted that the upstart Gibson surrender his title to me and his entire fortune to our sacred Treasure. When he rebuffed our entreaties, I ordered his abduction. That cowardly braggart died, whimpering, on this very gibbet. As a gesture of compassion, we sent his body in an oblong box back to his family.

"Gibson left his entire fortune to his spouse. No provision was made for the children from his first marriage. To everyone's surprise, Grace proved a dutiful stepmother. She set aside generous trust funds for both children. The newspapers lavishly praised her. The King was dead! Long live the Gold Queen!

"We allowed a suitable period of mourning before petitioning the newly-installed Gold Queen to settle her husband's debt. That interval proved costly, because it permitted Mrs. Gibson to secrete two-thirds of her holdings in trust. Nevertheless, we were willing to overlook this indiscretion in exchange for the remaining twenty-five million. Mrs. Gibson's response to our magnanimous offer was to surround herself and her step-children with bodyguards provided by the Pinkerton Detective Agency. A business trip to New York proved to be her

Waterloo. The Gold Queen's escort was easily slain when we abducted her from the Palais-Metropole Hotel this morning!

"The Gold Queen has refused to give us her wealth! Her blood is forfeit! There shall be blood for gold!"

"Blood for gold!" yelled the Minions of Midas.

"The Black Gulf in the Canyon of Death yearns for the Gold Queen's soul. The Dark Tyrant shall personally convey her there."

Advancing towards Grace, the Dark Tyrant took the noose and fastened it around her neck. The malevolent blue eyes of the masked executioner stared into the condemned woman's black eyes. The Dark Tyrant hoped to detect fear in the Gold Queen's eyes, but she faced her persecutor with courage. Grace spat into the Dark Tyrant's right eye. Then she quickly yanked off the hood of her momentarily startled nemesis. A mass of golden curls was revealed.

"The Tyrant's a woman!" shouted one of the Minions.

"We won't be bossed around by any woman!" hollered another. "We should lynch her alongside the Gold Queen!"

Pulling her mask out of Grace's hands, the unmasked blonde turned to face her rebellious underlings.

"Silence!" commanded Midas. "Our leader shall explain her deception. Only judge her after she has finished speaking."

"Yes, I am a woman! I never deceived you. A tyrant can be a woman. I am Josephine Balsamo! The police of three continents fear me as Countess Cagliostro! We talk of blood for gold! My bloodline is pure. The blood of Cagliostro runs in my veins! He sent the French King and Queen to the guillotine! I have sent the Gold King and Queen to the gallows!

"Together we have amassed a Treasure that exceeds the lost wealth of Monte Cristo!" Josephine raised her hood high. "To achieve our great victories, I hid behind a mask. Now I trust you with my true face."

Stepping to the edge of the metal platform, Josephine released the mask. It glided downward to land at the feet of the audience.

"Josephine de Beauharnais was my ancestor! With Napoleon as her consort, she became the most powerful woman in Europe. With Midas as my consort, I shall become the most powerful woman in the United States. Our Treasure will be used to purchase weapons for the new army that will conquer America! You shall be the generals of that army. You shall cease to be the Minions of Midas! You shall be the Marshals of Midas!

"This shall be your destiny if you embrace me as the new Gold Queen. Do you still desire my blood? Do you wish me life or death?

"Life!" screamed the ecstatic Minions.

"For the new Gold Queen to live, the old Gold Queen must die!" Josephine's left hand reached for the lever that controlled the trap door beneath Grace Gibson's feet. "Her death shall bring us one step further to confiscating the Gibson holdings."

"The Gibson fortune will never be yours!" insisted the prisoner. "Under the terms of my will, the fifteen million will be added to my children's trust. That money will be inaccessible for another decade!"

Josephine laughed. "Within the month, I shall exterminate your stepchildren like vermin. Their deaths shall nullify the trust fund. Their money will be inherited by their cousin in Pennsylvania. Hopefully, he will prove less stubborn than you. Any defiant last words, Gold Queen? The realization that your actions have doomed your two whelps has rendered you speechless."

While her left hand rested in the lever, Josephine raised her right hand towards Grace contemptuously and waved.

"As you contemplate your literal descent into oblivion, I bid you adieu."

As Josephine pulled the lever, a pistol bullet sliced through the air and cut through the noose. Grace fell safely through the trapdoor. Hitting the ground, she only suffered minor bruises.

The Minions of Midas found themselves confronted by thirty-five Pinkerton detectives armed with rifles. They were led by a bearded man with bronze hair. His left hand held a lantern while his right gripped a smoking Mauser pistol.

"Surrender or die!" commanded the bronze-haired man.

A vicious gun battle erupted. Midas and Josephine pulled their guns out of their holsters. Midas raised his firearm in the bronze-haired man's direction...

Suddenly, blood exploded over the mask. The bronze-haired man had drilled Midas between the eyes. The slain criminal fell into the empty tray of the golden scale. As another of the bronzes-haired man's bullets penetrates the heart of the Minion bearing the rifle, a vicious gun battle erupted between the henchmen of Midas and the Pinkerton posse.

Josephine leapt through the trapdoor of the scaffold. Landing on her feet, she stood directly in front of Grace. With the severed noose still tied around her throat, the Gold Queen lifted herself off the ground.

Josephine pointed her gun directly at Grace.

"Don't move, or I'll shoot you in the gut!"

The large chamber in which the two woman stood was illuminated only by light streaming from the open trapdoor. Still aiming her pistol at Grace, she walked towards a series of levers on the wall. Her left hand quickly lowered two switches. As the trapdoor shut, electric lights brightened the room,

The Golden Queen smiled mockingly. "Although you clearly would take great delight in killing me, your current circumstances necessitate my preservation."

"Very perceptive. If the Minions are defeated, I shall use you as a hostage to force the Pinkertons to allow my escape."

"This structure is made of no ordinary metal. Is it orichalcum from the secret kingdom of Ahaggar in North Africa?"

"How do you know of Ahaggar?"

"An ambitious engineer in my mining corporation heard rumors of that legendary land. Unfortunately, he disappeared in Algeria while seeking to verify the existence of Ahaggar. I imagine that the gold plundered by the Minions of Midas was used to purchase orichalcum."

"Soldiers wearing chainmail suits made of orichalcum will be impervious to bullets. I shall inaugurate my reign as the new Gold Queen by creating an invulnerable army. My orichalcum legions shall spread my tyranny throughout the continent."

Grace's right hand gripped the middle of the rope dangling from her neck. "Can I remove this? It's tickling my throat."

"No. Consider it a necklace fit for a Queen." Tilting her head back, Josephine roared with laughter.

Her gloating caused Josephine to shift her gaze away from her adversary for a handful of seconds. That brief interval was long enough for Grace to strike. She slammed the end of the rope against Josephine's wrist causing her to drop the gun. Swinging the rope like a baseball bat, Grace struck Josephine's face. As the blonde staggered, her foot unintentionally kicked the gun. It slid across the room until hitting a wall.

Grace lifted the rope again to strike, but Josephine seized her enemy's arm with both hands. With all her strength, she swung the brunette into the wall. The stunned Gold Queen dropped to her knees.

Consumed by rage, Josephine reached for the rope still attached to Grace's neck.

"You dare assault me, the true gold queen! Your temporary status as a hostage is revoked! I am thy executioner!"

Behind the slumped Gold Queen, Josephine yanked the rope. Gasping for breath as the noose tightened, Grace's right hand rubbed against the pistol on the floor. Grabbing the gun, she lifted it up over her shoulder and fired blindly.

The rope went limp and dropped downward. Turning around, Grace beheld Josephine grimacing in pain. Grasping her left side, the blonde staggered on her feet.

Grace pointed the gun at her wounded nemesis. "Josephine Balsamo, let this be your final epitaph. Tyrants die from their own bullets."

A second bullet plowed into the blonde's right side. Josephine toppled backward. The would-be Queen of America sprawled motionlessly on the floor.

The Gold Queen towered triumphantly over her vanquished foe. "I am the sole Gold Queen. All rival claimants to my throne shall suffer my justice."

Removing the noose, Grace noticed a folded stepladder reclining against a wall of the chamber. Opening the stepladder, she positioned it near the closed trapdoor. The Gold Queen decided that, in good conscience, she could not remain safe in this orichalcum chamber while brave men were risking their lives to liberate her. Josephine's gun still had three bullets. If the brutal battle between the Minions of Midas and the Pinkertons still raged, she would fight alongside her allies. She pulled the lever that opened the trap door.

"Iverton!" shouted a man's voice. "The trapdoor's open!"

Grace breathed a sigh of relief. Iverton was the supervisor of the Pinkertons assigned to protect her.

"Mr. Iverton!" shouted the Gold Queen, "Are you there?"

The face of a dark-haired man looked down through the trapdoor. "Mrs. Gibson! Thank God, you're safe. All the Minions of Midas lie dead or have surrendered. What about their female leader?"

"She died by my hand. I'm coming up."

Ascending the stepladder, Grace emerged into the open. She beheld Iverton and the bronze-haired man.

"Mr. Iverton, how did you locate this Long Island cave?"

"I don't deserve any credit, Mrs. Gibson. You have this gentleman to thank. He fortuitously was staying at the Palais-Metropole Hotel when the Minions of Midas kidnapped you. Identifying gypsum deposits left behind by the Minions' shoes, he concluded the gang's base was in the mine. It was also his marksmanship that prevented your execution."

"I owe you my life, Sir," acknowledged the Gold Queen, "but I don't know your name."

"You can call me Francis Ardan Sr. As we were advancing through the mine, we heard muffled fragments of the woman's speech. Did she identify herself as Josephine Balsamo?"

"Yes. Did you know her, Mr. Ardan?"

"I never had the misfortune to meet her in the flesh. I own a small notebook bearing a list of people that I have sworn to destroy. Josephine Balsamo is prominently on that list. I suspect that the true name of Midas is on the list, but my bullet's impact has made facial identification impossible."

"Does the name Jack Smith appear on your list?"

"There is a John Smith, Mrs. Gibson, but I have no idea whom he is meant to be. It's a very common name."

"When my husband was serving in the Colorado State Senate during the 1880's, the state was terrorized by a band of desperados known as the Black Gulf Canyon Gang. My husband organized a group of vigilantes to liquidate these murderous outlaws. Although Neil was victorious over the bandits, he was severely criticized for hanging members of the Black Gulf Canyon Gang without a formal trial. The consequential controversy caused Neil to abandon his political career."

"Didn't the leader of the Black Gulf Canyon Gang escape retribution?" asked Iverton.

"Yes, he vanished without a trace. His name was Jack Smith. Although the Minions of Midas have been active for the last three years, it was only until they began to persecute my family that they lynched their victims. Furthermore, Midas cited 'the Black Gulf in the Canyon of Death' while condemning me to be hanged. I suspect Midas was really Jack Smith."

"Perhaps removing Midas's robe and searching the clothes beneath will confirm Mrs. Gibson's theory," suggested Iverton.

Viewing the corpse of Midas residing on the scale's tray, Grace grinned at Ardan. "You transformed this scale of greed into a scale of justice. Midas gave his own blood for gold.'

Ardan stripped the golden garment from the slain ringleader's corpse. "His shirt and pants are made of chainmail. The metal seems to be identical with the platform's."

"It's orichalcum," divulged Grace. "Before I filled her with lead, Josephine boasted about her plan to equip an army with such suits. This must be an early prototype. Let me prove my hypothesis." She shot her gun into the corpse's chest. Reaching down and picked up the bullet, she showed it to Ardan and Iverton." The bullet didn't penetrate the chainmail. Its tip is blunted as if it hit an immovable object." Grace gestured towards the dead Minion who had earlier escorted to the gallows. "Clearly his followers weren't attired in orichalcum. You were fortunate indeed, Mr. Ardan, to shoot Midas in the head. Otherwise, your bullet would have bounced harmlessly off him."

"Not true, Mrs. Gibson. A bullet would still hit the chainmail with considerable force. The impact could result in injuries ranging from minor contusions to broken bones. The wearer of such a suit could even be knocked unconscious."

The Gold Queen's face turned ashen. "Josephine Balsamo! She may be alive!"

Grace ran to the trapdoor and looked inside the enclosed chamber. The body of Josephine Balsamo was gone. On the floor of the chamber, another trap door was open. "Josephine must have been wearing a suit of orichalcum chainmail under her robe. My bullets only stunned her."

Followed by Ardan and Iverton. Grace descended the stepladder. Ardan examined the open trap door on the floor.

"There is a narrow tunnel here through which a person can crawl. I'm going to see where it leads."

"I'm going with you," asserted Grace.

"It's too dangerous. I forbid it."

"Since you are neither my father nor my husband, Mr. Ardan, you have no authority over me.

"Iverton, restrain this woman."

"I'm sorry, Ardan, but under the terms of the contract that Mrs. Gibson negotiated with the Pinkerton Detective Agency, I must defer to her wishes."

It took Ardan and the Gold Queen half an hour to navigate through the tunnel. Reaching the end, they passed upward through an exit hole into a stables containing horses. Wheel marks on the ground indicted a carriage had just left.

Josephine Balsamo had again successfully eluded justice.

After leaving the Gold Queen under the protection of the Pinkertons, Ardan traveled to his house in New York City. The bronze-haired adventurer was informed by his wife that Junior was sleeping soundly.

Walking into his study, Ardan looked at a framed photograph on the wall. It had been taken more than a decade ago. The photograph depicted Ardan and his best friend and kinsman, Victor Savage. Ardan recalled Victor's brutal murder by a master criminal, Culverton Smith.

Unlocking his large safe, Ardan pulled out the notebook that he had discovered last year. Inscribed in Smith's hand, the front page bore the title "Black Coat Register." When Ardan had recognized the name of the notorious James Moriarty, he knew that the notebook was a list of Smith's criminal associates. Smith's motive in slaying Victor had been to secure an inheritance. Several murder cases in France had revealed the existence of a nefarious organization, the Black Coats, that specialized in assassinating the rightful heirs to family fortunes.

Ardan had crossed out the names of Moriarty and other malefactors who had perished over the years. He now crossed out another name.

"John Smith, you are the first Black Coat leader to die by my hand. Others of your evil brood shall follow. Your Minions of Midas were merely the fruit of a more monstrous tree. Victor Savage and the other victims cry out for justice. I dedicate the lives of myself and my son to the complete eradication of the Black Coats."

This story previously appeared in Tales of the Shadowmen 6 *in a slightly different form. It was revised for this republication to better conform with the chronology of Doc's family. We jump forward in time and find ourselves at the peak of the Great War, when we meet Doc Ardan, ready to embark, as usual, on a vital mission. Taking place just before Philip José Farmer's classic* Escape from Loki, *John's story aptly demonstrates that, when it comes to menace, men, not cannons, are indeed...*

John Peel: *The Biggest Guns*

The Western Front, March 1918

Francis Ardan Jr. first realized the trouble he was in when a burst of bullets slammed into the fuselage of his Sopwith Camel F.1. He banked to the left instantly to get out of the line of fire, and then scanned the skies for his opponent. He was near the operational ceiling for his plane—20,000 feet—and there weren't many enemy craft capable of catching him at this height. He was annoyed with himself for thinking he had been safe.

There—from the Sun! The enemy was instantly recognizable. A blood-red Fokker Dr.1 triplane, its twin Spandaus blazing, was screaming toward him. Only one person flew such a craft—Rittmeister Hans Von Hammer. Ardan knew the man's reputation; a total number of kills was hard to come by, but the ace had certainly shot down more than 50 allied aircraft.

It looked as if he was going to boost the Rittmeister's score today. He'd been caught badly by surprise, and Von Hammer had the height advantage. Still, Ardan was no novice in a cockpit and, as his friend Biggles had said often enough, "If you can fly a Sopwith Camel, you can fly anything." The aircraft took considerable skill, and had killed a number of over-confident or unwary trainees, but it repaid attention with amazing abilities. It was better than virtually any aircraft either side had in the air, at least in an even fight.

But this wasn't even. Ardan was skilled, and he managed to weave out of the next burst of gunfire, but Von Hammer was second only to Richthofen as an ace, and he wasn't about to allow his prey to escape.

Ardan twisted and rolled the Camel, trying to coax just a little more speed from the Clerget engine powering the craft. The Fokker was almost the match of the Camel in airspeed, but Ardan's plane had the slight edge in rate of climb. And the Camel had a slightly greater ceiling than the Fokker. If the young man could just push it enough to get above Von Hammer, he'd be safe.

He never got the chance. The enemy pilot was no fool, and he had clearly anticipated Ardan's reaction. With a sudden twist, the Fokker was aligned once more with the Camel, and the Spandaus chattered out death.

Ardan managed to spin to one side so that the bullets missed the cockpit, but they slammed instead into the Clerget. The engine started spitting smoke, and then fire. One of the fuel lines had clearly been severed, and the fire would be sucked back to the tank in a matter of seconds.

There was only one thing to do. The young adventurer grabbed the plate from the camera strapped to the side of the Camel and quickly slipped it inside his shirt. It was cold against his skin, but it should be relatively safe there. Then he stood up, and kicked himself free from the doomed aircraft. There was a rush of air, and he was thrown clear as the Sopwith lurched and fell. Barely five seconds later, it exploded in a smoky fireball.

Ardan was some 18,000 feet in the air and falling. He glanced around and saw the Fokker. Von Hammer tipped its wings in salute to his enemy, and then turned away to hunt more targets. Ardan was lucky that his opponent had been the Rittmeister, because many German pilots would also riddle the pilot, even if he appeared doomed. Von Hammer went only for the aircraft.

Besides, no one had ever fallen from 20,000 feet and survived, so leaving a man to die was barely a kindness. Many Allied pilots took their revolvers along on missions to shoot themselves in situations like this. A bullet in the brain was just as certain a death—and less drawn-out and terrifying.

One day, Ardan was convinced, parachutes would be packed into planes to enable men to fall safely to the earth. Experiments had shown that descents from balloons were possible using such devices, and even an aircraft or two. The Germans were reported to be experimenting with such devices.

Which was why the young man had done the same.

Ardan saw that the ground was approaching quite rapidly, despite his initial height. He could certainly pick out a great number of details on the farm below him. Wind resistance had stopped his acceleration, but he was falling quite swiftly. If he hit the ground—or even the pond he could clearly see—at this speed, he'd shatter every bone in his body. The important thing was to slow his descent, and that could only be accomplished by manipulating wind resistance. To do that, he needed to make himself larger.

He shed his flight jacket—a heavy leather garment that kept him warm but added to his mass. The wind chilled him, but briefly. He forced his trained body to ignore the cold, at least for the moment. Then he snapped the releases on his clothing.

His shirt and pants had been carefully constructed to his design by a French seamstress he knew. They were not a single layer of clothing, but several. Once the restraints were released, his shirt and pants blossomed out, like a flower unfolding. The strong cloth caught the wind, and he could feel that he was slowing down. The extra surface area was working! He spread his arms and legs, maximizing his cross-section as he fell, and the air resistance built up.

If only the stitching was strong enough to hold up under this terrible strain… This was his trial run of this new method, and he sincerely hoped it was successful enough to allow him future refinements…

Air ripped at him and his clothing. He glanced at the exposed seams. They appeared to be holding, but for how long? Well, there was nothing he could do now—if the threads failed, he would die—it was that simple. He had to assume that they would hold and give him a chance of surviving. He examined the ground that was drawing ever closer.

The pond was out. He was slowing as he fell, but at this speed, hitting the surface of the water would have pretty much the same effect as hitting a brick wall. It wouldn't be the wall that broke. What he needed was something compressible. That meant avoiding the farmhouse and the out-buildings, and the ground itself, of course. That left him only one possible target…

He wished that he had managed to invent some way of steering his fall. The only effect he could have on direction was to draw in or extend one of his limbs. It worked to a degree, but it was hardly very effective. That was something to consider for the next trial. Still, by using his limbs, he did manage to control his fall enough to head for the largest of the haystacks below.

And then, time ran out on him. He barely had time to hope for the best before he slammed into the hay.

It didn't kill him.

It did hurt. Quite a lot. His right ankle felt as if it was sprained, and he knew he would have extensive bruising over all of the front of his body. But he was alive, and had broken nothing. Not even the photographic plate he had risked his life to obtain.

As soon as he could breathe again, he rolled onto his back. Pain flared up all over, but that was a good sign—it meant that he was still alive, and hadn't broken his neck or spine. He moved slowly, every muscle in his arms on fire, as he unfastened his helmet and goggles and pulled them from his head.

There was a sound beside him, and he turned his head—slowly!—and saw that a curious pig had wandered across. It stared at him in some fascination, clearly wondering from where he had appeared.

"Don't worry," he told the shoat. "I'll be out of your way just as soon as I can move." He realized he had to be giddy with relief—talking to a pig! He closed his eyes again for a moment. A short rest, and then he'd start on his way. He had to get back to HQ to develop the photographic plate.

Two days later, Francis Ardan was in London. It was still slightly painful to walk, but he was getting better each day. And there simply wasn't time to rest—not with the evidence he had procured about the Boche plans. Right now, he needed expert assistance, and this was the best place to obtain it. He stopped beside the Georgian house in a fashionable section of Westminster. Beside the door was a small, simple plaque:

THE GUN CLUB
London Branch
Members only

Ardan wasn't a member, but that didn't worry him. Several highly-placed contacts in the *Société Secrète des Aventuriers* had vouched for him and made an appointment with the people he needed to meet. He sounded the pull-bell beside the door, which was opened quite promptly by a liveried retainer.

"Francis Ardan," he announced. "I believe I am expected."

"You are indeed, sir," the man agreed. He opened the door, allowing the young man to enter. "Allow me to take your overcoat and hat, sir," he offered. Ardan shucked the coat and handed across his Homburg. "The second door on the right, sir," the retainer announced.

The young man thanked him and strode down the wood-paneled corridor. There were prints on the walls of all manners of military guns and howitzers, many of which were unfamiliar to him. The floor was thickly carpeted, so he made no sound as he walked, his precious package clutched firmly under his left arm.

The second door was open, and Ardan saw that within was a large room. He knocked gently on the open door, and then walked into the room.

This room was also wood-paneled, and richly furnished. Large stuffed chairs were scattered about the room, close to small tables for refreshments or books. A larger table ran the length of the far wall, and two other walls were massive book cases, the shelves stuffed to overflowing with weighty tomes. There were electric lights in strategic spots to allow for reading. None of the people in the room were so occupied.

There were two men present, who rose as he entered. There was also a sole woman, who remained seated. One of the men was stout, balding and clearly in his 50s. The second was leaner, trim and had an amused cast to his handsome features. His skin was bronzed by the tropical Sun, showing he had traveled extensively, and his eyes were blue and piercing. The woman—well, she was quite startling. Aside from the simple fact that no clubs to the young man's knowledge allowed women inside their premises, she was one of the most startling beautiful women he had ever seen. She was young—perhaps only five or six years older than Ardan—and tall—again, almost matching him.

What was more surprising was that she somehow seemed familiar to him, though he thought he had never seen her before.

"Francis Ardan, I presume?" The older man moved forward and reached out a hand, which the young man shook.

"Just Francis—or Clark," he said.

"I am J.T. Maston," the man introduced himself. "Normally, I reside in Baltimore at our home office, but these, alas, are not normal times. This gentleman is Lord John Roxton. The young lady, of course, you already know."

Ardan was puzzled. "I am afraid I do not. There is something familiar about you, Miss, but I do not know your name."

The young woman gave him a wry smile. "Why, Clark," she murmured, "I don't know whether to be insulted that you don't recall me or flattered that I must have changed so much. We now share our last name, if that helps you to place me." Her voice was strong and pleasant, and had a decided French Canadian sound to it.

"The same name?" Ardan was startled. "Yes, of course! Aunt Pamela!" He blinked. "The last time I saw you was at Uncle Alex's wedding!"

His cousin laughed. "Yes, that was five years ago. I have changed a little. Child-bearing has a way of doing that to a woman."

"How is your daughter... what's her name?... Patricia?"

"Four, now. You should see her. She's a real little terror," she said laughing.

Pamela May Thibault had married an uncle of his, who had moved to the backwoods of Canada almost 20 years ago. Ardan had pretty much lost touch with him as a result, and had only seen her once in his life, at their wedding. No wonder he had not managed to recognize her—and why Maston had assumed he knew her.

"What are you doing here?" he inquired.

"The Thibaults are long-standing members of the Montreal branch of the Gun Club," she explained. "I happened to be in London, and when I heard you wished to consult the members here, naturally I arranged to be present."

"Naturally." One thing Ardan did recall about his Canadian aunt was her pronounced sense of curiosity and her fascination with excitement.

"I hear you have somethin' special for us, young man," Lord Roxton said, clearly eager to get down to business.

"It is something you might be able to help me with," Ardan agreed. He removed the photographic plate from the bag he carried and laid it on the nearest table. Roxton and Maston bent to look at it, and Pamela shifted in her chair to get a better view.

"Must have been risky gettin' this," Roxton murmured.

"Slightly," Ardan agreed, not wishing to detail his adventures. "It was taken at a height of about 1000 feet. It is an enlarged view of the interesting area of the resulting picture."

"I'll say," Pamela agreed. "It's a railway gun, clearly."

Ardan knew this much, but little more. "It's a new Hun weapon," he explained." The barrel is approximately 100 feet long. It is mounted on a railway flatbed to enable it to be draw by an engine."

"Must have an impressive range," Roxton offered.

"It has," Ardan agreed. "It is located in the forest of Coucy, and it has been shelling Paris—at a distance of 75 miles—since March."

"Ah!" Pamela exclaimed with delight. "The famous Paris Gun! I've long wished to see it!"

"So have the Allied High Command," Ardan informed her dryly. "And they wish to destroy it. But it is well defended and mobile to a degree."

"At those sort of ranges, it can't be too ruddy accurate," Roxton said.

"It doesn't have to be," Ardan said. "It can shell Paris without any warning, and causes a great deal of panic. No one can tell when the next bombardment will commence, or what may be the target. It is a weapon more of terror than siege, but it does its job well. Morale in Paris is low."

Pamela sighed. "And I assume your task is to destroy it? It does seem a pity."

"The inhabitants of Paris might not agree with you," Ardan said, dryly.

"Oh, I understand that," Pamela said hastily. "And I quite agree. But..." She picked up the plate. "It is *such* a magnificent gun. Made by Krupp's, obviously." She had named the largest German manufacturer of weaponry. "And designed, undoubtedly, by Von Kimmel."

"Yes," Maston agreed. "He was a member of the Gun Club before the War," he explained to the young man. "He often spoke with me about his wish to produce the biggest gun in the world. It would appear he has achieved his aim." He shook his head. "Such a perversion of all we stand for."

Ardan looked at him curiously. "But what other point is there in building guns if not to destroy life and property?"

Maston was shocked. "Sir!" he exclaimed. "The *point*, as you put it, is to *learn*. We strive to extend the frontiers of man's knowledge, to discover his capabilities."

"Besides," Pamela pointed out, "it was a gun that launched your grandfather—and Mr. Maston's father, along with Mr. Barbicane—on their wonderful trip to the Moon."

"Considering the forces involved, they were all astoundingly lucky not to have perished in the attempt," Ardan replied. "And one exception does not negate my point—the sole reason to build such guns is to kill and destroy. Men can advance their knowledge in far more peaceful ways."

"But not as much fun," Pamela complained.

"I think we'd best leave philosophical matters to the philosophers," Ralston said. "I meself am a man of action, and it's clear that's what is called for here. Do you have a plan, young man?"

"My thought is for a small band of men to penetrate the German lines," Ardan stated. "Less than five would stand the best chance, and three might be optimum. Well-placed thermite charges should cause sufficient damage to the barrel to prevent it from functioning."

"That might work," Pamela agreed. "Provided there are no spare barrels."

"Why would the Germans have any spares?" Ardan asked.

"Because of the tremendous velocity the shells will achieve on being fired," she explained. "Simply firing a shell would cause measurable wear inside the barrel. The barrel would need to be replaced on a regular basis or else the weapon would be rendered useless."

Ardan had failed to consider this, and he felt a pang of embarrassment. It was his way to attempt to consider all the possibilities, and he had overlooked this one. "Then more than the barrel must be destroyed—the rail car itself. I cannot be certain that the Huns do not have more of these weapons ready to replace the gun, but it would seem unlikely. Given the state of the war, they would surely have utilized them."

"Agreed," Maston said. "And casting and placing such a weapon would be a delicate and far from simple process. There is a likelihood that spare barrels have been cast—but it would take considerable time to install one and align it. A variation of even a fraction of an inch from the bottom to top of the barrel could be disastrous."

Roxton gave a barking laugh. "It sounds extremely chancy and dangerous to me, young fella. Count me in—I wouldn't miss it for the world."

"Me too," Pamela said, eagerly. "Next to building a gun like that, blowing one up is probably the most fun I'll have had in years."

Ardan stared at her, aghast. "You are most certainly *not* coming along on this mission. It is far too dangerous for a woman. If we are captured, we will be shot as spies—and the Germans have proven that they are quite as happy to execute women as men."

Pamela's eyes blazed. "Clark, I did not think you would be such a chauvinist! Do you think women have less courage than men? That we would shirk our duty because we are more afraid of consequences than you?"

"War is no place for a woman," Ardan said, firmly.

"It's no place for men, either!" she snapped. "But while war exists, we must all do our duty and attempt to bring it to the swiftest end. I am coming, and that's final."

Ardan looked to Roxton for help. "Surely you agree with me?" he asked.

"On general principals, certainly," the English Lord said. "However, in this particular circumstance, I have to agree with the young lady."

"What?"

"Certainly." Roxton gave him a frank look. "Miss Thibault has shown that she is the expert here in the matter of the Paris Gun. She has already made one good point that you overlooked—not your fault, of course, you can't know everythin'—and she may be able to make more on the spot. If you really want that gun blown up, then I'd say she'll be an invaluable member of the team."

"Thank you, your Lordship," Pamela said, smirking at her nephew.

"Don't thank me, young lady," Roxton replied. "Our young Mr. Ardan might well be right, too—this is a very dangerous mission, and we might all end up dead and the gun untouched. But I've fought dinosaurs and men, and I'm not goin' to sit this one out."

"And nor am I," Pamela said, firmly, glaring at Ardan and daring him to disagree.

What could he do? Much as he hated the idea of leading his cousin into danger, she and Roxton had a valid point. She clearly understood this weapon better than he did, and it was imperative that it be destroyed.

"Very well," he said, gritting his teeth. "We leave at 4 a.m.—perhaps you had best prepare for this mission by writing out your will."

"Did anyone ever tell you that you're a sore loser?" Pamela asked.

"I do not make it a habit to lose," Ardan informed her.

She gave him a sweet smile. "I'll try and make it as gentle an experience as possible, then," she promised.

Ardan could see that this was not going to be easy on his nerves...

Getting across the English Channel to France was simple enough, if a little wearing on Ardan's nerves. Pamela, it seemed, threw herself into every endeavor with a wholeheartedness that worried him. She had read up on the Coucy region where the gun was based and memorized pages of information. That was all well and good, but he hoped it would not make her over-confident when they arrived. She had managed to confine her changes of clothing to a minimum—not a simple thing for a woman in the young man's experience. And she had brought along a small arsenal.

Ardan distrusted guns. Even the best of them had the potential to jam at the moment you needed it most, and he tried to avoid using them unless absolutely necessary. Pamela, however, having been brought up in the backwoods of Quebec, had been hunting since she was a child, and had several rifles and a pistol, all of which she had obviously cleaned on a regular basis. He could hardly forbid her from bringing them along—they would probably be absolutely necessary. Besides, Roxton had his own bag of rifles and he could hardly forbid Patricia what his other companion was carrying. But it disturbed him to see a woman with a weapon.

He had trouble understanding women. Partly, he knew, it was simply that he was unfamiliar with them. His mother Jacqueline had died when he was a child, and he had been raised by his father and a group of all-male tutors. The other part was that he simply did not know how they thought. Pamela, for example, was clearly very intelligent and insightful, but he could never predict what she might be capable of saying next. He wished over and over that she had not come along on this mission.

The trip to the forest of Coucy was long but uneventful until the final stretches. Once they entered the area under German control, Ardan halted their advance for a quiet conference. They all wore identical clothing—dark pants, a long, dark great-coat and dark hats. These served to cover his and Patricia's light-color hair, which might otherwise give them away. Roxton and Pamela both had rifles slung over their shoulders and pistols in holsters at their waists. Ardan had no gun, but carried his usual supply of scientific devices he preferred to utilize secreted about his clothing.

"The Boche patrol these woods on a regular basis," he informed his companions softly. "We shall have to take great care from here on. Make as little noise as possible, for stealth is essential."

"Teach your grandmother to suck eggs," Pamela jeered. "Roxton and I are both hunters, and if we weren't adept at silence, we'd hardly catch much, would we?"

Ardan strove to keep his temper in check. "I am merely reminding you both," he said. "You do not have to take every comment as a personal challenge."

"If you didn't mean them to be, it would be a lot simpler," Pamela retorted. "I know you resent my being here, but I *am* here, so stop acting like I'm a liability and allow me to do my job."

Ardan nodded, stiffly. "I am endeavoring to do just that."

"Under protest," his aunt argued.

"Um, please," Roxton broke in. "Let's not have this discussion again, eh? We're here, the gun's there, and we'd better be on our way, eh?"

"Right," Ardan agreed. "Come along."

As the slipped through the thick woods, the young man realized that Pamela had been quite correct—she and Roxton made almost as little noise as he himself did. Both were clearly excellent hunters and adept at stealth. Why, then, did this information not make him feel any better about his aunt being there?

Was it possible that she was correct, and he *was* a male chauvinist?

They passed close to three patrols, all of which they detected soon enough to enable them to hide until the enemy had passed. It was clear from the casual manners of the soldiers that they feared no Allied attacks this deep in their occupied lands. That confidence, if shared by the rest of the Huns— might make their task a whole lot simpler.

A short while later, Roxton tapped him on the arm and pointed. Through the trees ahead he saw the glint of metal on the ground—the railway line to Paris. They were getting closer to their target and had to take even greater care as they moved.

There were more patrols, and these were more alert than the farther-flung ones. They were close to their superiors and wanted to make a good impression. In each case, though, Roxton and Pamela hid in the undergrowth while Ardan took to the branches of the trees above. In the event any of them were discovered, then the others might be able to offer assistance. It turned out to be unnecessary, however, as their approach remained undetected.

The Paris Gun itself was surrounded by a battery of smaller guns for protection against any Allied raids—as well as by the flyers of Rittmeister Von Hammer's squadron, who would fly over the site on regular patrols once it was light enough. Probably in less than an hour. It was a little incongruous in the depths of the woods to see the guns manned by sailors, but the Paris Gun was commanded by a German Admiral as it was technically a naval gun, even though they were far from the ocean. The Huns were sticklers for protocol. So the guns were all operated by men and officers of the Navy, while the patrols were regular Army.

Ardan and his companions moved slowly and stealthily through the enemy forces, skirting the guns as widely as possible. And their target came into all-too-clear sight.

Even though he had seen it from the air, Ardan was still startled by the sheer size of it. The barrel was almost 100 feet long, and had to be strongly braced lest it might bend even a fraction of an inch. It sat on a large flatbed, which stood itself upon a concrete base to take the weight, which had to be in excess of 200 tons. Shells for the gun were in smaller, separate trucks. The flatbed was placed on a turntable to allow it to be aimed, but it clearly would take a long time to reposition it.

He, Pamela and Roxton studied the gun from concealment, and then crawled away some distance before they discussed their options.

"What do you think?" he asked Roxton, softly.

"Well, there's several points where we can destroy it," the hunter replied. "The supports for the barrel, for one thing—shear them and its own weight will bring the blasted thing down. Even simply cracking the concrete supports or blowin' up the railcar it's on would do the trick. A few sticks of dynamite down the barrel..." He shrugged. "Plenty of possibilities, m'boy."

"Not one of which will work," Pamela stated firmly, echoing Ardan's own fears. "Oh, they'd all do the job fine—provided we can get close enough to the gun to actually *use* one or all of them. But there's over 200 men surrounding that gun." She glared at her nephew. "I don't care how quiet you are, or how stealthy—nobody could get through those men and plant any bombs unseen. *Nobody*."

"I agree," Ardan stated, and he saw the flash or surprise in her eyes. He cracked the smallest of smiles. "I don't disagree with you purely as a matter of principal, you know."

"I was beginning to wonder," she murmured. "So, what do we do?"

"The two of you will destroy the gun," Ardan said. "Any of Roxton's suggestions sound fine to me. Or you could try this." He pulled a small container from his clothing and handed it to Pamela. "A thermite paste of my own devising," he explained. "Smear some of this on a few of the projectiles. The heat from firing the gun and the friction of the projectiles in the barrel will cause it to heat up and expand the projectile."

"Trapping it in the barrel," the young woman said gleefully. "I like it." She took the container. "But we still can't get close enough to use it."

"I will create a diversion," Ardan assured her. "As soon as it commences, the two of you head for the gun."

"What are you plannin'?" Roxton asked curiously.

Ardan smiled. "There are a lot of men on the ground around the gun. But not one *above* it..."

Getting to the German airfield wasn't too difficult now that he was on his own. Francis Ardan used all of his skills to slip silently through the woods, and avoided all of the patrols. At the edge of the field, he paused to reconnoiter. There was a fair amount of activity, with mechanics checking over various aircraft. Workers were fueling a few of the craft, so it looked like an aerial foray was being readied. With a smile, he spotted Von Hammer's blood-red Fokker sitting alone. A worker was driving a fuel truck away from it, so it was clearly ready for flight, and merely awaiting the arrival of the aviator himself.

What better disguise could he employ? The young man moved from cover, and sauntered toward the craft. His long, dark coat looked sufficiently like a flying jacket that he aroused no suspicions. It was early and no one was expecting any intrusion at this remote, guarded field, and this played in his favor. As soon as there were no eyes upon him, he sprinted for the Fokker and swung into the cockpit.

He'd never been in a Fokker tri-wing before, but he knew that if Biggles were here, his friend would be saying, as ever: "If you can fly a Sopwith Camel, you can fly anything." The controls were basically very similar, though Ardan was certain the Fokker would handle very differently once he was aloft. This should prove educational...

Once he had fired up the engine, he received some attention—especially since the ground crew knew that Von Hammer had not yet arrived. A handful of people started to move, puzzled, toward him, as he taxied and then began gunning the engine to gather speed. The ground had been cleared and roughly leveled, but the plane shook and bumped. Then he had sufficient speed to get aloft and he hauled back on the stick.

Mechanics flattened as he flew low over their heads. He was starting to get the feel of the controls as he maneuvered for height. It would be a while before anyone would be able to get aloft after him, but he couldn't spare too much time to experiment. Instead, as soon as he was 200 feet up, he turned the plane and headed back toward the Paris gun.

He checked the craft's Spandau's, firing short bursts from both to be certain they were working properly, and smiled grimly. He was now ready.

The flight back was swift, and it was barely five minutes before he could see the huge barrel looming ahead of him. Men were working on it, and he realized that it was being readied to be fired. Paris would suffer another terrifying barrage if he and his companions didn't succeed.

He sent the Fokker into a downward spiral, and held his thumbs over the firing controls. Despite the fact that they were enemy soldiers down there, he was reluctant to actually take a life. After the war, he intended to train as a medical doctor, and he preferred to save life rather than kill. Accordingly, he sent his first burst slightly to the side of the gun.

Incredulous eyes glanced up, and obviously saw that their attacker seemed to be their own top ace. Accordingly, nobody moved initially. Ardan sprayed a second burst closer, and now saw realization and panic set it. Men threw themselves from the gun and ran for cover. It was a shame he had no bombs aboard the Fokker—he might have caused serious damage if he had—but he kept up a continual stream of fire as he passed over and over the gun. He saw the gun crews heading toward the anti-aircraft guns, having finally realized this was an enemy and not their defender. The sky would start getting uncomfortable for him very shortly.

Then he saw two figures running *toward* the gun—obviously Roxton and Pamela. He swooped in lower to provide them covering fire as they committed their act of sabotage.

The Huns had managed to get one of their ack-ack guns in operation, and started firing in his direction. Dodging the one gun wasn't too difficult, but then a second and third came into operation, and the sky was starting to get very unpleasant. At this altitude it wouldn't be long before he was hit. He strafed the emplacements as best he could, but they were dug in well, and impossible to hit. Glancing back at the Paris Gun, he saw that Roxton and Pamela were retreating back to the forest, their work presumably accomplished.

Now he could break off his attack and retreat. Stretching the Fokker to the limit of its endurance, he made a sharp left wheel. He could hear the fabric and wires groaning about him as he did so, but in moments he was out of the range of the enemy fire.

But only for seconds. Then a stream of bullets from *above* slammed into the right side of the plane. Ardan glanced about ands saw three more Fokkers—all metallic gray—swooping toward him. He tried to whirl out of their way, but he was still not an expert at the controls, and the plane was sluggish. More bullets tore through his wings and came dangerously close to hitting him.

Von Hammer had arrived...

His own guns were almost empty by now, so attempting to fight was impossible. The Rittmeister knew these planes far better than he did, and this would be a fight Ardan would lose. He did the only thing he could in the circumstances—pointed the nose of his plane down, and aimed to land.

Von Hammer held his fire—he was not a brutal man, and there would be no glory for him in killing an opponent who was clearly surrendering. Besides, he probably wanted his own plane back.

As Ardan taxied to a halt, German soldiers surrounded him rapidly, their rifles raised. The young man cut the Fokker's engine and clambered slowly out of the craft. A Captain, his Luger carefully aimed at Ardan's head, came forward.

"I surrender," the young man said calmly.

"A wise move. Your attempted attack has failed." The German smiled. "Paris will be shortly under siege once more." He gestured toward the big gun, where activity had commenced again. Men were loading a shell into the huge breach. There was no obvious signs of damage, and he could only trust that his companions had achieved their mission. His captors led him away.

There was a transport truck waiting on one of the roads away from the rail line, and the Captain gestured the young adventurer toward it. "You are not the first of today's captives," the German said with satisfaction. "You will join your companions."

Ardan felt a momentary tightness. Had Pamela and Roxton been caught? He was prepared to suffer what he must, but the thought of his pretty aunt as a prisoner of the Boche was almost unbearable.

Then all Hell broke loose. There was a tremendous explosion, and a wave of fire. Ardan was completely deafened, and blown off his feet. He shook his head, attempting to clear it, and saw that the Paris gun was in flames. The barrel was shattered and twisted, and the rail car warped. Germans—some with their clothes aflame—were running for cover. They were probably screaming, but the young man could hear nothing.

His companions had performed their task well. For the first time in his life, Ardan realized that sometimes having people with him to aid him might not be such a bad idea. People like Roxton and Pamela, people he could trust and rely upon... Though it was rather academic at the moment. He was a prisoner still, and unlikely to be doing any more fighting for the foreseeable future.

His hearing gradually began to return, and he could hear feverish commands being yelled in German. People were attempting to quell the fire before it spread to the ammunition cars. Ardan staggered uncertainly to his feet, and checked himself over. There was a web of blood upon his forehead where a small piece of shrapnel must have struck him a glancing blow, but otherwise he was unharmed.

"Get those prisoners out of here," someone called in German. His hearing was returning, thankfully. The Captain used his Luger to gesture the young man into the waiting truck. Two of the armed soldiers followed him to act as guards. As he stood ready to climb aboard, friendly hands reached out to help him clamber aboard. With great relief, Ardan realized that they belonged to two men he had never seen before. So Roxton and Pamela had made good their escape! That made him feel a lot better.

"Come on, you hairy ape," one of the men grumbled. "Let's get this hero aboard." He was a tall, slender man with impeccable, unbelievably neat clothing.

His companion was shorter and stockier, and indeed looked almost more anthropoid than human. "I'm not the one slacking off, you over-dressed shyster," he complained. Then he gave the young man a massive grin. "Nice work, partner. It's good to see that gun out of action."

"Much as it pains me to ever agree with you," his companion said, "in this case, I concur."

Ardan settled onto the floor of the truck with the two of them. The guards sat on small benches, keeping an alert eye upon the captives. The van started up with a jerk, and then rumbled away. The other two prisoners had started up some argument about who it was of them that had managed to get them both captured. The young man ignored them as best he could, instead watching with considerable satisfaction as the Germans strove to save what they could from the disaster. Then the van turned away, and he could see the destruction no more.

Yes, indeed—having people he could trust and work with had been a great advantage here, and might well be again. It all depended upon him finding the right people, of course.

"You monkey-brained, prehistoric remnant!" the natty dresser yelled at his companion.

"Yeah? What do you know, you fashion plate?"

It was going to be a long trip...

As we mentioned in our introduction, during the 1920s, Doc Ardan was often encouraged by his father and by Dr. de Grandin to take breaks and go on exploratory journeys to remote locations. Here is one of his adventures, previously published in Tales of the Shadowmen 2...

Jean-Marc Lofficier: *The Star Prince*

Moroccan Desert, The Early 1920s

"If you please, draw me a dinosaur!"

Francis Ardan looked at the golden-haired boy. He was dressed in an operetta-style costume, wearing a long blue coat, white shirt, pants and shiny boots. The aviator had been forced to make an emergency landing in this deserted part of the Western Sahara and was busy repairing the engine when, suddenly, the boy had appeared out of nowhere.

"What are you doing here?" asked Ardan.

"If you please, draw me a dinosaur," asked the boy.

It seemed churlish to refuse. Ardan took out his logbook and pencil and began drawing.

"Who are you?" he asked.

"I come from above," said the boy, pointing at the starry sky. "I am so bored up there."

"How did you come here?"

"It is difficult. And very painful. When I leave, I die a little. So I only come when someone is around. I can only come here because that's where they are. The machines."

"The machines?"

"They're buried deep in the sand. There used to be a sea here, and dinosaurs and other children with whom I could play. But everything is gone now. And I am all alone."

Ardan had finished the drawing. He gave it to the boy.

"It is very beautiful," he said. "Just as I remember them. Thank you. I will treasure it forever. It was worth it."

"Can't you come more often? Reach other people?" asked Ardan. "There is so much we could learn from you."

"I don't have enough power. I'm sorry. I'm only a very little star," said the boy, as his made-up body slowly began to crumble into dust, mingling with the sand that covered the ancient machines.

Vincent Jounieaux' tale as written for another anthology, The Shadow of Judex, *devoted to the black-cloaked French Avenger. Here, Doc Ardan, almost out of medical school, and ably assisted by Inspector Ménardier, last seen in the classic novel* Belphegor, *faces a terrible conspiracy...*

Vincent Jounieaux: *The Dreadful Conspiracy*

Paris, 1925

Inspector Ménardier wrinkled his nose when he stepped into the interview room at the Quai des Orfèvres. A strong smell of mildew permeated the small room because of its peeling wall paper. On the ceiling, only two bulbs out of four were working.

It seems President Doumergue is still powerless to change the mind of the Banque de France, he thought. *Times are tough for public services. I think we'll still have a long wait before they fix the ventilation or replace the lights...*

He sat down in front of a metal table, across from the empty seat that would soon welcome his suspect. Ménardier thought that the modern psychological theories that encouraged the police to put the perpetrator in a position of inferiority were absurd; he didn't care in which chair the suspect sat. He glanced at the one-way mirror, behind which stood one of the faceless minions of the Préfecture de Police. The interview would be recorded for later analysis.

"Bring him in."

Someone heard his command and the door creaked open. A tall, young man with a light bronze complexion was ushered into the room. His hands were cuffed behind his back. Because of his size, he had to bend a little to cross the threshold. His powerful muscles stood out under his khaki-colored shirt.

"You may leave us," Antoine said to the policeman who was escorting the suspect.

The man gave a brief salute, complied, and closed the door on the two men. The inspector began the interrogation:

"Are you Monsieur Francis Ardan? Or do you prefer to be called Clark Savage Jr.?"

"I'm the only one here, am I not?" replied the young man, still standing up. He eyed the policeman suspiciously, hostility burning deep inside his golden eyes.

"Whom have I the honor of addressing?" he then asked.

"I'm Inspector Ménardier of the Police Judiciaire."

"I wish I could say I was pleased to meet you, Inspector, but I'm not."

"I'm sorry to hear that, Monsieur Ardan. I know it's always painful to be brought before the police..."

"Only if you've done something wrong—which I didn't."

"That is for me to determine."

"I fear that this conversation is starting out on the wrong track, Inspector. As an American citizen, I have rights. I demand that you contact my attorney, Mr. Theodore Marley Brooks of New York."

"Calm down, Monsieur Ardan. You're not in America here! You're in Paris, at the Quai des Orfèvres. Right now, the only person who can say what rights you have is me, and I'm telling you to sit down!"

"For a policeman, you seem to be singularly disrespectful of the Law."

"And for a student of medicine, you look like a fairground Hercules."

Ardan ignored the sarcasm but, under Ménardier's astonished eyes, he flexed his biceps; the veins of his arm swelled and the muscles tore the seams of his sleeves. There was a loud snap and the handcuffs fell to the ground. The man of bronze leaned forward, pressing his fists on the table. The inspector remained impassive, with only a discreet smile on his lips.

"Monsieur Ardan, do not aggravate your situation!"

"What am I accused of?"

"You are accused of the murders of Baron Hampain, Ferdinand Finalit, Horace Dasseaux and Serge Bouriet, all punishable by the death penalty under Article 295-298 of the French penal code."

Ardan clenched his fists; his knuckles turned white.

"And why would have I done that?"

"For the money, of course! They were four of the largest fortunes in France..."

"Ridiculous! I have more wealth that I could ever spend in a lifetime."

"Ah, yes! I forgot! Your father's Central American gold mines!"

"Indeed. And the income generated by the Hidalgo Trading Company which guarantees me a very comfortable standard of living..."

"While it is true that my meager pay does not allow me to look at this business with complete impartiality, it seems to me that wealth always creates a desire for more of the same. The thirst for it is insatiable..."

"Let me call my lawyer. Ham will soon get to the bottom of this."

"Unfortunately, we have too much evidence against you. I am forced to incarcerate you at La Santé prison."

"You're making a terrible mistake..."

"I don't think so. Unless I'm in error, you are soon scheduled to present your doctorate thesis at the Medical School of La Sorbonne, is that right?"

"Yes, but I don't see the connection..."

"And your research is about...?"

"I doubt that you're educated enough to grasp it."

"Let me be the judge of that, please."

"Well, my thesis deals with the after-effects of partial lobotomy on human behavior."

"Good. We're making progress! Now, let me introduce you to some of the evidence against you. First, all four victims suffered from some odd brain surgery only a few weeks before they were killed; second, they all developed abnormal behavior and emptied their bank accounts in a totally irrational fashion before their alleged suicides; third, we found your student card under the sofa at the home of the banker, Serge Bouriet—the last victim! You see, Monsieur Ardan, we know a lot about you..."

"You know nothing! Someone is obviously trying to frame me for this."

"Really? What about the billions of francs that Bouriet transferred to your bank account before he died? I'm referring to the account held in your name at the Depository Bank of Zurich. It belongs to you, doesn't it?"

"..."

"I see that I've managed to surprise you at last... You see, even a lowly French official with a questionable level of education might know a thing or two about tax havens. Finding your trail was difficult but not impossible... I wish you good night now, Monsieur Ardan. I hope your bed at La Santé won't be too hard!"

Winter was rapidly approaching; the days were shortening; the weather had turned cold and damp. On the Rue de Turenne, under the wan light of the street lamps, the passersby were raising the collars of their coats and burying their hands in their pockets.

The offices of the banker, Berthelaux, occupied a building at the corner of an upscale street in Le Marais district.

"Vallières! You're still here? Excellent! Bring me the file on the Industrial Bank of China. It's in the safe in my room. I left it open... Stop dilly-dallying and hurry up!"

Silently, Berthelaux's personal secretary obeyed the order. The early night had surprised Berthelaux at work. After Vallières had left the office, the banker stretched in his chair and looked at his books filled with carefully calligraphied figures in black ink. His bronze art deco desk lamp cast a shadow on his worried face. With his fingertips, he prodded at the back of his neck... What had happened to him? That morning, he had to twist in front of the mirror to catch a glimpse of a thin, white scar. His hair had been cut there but was already regrowing. Someone had performed some kind of surgery on him, maybe a week or ten days before, judging from the hair, but he had no memory of it...

"I've got it, Monsieur."

Berthelaux was startled; he had not heard Vallières return. The old secretary stood at the door, file in hand.

"Damn! You scared me! Next time, knock on the door will you? Leave the file here. I'll look at it alone. See you tomorrow, Vallières. Be on time."

"Yes, Monsieur. Certainly, Monsieur."

With the corner of his eye, Berthelaux stared at the departing secretary. The man was tall, seemingly alert, but his temples were covered with pure white hair. He couldn't tell his age... Forty? Fifty? Older? The secretary hadn't seemed to notice the banker's concerns, which suited Berthelaux well. Vallières' absolute discretion was, on occasion, verging on naiveté. Berthelaux never had to complain about the man's professional behavior. Vallières was an ideal employee, hardworking, effective, even-tempered and loyal to the point of stupidity. Even today, the secretary had not questioned any of Berthelaux's unexplained absences.

I should give him a raise, he thought before returning to his main subject of preoccupation.

His inexplicable amnesia worried him. There was no way he could tell the police. With all the evidence of his financial wrongdoings lying around, he would be the one to find himself behind bars! He could consult his physician, but the strange scar night trigger a cascade of investigations and interrogations... Who had kidnapped him? For what reason?

The problem haunted him and disturbed his thoughts. He did not remember anything... Simply waking up one morning fully dressed with a raging migraine. Panic had overwhelmed him, prompting him to burn his accounting books and destroy all incriminating documents. But he had saved the file on the

Industrial Bank of China because it was his highest concern. He, Hampain, Finalit, Dasseaux and Bouriet had started it, supposedly to finance French industrial expansion in the Far East. In reality, the bank allowed them to siphon away the savings of small French investors and divert investment from the Chinese government... The scandal had broken in 1921, but it had been quickly stifled and Berthelaux had been sentenced to only a ten year loss of his civil rights—a trifle!

Today, the newspapers had reported the death of his fourth partner! What a strange coincidence—or was it? This series of murders may have been committed by one of the many French investors ruined by the scam. Could someone have decided to wait four years before taking his revenge? Was he next? He glanced at the file labeled BIC and threw it into the fireplace. Then, he lit a match after dousing it with rubbing alcohol and watched it burn.

"All the evidence is going up in smoke!" he said to himself.

Vallières slammed the outside door when he left the house. The aged secretary, his hands in his pockets, plunged into the Parisian night. At the end of the street, he glanced back. One could see Berthelaux's shadow illuminated by bursts of light from the fireplace, on the curtains of the first floor windows.

"Damn you, Berthelaux!" muttered Vallières. "Your time has come, villain... I see that fear is driving you to try to destroy the evidence against you... But you'll soon discover how useless it is…"

Berthelaux was his mortal enemy! The man had set up shop again, but his public notoriety was merely a front; behind it hid one of the worst villains of the world of finance. Not just any crook to Vallières, but one of the men who had conspired to ruin his father, the Comte de Trémeuse. Buried under his debts, and the schemes of the bankers, the unhappy nobleman had committed suicide. It all dated back to before the Great War, when he was but a child. Over the years, he had grown into a fearsome crime-fighter called Judex, who had succeeded in avenging his father and was now going after the criminals of high finance who destroyed the lives of their victims, but were rarely pursued by the Law. For the identity of Vallières was but a mask, a disguise useful to infiltrate the privacy of the scoundrels he hunted.

An odd couple was strolling through the streets of Paris. One was a dapper dandy, carrying a thin black cane; his companion looked more like a gorilla than a man. The dandy was the lawyer Theodore Marley Brooks, a.k.a. Ham; his burly friend was Andrew Blodgett Mayfair a.k.a. Monk. They always seemed ready to jump at each other's throats and neither missed an opportunity to hurl insults at the other. Yet, Ham had often risked his life to save Monk, and vice versa. The lawyer, used to the square grid of New York streets, felt lost in the maze of the French capital and blindly followed his friend. Monk, his bushy eyebrows furrowed, studied a map of Paris.

"Right, then right again, then left" he announced. "It isn't very far! Here, look: a café! I would love to have a *petit blanc*, as they say around here... What do you think, Ham? It would do us a world of good before we have to wrestle with that undertaker!"

"God, no! Not on an empty stomach! Besides, we don't have time. Sorry Monk, it'll have to be another time!"

"That's fine, I can wait until tonight. How about we go and listen to our compatriot at the Dome?"

"What on Earth are you talking about?"

"Josephine Baker! The singer, you idiot! The one who walks in the streets of Paris with a Panther on a leash! They call her the Queen of Montmartre!"

"The name does ring a bell," the lawyer admitted.

"I have two *amooouuurs*…" Monk began to sing.

"With your face, just one would be a miracle."

Monk growled, baring his fangs and gave his friend a small blow to the solar plexus. The young lawyer, breathless, was forced to listen to the entire song...

The telegram reporting the arrest of Francis Ardan had been delivered to the Empire State Building the day before. It had been received by Colonel John Renwick a.k.a. Renny, who had immediately notified his two associates Thomas J. Roberts, a.k.a. Long Tom, and William Harper Littlejohn, a.k.a. Johnny. All three were ready to travel to France, but the Atlantic crossing proved impossible! Traveling by boat would have taken too much time, and the test flight of the dirigible *Graf Zeppelin X1* between New York and Cherbourg wasn't scheduled for another few weeks.

Monk and Ham, however, were already in England, each attending professional conferences, Ham on International Law in Cambridge and Monk on chemistry in Oxford. It was child's play for them to take the first ferry from Dover to Calais. Meanwhile, Long Tom, Johnny and Renny had set up a hotline at the Empire State, in case their help became necessary.

Ham had a lot of professional contacts around the world and knew Mr. Ferval, the Director of the Police Judiciaire. The two had met at Harvard the year before and had immediately hit it off. At the time, Ferval had been in Boston to acquaint himself with the modern methods of American policing. His support would be invaluable in helping Ardan prove his innocence.

Ham and Monk had arrived in Paris the day after the arrest of their friend. A telegram from Johnny was already waiting for them at their hotel. They were to proceed at once to the hospital of La Pitié-Salpêtrière where the autopsy of the latest victim, Serge Bouriet, was being conducted. Then, a meeting at the prison of La Santé with Ardan, Ferval and the arresting officer, Inspector Ménardier, had been arranged.

Once the two Americans reached the Boulevard Saint-Marcel, they looked at the map and quickly located La Pitié-Salpêtrière. There, the receptionist gave them directions to the pathology department where the Morgue was located. They introduced themselves to an orderly and sat patiently in the waiting room.

"I hate the smell of hospitals," muttered Monk, wiping the sweat beading on his forehead with one of his paw-like hands.

"You mean that irresistible fragrance of ether and excrement?"

"Yes! With a touch of mycosis."

"Stop being such a girl."

"And if you keep making fun of me, I'm leaving you here alone here to deal with the Frenchies!"

Monk was pretending to leave when a door opened and a voice called out:

"Mr. Brooks? Mr. Mayfair? The Doctor will see you now."

A thin, lanky, orderly, reeking of formaldehyde, invited them to follow him.

"Doctor de Grandin apologizes for the delay," he added. "He just finished the autopsy and immediately sent me to fetch you."

"Excellent," said Ham. "It is very kind of Doctor de Grandin to see us so quickly. This is a matter of grave urgency. The clock is ticking!"

The orderly looked at him, a little shocked by his bluntness... He took the two Americans into a room filled rows of gleaming stainless steel tables, upon which were cadavers. Some were wrapped in a black plastic sheath, but the vast majority were naked, some as pale as snow, others mottled with cyanosis. Monk almost had a heart attack when he saw the grisly scene. At the end of the room was a doctor in a white coat, mask, gloves and goggles.

"Come in, gentlemen!" he shouted to the newcomers. "I've just finished the autopsy of our 'client.' Step right up! I think some my findings are bound to be of interest to you...

The remains of Serge Bouriet rested on the autopsy table, his skull opened and his thorax ajar. Various bloody bodily fluids had collected in the metal gutters. Monk turned green at the sight of the dismembered corpse.

Doctor Jules de Grandin, of the Ecole de Médecine of the University of Paris, was a small blond man with a beautiful waxed mustache and extraordinarily piercing blue eyes He appeared perfectly at ease as he completed his gruesome task. He told the two Americans that Bouriet had died of asphyxiation by hanging, as evidenced by a pulmonary edema and a tracheal cartilage fracture. But a strange scar on his neck had captured the doctor's attention.

"You see, right there!" he said, animatedly. "This scar is relatively recent, less than four weeks-old. It is clean; the work of a surgeon, made by a scalpel and professionally stitched. I'm still trying to figure out its purpose… As you can see, the left trapezius and complexus muscles were cut and then stitched back together. There is a small swelling right here…" added the doctor, inserting a gloved finger inside the body/ "Ha-ha! I feel something!"

"Have you found something?" asked Ham.

Monk, his mouth half open, stood speechless, unable to tear his eyes away from the opened skull.

"Yes! *Par la barbe d'un bouc vert!* It's something small—and metallic! I'm going to pull it out…"

Making a careful excision took some time, but de Grandin finally extracted a small, black, metallic sphere, the size of an olive, with very fine, silver filaments hanging from its ends.

De Grandin deposited the object in a basin and, adjusting magnifying lenses over his glasses, returned to his study of the dead man's brain.

"I'm cutting through the ligaments to study the lower segment of the medulla oblongata. *Parbleu!* The columns of Goll and Burdach are riddled with microscopic holes..." De Grandin adjusted his magnifying glasses. "The holes are pointing towards the cerebral protuberance. It's impossible... How could this man have endured such an intervention? It's..."

The rest of his words became lost in incomprehensible medical jargon. Ham suddenly felt a nagging doubt. Ardan had come to France to complete his medical studies and benefit from the teaching of Clovis Vincent, the famous neurosurgeon. Could this be their friend's work? No! He couldn't believe it! Maybe the analysis of the strange metallic "olive" would provide a clue towards the solution of this puzzle?

Suddenly, a loud thud interrupted his thoughts: Monk had just fainted.

Monk quickly recovered from his shock and the duo soon joined Monsieur Ferval and Inspector Ménardier at the prison of La Santé. The meeting between Ham and the Director of the Police was enthusiastic, and the smartly-dressed lawyer even allowed the Frenchman to hug him.

Ferval used his position to take them inside the prison without the usual searches, etc. They expected to find their friend laid low by this terrible trial. But that would have been a mistake! Instead, Ardan welcomed them with good spirits and open arms and only the short stubble on his cheeks testified to his incarceration...

He had taken advantage of his day behind bars to continue writing his thesis, between his usual tough training sessions. His incredible skills were not the result of magic, but of great physical and mental discipline. His perfectly proportioned body and vast intellectual abilities were the result of intensive training, scientifically designed by his father, who had begun to work with his son in the cradle...

Ardan thanked his friends for coming so quickly. Ham introduced him to Monsieur Ferval and the two men bowed to each other. In the prison's parlor, they quickly reviewed the situation. Ferval had asked Ménardier for a copy of the file in order to form his own opinion. It appeared that the four victims had several things in common: they were all involved in the scandal of the International Bank of China, they all had undergone some strange surgery during which a mysterious artificial implant had been connected to their brains, and finally, they all had emptied their bank accounts before committing suicide.

The first three men had transferred their assets to banks located in the Far East, but the latest victim, Serge Bouriet, had transferred his money to an account in Switzerland in the name of Francis Ardan...

That, in addition to his student card, unexpectedly found at the crime scene, seemed to incriminate him; but Ferval was suspicious. Ardan explained that he had no recollection of when the card had disappeared from his wallet.

The only lead left to the police was to interview the last surviving founding member of the International Bank of China. The man's name was Berthelaux. Ferval asked Ménardier to call on him and place him under police protection as soon as possible.

Ardan asked to attend, or even participate in, the analysis of the strange olive-shaped implant that was to be performed by Doctor de Grandin that same night. Ferval was, at first, reluctant to authorize it, but Ham suggested that, if his friend was accompanied by a police escort, gave his word of honor not to attempt to escape, and deposited a large sum of money with the Caisse des Depôts & Consignations, then bail was possible.

"But you need to obtain authorization from the Investigating Magistrate," said Ferval, still hesitating.

"You mean, this kind of authorization?" said Ham, smiling, producing a letter signed by Judge Coméliau, whom he had met before they even got to La Pitié-Salpêtrière Hospital.

Ferval smiled. Certainly, his friend from Harvard had not usurped his reputation as one of the finest legal eagles of the bar!

It was five o'clock when Judex / Vallières heard a Talbot turn into the Rue de Turenne accompanied by a howl of screeching tires. He drew aside the curtain of the first floor window and saw two men jump out of the car and walk at a brisk pace towards the Berthelaux house, They were followed by the well-known figure of Inspector Ménardier.

The police!

The net is closing, thought Judex. *I do not know what you did during your unexplained absence, Berthelaux, but the police are on to you. You can't escape me though... You belong to me!*

He let the curtain fall, as he heard the police ring the doorbell several times.

"Monsieur Berthelaux?"

"This is he."

"I'm Inspector Ménardier of the Police Judiciaire. May I come in?"

"May I see your badge?"

The badge flashed, revealing a quick glimpse of the service pistol under the inspector's jacket.

"Fine, Inspector! What can I do for you?"

"Let me introduce you to my two friends: this is Mr. Brooks of the New York bar, and Mr. Mayfair, also an American. I'm sorry to burst in on you like this, but we have evidence that leads us to believe that you're in great danger."

"That's ridiculous! I'm an honest businessman. Who on Earth could want to hurt me?"

"It's about the International Bank of China."

"Sorry, Inspector, but that's all in the past. However, since you've come all the way here on my behalf, you might as well follow me into the library..."

The three men accompanied the banker to the other side of the house. The library was a sumptuously decorated room, filled with ivory carvings, and a collection of small *objets d'art* made of wood or terracotta lining the shelves.

Berthelaux sat in an impressive armchair in a corner and silently invited his "guests" to take the remaining seats.

"As I said," began Ménardier, "we're convinced that four of the founders of this bank, Baron Hampain, Finalit, Dasseaux and Bouriet, were murdered. You are the last surviving member of that group. But don't worry, reinforcements are on their way. You've got no reasons to be concerned…"

"Tell that to my dead colleagues!" said Berthelaux bitterly.

"Is it possible," interjected Ham, "that the problems at the International Bank of China might have injured a Chinese tong? Two years ago, a colleague of our friend Ardan, Dr. Lyndon Parker, faced such an organization called 'Si-Fan.' Could the same thing have happened here, and it is that organization which is now seeking revenge on those it holds responsible for their losses?"

Berthelaux thought for a moment, then said:

"Well, now that you mention it, one of our most important Chinese depositors, who, of course, lost all their money in the bankruptcy, was called Ming Tsai Tsu. He was the head of a consortium known as the Shin Tan..."

"The Shin Tan?" exclaimed Ménardier. "Over the years, I've had to investigate matters relating to Orientals. It is a little known fact, but there are many Far Eastern secret societies operating in France. They are extremely powerful and have branches throughout the world... The Shin Tan is one of them. Their Master is said to be a Mongol 'demon' known only by the nickname: the 'Yellow Shadow.' The few informants who told us about him died suddenly—and not from old age. They all perished from unexplained causes."

"If this Ming character was hurt by the collapse of the International Bank of China, it isn't surprising that he seeks revenge," Ham said. Turning to the banker, he added: "I'm afraid that your financial shenanigans, Monsieur Berthelaux, have had unhappy and unforeseen consequences!"

"Or perhaps," said Monk, "it's a reprisal against the French government's involvement in the death of 52 demonstrators in Canton last June?"[23]

"In any event," said Ham, "this cannot but stir the ardor of the defenders of the Treaty of Versailles and ruin the Franco-German *rapprochement* advocated by your President, Monsieur Heriot, and President Von Hindenburg."

---

[23] On 23 June 1925 in Canton, British and French troops opened fire with machine guns on Chinese demonstrators, killing 52 people and injuring over 100.

"One thing is certain," concluded Ménardier, "all trails lead to you, Monsieur Berthelaux!

That night, at the laboratory at the Sorbonne, Doctor Jules de Grandin, assisted by young Francis Ardan, examined the microscopic metallic olive found in the victim's skull.

The analysis revealed a very advanced technology, well beyond the capacities of either France or the United States.

De Grandin consulted some old books and various documents that he kept locked in a safe. Then, after carefully putting them back, he said:

"In 1901, a man known by the pseudonym of Anton Zarnak spent twenty years in Tibet studying the occult with those he called the 'Masters of A'alshirie.' I had access to some documents kept secret by Zarnak, and the components of this 'olive' appear identical to their technology. I do not pretend to understand it, but I know that its power can affect the mind."

"What if the bankers were remotely mind-controlled?" said Ardan. "That 'olive' turned them into human robots, subject to the will of another—the inventor of this devilish device—who forced them to empty their bank accounts, and then to commit suicide!"

"It is indeed quite possible," nodded de Grandin, stroking his mustache. "Anyway, my young friend," he added, with a friendly tap to Ardan's shoulder, "that's what I intend to write in my report. *Par la barbe d'un bouc vert!* You will not spend another night in our jail at the French taxpayer's expense!

As Ménardier had said, the Police Judiciaire's archives contained very little information about the Shin Tan. There were some extremely sketchy reports from informers, and a document written by the "King of the detectives," the great Chantecoq himself. He had identified one of the few French agents employed by the Shin Tan, a man named Leclerc, who served as a cover for the organization when conducting a number of secret transactions with the French underworld, whose well-known patriotic fervor would not have easily accommodated the notion of dealing with Oriental heathens.

Leclerc's family, according to a report from the last century, written by none other than Chevalier Dupin, had served the Shin Tan for several generations. Leclerc himself met his masters every week at six a.m. at the Notre-Dame Cathedral. Ménardier and his men had only a few hours to get ready.

Ménardier was hiding inside the Saint Denis portal. He was on the lookout in the shadow of the cathedral, his eyes piercing the darkness broken only by the feeble light of candles.

The four bells of the north tower, the Benjamines, struck six o'clock. The Inspector pulled up his overcoat and, by reflex, checked the time on his pocket watch. Leclerc had entered the empty cathedral by the north transept five minutes earlier. The police, as a precaution, had evacuated the church personnel and the few church goers, replacing them with officers in disguise. The man had stood for a moment on the porch, scanning his surroundings. Apparently reassured, Leclerc had then crossed the cathedral without noticing the presence of the police, and gone towards a confessional. Still lurking in the corner of the chapel, Ménardier had seen him enter the booth and sit at the place normally occupied by the priest.

Now, the wait was on...

Ménardier had begun to doubt the arrival of the minions of the Yellow Shadow when, suddenly, an electric torch was lit several times on the other side of the nave. The signal came from Brooks, lurking on the other side of the cathedral.

Ménardier looked up at the side entrance. *Here we go*, he thought, checking his 9 mm Luger. *Si vis pacem, para bellum*, he added, because he hardly knew what to expect from the Shin Tan...

With an undulating walk, a Eurasian woman had suddenly appeared and slowly approached the confessional. Tall, beautiful, she wore a black silk dress that molded her beautiful, slim body. The top of her dress did nothing to hide her voluptuous chest. A long string of pearls hung around her neck. Her proud bearing and extreme sensuality clashed with the austerity of the cathedral.

The young woman slipped under the short curtain of the confessional and knelt with a grace so full of lust that the Saints themselves would have sighed in despair. Ménardier twitched when she rummaged in her bag, but she only pulled out a wad of bank notes, which she handed to Leclerc. The latter began to count them feverishly. Then, quietly, the woman got up and left the confessional.

This was the moment that Ménardier chose to leap from his hiding place and shout:

"Police! Nobody move!"

The door of the confessional suddenly burst open and Leclerc rushed into the nave. Ménardier aimed his gun at the villain, but, faster than lightning, the man had already vanished in the darkness between the stone pillars.

The Eurasian woman took advantage of the moment of uncertainty to scamper towards the choir. Ménardier turned his gun on her. He did not intend to kill her, just to stop her with a bullet in the thigh. He was going to fire when Monk broke into the cathedral, blocking his aim. The Inspector lowered his gun, afraid of harming the American who was now in his line of fire.

Monk, spreading his arms, prepared to intercept the Eurasian woman, but she executed a perfect roll that placed her directly between the legs of her adversary. There, she struck him a hard blow to the groin. The gorilla-like Monk bent under the pain of the blow, but riposted immediately. His left fist described a curve, but encountered only emptiness. However, it had been but a feint. He followed it immediately with a right hook that the Eurasian could not avoid.

The woman uttered a sharp cry of pain. Monk thought he had won, but as he was preparing to grab her, the Eurasian dealt him a violent karate chop to the larynx.

Monk let out a rumbling noise and collapsed, nearly asphyxiated. Bug-eyed, helpless, he saw the woman step over him and fade away into the night.

Meanwhile, Ham. who had observed the whole scene, had rushed out in pursuit of Leclerc, whose stocky body zigzagged between the pillars of the cathedral. The lawyer was gaining ground on his prey, and was about to tackle him to the ground, when the villain suddenly collapsed to the ground, uttering a horrible groan.

Ham looked at Leclerc whose face was becoming swollen.

"The Yellow Shadow... lachrymatory..." the man had time to whisper before he died with a gasp.

His head rolled to one side. His black tongue, abnormally large, jutted from his open mouth like a tumor.

"He's been poisoned," said Ménardier who knelt beside the lawyer.

"Look! The bank notes!" exclaimed Ham.

In the white circle reserved for the watermark in the center of the notes from the Banque de France, which normally depicted a blacksmith and a pretty girl in a toga, a grinning Tibetan demon mask had just appeared!

The mark of the Yellow Shadow!

"He poisoned himself by licking his fingers while counting the money," said Ménardier. "I saw him do it. It's diabolical!"

They were then joined by Monk, who muttered in a hoarse voice:

"That devil woman is gone!" Massaging his sore neck, the 'gorilla' added: "Right now, a shot of bourbon would do me the greatest good..."

Ham smiled, pleased that his friend had recovered his usual banter.

"I just searched the victim," said Ménardier, "and I haven't found any papers on him. Unless the post-mortem turns up something..."

"Shit!" growled Monk. "Another dead end!"

"Not necessarily," said Ham. "I carefully memorized his last words... It's amazing how death loosens tongues!"

The Paris catacombs were spread before them, like a deadly maze winding through the darkness.

Ménardier, Ham and Monk were marching in a line, their crepe soles stifling the sound of their steps. On each side of them, piles of human bones and friezes of skulls shone softly under the light of their electric torches.

Ham shuddered. He had not taken the time to dress himself warmly and the stress only added to the chill generated by the ambient 57 degrees F. He had drawn his sword from the scabbard of his cane and followed Ménardier and Monk, who were both armed with crossbows. Behind them came a small squad of policemen, armed with Thomson submachine guns, dispatched by Commissaire Valentin of the notorious *Brigades du Tigre*.[24]

Meanwhile, several elite policemen stood guard at the home of Berthelaux, which had been converted into an impregnable citadel. Ferval believed firmly that the banker would be the next target of the mysterious Mr. Ming...

As for Francis Ardan, the file requesting his release was now on Judge Coméliau's desk. There was no doubt that he would soon sign it, and that the young man would be free before the end of the day. However, Ménardier had not seen fit to wait for Ardan's release to launch his offensive.

Leclerc's last words seemed to indicate that the Parisian lair of the enigmatic Mongol—whom no one doubted was behind the mysterious "olives" implanted in the villainous bankers' brains—was located near the lachrymatory, one of

---

[24] The so-called "Tiger's Brigade" were created in 1907 by President Georges Clemenceau, whose nickname was the "Tiger," hence their name, to serve as the first, modern crime fighting unit, not unlike London's Flying Squad created in 1919. They formed the basis of a popular French television series which ran from 1974 to 1983, referenced here.

the famous tombs located in the Paris catacombs. Ferval orders were clear: to protect Berthelaux on the one hand, and to invade the ossuary.

Around noon, the task force sent by Valentin quietly joined the trio at the entrance of the catacombs. Silently, the dozen men made their way into the depths of the capital. Like an army of ghosts, in absolute silence, they rushed down through an endless succession of aqueducts and winding quarry tunnels.

When they reached the ossuary, the access of which was blocked by a heavy metal door, Ham shuddered at reading the words carved on the lintel: "*Stop! Here begins the realm of Death...*" The curator of the Carnavalet museum had handed him a key and Ménardier used it to unlock the enormous metal bolt as discreetly as he could.

The expedition resumed its macabre progression, heading for the crypt of the lachrymatory. Suddenly, Inspector Pujol, one of Valentin's men who had gone ahead as a scout, warned them of the presence of guards preventing access to the tomb. Ménardier asked the men to extinguish their torches and they continued their advance in the most complete darkness, walking silently in single file. Ham shuddered again.

Soon, they reached the crossroad where Pujol waited. With a gesture, he showed them the tenuous glow of torches shining at the end of a gallery leading to the tomb.

They tip-toed forward, hugging the damp walls. As they reached a column of bleached bones, Ménardier beckoned Ham to join him. The lawyer walked silently and cast a wary eye behind the pillar.

Two figures stood there, motionless. There were two *dacoits* with long hair and dead eyes, armed with large knives, guarding the crypt. Ham turned around and ran his thumb across his throat. The message was clear! Monk and Ménardier took aim with their crossbows in perfect synchronicity and shot. Whistling through the air, the bolts pierced the necks of the sentinels, who barely had time to cough up some blood before expiring. Their bodies had not even touched the ground when they were picked up and removed by the policemen.

In the center of the darkened hall stood the lachrymatory, the famous tomb of the poet Nicolas Gilbert, bearing the famous inscription: *Au banquet de la vie, infortuné convive, j'apparus un jour et je meurs...* [25] There was no sign of life, or activity. The echo of the removal of the dacoits had not raised any alarms...

Pujol and his colleague Inspector Terrasson went to check the neighboring tunnels and quickly returned, gesturing to certify that the premises were secure.

The squad then began to conceal themselves around the tomb, and the interminable wait amongst the remains of six million dead began. The strangeness of the place, the threat of the Shin Tan, the ominous Mr. Ming, all these things worried Ham. To add to his torment, Monk taunted him by making constant, apelike grimaces at him.

At about six o'clock in the evening, they heard a creaking sound echoing through the tomb; a stone rubbing against another stone. Ham, shivering with cold, stood up. Around the room, the policemen, alert, stood up quietly, ready for action.

A sliver of light appeared on the wall behind the tomb, then widened to reveal a secret passage from which emerged a silhouette. It crept cautiously into the tomb. Monk immediately recognized the Eurasian woman whom he had fought at the cathedral. Her right arm was in a sling. She emerged from the shadows. She was just as stunning as she had been at Notre-Dame; this time, she wore a short dress made of silver *lamé*. She inspected the tomb with a flashlight, but did not detect any danger.

The Eurasian woman then went to the sarcophagus and touched a secret mechanism, which revealed another secret passage. The sarcophagus opened over a narrow stone staircase which the woman took, hurrying down. Already, the sar-

---

[25] At the banquet of life, unfortunate guest, I came one day, then died.

cophagus was about to close when Ménardier, rushing forward, slid his crossbow inside to prevent the mechanism from shutting down. The weapon bent, the wood groaning under the strain, but the opening remained ajar...

The Inspector quietly slipped through the passage, immediately followed by Monk, Ham, and the men of the *Brigades du Tigre*. The spiral staircase curved through countless strata of bones carved with runes and ended up in a narrow gallery. Below it was a vast cavern, carved out of the stone, illuminated by a pulsed light accompanied by a low hum.

The policemen, holding their guns at the ready, looked into the cavern, which was filled with banks of scientific-looking machinery. At the center of the room was the Eurasian woman. She stood in front of a human-sized glass jar; inside which was a dark, motionless humanoid form. It was a bald man with amber-colored eyes, wide open, in an olive face, dressed as a clergyman, seated in an armchair, the high back of which was carved with dragons and chimeras. His head was under a transparent helmet bristling with coils, conductors, and resistors.

The dreaded Mongol was bathed in the same murky light that seemed to come from nowhere.

"The Yellow Shadow," whispered Ménardier.

Suddenly, Ming seemed to awaken from his trance. With a gesture, he removed the helmet to which he had been attached. Then a mechanism caused the glass jar to lift upwards.

Ming rose.

"Ivana," he said, addressing the Eurasian woman, "have you accomplished your mission?"

"Yes, brother," she replied. "Leclerc will never speak again. But the police are on our track. I'm afraid..."

"I know her, now," Ménardier murmured. "She is Ivana Orloff, a Russian princess related to the Counts Boehm of Germany. Much was made of her in the press recently when she arrived in Paris..."

"Drop your weapons!" said a heavily accented voice.

Ménardier, Ham and Monk turned around and discovered a horde of dacoits, each more sinister than the other, pointing the barrels of their guns at them. They all wore strange dark glasses. Rather than comply, the police went on the attack and opened fire on the dacoits.

Taking advantage of the melee, Ming took a small crystal ball filled with a greenish liquid, which had been resting on a work table, and smashed it on the ground. Immediately a ray of blinding white light flooded the room. The brightness of the rays burned the eyes of the police. Ham howled in pain. He understood the reason for the strange glasses worn by the dacoits: they shielded their eyes from effects of the weapon used by their master!

He heard hurried steps, then words spewed in a dialect unknown to him. The lawyer dropped his sword for fear of hurting his friends. A pair of arms seized him. He delivered a series of blows to defend himself, feeling jaws crunching under his fists. But a hard object hit his head, making him see a thousand stars in the bright afterglow. Ham fell to his knees. His tongue welded to the palate of his mouth, he could not call for help. His legs and arms hurt... The second blow mercifully rendered him unconscious...

When Ham came to, he felt as if two red-hot pincers were crushing his skull. He saw Ming look at him:

"Are you in pain, Mister Brooks? Good—but try not to die... You think you may have won the war, but you have won but a single battle! Tell your friend Ardan that I shall ruin his plans for peace! You Americans, you only want to get rich on the backs of the less advantaged... You wish to forget that there are wars and revolutions, but I'm here to remind you... I will foster a future darker than your worst nightmares!"

Ming laughed a long and cruel laugh, like the growl of a tiger.

Before passing out again, Ham saw him smile and disappear with his sister, Ivana Orloff in tow. Then he sank back into unconsciousness and a mindscape of fragmented arabesques...

A policeman lifted his eyelid and shouted something that Ham did not understand.

The man turned him on his stomach and he felt the blade of a knife sliding between his wrists, cutting the ropes that had hindered him, freeing his hands from behind his back.

Ham huddled on the cold ground, wet, dazed, vaguely discerning Monk at his side.

Acrid smoke filled the cavern. He heard a series of explosions and chunks of ceiling crashed near him. The lawyer didn't care. The only thing that existed for him was his violent headache. He could barely move. The bitter taste of bile was in his mouth... *Above all, don't move*, he said to himself.

He saw Ménardier haranguing his troops... So the Brigades du Tigre had won the battle after all!

Then, he saw the familiar figure of Francis Ardan, accompanied by Doctor de Grandin, who was busy dismantling Ming's diabolical machines. Naked filaments hurled showers of sparks in the air.

We have to get out of here asap, Ham thought in a flash of lucidity. *Everything must be booby-trapped. The Yellow Shadow wouldn't want anyone unlocking his secrets...*

There was another blast, followed by another blackout. Time stretched endlessly. Someone tried to lift him.

"No! I beg you... Evacuate the room!" urged the lawyer.

He hardly recognized the man built like a gorilla, his face bloodied, who grabbed him under the arms and carried him to safety.

A pale sun rose over the rooftops of Paris, dissipating the opalescent dawn.

Ménardier had been pacing the sidewalk for five minutes when the automobile appeared at the corner of the Rue de Turenne. The Inspector saw the tall figure of Ardan, followed by the massive one of Monk, get out of the vehicle, not without some difficulty.

"I've been waiting for you," he grumbled.

"Sorry," said Ardan. "We had to go to the emergency room of the Hotel-Dieu to check on Ham and take care of Monk's head..."

Monk's flat forehead was bandaged, and the left side of his face showed numerous scratches. His clothes were spotted with blackened blood stains. Ménardier, turning to Ardan, asked:

"How is Mr. Brooks?"

"A skull fracture. He was being taken into the operating room when we left... But I'm assured that his life is not in danger.

"Thanks for arriving at the last minute with those reinforcements Ardan. Without you..." The Inspector shuddered at the thought of the gruesome fate that the Mongol could have inflicted on them.

"All the credit should go to Doctor de Grandin," said Ardan. "It was he who designed a machine capable of tracing the source of that mysterious 'Mega Wave' used by Ming to enslave his victims, allowing us to arrive just in time to lend you a helping hand. De Grandin drew on the work of an English physician, Doctor Septimus, whose book on the subject was published in 1922, but..."

But Ménardier wasn't listening anymore; the Inspector had turned around and was heading toward the steps of Berthelaux's home.

The curtain was about to fall!

Some police officers stood on guard in the lobby, searching the visitors. In an adjacent room, they saw more policemen and de Grandin seated before his electronic equipment. A small parabolic dish on top of it turned slowly, while the round, grey screen showed a tiny, erratic sinusoid green line.

Ménardier observed the light patterns without understanding. This modern technology was beyond his comprehension...

"Still nothing to report, doctor?" he inquired.

"Nothing," replied de Grandin; his eyes were underlined with dark circles due to the lack of sleep from the night before.

He was trying to modulate the reception of the signal when Berthelaux appeared in his dressing gown, walking down the stairs leading to his living room.

"What's all this fuss?"

Ardan, who had hitherto remained silent, jumped on the banker and seized him by the throat, lifting him up off the ground. Berthelaux, his neck caught in that giant grip, kicked at the air with his legs.

"Help!" he cried. "Who is this madman? I'll ruin your career, Inspector! I have friends in high places!"

The man of bronze man forcibly turned the banker's head, revealing the short white scar on the occipital bone on the back of his head. He then said coldly:

"Just as I feared, we're too late. This man has already undergone Ming's operation. He's under the control of the Yellow Shadow. It is through this abominable scheme that Ming grabbed the fortunes of the first three bankers who'd robbed him, and tried to frame me for the death of the fourth..."

Ardan dropped Berthelaux, who fell heavily into a chair, coughed, gasped, struggling to catch his breath. Ardan went on:

"But now, we're on to you, Ming! We know the directional nature of the Mega Wave and Doctor de Grandin's equipment will find you, wherever you are!"

Berthelaux continued to squirm in his seat, uncomfortable. Ménardier turned towards him.

"What do you say to that, Monsieur Berthelaux?"

"Inspector, I have no idea what this man is talking about! I know nothing about a Mega Wave or anything else, I swear... It's true, I woke up two days ago with that scar, and I can't remember how I got it. I must have been kidnapped and drugged, but I don't remember anything!"

"Of course, you didn't see fit to call the police..."

"I was going to, but I was scared! You understand... A man in my position! I thought that it may have been someone upset with his investments... But my intention was always to contact you and help you with your inquiry..."

"Nonsense, Ming!" interrupted Ardan. "Your plan is subtle, but we now know that you're in control of Berthelaux through that olive implanted in his skull. I want to know what you real goals are!"

"You're crazy! I may have that thing inside me, but right now, I am the banker Berthelaux! I demand a lawyer! Inspector, I order you to take me to a hospital in order to have that thing removed…"

Suddenly, a bell rang.

"8:59 sharp!" said the banker. "No one is more punctual than my good man Vallières..."

Soon, Vallières entered the room, carrying a tray with tea and coffee which exuded a powerful aroma and another, more subtle smell, undetectable by all, except for Ardan's olfactory sense, trained since birth to uncover traps of all kinds.

"No!" yelled Ardan, realizing what was happening. "It's Ming! You mustn't ..."

Then, he lapsed into unconsciousness, joining Monk and the police already asleep from the effects of the soporific gas made from a rare species of mushroom of which only Judex knew the secret.

"Justice is done," murmured the avenger, carrying the body of Berthelaux and disappearing towards the roof.

When the police came to, Ménardier rushed into the lobby. Short of breath, his eyes still tearing, he asked the policemen on guard:

"Tell me that you saw something...?"

"Nothing, Inspector! We saw nothing at all!"

Ménardier was about to unleash a volley of oaths when Ardan pointed to something white fluttering through the room. It was a dove, which, cooing, landed on Berthelaux's desk, then flew away and disappeared through an open window in the morning sky of Paris.

"Shit!" swore Ménardier, his face crimson. "It's Judex! He's got Berthelaux!"

"Judex?" asked Ardan.

"A vigilante who goes after crooked businessmen and crazy industrialists... There's a good chance that we'll never see Berthelaux again..."

"The only victim of Judex that we've ever identified," added Jules de Grandin "and that was purely by accident, was located by Chantecoq. It was Gontran, a billionaire and a madman. Judex had performed plastic surgery on him, making him completely unrecognizable. He had also undergone some kind of lobotomy that had left him a wreck. He lived like a bum under a bridge in Paris... He was interned. What a mess... If only this man used his talents to rehabilitate criminals, instead of punishing them..."

The expression on Ardan's face became pensive.

"Rehabilitating... Yes, that's a thought," he murmured.

"What will you do with Bouriet's fortune, which you now own, albeit unintentionally?"

"First, I'll compensate all the victims, of course. Then, I think I'll set up a fund to support Aristide Briand. I believe in him. He advocates reconciliation between France and Germany... Because I fear that the Yellow Shadow may already be fomenting a new war..."

(translation by J.-M. & Randy Lofficier)

Jason Scott Aiken's tale, previously published in Tales of the Shadowmen 12, *is based on* The People of the Pole, *a remarkable 1907 French proto-*Lost World *novel by Charles Derennes, translated by Brian Stableford, available from Black Coat Press, ISBN 978-1-934543-39-9. In it, Doc Ardan goes looking for a mysterious race of intelligent reptiles...*

Jason Scott Aiken: *Ardan at the Pole*

January 3, 1928, Baltimore, MD

This afternoon, I had lunch at the Baltimore Gun Club in the company of Mr. Hareton Ironcastle. A naturalist and renowned explorer, he had sponsored my membership into the club several years ago. Although, Michel Ardan (a distant relative of mine) has his picture placed prominently on the wall of the establishment, this connection didn't guarantee my admission to this selective group. Ironcastle's heartfelt recommendation, along with my military record and scientific background were vital in acquiring membership.

Ironcastle, a good friend of my father, related tales from some of their adventures to me. He was able to fill in some gaps about my father's life that I hadn't been aware of. Mr. Ironcastle was also interested in my days as a pilot in the Great War. He seemed fascinated with aviation in particular.

When he asked about the possibility of Arctic flight, I raised my eyebrows. Knowing I was onto his leading questions, he produced a rugged, well-traveled satchel from beneath his chair. The veteran explorer reached in and withdrew a manuscript, then placed it on the table for me to examine. I judged it to be an older document, close to 20 years old. The text was in French, but for the sake of ease, I will list the English translation here.

The People of the Pole
Written by Jean-Louis de Venasque
Transcribed by Charles Derennes
Completed November 25, 1906

I looked at Ironcastle inquisitively. Over the years, I had heard rumblings of the de Venasque manuscript, but up to this point, I had never met anyone who had seen it, let alone owned an actual copy of the document. I inquired if this was in fact the original document. Ironcastle stated it wasn't the original, but the one and only copy of Derennes' transcription of de Venasque's original document. This was Derennes' own copy, and he never produced another.

According to Ironcastle, the original de Venasque manuscript was in the private collection of the anthropologist who discovered it, Louis Valenton. He is a professor at the College de France. The manuscript was found in a petrol canister by Valenton while on the Yalmal Peninsula, near the mouth of the Ob. It was Valenton who allowed Derennes to make a copy.

Valenton and Ironcastle were old acquaintances. At some point, three years ago, Derennes sent the copy to Valenton unexpectedly, instructing him to find a proper home for the document. Valenton had no need to have the original manuscript and the copy. He also wanted to follow through on friend's wishes. This led to him sending the manuscript to Ironcastle.

Ironcastle asked if I would read it and provide an opinion on the veracity of Jean-Louis de Venasque's account. He didn't have to ask me twice, for my curiosity was piqued. He excused himself from the table to allow me time to read the document.

Although the account was quite lengthy, my skill at speed reading allows me to read, and comprehend, written documents in a quarter of the time as the average person. The contents were engrossing, and I found myself rapidly turning the pages. I will summarize the account of de Venasque below for a frame of reference.

On April 26, 1905, Jean-Louis de Venasque, a French nobleman, and his acquaintance, Jacques Ceintras, an engineer, departed in their dirigible from Franz-Josef Land in an attempt to reach the North Pole. The pair piloted the vessel across the frozen plain until they reached a violet-lit area that is the North Pole, complete with flora and fauna. They found miniature pterodactyls and a race of intelligent humanoid iguanodons that lived in a subterranean realm beneath the pole.

The mental state of both men seems to deteriorate over time. Ceintras went mad and eventually killed a number of the iguanodons after they prevented the pair from leaving in their dirigible. This was thanks to a type of magnetic locking mechanism the creatures employed, which anchored the aircraft to the ground. Eventually, Ceintras and Venasque parted company. Ceintras chose to walk across the frozen plain to certain death. Venasque stayed at the pole and chronicled what transpired. He placed his manuscript in a petrol canister and threw it into the nearby river, hoping it would make its way out to sea.

Once I finished reading the manuscript, I sat at the table in silence for fifteen minutes. There have been a handful of explorers who have claimed to reach the North Pole since de Venasque and Ceintras attempted the feat. The claims of these explorers remain questionable to this day, but none claimed to have seen the fantastic sights de Venasque described. The situation with the de Venasque account was quite unusual. I had to admit to being a bit skeptical of the source, Valenton. If the claims were true about the iguanodons, the manuscript would support Valenton's own theories, which weren't widely accepted by the scientific community.

In 1906, after returning from an expedition in northern Asia, Valenton brought back the bones of a previously undiscovered creature. He dubbed it the *anthroposaurus*. He postulated it was an amphibious reptile that possessed both intelligence and reason. Valenton believed the anthroposaurus to be a contemporary of the first humans. He conceded the species was now extinct, but perhaps some had survived and evolved. If true, the iguanadons mentioned in de Venasque's manuscript could be the descendants of Valenton's anthroposaurus.

I can't say my doubts ended at Valenton. The writings of de Venasque himself were also a bit troubling. Even when taking into account that he was writing these documents in complete human isolation, expecting to perish in the coming days, there was something not quite right regarding his demeanor. This account might very well have been an elaborate fantasy written by a psychotic who murdered his friend, and attempted to justify it by creating his own warped reality. The violet light, iguanadons, the miniature pterodactyls, and underground realm may all have been fictitious. The two explorers didn't have the friendliest of relationships to begin with. Perhaps their dirigible suffered a catastrophic failure and they became stranded at the North Pole. The animosity between them may have risen to the surface, and a life was taken as a result.

Yet, if this was the work of a madman, it was very well constructed and full of some interesting concepts. Especially when one considered when it was written. It was too bad de Venasque hadn't made it back to civilization. Had he returned to France, he would have had a future as a fiction writer.

When Ironcastle returned I related the above conclusions to him. He listened intently, but didn't show any emotion until I stated my final thought on the matter. The only way to verify the account would be if someone journeyed to the North Pole to investigate. Ironcastle smiled and nodded in approval. He asked me if that was my way of volunteering. I paused for a moment, and stated that it was. Ironcastle was pleased; he proclaimed he had reason to believe portions of de Venasque's account. I asked him to enlighten me, but he looked around the room and shook his head. He then told me it wasn't the time or the place to discuss such things.

Ironcastle and I left the Gun Club together. He wished me luck and instructed me to reach out to him should I need anything. I began planning once I got back to my lodgings, which my cousin and his bride have allowed me to use while in Baltimore. I'll be leaving tomorrow morning to gather resources and begin planning the expedition.

March 12, 1928, Kabarova, Russia

I have spent the last two weeks in this small Samoyed village situated south of the Jugor Straight, near the entrance to the Kara Sea. This is the same village where de Venasque and Ceintras prepared for their voyage in their dirigible. All inquiries made around the village support their presence here in 1905. Some of the villagers who were children, or young adults, remembered the pair very well. From the descriptions of the villagers, I was able to sketch the appearances of the two and have the townsfolk confirm my accuracy.

Tracking down the lover of Ceintras proved to be quite easy. I spoke with her... and her son who is now 23 years-old. She accepted the fate of Ceintras long ago, but in private, she asked me to bring back his body, if there was one to be found. I made no inquiries on the parentage of her son, as it was simple to deduce.

My means of travel will be a Boeing Model 40 A. It's one of only twenty-five built. I'm making some customizations to the engines and frame to allow for better performance in cold temperatures. The craft must also be modified to allow for additional fuel. Luckily, compartment space is plenty. If need be, I can easily fit a passenger in the cargo hold with my equipment.

Preparations are going splendidly. I hope to have the modifications completed in the next few days, followed by a test flight by the end of the week. If successful, the aircraft will then be transported by ship to the southern tip of Franz Josef Land, just as de Venasque and Ceintras transported their dirigible. My cousin has graciously lent me the use of his ship, the *Faucon Occidental* for transportation.

March 16, 1928, Franz Josef Land, Russia

The test flight was a success. I arrived this morning in Franz Josef Land aboard the *Faucon Occidental*. Camp was set up. All preparations are set for a sunrise flight tomorrow morning. My plan is to spend the rest of the night in my mind palace in preparation. If all goes according to plan, my next journal entry will be from the North Pole. For purposes of record-keeping, I will use a chronometer of my own design to keep track of the time, and day while at the pole.

March 17, 1928, The North Pole

Although the area surrounding the pole is in total darkness this time of year (with the sun due to rise in the next few days), I was guided to this spot by an orange light on the surface. Upon landing, I observed the obvious lack of violet light, as well as any plant or animal. The ground was a solid sheet of ice, with no sign of any river or stream. The source of the orange light I observed from above was a small signal fire. I quickly unpacked my supplies and set up a tent for shelter. I plan to use this as my base of operations while investigating the surrounding area. I'm going to take refuge from the cold and attempt to get some rest before exploring the area further.

March 18, 1928, The North Pole

I woke feeling refreshed and eager to begin my investigation. After eating my morning rations, I returned to the fire. Utilizing the flames, I ignited a torch. Around the blaze I observed a path of well defined footprints that led to the fire. The footprints then circled around the fire, and disappeared back into the darkness. The tracks made a large horseshoe shape. Judging by the depth and rendering, the same person must have been walking over their own footprints for some time.

The below zero temperatures at the pole required me to bring some prototypes I recently completed. I'm particularly proud of the undergarments that prevent my body heat from escaping. Pair these with the heat packets I inserted in my boots and gloves, and I was able to stay out in the open for hours at a time. I've been letting my hair and facial hair grow since leaving for Russia, and it has come in very thick. Every little bit helps. I donned a pair of pilot goggles as well. After checking my handset to ensure the tracking device on the plane was functioning, I pursued my investigation of the footprints.

I walked parallel to the trail for ten minutes before my vision started to blur. After approximately two more minutes, I began to lose my equilibrium. My knees buckled, forcing me to stop my trek. I closed my eyes and concentrated on my breathing, taking an internal diagnostic. Before I could complete a hypothesis, the sensation faded. My vision cleared and I was no longer off balance. I decided to continue following the trail, when I noticed the footprints were no longer visible. After circling the area, I was unable to find any sign of the tracks. The only footprints I could locate were my own. Not only that, but I noticed I felt a bit winded, as though I was at a higher altitude than before.

An examination of the horizon revealed I was on a plateau between two mountain peaks. This shouldn't have been possible. I posited that I may have blacked out during my trek and somehow ended up there, thanks to my prodigious physical abilities. Even for me, that situation seemed remote. I consulted my hand-held tracking device, but the screen gave no indication of my aircraft's presence. The device was functioning, as the dot indicating my position was active, but there was no sign of my plane.

When modern technology fails me, I'm always open to more archaic methods. So I looked to the stars. I had studied the arctic sky upon landing the night before. Gifted with an eidetic memory, I can assure you the sky I was observing was no longer the same sky. Even the Pole Star, Polaris, proved difficult to identify, as it was out of position.

With both technological and archaic means of navigation

failing me, I chose to attempt to retrace my footsteps. I turned around and began trekking back in the opposite direction. Continuing on the same course away from my shelter and means of egress would have been most unwise, regardless of how far away I actually was.

As I turned back, I noticed movements in my peripheral vision. I was being flanked on both sides.

I had just enough time to pivot and execute a *baritsu* technique on the assailant on my right, which flung him into the attacker on my left. Both fell to the ground on impact. The two tripped over each other trying to get back their footing.

They growled at each other in their disorientation. Clearly, these beings had never encountered the martial arts before. Their confusion was to my benefit, as it provided me time to study their appearance. I also gave some ground to put some distance between us, as to better observe them.

They weren't human. Well, they weren't *homo sapiens*, that much was obvious. Their faces resembled Neanderthals'. They snarled and made gestures at me. I would describe their skin pigment as yellow, and they had thick black manes. The beings wore white animal skins, presumably of the polar bear. They were squat, approximately 5'4" in height, but they were stocky. They were especially broad in the shoulders. These were powerful-looking creatures. Judging by their heads and hands, they had large skeletal structures as well.

As I prepared for their attack, two more creatures appeared behind them. Then two more behind those. The initial two creatures I encountered had their blood up and this worked up the other four into a frenzy as well. It's my belief that they were verbally communicating with each other. They kept staring at me with what I can only describe as murderous intent. Finally, they reached beneath their cloaks and produced daggers made of bone.

It was my estimation that I was capable of snapping their necks or backs with my bare hands on an individual basis. However, this would be a difficult task when fighting them simultaneously. It was evident if all six were to rush me at once, there would be little I could do. Even a smoke pellet from my vest would only delay the inevitable. I was outnumbered six to one on an icy plateau with no escape. Coming to the conclusion that I was faced with a fatal outcome, no matter the situation in hand to hand combat, I decided to engage them with a weapon.

I reached into my belt and drew my dagger, the God Slayer. This is an ancient blade I discovered on an archaeological expedition in the Caspian Sea. The name is derived from the scrolls found cached with the blade, which claimed it once slew a deity. The blade was razor sharp and made of an alloy that I haven't been able to identify. I had little doubt in its capabilities to sever the thick muscle and bone of these creatures.

If the creatures had attacked first, I wouldn't have been able to defeat their superior numbers, so I took the initiative and launched myself at the first two creatures. Gripping the blade with a backhanded grip, I made a single arching cut across the throat of one creature, severing his jugular. I grabbed the second creature by his mane and drove the blade through his forehead and twisted for good measure.

Two others came at me, but they attacked head-on and I had the advantage of a longer reach. I kicked one squarely in the face to buy some time. Then I spun behind his partner and attempted to sever his spinal cord at the base of the neck. I did cut him, but evidently not deep enough. The creature attempted to get back to his feet, but I stabbed down and embedded the dagger in the top of his skull. Expecting attacks from the final two, I spun around and prepared to defend or attack. But the final two weren't attacking. As a matter of fact, they were giving me some ground. I was about to back away and go about my business when I discovered the reason for their hesitation.

Out of the darkness walked even more creatures. A quick count put their numbers at roughly a hundred. These creatures were garbed in thicker animal hides, and all carried spears. It was apparent I had only met the forward scouts of this larger army. The remaining two scouts eyed me with sinister intent. The joy was apparent on their cruel faces. The situation looked grim until the scout closest to me looked puzzled and began sniffing the air. He looked to his right, pointed and yelled in alarm.

In the direction he pointed was a large group of warriors, their bronze armor and swords gleaming in the moonlight. I counted their number to be at sixty. They didn't have the superior numbers, but this didn't seem to faze them. Their leader shouted: "*Lomar rus!*" as he led the charge into the fray.

It was an epic and savage battle, with both sides rending flesh and bone all around them. As much of a spectacle as it was, I didn't think it would be wise to be around to answer to whomever the victors might be. I retreated and took the opportunity to quickly rehydrate and consume some rations. Then I made my ultimate exit from the scene.

I approximated the direction where my aircraft was supposed to be to the best of my ability, and began running in that direction. I needed to get away quickly, but didn't want to burn excess calories due to my situation. My rations were limited. So I jogged lightly, and went into a wolf trot once I felt I was far enough away from the battle. According to my chronometer, I wolf-trotted for a half hour. The peak I was running toward didn't seem to be getting any closer. I continued my pace until I became overcome with disorientation once again. Closing my eyes and focusing on my breathing got me through the episode once more.

When I opened my eyes, it was to a violet-lit sky. I wasn't standing on ice any longer, but grass. A feeling of warmth came over me. Twenty yards in front of me was a flowing stream. I was now at the very place described by de Venasque. Seeing the stream, I knew the dirigible and entrance to the underground tunnels must be nearby. I crossed the stream and made my way over a small hill. On the other side was the dirigible, still anchored to the surface. I crouched down and produced a pair of binoculars, then scanned the area.

I saw no signs of movement at first, but I did spot the door to the tunnels described by de Venasque. I remained in a crouched position at this location for several minutes before venturing down to the dirigible.

On my way down, I observed footprints both human and non-human. The human footprints were consistent and appeared to belong to the same person. While the non-human footprints were inconsistent and seemed to belong to different individuals. Before approaching the dirigible, I buried the God Slayer. If the magnetic clamps were still active beneath the vessel, I didn't want to have my dagger pinned to the surface as well. As I rounded the base of the dirigible, I noticed a small campfire that was still burning. The remains of a small fowl-like creature were still on the spit roast.

I proceeded to enter the dirigible by knocking on the cabin door, but no answer was given. I entered and saw the reason why: there was a man on the floor curled into the fetal position. I crouched down and examined him. He was a little bit older, but it was without a doubt de Venasque. However, he didn't look nearly as aged as I expected him to. My diagnosis was he was suffering from malnutrition from a lack of a balanced diet. From the scraps around the room, it appeared his only source of nourishment was from meat of the fowl-like creatures. I felt his abdomen and it was rock hard as well. I deduced he must be having difficulty passing stool, causing him added discomfort.

I undressed out of my heavy arctic garb and unpacked the supplies. My first order of business was to get some nutrients in his system. I administered an IV solution mixed with ingredients from my first-aid kit. I also performed an enema to help him with his abdominal discomfort. While he didn't awaken for nearly three hours, his bowels did vacate multiple times. I observed the look of discomfort on his face disappear. The man was a bit confused when he first woke up, but this was eclipsed by his joy at how much better he was feeling. He thanked me for my help and introduced himself as Jean-Louis de Venasque. I shook his hand and introduced myself, before he drifted back off to sleep.

To say this has been a busy day for me is an understatement. According to my chronometer, it's now 22:00. I can't begin to understand the events of today, but hopefully tomorrow will bring some answers. I'm going to refill Venasque's IV bag and get some rest myself.

March 19, 1928, The North Pole

After awakening at 07:00, I checked on de Venasque. Upon measuring his pulse, he jolted upright. Not used to having anyone touch him for quite some time, this startled him out of a dead sleep. He then remembered the situation and my name. I explained to him how I came to be there and what I had discovered since arriving at the North Pole. I explained the periods of disorientation to de Venasque and he stated it started happening to him as well. De Venasque proved to be quite sound of mind despite my earlier conclusions drawn from his manuscript. He appeared to have overcome the mental stress inflicted upon him.

De Venasque indicated he has been the one lighting the signal fire, and if I had followed his footprints exactly, I would have reached his location much sooner. Apparently, the North Pole is in a state of flux due to the Earth's magnetic field surrounding it. This has caused a strange phenomenon to develop. De Venasque calls them "invisible doors," but I believe they are rifts in space and time.

When one travels through them, they visit the North Pole, but not necessarily the native North Pole of their own time or dimension. It's just a theory and I have no way to prove it, but, "once you eliminate the impossible, whatever remains, no matter how improbable, must be the truth".

The Great Detective's logic is ever sound, and proved quite reassuring. Especially in the face of what could be considered a supernatural event.

I indicated to de Venasque, that if he could lead me back to the signal fire, I had an aircraft ready. I told him I was willingly to fly him and Ceintras back to Russia, or anywhere else they would like to go. The mention of Ceintras' name caused a frown on de Venasque's face. He relayed that he hadn't seen Ceintras since he left the camp of his own will. De Venasque told me he kept track of the days by when he fell asleep. However, once he became ill, his sleeping habits became too erratic to be accurate. By his estimation, five years had passed, possibly more (which again tells me there is a peculiar distortion surrounding the North Pole). De Venasque stated Ceintras was surely dead by now. He explained he had only managed to survive by consuming the miniature pterodactyls and their eggs. His only source of water came from the stream.

When I asked him about the iguanadons, a look of fear washed over his face. According to him, when Ceintras committed his act of murder, it was like a ripple in a pond. Ceintras introduced the concept of murder into their culture, and they haven't been the same since. Although they still allowed de Venasque to live on the surface, the iguanodons would attack him if he entered or approached the tunnel. I asked him if he had had any luck with the magnetic clamps, but he said he gave up finding a solution some time back. He told me the door to this dimension he and Ceintras accessed in the air would be very difficult to find now anyway. He suggested we both leave on foot via the ground "door" which he used to keep the signal fire lit.

I agreed, but didn't wish to leave right away. After traveling all this way, I intended to visit the underground tunnels and observe the iguanodons. We left the dirigible, and I retrieved the God Slayer. De Venasque walked me to the rift he used to return to our native pole, and I instructed him to wait there for my return. I couldn't enter the tunnels without a disguise, so I made use of iguanodon skins de Venasque had in his possession, as well as a fresh iguanodon corpse found near the stream. The corpse had its throat torn out, but it could still be made into a suitable mask. De Venasque indicated this type of martial combat was becoming more and more common among the People of the Pole.

Once completed and donned, I asked de Venasque for his opinion. He gave me high marks, but stated I would most likely be the largest iguanodon in the tunnels, and would be sure to stick out. This was especially true if they happened to look down at my legs and feet. I decided to go forward with my plan despite the dangers. My examinations of the iguanodon corpse led me to believe the creatures didn't seem to be very physically imposing. But clearly their teeth and claws could be deadly. Before leaving, I had de Venasque sketch me a map of the tunnels so I could better navigate them.

I parted ways from de Venasque and trekked back towards the dirigible. The entrance to the subterranean realm was an iron door nearby. Although the door was heavy, I opened it with relative ease. I shut it behind me, and made sure to test it still opened before descending into the tunnel. Feeling no danger of being trapped from within, I allowed my eyes to adjust to the darkness and followed the tunnel down into the earth.

I can confirm everything de Venasque reported in his account as accurate. While cautiously making my way through the underground labyrinth, I observed the machine which supplied the violet light, as well as the rookery. The map de Venasque provided proved to be no longer complete, as the iguanadons have continued tunneling deeper into the earth since his last visit. I cautiously proceeded, deeper than de Venasque ever ventured.

The People of the Pole have been busy. I traveled for nearly ten minutes before discovering a side cavern they had hollowed out. I entered and lit a small torch. A hideous figure met my gaze in the form of an idol resting on an altar in the middle of the room. It was a grotesque toad-like figure with a rounded belly and a haunting smile. De Venasque's original account made no mention of any deities worshiped by the iguanodons. However, judging by the craftsmanship, it couldn't have been made at the hands of the iguanodons. I have to conclude that they found the statue while tunneling. What ancient civilization worshiped this creature as their deity

I don't know, but I intend to look into it.

I attempted to move closer for a better look, but I was interrupted when one of the iguanodons entered. I did my best to avoid conflict, but I was unsuccessful. As I tried to slip out past him, the creature noticed my lower body and began to scream. It then snapped at me with its teeth. I swayed back to avoid the bite, then clasped its jaws in my hands. It was unable to open its mouth further, but it was already successful in raising an alarm. The sounds of more creatures approaching could be heard echoing from further down the tunnel. It was apparent I needed to make an expedient exit. I snapped the neck of the creature, and removed my disguise so I could run at full speed. Not having the disguise on also let me use the God Slayer freely.

The creatures never caught me from behind. I had a large enough head start on their pursuit, but I did run into many creatures (literally) on my way through their community. Most I knocked over without incident, but I did have to use the knife on a few who aggressively charged me. I made short work of them, and I escaped back to the surface without any trouble. Once on the surface, I ran to where de Venasque was waiting for me and we entered the rift back to our native dimension.

De Venasque said we shouldn't worry about being followed, as the iguanadons never venture anywhere close to the rift.

Tonight, we will spend the night in my tent before embarking on our return flight to Franz-Josef Land in the morning.

March 21, 1928, Kabarova, Russia

It's been an interesting two days. De Venasque and myself have returned to Kabarova for the time being. I plan on returning to New York City tomorrow morning, but I have much to do before my departure. I have written a private account detailing the expedition that I will personally deliver to Hareton Ironcastle once I reach the United States. I have asked for him to keep all of my findings confidential for the time being, and I'm sure he'll agree.

Also, I have decided to keep the personnel I contracted for this expedition in my private employ, and I've hired de Venasque to oversee them. The North Pole is a mysterious place (one must wonder if the South Pole has similar phenomena surrounding it, but that's a question for another day). As unusual as it may be, I believe the pole would make a great location for private reflection. I plan to have de Venasque and the workers construct a base of operations for me near the pole, outside of the area of the anomaly.

I will spend my final night in Kabarova sketching out the design of the base in solitude.

Dedicated to the late, great Philip José Farmer and the members of The New Wold Newton Meteoritics Society who paved the way. The author would like to give special recognition to Rick Lai. Rick first postulated that Doc constructed his retreat after saving arctic explorers several years prior to the author independently conceiving this story.

In the time travel epic that follows, Travis Hiltz brings together several members of the "Ardan family," starting with the great Michel Ardan, the hero of Jules Verne's 1865 classic From the Earth to the Moon...

Travis Hiltz: *Family Reunion*

1875. In the vicinity of the North Pole

The dog sled sped across the ice field. Its sole occupant huddled deeply into his furs.

The sled was a unique contraption. It was a bit larger than the usual dog sled and was pulled by a single dog, a massive metal beast, steam pouring out from its ears. Its steady chugging noises were the only sound to be heard for miles.

Wires, tied together with string, trailed from the hound's flanks to the handles of the sled that the man used to steer and control the rate of speed.

Michel Ardan, French explorer and adventurer, had volunteered to not only test run the steam dog but to explore the North Pole, recently purchased by the Gun Club of Baltimore. After a failed attempt to cultivate the huge coal deposits, they had lost interest in it.

Seeing a chance for a new adventure, Ardan had happily agreed to go see what was to be seen.

The ice field took on an uneven quality, as though an ocean had been flash-frozen. Ardan fumbled with the controls, attempting to slow his speed. One of the runners caught the edge of an ice crest and the sled began to tip. Startled, Ardan clenched his hand and the sled took off in a burst of speed and hit the next ice wave at full speed, leaving the ground for several feet before hitting it on its side. The sled skidded, the metal dog's legs still chugging, before crashing into a small hill.

There was a loud cracking noise, which Ardan realized was—luckily—the ice rather than any of his bones, or his dog.

The Frenchman sat up, rubbing his head. He then attempted to scoot away from the ice wave that he had hit.

Just below the surface was a bizarre and startling figure: a large reptile that stood on two legs like a man. One of its arms seemed to be reaching out. It clutched something in its hand.

The cracking and the sudden outpouring of super-heated steam had caused the ice to partially melt away, and the green, leathery hand was soon free.

Ardan got to his feet, pushed his goggles up to his forehead, and peered intently at the amazing creature.

Curious, he pried the webbed fingers apart, revealing an orange gem, about the size of a grape, which seemed to pulse with an inner light.

Pulling off one heavy mitten, the Frenchman reached out and picked it up.

He was hit by a sudden wave of vertigo; there was a flash of light and, when it faded, the frozen lizard man and the metal dog were left alone on the ice.

1929. Somewhere in Africa

Francis Ardan ran down the stone corridor, the primitive guards close behind him.

His expedition to find the rumored ruins of Atlantis had proved to be a little too successful, and now he was exerting a great deal of thought and energy towards getting away alive from the fabled lost city.

He raced around a corner and skidded to a halt at a T-junction. Down the left corridor, Ardan spotted a heavy oaken door.

He shoved it open, ducked inside, closed it and immediately began scanning the room for something to brace the door with. Seeing no furniture or suitable objects, he took off his belt and tied it between the two large iron hoops that served as door handles.

He then gave a relieved exhale, wiped an arm across his brow, and turned to survey his temporary sanctuary.

The room was round and quite large. Its outer wall was ringed with alcoves, each containing the statue of a man coated with some kind of unusual lacquer.

In front of each alcove was a small dais, made of polished stone.

As Ardan walked along, he noticed that each dais was topped with a cloth and, resting upon it, was some form of jewelry: a golden ring on one, a silver tiara studded with blue gems on another...

He continued circling the room, until he came upon a podium upon which rested a single gem: it was the size of a jellybean and shined with a soft, orange light.

Unsure of why, the young explorer reached out to touch it.

He felt a slight dizziness and his eyesight blurred.

When the guards finally broke open the door to Antinea's gallery of suitors, they found it empty.

1947. A planet orbiting Psi Cassiopeia

Dale Ardan ran through the jungle, batting aside vines and branches with her free hand, while firing off the occasional shot from her ray gun with her other.

Her pursuers were fearful of her weapon, but either too fierce or foolhardy to give up their pursuit.

Convinced by her friend, Professor Zarkov, that he had calculated the final landing place of the famed lost spacecraft of Professor Selwyn Cavor, and with things surprisingly quiet on Mongo, Dale had volunteered for what had sounded like a restfully boring excursion.

Then the blue monkey men had attacked and she'd been separated from Zarkov. She wasn't too sure she could find her way back to their rocket ship either.

Firing a few parting shots, the young reporter from Earth scrambled up the nearest tree.

Once she had a bird's eye view of her surroundings, Dale scanned the thin path that ran through the trees. Stumbling on the slippery bark, she reached out to steady herself, and her fingers brushed against a small, orange gem lodged inside the bark.

She gasped as she lost her balance.

When the trio of blue aliens reached the treetop, there was no one there.

Somewhere else

Michel Ardan found himself standing in a field, the dry grass crinkling beneath his boots. He pulled back his parka hood, and got rid of his remaining mitten.

Squinting towards the mist-shrouded trees at the edge of the field, he thought he could glimpse figures moving.

"Hello…!" he shouted, bewildered. "Where in the Hell am I…?"

"Hello…?" a voice behind him hollered in reply.

The explorer spun and found himself facing a tall, tanned, muscular young man with close-cropped hair. He looked to be dressed for safari, along with a multi-pocketed, sleeveless vest.

"Ah, well," the older man started. "I seem a bit…"

"Great-grandfather?" the younger man said, peering at the other's face. "Is it you…?"

"I can assure you, I am me," Michel said. "Now, be so kind as to tell me who you are?"

"It's I! Francis! Your great-grandson!"

"My…what…? But I don't…!"

"Francis…?"

The new voice was female and startled both men. Running towards them was a young woman clad in yellow, skin-tight trousers, a blue tunic and a silver gun belt.

"Who…?" Michel started.

"Do I know you?" Francis said.

She ran up and hugged the young man, who, after a moment, awkwardly patted her back.

"It's me! Dale! Your cousin!"

Francis then held the young oddly dressed woman out at arm's length.

"My cousin?"

"Yes! John's daughter."

"This conversation seems to be going in circles," Michel said, undoing his parka and fanning himself, lazily with his gloves.

"But how?" Francis asked, puzzled. "I haven't seen you since you were eight! And now you look..."

"I'll be 30 next month," Dale replied.

Francis took a step back and rubbed his chin in thought.

"So you're from 12 years in my future..."

"Allow me to introduce myself," Michel said, taking Dale's hand and giving it a gallant kiss while making a slight bow. "I am Michel Ardan, explorer and gentleman of fortune. *Enchanté, Mademoiselle.*"

"Michel Ardan?" she breathed. "Great Uncle Michel…but, you can't…? You're…you passed away in…"

"Dale!" Francis snapped. "Don't!"

Both the young woman and the older explorer froze, Michel still holding Dale's hand.

"Don't you see what's going on?" Francis continued. "This is time travel… of some kind… I'm not quite sure how or why… We have to watch what we say!"

"So this young lady is also a relative!"

Dale opened her mouth to speak, glanced over at Francis, and shut it again, her brow furrowed in thought.

"This is very strange," she said, eventually. "And I've been to…"

"No!" Francis snapped. "Don't say anything!"

"This is giving me a headache," the older Ardan said.

He rummaged through his jacket pockets, coming up with a much-abused looking silver flask. He took a healthy swig and then held it out to the others.

Francis shook his head and turned to study their surroundings. Dale shrugged and took a drink.

"I have seen some amazing things myself," Michel smiled, between sips. "While I promise to keep any questions I have about the future to myself, I will say I approve of women's fashions."

"Oh," Dale said, shaking her head. "I see that Mom's stories about you weren't exaggerations."

Taken slightly aback, Michel frowned, tucked away his flask and glanced around thoughtfully at their surroundings.

"So, if we cannot talk about our places in history," he mused, "can we talk about where we are? Reminds me of the moors around the country home of a friend of mine…"

"I don't think we're in England," Francis said, intently. "Something is… different. The air… it… tastes wrong."

Dales brow furrowed as she looked around.

Michel took in a mouthful of air and ran his tongue across his teeth.

"We probably shouldn't be standing out here in the open, until we have a better idea what's going on," Dale suggested, her hand moving to her holster, unconsciously.

Francis nodded, and gestured towards the tree line.

"There's a path over there," he said.

Reaching into an inner pocket, Michel brought out a revolver and led the way. In single file, the odd trio jogged across the field, making for the row of thin, grey trees that surrounded it like a fence. There, they found a narrow path, snaking its way deeper into the forest.

They moved a few yards along, so they had some shelter amongst the trees while still being able to keep an eye on the field. Michel leaned against a tree, keeping watch, while Francis and Dale scanned the woods for any signs of life or civilization.

There were faint rustlings that might have been animals, or perhaps people moving about. Their eyes shot about, moving, along with their guns, towards the direction of the noise.

"I don't hear anything anymore," Dale said, after several tense minutes had passed.

"I still do," Francis said, gesturing down the path. "That way. There are people moving around."

He turned and headed off down the path. The other two watched him go and looked at each other. Dale shrugged and made an "after you" gesture.

"No, no," Michel said, shaking his head. "I am nothing if not a gentleman. Mademoiselles first. *Après vous, je vous en prie.*"

Dale gave a mock curtsy and then headed after her cousin.

They walked through the woods, Dale and Michel starting at each new noise, Francis focusing on the path, seemingly unfazed; yet, his hands were tensed, ready to strike if needed.

The trees began to thin out and they caught glimpses of movement. Francis slowed down, and Dale almost collided with his back. She and the older explorer peered around their relative's broad shoulders.

When Francis suddenly crouched down, the other two Ardans were momentarily startled before joining him.

Laying down in the tall, dried grass, they gazed upon several dozen uniformed men who appeared to have set up a makeshift fortified camp.

"Are those World War I uniforms?" Dale asked, puzzled.

"World War what?" Michel asked, distracted from the soldiers.

"Forget I said anything," she muttered, before turning to Francis. "But are they?"

"Yes," he said with grim certainty. "French."

"Is it my old eyes," Michel asked. "Or do they look a bit… blurry…? I'm having trouble making out their faces."

"They look… faded," Dale nodded. "Like ghosts…"

"Ghosts?" Michel muttered. "Are we ghosts as well? All that babble about time travel, but perhaps the truth is more dire…"

"We're not dead, if that's what you mean," Francis said. "I've trained to be aware of my body and can feel my pulse and circulation. Plus, it's chilly enough that I can see occasional wisps of my breath when I exhale. We're all alive…"

"We are," Dale interrupted, "but what about them?"

"I… I haven't worked that out quite yet." Francis replied, sounding slightly uncomfortable at having to admit out loud to not knowing something.

"Seems there's an easy way to find out," Michel said, getting to his feet.

"Don't…" Dale said, then turned and touched her cousin Francis on the arm. "Should we…?

"Let him go," Francis said, getting to his feet as he watched his great-grandfather push his way through the underbrush and into the field.

"Are you going to do something?" Dale asked, joining Francis and sliding her ray gun out of its holster. "Help him, or are you just going to use him as a stalking horse?"

Francis gave the bare minimum of a shrug, as though unsure himself which option to choose and kept his attention on his older relative.

Michel strode into the field, one hand resting jauntily on his belt. His expression was that of a man who has just entered a café and seeks the headwaiter's attention rather than that of a time-lost stranger that has just walked into a military camp.

He stood there in plain view for several minutes before a few of the bustling soldiers took notice of his arrival.

As they moved towards him, rifles up, their ghostly expressions anxious, Michel raised his hands.

"*Bonjour!*" he said, smiling in what he hoped was a friendly and unthreatening manner. He'd had great luck with it on young women, but this was his first attempt at ingratiating himself with soldiers.

It must have been fairly successful as no one shot him, but not a complete success, as no one lowered their guns or smiled back.

Francis moved closer to his relative, but kept the trees and underbrush between him, Dale and the soldiers.

The young woman took a step forward, but her cousin stopped her with a gentle touch on her wrist and a shake of his head.

They watched, as the soldiers gestured with their rifles, where they wanted Michel to go. They grunted questions at the polar-clad Frenchman. They seemed to find his arrival surprising and, despite him being a fellow countryman, and his reassuring and gallant smile, they seemed distrustful.

Moving stealthily through the trees, Francis and Dale kept sight of them and followed their progress through the makeshift camp.

At one point, Michel, enthralled by his unusual surroundings, missed a turn and one of the soldiers lunged forward to grab his arm.

The trees and the soldier having his back to Francis kept him from getting a good look at what occurred. All he and Dale could see was the three men stopping and looking puzzled at something.

Michel took a step back from the soldiers, his hands raised once more. His look of nonchalance melted away, leaving his features grey and shaken.

"Something is wrong," Francis muttered.

"And we aren't going to find out what by sitting in these bushes!" Dale snapped, grabbing a hold of his arm, as she got to her feet. "Study time is over. At least with Flash, I don't have to worry about him over-thinking things. Let's go!"

After being dragged a few steps, Francis gave up any hope of getting his cousin to slow down and quickly jogged past her, bursting from cover with the plan of reaching their older relative first.

Since they had arrived in this mysterious place, Francis had focused his keen senses and intellect pondering their dilemma and its solution. This tactic had unfortunately been seen as reluctance on his part or outright unwillingness to take action.

Nothing could be further from the truth. Francis was just not as impulsive as his other two relatives. He had a distinct idea in his head of when it was time to observe, and when it was time to move.

He was a bit perturbed that the initiative was being taken by Dale and Michel's actions, but once the time to act had come, there was no hesitation on his part.

Leaving his female cousin easily behind, Francis quickly moved from the forest to Michel's side, taking a defensive stance, ready to fight off the soldiers if necessary.

"Are you all right?" Francis asked his great-grandfather.

"I… do not know," Michel muttered, rubbing at his arm and studying it intently.

The soldiers took several steps back and raised their guns at the new arrival. Other soldiers approached, several running up, others moving slower and more cautiously.

"What happened?" Francis asked.

"He grabbed my arm…" Michel muttered, looking from his arm to Francis, his expression completely bewildered.

"Hold on boys!" Dale shouted, catching up. One of the soldiers turned and, after an appreciative glance at her skin-tight outfit, moved to block her path.

To both their surprise, she ran through him, as if he were no more solid than a waterfall.

Dale skidded to a halt, then turned and stared at the soldier.

The soldier stared back, dropped his rifle and frantically felt his chest.

Puzzled, Francis glanced from Dale to Michel, and then threw a punch at the nearest soldier. It passed right through the soldier's chest. Francis withdrew his fist and flexed his fingers.

"Interesting," he said.

"They're ghosts!" several of the French soldiers announced at once.

"We're not the ghosts!" Michel snapped at the soldiers. "It is you who are deceased! I am hale and hearty!"

"No one is a ghost," Francis said, not raising his voice, but his tone drew everyone's attention.

"She walked through me!" one soldier protested, pointing accusingly at Dale.

"Um…sorry," she muttered, lowering her gun, as she was unsure where to point it or even if it would be of any help.

"Everyone calm down for a moment," Francis advised, raising his hands in a placating gesture. He turned to the nearest soldier. "What's today's date, private?"

"Um…I'm not entirely sure," the soldier replied. "To be honest, we have… it's… just…"

He looked around at his comrades for support. They, too, all appeared either reluctant or unable to say when it was and what they were doing here.

"We aren't sure how we got here from… um… and we never made it back…. Best if you spoke to the Lieutenant…and the Professor," he finally stammered. "Follow me…you too, mademoiselle…"

Dale acknowledged his awkward good manners with a nod and a smile and followed the young soldier and her two male relatives. Michel glanced around him thoughtfully.

Francis attempted to study further, but kept being distracted by a poking at his bare right arm.

"What?" he asked, peering over his shoulder at Dale.

"Just testing," she replied, absently.

"Testing what?" he said, realizing that this cousin was no less aggravating as an adult then she had been as a child.

"We can touch each other," Dale replied, thoughtfully. "But…"

She reached past Francis and put her hand through the shoulder of the nearest soldier. He twitched slightly, but it didn't seem to affect him enough to turn.

"Stop that," Francis chided her.

"So, how come?" she asked.

"I don't know everything," he replied.

"Could have fooled me."

"My best guess is different… methods of time travel operate at different frequencies," Francis shrugged.

To his surprise, rather than asking more questions, Dale merely nodded and sank back into thoughtful silence.

The group made their way through the makeshift army camp to large tent at the far corner. The young soldier led them into the cluttered interior. It looked as though someone had dumped a university science lab and a bootleggers' back room into a sack, shook it and then dumped the contents inside this tent.

In an oasis, two men stood, with their backs to the Ardans, intently working on some unseen project.

One was a shorter, compact man in a bottle-green frock coat; the other wore the robe and headdress of a Bedouin.

"Scuse me, sirs…?" the young soldier said, after they had stood by, ignored for several minutes.

"Duranton, we can't be interrupted if we…" The tall Bedouin said, in a clear French accent.

Both men turned, revealing the shorter man to have a neatly trimmed beard and a pince-nez perched on his bulbous nose, while despite his attire, the Bedouin was obviously a blonde European. One eye was scrunched up in a squint, indicating an injury.

Both men paused, blinking in surprise at the new arrivals.

"What in blazes…?" the man in the frock coat muttered, more irritated than surprised.

"Who…?" the taller man added. "How…?"

"We were rather hoping you could answer those questions," Michel said.

"This may be hard to believe," Dale said, "but, we think we came here through time travel."

The two men shared a glance and the taller gave a small smile.

"You knew that already, though," Francis said, looking around the cluttered tent.

"We were told you could explain what's going on?" Michel added, in a faintly challenging tone.

"It's difficult…" the tall man began.

"Oh, balderdash!" the bearded man grumbled. "Basic temporal theory and mechanics."

"I am Lieutenant Henri de Lanselles," the tall man said. "My friends call me Monocard, due to…" he trailed off and gestured towards his afflicted eye. "By default, I am in charge of these men. We came across a… device that transported us from the frontlines to 13th century Spain… there were complications… some made the return trip. We were not so fortunate."

"What he's attempting to convey," the bearded man interrupted, "is that all the men here were left behind in the 13th century, and so experienced the rather unique… um…experience of dying several centuries before they were born. This created rather a sizable ripple in the time stream."

"You seem to know a great deal about all this," Francis mused. "They referred to you as Professor. I take it you do not belong to the Collège de France?"

"Not in the least," he stated, puffing up with pride, adding perhaps an inch to his less than impressive height. "I am Professor Helvetius, a student of the myriad facets of the flow of time. It was during my studies that I became aware of the troopers predicament and the damage it could cause. I used my own personal transport…"

He nodded towards a metal contraption wedged into the corner of the tent. It looked like a diving bell.

"…To retrieve them and transport them somewhere, relatively safer and less likely to damage the fabric of the continuum…"

"Did that make any sense to anyone else?" Michel asked, making no effort to hide his bafflement.

"A little," Dale shrugged. "Where are we?"

"This is a little…pocket, an oasis, set slightly to the side of history," Helvetius said, his hands clasped behind his back, projecting the air of a university lecturer. "For the moment, they, and the flow of history, are safe, unfortunately there are complications…"

"Are you using a molecular transponder?" Dale suggested.

"Ah-ah! A scientist!" Helvetius beamed.

"I hang out with one," she replied. "How are you keeping it stable with a group this big?"

"That's one of those complications," the bearded savant explained. "I can stabilize this little limbo, but that takes all the energy I can generate, which means we can't actually leave. I've been trying to find an alternative power source, but instead, I somehow ended up bringing you three here… that was a bit of a puzzler…"

"And who are you expecting to attack?" Michel asked, causing everyone to turn and look at him. "Why would you have a fortified military camp unless they was an enemy."

Dale gave her relative and appreciative nod.

"We are not sure who, or even what, they are," Monocard replied. "The Professor says they are cousins to man, but all we have encountered are beasts."

"Yes, yes," Helvetius said, brushing away Monocard's concerns with a frown and a faint gesture. "The Morlocks' arrival is unfortunate, but inconsequential. The real problem is maintaining this pocket dimension, or returning the soldiers to the proper time stream, and both of those options require a stronger energy source!"

Muttering to himself, the little scientist stalked off, soon lost to sight amongst the clutter.

The rest of the group stood about, feeling a bit confused and awkward.

"Well, it sounds like we've got two problems then," Francis said, breaking the silence. He crossed his arms, his tanned forehead crinkling in thought, before turning towards the Frenchmen in desert garb. "Can your men handle these... Morlocks?"

"We've been able to hold them off so far," Monocard shrugged.

Francis nodded and turned to his relatives.

"If I attempt to help Professor Helvetius," he said. "I know, grandfather, that you have some experience... How about you Dale?"

"How about me, what?" she asked, baffled.

"Where would you be able to help best?" Francis asked. "The science or the fighting?"

"Shouldn't we be...?" Michel began.

"If you're about to suggest finding a safe place for me..." Dale said, her hand resting on the butt of her ray gun.

Michel glanced at his great-grandson, seeking either support or advice, but saw from his stoic expression that he would be getting neither. He chose the better part of valor and gave a brief bow and a "please continue" gesture.

"I'd probably be more help in defending the camp," Dale said. "Most of my knowledge is second hand, and this is beyond anything I've encountered."

Francis nodded then returned his attention to the time-lost soldier. Monocard then moved to the flap of the tent.

"Jasim!" he called, leaning out.

A disheveled soldier, with some odd bits of braid and patches on his uniform, came jogging up.

"This gentleman and mademoiselle are volunteering to assist with the defenses. Show them the mess tent and then a posting."

Jasim gave his commanding officer a questioning look, then shrugged and lead the pair off.

"What about you?" Monocard offered, returning to Francis's side. "What do you have in mind?"

"I'd like to see what Professor Helvetius is working with," Francis replied. "A great deal of this is beyond me, but I have studied enough science to understand the basic principles… perhaps I can help, or at least, puzzle out how his search for an energy source scooped the three of us up."

Monocard nodded and raised his hand to help guide the adventurer to the right area, when a clatter from amongst the clutter distracted both men. They could see Professor Helvetius' head bobbing around amongst the collection of scientific bric-a-brac, muttering darkly.

A wooden stool, piled unsafely high with tools and bits of wire, tipped over, crashed to the ground and a small boy came running out, followed by the scowling scientist.

The child, a boy, sported a straw boater over a blonde pageboy cut. His knickers and shirt had last been fashionable at the turn of the century.

He collided with Francis's muscular leg, clamped one hand onto his hat and peered up. His dirt-smeared face breaking into a smile.

"Cousin Francis!" he exclaimed. "You got tall!"

"Button Bright?" Francis muttered. "What are you doing here?"

"I got lost," the boy shrugged.

"You know this urchin?" Helvetius demanded, leaning against a computer bank and dabbing at his face with a large floral-print handkerchief.

"He's my cousin," Francis said, still peering down at the young boy, puzzled.

"Another one?" the savant grumbled. "This has to be significant… But how?"

"Why were you chasing him?" Francis asked.

"He tried to take my marble away," Button Bright accused, his face taking on a serious expression.

"What?" Monocard asked.

Button Bright dug in his pants pocket, coming out with a piece of twine, a small brass gear, a molasses candy and an orange gem about the size of a jelly bean, that seemed to glow faintly.

"Where did you get that?" Francis asked, crouching down, while reaching into one of his vest pockets. "Did you take it from… no, wait…!"

He took out the gem he'd found in the vault in Atlantis. He held it between thumb and forefinger and reached forward to compare it to the one his young cousin had.

"Don't let them touch!" Helvetius suddenly shouted, causing Button Bright to start and close his fist around his gem. "Where did you get those?"

"Found it," Button Bright informed him, defensively.

"Mine was in… uh… an archeological site in the Hoggar," Francis said, feeling the full story would just further complicate the situation.

"Do the others have gems with them?" the old scientist asked.

"I believe so," Francis responded. "Dale had one when she first appeared here, and I think grandfather said something about finding one, as well… Are they the power source you were looking for?"

He brought his up to his eye and studied it intently.

"Oh yes, I believe they will do," Helvetius smiled, digging into a vest pocket and pulling out a jeweler's loupe and screwing it into an eye. "They positively reek of temporal energy and causality."

"All four of you found one of those gems?' Monocard asked, leaning over Francis's shoulder to study it as well.

"No," the Professor said, straightening up and taking the lens from his eye.

"What do you mean, 'No'?" Francis asked, standing up.

He picked up the toppled stool, then picked up Button Bright and placed him on it.

"Oh, it's even better than that," Helvetius replied. "The four of you have only one gem between you!"

"Is that supposed to make sense?" Monocard asked.

"Are you saying, we each found *the same gem*, but at different points in history?" Francis asked. "Is that possible?"

"Oh, yes," Helvetius nodded, his voice taking on a pleased tone. "Just quite tricky and fairly dangerous. This is a very special artifact. It's one of only a handful of such items to be found in all of time and space. It's crystallized chronal energy and... well, can't stand about... Come along, we've work to do, I'll explain further while we put them to good use!"

"I'm hopelessly out of my depth here," Monocard said. "I'll go check on your companions and the troops. Good luck."

Francis nodded, scooped up Button Bright, and attempted to follow the bearded man through the jumble of scientific clutter.

Professor Helvetius pulled out a metal tripod on which was perched what looked like a metal phonograph. Instead of one needle arm, this one had four.

The short scientist bustled about the device, making adjustments, attaching cables and unfolding the needle arms. He held out a hand and made an impatient gesture.

"Is he waving to us?" Button Bright asked, tilting his head.

"The gems!" the bearded savant grumbled, glaring at the duo.

Francis handed over his gem.

"How is this going to work?" he asked.

"The gems themselves are basically droplets of time," Helvetius explained in his lecturer tone. "Some believe they are all that remains of dead chronovores. When anything or anyone travels through time, they accumulate chronal energy. Add the paradox of four versions of the same object being gathered in one place, and then the ripples caused by the coincidence of four members of one specific family bringing these gems together, and we should have enough energy to easily return everyone to their rightful place and adjust the fabric of time like if it were a child's jigsaw puzzle..."

"Good," Francis nodded.

"Or the resulting outburst of energy will reduce everyone in this pocket dimension to component particles and scatter them like grains of sand in a hurricane..." Helvetius continued in the same drone of a lecturing professor.

"Can't say I like the sound of that," said Button Bright.

Francis frowned. He held out his hand and gave his young cousin a stern look, until the child reluctantly dropped his time gem into the older man's palm.

Once Helvetius had the two gems, he set them on the device's disk and then placed a needle upon each gem. The machine began to hum.

"That's a good sign?" Francis asked, concerned.

"Yes, it's doing fine," the older man replied, not looking up.

There then came a rhythmic roar that seemed to come from outside the tent.

"What is that?"

"Nothing to worry about," Helvetius muttered, adjusting several dials. "It's most likely the Morlocks making another raid..."

"What?" Francis asked, incredulously.

"What's a Mo'luck?" Button Bright asked.

"Michel and Dale and their gems are out there," Francis said.

He deposited his young cousin on what looked like an old fashioned barber's chair.

"You stay here and do not pester the Professor and I'll try and bring you back a Morlock," Francis instructed. "Or a new marble, OK?"

The boy gave it a moment of serious thought then gave a nod of agreement.

"Good boy," Francis said, with a brief smile.

Then he quickly made his way through the tent and out into the camp...

Dale and Michel were settled in a crude guard post. Its rough walls and the bench they sat on were all made from wood and branches from the surrounding forest.

They had discovered, to their dismay, that the difference in their time frequencies meant that, not only they couldn't touch not the soldiers, but also their equipment, including food and drink. So, all they had were Michel's flask, some dried strips of meat, and a few hard candies from his knapsack.

Neither was looking forward to the idea of this being a long stay.

The pair sat, quietly, intently scanning the surrounding woods.

"I… um… wished to apologize, if my earlier comments offended you," Michel said, breaking the silence, but also deliberately not shifting his gaze away from the trees. "You seem a most… um… competent young lady."

Dale glanced over at her relative, noting his discomfort and smiled.

"Apology accepted," she said. "You meant well, and I will admit to having been, on occasion, a damsel in need of rescuing. Everyone needs help sometime."

Michel turned and smiled back at her.

"I'm sorry to hear that history is going to keep us from getting better acquainted," he said.

"Well, it is mother's stories about you and Francis' father that have inspired me," Dale explained. "I became a journalist, got to see some of the world and then… Well, let's just say I got to do quite a bit of traveling."

"Good to hear the thirst for adventure still runs in the family," Michel said, offering Dale his flask.

She accepted with an appreciative nod and took a sip.

"I think you'll find that Francis and I are doing our part."

A thin soldier in a threadbare uniform came into the guard post.

"Excuse me, Monsieur and mademoiselle," he said, in a hushed tone. "Just wanted to warn you. We've spotted some movement in the woods. It looks to be Morlocks, so keep sharp. They can be a bit… um…off putting first time you see them, but as soon as you spot one, shoot, 'cause they're vicious bastards… sorry, pardon, Miss…"

"Thank you," Michel said. "We'll keep an eye out."

"Appreciate your concern, but if you guys can't touch us, we're probably safe from your Morlocks," Dale shrugged. "So, we're not sure what we can do to help."

The soldier gave an absent minded nod and a slight shrug of his own.

"Well, the Lieutenant thought it best you knew," he explained. "If they get past the fence, head for the field hospital. It's the best fortified."

He gave a salute and then left.

"What is a Morlock, I wonder…?" Michel muttered. "It seems to have these fellows anxious."

"No idea. I've seen some strange creatures," Dale mused, "but I never heard of them…wait, I think I see something!"

She pointed toward the trees, and they spotted a half dozen life-forms creeping among the trees. Both time travelers slid their weapons out of their holsters.

The Morlocks moved more like apes than men. They were hunched over, and there were no signs of helmets of firearms.

"There's a great many more of them than I'd expected," Michel muttered. "I almost find myself hoping you're right, and they'll be as ghostly and insubstantial as the soldiers. Here they come!"

The duo could hear shouts going down the line of the makeshift fort, as the Morlocks burst out of the forest.

Their resemblance to apes was more distinct, seeing them in the dim, grey light. They ran like primates, using their arms, as much as their legs to propel them along. They were covered in dingy white fur, their only clothing being belts and harnesses.

Their eyes were large, round and glassy, like polished opals.

"Beast men?" Dale muttered, bringing up her ray gun.

"Dear Lord!" Michel added.

Between the forest and the camp was a short field of unkempt grass that rustled as the Morlocks ran towards them.

Added to that was an odd hum, almost a growl, that came from them, whether it was language or merely an inarticulate roar was unclear, but either way it was unnerving.

Dale had seen her fair share or unearthly creatures, but there was something disturbing about the Morlocks. There was a feeling that while they were different, they were not aliens. They hadn't come from some far off realm, but were rather men—men gone wrong.

Adding to that unnerving quality was the fact that they were concentrating their attack on the corner where the two of them were stationed.

Michel fired off two shots in rapid succession; Dale found herself feeling slightly relieved when they passed right through the bestial beings.

The Morlocks had soon crossed the field. A few fell to the French Soldiers' bullets, but the majority reached the crude, wooden wall.

"What should we do?" Dale asked, uncertain if there was any point to staying where they were, let alone fruitlessly shooting at the Morlocks.

That moment of hesitation was a moment too long. The Morlocks were at the wall and clambering over.

The first two reached the top and lunged at the two time travelers.

Like with the soldiers, the furred creatures passed through them. But unlike the soldiers, both Dale and Michel felt their passage, like a gust of freezing wind, or the blast of heat when a furnace door.

Michel shuddered and stumbled back a few steps, leaning against the wall.

Dale flinched and reflexively fired. The blast from her ray gun passed through the Morlocks, and they toppled to the ground, twitching and growling.

"What…?" Michel muttered. "What did you do…?"

"I don't know!" was all Dale had time to say before the next wave of Morlocks were clamoring over the fence, hands flailing and grasping at the pair.

Some of the soldiers joined the fight, pulling the Morlocks off the wall and grappling with them. Even while fighting the time-lost soldiers, the Morlocks still seemed intent on attacking the Ardans.

"Why are they after us?" Dale asked, firing at any Morlock that came too close.

"They... I think... can touch us," Michel muttered, one arm hanging limply at his side. "I felt... something..."

"It doesn't make sense!" Dale shouted over the noise of the battle going on around them. "Michel...!"

A section of the wall near the older Ardan cracked and several clawed, white-furred hands burst through, grabbing hold of his coat. While they passed through his arm, he flinched, and the fabric of his coat sleeve could be seen tearing.

Dale fired off several frantic blasts, further splintering the wood and driving back the Morlocks. She lunged forward, grabbed hold of Michaels' other arm and dragged him to the relative safety of her corner of the guard post.

They huddled in the corner, Michel tending to his unusual wounds and Dale shooting sporadically, with no real idea of what their next move should be, as the battle swirled around them.

The sidewall finally cracked and a half-dozen Morlocks came pouring through.

Dale blasted away, the beam flickering and her ray gun made a groaning noise.

She gave it a shake, fighting off a trickle of panic as she scanned her surroundings, looking for any kind of escape route.

Suddenly, Francis vaulted over the back wall and landed in a crouch next to his relatives.

"We need to get out of here," he said, firing off a couple shots and then scowling at the lack of results.

"We are open to suggestions," Michel commented.

"Do you both have those strange gems you found?" he asked.

They nodded, confused by this odd digression.

Within seconds, Francis had scanned their surroundings, their attackers, and the soldiers struggling to drive them back. He sighed in annoyance and holstered his gun. He grabbed his two relatives, flung them over his shoulders, lurched to his feet, and then made a standing jump at the wall.

Like some kind of surreal fox hunt, Francis ran, his two relatives slung over his shoulders, Dale still firing at the pack of Morlocks, fighting free of the soldiers and scrambling after them.

Francis wound his way through the camp, dodging Morlocks, until they reached Professor Helvetius' tent.

He dumped them inside.

"Go find the Professor," he told them. "Far right corner. Give him your gems."

He ducked back out and sealed up the flaps behind him.

Dale and Michel got shakily to their feet. The older man was limping as they hurriedly made their way through the clutter, the young woman trying to adjust her ray gun in case the Morlocks caught up with them.

"What is going on?" Michel exclaimed, coming across Helvetius and the strange phonograph, trailing tubes and wires.

"Button Bright?" Dale yelped, startled at discovering yet another relative.

"Dale!" the young boy called back. "Everyone is tall. Hello, sir."

Michel nodded in reply.

"Good, you're here," Helvetius said, straightening up. "Hand them over."

Both Ardans fumbled about and held the gems out to the blustery scientist.

"Don't let them touch!" he snapped, startling them and causing Dale to almost drop hers.

"You have marbles too!" Button Bright exclaimed, more entertained about events than anyone else involved.

Helvetius snatched the offered gems, holding them in separate hands, and then delicately placed them on the clunky device and adjusted the needle arms. He then turned the small metal crank on the side and the device began to vibrate and hum.

"Hmmm," the old time traveler mused, stroking his beard and then adjusting his pince-nez. "You might want to take a step or two back," he added, turning to the trio. "The results may be… unpredictable."

Michel scooped up Button Bright and then he and Dale dove behind a roll top desk as the machine began to glow a bright orange.

"It was a pleasure meeting you all," Michel said, as the glow brightened and the furniture began to rattle. "It'll be even better if we survive this…"

"That it will," Dale said. "It feels like we're about to find out. Good luck in the past."

"And you, in days to come."

Outside the tent, Francis stood like a bronze sentry as a quartet of Morlocks came shambling around the corner of the field hospital and raced at him.

He fired a few shots into the air, knowing it was unlikely he could fight them off; his plan was merely to stall them long enough for Professor Helvetius to do whatever it was that he thought the four gems would accomplish.

"I don't know what you are," he said in a commanding voice, "but this is as far as you go."

The Morlocks came to a halt, a few feet away, unsure how to deal with this new opponent. They huddled together, conversing in the coarse snarls that passed for their language, and then lunged for the young adventurer.

Like with the others, they passed through him, causing a strange distress, but little in the way of physical hurt.

Francis clasped his forearm, expected a wound, only to see unmarked skin. He swung a fist, passing through the nearest creature, which stumbled into several of his mates.

"OK, we can't exactly hit each other," he muttered, thoughtfully, "but whatever we are doing, whatever similar frequencies we are on, doesn't create a pleasant sensation. Let's see who can last the longest."

What occurred wasn't so much a fight as some sort of bizarre ballet. Blows didn't connect, but resulted in a strange phantom pain, like a low level shock. Francis focused on dodging his opponents' grasp, while making just enough contact to keep them off balance.

His skin soon glistened with sweat and his movements became sluggish.

At first, he wrote off the odd blurring effect of the dull, grey sky and surrounding trees to be caused by fatigue, but then the Morlocks ceased their attack, looking about them in anxious bewilderment. He also heard the concerned shouts of the French soldiers.

"I hope you know what you're doing, Helvetius." Francis said, seconds before a wave of orange light washed over him and he felt his body go boneless...

When the light faded, Francis Ardan was standing in the hall of Atlantis, feeling a bit light-headed as he watched the guards fleeing from the room.

He blinked his eyes and soon regained his equilibrium.

"It must have been quite an entrance I made," he muttered. "I doubt it'll keep them away long. I'd best be on my way."

He glanced over at the dais where he had found the time gem. There now rested a heavy, creamed-colored envelope, with a seal of wax, in a familiar shade of bottle green.

It was a day later, after he had managed to put some distance between himself and Atlantis, sitting by a small campfire, back out in the Sahara desert, on his way home, that he had the time to finally read the single page filled with a tight scrawl.

As he'd expected, it read:

All went well. I was able to relocate nearly everyone back to his or her proper time.

As for the Lieutenant and his troops, their "deaths" are a matter of historical record, so I merely shifted them to a time period where their presence won't result in a paradox.

The Morlocks have grown into an arrogant civilization. I think that, in the long run, having neighbors capable of fighting back will do them some good.

Your relatives have been returned to where time took them, save for young Button Bright. Curious child. I cannot imagine where he wandered off to.

Looking forward to renewing all your acquaintances in...

Here there was a smudge, as though reaching to refill his pen, the Professor's coat sleeve had rubbed across the page.

After several minutes of fruitless attempts to decipher the last word, Francis merely shook his head and lay back upon his bedroll.

"Time will tell," he said, to the open star-laced sky.

There are a number of parallels between the great Belgian science fiction author J.-H. Rosny Aîné (1856-1940) (whose collected works are now available from Black Coat Press) and Philip José Farmer. Both brought a mature, adult perspective into the genre; both tackled biological, sexual and moral issues in ground-breaking fashion and, finally, both were masters of the "Lost World" genre. It was, therefore, particularly fitting that Farmer adapted and retold Rosny's L'Etonnant Voyage d'Hareton Ironcastle *(1922) into English in 1976. Win Scott Eckert, teaming up with fellow Farmerphile Christopher Paul Carey, has drawn from these prestigious sources to create another wonderful Lost World saga (previously published in* Tales of the Shadowmen 5*), which brings together a bevy of characters from unexpected sources...*

Christopher Paul Carey & Win Scott Eckert: *Iron and Bronze*

Sub-Saharan Africa, November 1929

A dark form, silhouetted against the backdrop of a million brilliantly scintillating stars, loomed above Hareton Ironcastle. The shadowy shape might have been the same monstrous dreamworld being that had just startled him awake. But no. The sheen on the form's exterior was just starlight glancing off skin. Human skin.

Unnerved, but also irritated, Hareton's pulse raced. He wanted to shout at the man who stood over him, demand what the Hell he was doing staring down at him like some fiendish ghoul. Instead, Hareton feigned a yawn, ran his fingers through his straw yellow hair, and said calmly, "Having problems sleeping, N'desi?"

N'desi's only answer was to remove from a pouch at his hip a small stone, which with slow, graceful strokes, he began grating against the sharp edge of his strange square-ended, slightly curving sword. The iron weapon gleamed hideously in the starlight.

Hareton sighed. The man had been acting queerly since they had picked up the telegram in Fort Lamy that sent them on their new mission, refusing to leave Hareton's side for even a moment. This despite the fact that N'desi was no longer technically in the American's employ. Stranger still, the man had begun uttering strange pronouncements in his native Bantu dialect whenever he caught a glimpse of the glittering ax which, less than a month ago, they had recovered from the forbidden ruins in the high reaches of the Tibesti. Perhaps the fellow was taking *taduki* again. He had seen N'desi light a blue flame in the desert a fortnight before they had come upon the ruins, and the unmistakable sweet aroma of that rare herb had drifted to Hareton upon the cool arid breeze.

Time seemed to shatter like a brittle stone and the strange dream from the night N'desi took *taduki* settled over Hareton. A dream of the same nightmare creature that had just now visited his sleeping spirit–a towering being, with a roughly human-shaped body, with rippling plantlike skin mottled with many deposits of sparkling silicate crystal, and thick trunk-like limbs that shot into the ground like tree roots. In the dream, the creature led him on a secret way through the mountains, its body stretching from its lower torso, twisting over the seemingly unending desertscape, while its legs remained rooted beneath the sand miles behind. When Hareton awoke the next morning, he had followed the dream path and discovered an old hermit watching over the crumbling foundations of a primordial mountainside settlement. To the protests of the hermit, Hareton, as if possessed by some feverish delirium, had with his bare hands unearthed a stone altar in the ruins, long buried by the dust of time; and upon the altar found the very prize he had come to Africa to obtain: the ax known as the Reaver of Worlds.

Had the *taduki* Hareton so faintly inhaled given him a vision, as it was so reputed to do? And if so, by what strange mechanism did the herb open up the doors of time and space and bring him to his goal? And for what sublime intent?

He felt the bulge of the ax in the pack at his side. Yes–it was still there. Feeling its hard substantiality somehow seemed to mend time and return him to the present.

"It is *xanigew*." N'desi's deep voice, so rarely used, startled Hareton.

"What? You mean the ax? It's what, did you say?" Hareton took care to impart an air of indifference. He did not want to egg on the man's superstitions, which ran thick in his bloodline. After all, N'desi's grandfather, Mavovo, had been a pupil of the great Zulu witchdoctor Zikali.

N'desi remained silent for nigh a minute. Then he said, "The glittering stone you carry disturbs your sleep. As it does mine."

Getting up from his sandy bed, Hareton shot the man an accusatory look. "The ax is cursed," he said flatly, "that's what you're saying. Or *xanigew* or whatever you called it. But I don't think it's that at all. You know something more than you've been letting on." A shiver seized Hareton, which he disguised by rubbing his arms as if chilled by the early desert morning. But an uncanny realization now came over him: meeting N'desi in the bazaar in Marrakech had been no coincidence. The man must have sought him out when he heard the famed American explorer was searching for the Reaver of Worlds.

The ax. It all seemed to come back to the ax. The stories of the natives in eastern Niger said the glittering, iron-headed weapon had been crafted from a splinter of a much larger one. The latter was reputed to have been cast to the Earth by the natives' gods, the Sky People, and wielded by a giant who, in his great anger, had smashed the ax into the Earth countless generations ago, giving rise to the Tibesti Mountains and unleashing a cataclysmic torrent that gushed from the belly of the Great Mother goddess and consumed the world. The legend of the ax, and a tip off from the wise and trusted old mystic Hâjî Abdû that the Reaver of Worlds was in truth a very real artifact, is what had launched Hareton on his recent quest.

N'desi, half a head taller than the six-foot-two American, looked down at Hareton, his dark eyes glowing dimly in the sand-reflected starlight. "The search for your countryman is noble. But it will lead to the rise of a great evil. Leave him to die in the Hoggar."

"Is that what the *taduki* has told you? That I should let the son of my greatest friend die, and place my faith in your depraved addiction to that mind-numbing herb?"

So that explained the man's odd behavior since Hareton had received the telegram from New York. Partaking of the herb had caused some errant signal in N'desi's brain to connect two unrelated events–the finding of the ax, and the search for the son of Hareton's friend, whose plane was last sighted two weeks ago by French military intelligence on a precise course for the Hoggar's Mount Tahat. Now, because of the herb's rewiring of the Zulu's gray matter, N'desi believed the ax had somehow cursed Hareton's new mission.

"Your heart knows the truth." N'desi placed his sharpening stone back in its pouch and returned the long iron sword to its wooden scabbard. "Do not forget the dream which led you to the ax you sought."

Hareton guffawed. "Coincidence! That smoke of yours fouled up my mind and sent it spinning backwards. The local hearsay brought me into the general vicinity of the ruins. It was luck we found it, I'll say, but the herb only tricked me into thinking I knew the route to the ax ahead of time. That's how the psychologists explain déjà vu, you know–the mind working backwards to solve a problem that's already been solved?"

N'desi lips stretched into a rare smile. "And what of the old hermit seizing up and dying at the very moment you raised the ax from the dirt?"

Hareton said nothing, but his own grin faded. N'desi, perhaps sensing he had won the battle but lost the war, began breaking camp. Already in the east the desert night's sable blanket faded. Soon the blood-red orb of the Sun would again bake the sands and Hareton would welcome the shadows of the Hoggar, curses or no.

Harry Killer was not dead.

He reclined on the throne, padded with luxurious gold-laced pillows, and snapped his fingers. A man shambled over bearing a jewel-encrusted bowl filled with olives and cheeses. The servant was hunched over, back and arms bent at almost simian-like angles. The dim light provided by elaborate copper oil lamps suspended from the cavern ceiling shadowed the man's face.

Killer waved the servant away and pointed him toward the cavern's other occupant.

Queen Antinea was on her knees at the base of her throne. Black circlets of metal banded her wrists in front of her, as well as her ankles. Thick chain links connected her manacles.

The servant loped toward Antinea and shoved the bowl under her face. Her lustrous dark hair waved and she shook her head in apparent disgust. Killer knew the revulsion she must feel at the man's fetid breath, his heavy, fur-covered brow, his protruding yellowed teeth.

The juxtaposition of the young chained beauty and the panting beast-man amused Killer. He admired her, the curve of her hip, the swell of her breasts under the thin gown he allowed her.

But most of all he admired her youth. He wanted it.

By rights, Harry Killer should have been dead. He should have been killed when Blackland, his criminal outpost in the Sahara, was blown to bits almost 30 years ago.

Instead, he had awoken deep in the rubble and foundations of the City in the Sahara, buried in dirt and grit and concrete. There had been a shimmering glow in the darkness where none should have been, an almost crystalline light. When he had reached out and grasped this beacon, time swirled and space inverted. The glittering light expanded and enveloped him, and he saw a vast and hidden underground realm buried in a rocky and barren mountain range.

And Killer saw the nude woman, the raven-haired queen of indescribable beauty, with haunted green eyes and a lush red mouth. This woman, posing with nonchalance and shaking her head, as if to say to him, "No, you cannot have this, Harry Killer, this is not for you."

Then time righted itself, and the crystal light was solid. It wrapped around his legs like a sea-birthed tentacle, dragging him gasping through the sand, until it thrust him upward into the air. Killer had hacked and spit up dirt and grit, and lay there on the ground for what seemed like hours, chest heaving. Then, gathering his wits, he was finally able to sit up and look around him.

The smoldering ruins of Blackland were nowhere to be seen.

Harry Killer crawled out of the desert and headed south, holing up for half a year at a native village. Scars and burns pulled his face into a ghastly skull-like visage, and his previously bushy eyebrows, burned in the explosions, were now thin and sparse. As he healed, the Wantso villagers who had initially taken in this broken and burned husk of a white man grew to be more and more afraid of him. More strength flowed into his massive frame with every passing day. And with every passing day, he took more and more liberties, eating their food, using their women.

Finally, one day, he heard some of the men complaining about him. Killer was not a linguistic expert, but he was sharp enough to pick up much of the villager's language within the six months of his stay with them. The native men spoke unthinkingly in front of him, while Killer grinned his death's head grin and bobbed his head like an idiot, and listened intently.

They planned to kill him. Dismemberment, preferably while he was still alive, was not too good for him.

Though huge and muscular, Killer was no match for a whole village of men, and he knew it. When he stole away in the dead of night, he thought about razing the village, but decided that would give any survivors even more reason to seek vengeance and come after him. If he left quietly, they might just leave him alone and not give chase.

Finally Killer made his way to the coast and from there to Europe. He traveled the globe and rebuilt his criminal enterprises, this time choosing to remain mobile rather than once again banking all his resources on one base which could be destroyed. He diversified.

There was one other thing.

Harry Killer did not age. When Blackland had gone up in flames, he had been in his mid-forties. A decade later, he felt as he had when he was 30.

War to end all wars came and went, the trenches of Europe filled with lost souls while Killer got rich dealing in the weapons of German scientists like Herr Doktor Krueger.

Another decade later, and he still felt the same. The crystal light, he realized, in the bowels of Blackland, must have saved him, even rejuvenated him.

But the effects were not permanent. By 1926, he was almost a cripple, dying.

It was chance that gave him a clue. Boredom had led Killer to the ship's library on the *Ile-de-France*, a steamer on Compagnie Générale Transatlantique's New York-Le Havre route, and thus to the fantastical memoirs of Lieutenant Ferrières, of the 3rd Spahis. As Killer read Ferrières' account of Queen Antinea's hidden lair buried in the Hoggar Mountain range of Africa–so close to the Saharan location of Blackland!–and the Queen's apparent everlasting youth, he became convinced there was a connection to his experiences and the visions he had experienced in the wake of Blackland's destruction.

Within a month, he had mounted and fully stocked an African expedition. He planned a detour to a hidden valley he had discovered in his post-Blackland wanderings, there to recruit some local "muscle:" degenerate para-anthropoids of a lost race who called themselves the Wandarobo.

With the Wandarobo beast-men in tow–or rather with him in tow, borne through the jungle and then the rocky desert in a covered litter, as he became increasingly weak–Killer descended upon Hoggar. Antinea's hideaway was ridiculously easy to find. Benoit, the editor of Ferrières' memoirs, had not taken the pains to alter names and places, trusting that the Lieutenant's account was so fantastic it would be viewed as complete fiction–as it likely would have been if not for Killer's visions.

As simple as it was for Killer to locate the decaying empire in the volcanic landscape, Mount Tahat looming in distance, it was even easier to conquer and secure. Antinea's highlands realm, the Mountain of Evil Spirits, once a flourishing community, was reduced from its former glory. Many faithful servants, handmaidens, farmers, and Arabian guards remained, but not nearly enough to repel Killer's swarming Wandarobo.

And so Harry Killer sat upon the plush throne of Antinea's Hoggar sanctuary, while the Queen knelt defiantly before him in chains.

Antinea swung her chained fists at the beast-man, sending the bowl of olives and cheese flying. She spat at Killer, her eyes cold with fury.

"Now, now, my Queen," Killer said. His dried skin pulled tightly about his skull as he forced a smile. "That will get you nowhere. You know what I want. You're older than I am; you must be much older, in fact. Yet you don't look a day over 20. I've been here two weeks. I've been gentle with you so far, but my patience wears thin. I won't wait forever."

"Gentle? Ah…You have thrown me in a cell in my own dungeon. I've no pillows to rest upon and no coverlets to warm me at night. My bath is a cold bucket of unscented water, dumped on me in the morning as I sleep. And you dare cast your treatment as gentle?"

"A little hardship in life does us all good, my Queen. It builds character."

"Then, indeed, your life to this point must have been one of unparalleled luxury."

"I'd revel in this banter with you, draw it out for days, weeks, my Queen, if I had time." A dry rattling cough wracked his body, and he recovered. "I promise you, if you don't tell me what I want to know, and soon, I may die, but if I do, the Wandarobo will tear you limb from limb while you still live. You'll beg for them to dispatch you cleanly before they're done with you."

At this threat, Antinea's imperious anger evaporated. Killer watched her smile serenely at him, then turn her gaze to the three Wandarobo guards crouched at the entrance of her cavernous throne chamber. She stood, her movements slow, sinuous. Then she reached up to her neck, unfastened the gown, and at a leisurely pace drew it down her body, like honey flowing down a spoon.

Antinea stood nude before the panting Wandarobo. They stared, hypnotized as one, at her magnificent, uplifted breasts. She continued to smile at Killer.

He was transfixed, just like the primitives who served him. Antinea appeared just as she had in the crystalline vision years ago.

Antinea's voice punched through the memory. "I think there will be no tearing limb from limb any time soon."

Killer saw red, and yelled at the Wandarobo. "Get her out of here. Back to her cell!"

He watched Antinea continue to smile. The guards didn't move. Then she nodded slightly at them in acquiescence. Or was it command? Rough Wandarobo hands eagerly grasped her slender, pale arms and drew her away.

The beautiful Antinea, who reminded them so much of their own ruler before their exile to the squalid outpost where Killer had found them, was once again locked away in her cell. They had stood gazing dumbly at her for minutes, which would have dragged into hours, if she hadn't finally dismissed them with promises of more delights, visual and otherwise, later.

Now the three tramped through the dank caverns, grunting and bragging and arguing about which of them had captured Antinea's green-eyed gaze the longest.

As they rounded a darkened bend, a bronzed and heavily sinewed arm reached out and encircled the latter Wandarobo's neck, pulling the beast-man silently into the shadows.

His two companions lumbered onward, oblivious.

"Well, my Queen, how are you doing it?"

"Doing what?" Antinea responded to Harry Killer's question. Her ever-serene smile belied her innocence.

"You know what!" he practically shrieked. He inhaled deeply to calm himself, and, not for the first time, wished he hadn't become a teetotaler after the destruction of Blackland. He could use a snort right now, but alcohol had never tasted quite the same after he'd seen the crystalline light.

More calmly, Killer continued: "Over the past three days, half of my men have disappeared without a trace. The first, right after I sent you back to your cell following your burlesque display."

"I have no idea of what you speak."

"Never mind!" He took another deep breath. He really could use that drink. This woman was getting to him. "My men are disappearing, and they're all whispering that the *ilhinen* have come to get them."

As Killer spoke the word *ilhinen*, the Wandarobo guards in the chamber stirred and rocked back and forth, howling and making signs to ward off evil spirits.

Killer glared at them, and when they quieted somewhat, Antinea remarked, "*Ilhinen*. That is not good."

"Of course it's not good, you traitorous bitch!"

"Traitorous? I owe you no allegiance. I'll see you in the Hall of Red Marble before this is over."

Killer would have stomped his feet on the stone floor, if he had had the strength. But his energy was fast fading.

"I have no plan to become one of your lovers, or rather your victims, my Queen. Tell me what I want to know, and I'll leave."

Antinea smiled faintly.

"I'll give you one more day," Killer said. "I have no more time to play with you. Tomorrow, we start removing fingers. Then toes. Then the other extremities. I guarantee the Wandarobo won't pant at you after that. But it doesn't have to come to that. Tell me the secret of rejuvenation. We've searched everywhere. It must be here. Where is it?"

The Queen continued to gaze at him in silence, resolve showing in her cold eyes.

"Take her away," he ordered the guards, gesturing to the cavern entrance, and buried his head in his hands, exhausted.

Antinea went willingly. Before she stepped into the carved entryway, she paused and looked back.

"Ah, Monsieur Killer?"

He looked up.

"*Ilhinen!*"

The Wandarobo started howling and jumping again, and Killer plugged his ears, screaming in frustration.

Deep in the bowels of the Mountain of Evil Spirits, a group of Killer's Wandarobo guards sat at a long table with wooden benches running along each side. They slurped watery gruel from Antinea's scullery and grunted back and forth about their rapidly disappearing comrades.

One of Antinea's Arab servants, a larger man in hooded robes, set down a large tray at the end of the table, handed out fresh bowls, and began to load up the empties. Despite what must have been long years spent laboring in the dim cavern complex, the muscular hands extending from the robe's sleeves appeared to be dusky and tanned.

The beast-men ignored him, their faces pressed in their bowls, long tongues scouring for every last drop.

When they looked up, a few of them sensed something was amiss. Were their numbers fewer? Perhaps one or two had left to relieve themselves…

One Wandarobo, a shade more intelligent than his companions, whispered, "*Ilhinen*…"

Antinea was face down on a stone pedestal, held on the left by one of Killer's beast-men, her right arm extended straight out and held down at the wrist by another. Killer held a long sword poised above her splayed fingers.

"Last chance, my Queen."

Antinea sighed. "Very well."

"What?"

"I said, very well. I will show you."

Killer signaled and the Wandarobo let her loose. Antinea sat up, rubbing her wrist. She wrinkled her nose at the stink of the nearby beast-men. "Would it hurt for them to bathe occasionally?"

"Quit stalling."

"As you wish." Antinea rose to her feet–still chained, as were her wrists–and shambled toward her throne.

"What do you think you're doing?" Killer asked.

"Getting you what you want. Shall I stop?"

"No, get on with it."

Killer watched as Antinea stood before the throne and uplifted her arms, as if praying to an altar. The throne began to rise, stone scraping on stone. The base then slid backward on unseen mechanisms, revealing a staircase below. She began to descend but Killer shoved her aside and went first. He heard her follow him down, as best as her chains would allow.

At the base of the stairs was a small, cubicle chamber carved into the stone. Killer saw a small stone dais, upon which rested a simple metal bowl. A single item lay within the bowl. It resembled a broken and lifeless tree branch, or root, peppered with dulled silicate crystal.

That was all.

He turned to the smiling Antinea, enraged. "This? This is the mighty secret of everlasting life?"

"It is," Antinea replied.

Her calm infuriated him even more. He turned back to the branch, his frustration mounting. "It's not working. It looks nothing like what I saw years ago."

"What did you see?"

"Glowing light. Crystalline. These mountains. You."

Antinea raised and lowered her shoulders. "You said yourself there is no way I could be so youthful. I sit above this every day, on my throne, to ensure my exposure to it. It is the secret you seek, I assure you."

Harry Killer contemplated the branch for a long time. Then he turned, grabbed the chain that hung between her wrists, and hobbled up the stairs, tugging her behind him. At the top, he called over one of the Wandarobo.

"Take her away."

Before the order could be carried out, however, there was commotion and shuffling outside the throne chamber. The rich tapestries covering the carved entranceway were thrown aside, and four beast-men entered the cavern, grasping between them a man, either European or American, in well-worn khakis, jodhpurs, and dark brown boots, accompanied by a native African.

"Master," one of Wandarobo rumbled in guttural tones, "an intruder!"

"Who the Hell are you?"

The man removed his safari helmet and held it in his hands.

"Hareton Ironcastle, at your service."

The heavy iron door shut, leaving Hareton and N'desi in utter blackness.

"Don't say it, I know, it's the cursed ax." Hareton's humorless voice sounded muted in the confined space. He began tracing his hands over the rough basalt walls of their cell, thinking of how Muriel would react if he failed to return from

Africa. His spirited daughter wouldn't just send her husband Phillippe and her cousin Sydney Guthrie to search for him–she would come along herself... and fall into the very trap he had.

Hareton had just about completed a circuit of their tiny prison, cursing as he tripped and overturned a half-filled, stinking chamber pot on the floor, when a dim light suffused the chamber from above. At the same time, he heard a door groan on metallic hinges, shuffling feet on the stone floor, and then the deep boom of the door slamming closed. The faint light emanating from a hole near the ceiling disappeared.

"Who's there?" Hareton shouted, hoping his voice would carry to what was obviously an adjoining cell.

For a moment, silence; and then, in haughty, feminine tones: "A queen without a throne." The words, though English, belied the speaker's native Arabic.

"Antinea!" Hareton breathed. He had thought reports of the woman and her spider-trap in the desert to be mere fiction, although his doubts had soon evaporated as he crossed the very distinctive terrain in the Hoggar which he recognized from Ferrières' famous account. And now here lay the queen spider herself, trapped by the treachery of her own web.

"What goes on here?" he asked, resolving not to judge the woman on hearsay. "Who is this man who has invaded your lair and imprisoned us?"

"A man, like any other," came the silken voice. "Except for one thing. He has no soul."

"Otherwise he would have fallen under the spell of your beauty, no doubt." He could not help himself. He had to probe her motivations, get a sense of her character.

"You have heard of me? I should not be surprised. I would have left this grotto long ago and avoided those who would seek me out, had these tunnels not housed the very thing which brings the man known as Killer. But I am patient. Soon enough will he make his home in the Hall of Red Marble."

Hareton repressed a shudder in the darkness, recalling what he had read of the woman's predilection for killing her former lovers–once she had tired with them–and embalming their bodies with orichalcum, that rare element utilized by the metallurgists of the dead civilization described by Plato in the Critias.

"Atlantis!" Hareton said aloud, feeling awed. He could hardly believe it, but had he not seen the seven dried-up canals surrounding the city, exactly as Plato had written? To think, the lost culture that so many had sought in the Atlantic lay buried here–high atop the Hoggar in the middle of the Sahara! The first thing he would do if he ever made it back to his private library in Baltimore would be to burn his copy of Donnelly's *Atlantis*–so what if it was one of Aunt Rebecca's favorite tomes.

"This land was not always desert," Antinea said, as if reading Hareton's thoughts. "Once a great water lapped the sides of my mountain home, which was then but one city in a vast and powerful empire. But if other cities survived the Reaver of Worlds, I have not heard of it. My fortress alone endures."

At hearing the phrase "the Reaver of Worlds"–the same words used by the local tribes to describe the ax he and N'desi had uncovered in the Tibesti–Hareton's entire frame buzzed as if he'd been struck by a god's hammer. But local folk tales did not matter–he could not allow his curiosity to distract him. The man who had imprisoned them meant business.

"What is this thing you say brought this Killer fellow to the Hoggar? And now that he has it, why hasn't he gone on his way?"

A low laugh purred in the darkness. "Have I said that he has it? No, only that he seeks it. And as for what it is, I know not myself, although long have I gazed into its mystery. And what I have seen–"

From the hole connecting the two cells Hareton heard the sound of metal grating against metal–the iron bolt sliding open in the door to Antinea's prison. Then metallic hinges groaned and again a dim light came from above. A moment later, the door to Hareton's cell opened. A large robed figure filled the narrow tunneled hallway outside, a white burnoose hiding the towering newcomer's face.

"I took the liberty of retrieving these," the man said in surprisingly well-modulated American English. The Reaver of Worlds appeared from beneath a robed sleeve, proffered to Hareton handle-first in a large, deeply tanned, corded hand. Then, from beneath his robes came N'desi's square-ended iron sword.

Hareton took the ax, glittering in the orange light of the tall man's torch, while N'desi's teeth gleamed like a vista of snow-peaked mountains as he grasped the hilt of his own weapon.

The giant robed man turned to Antinea. "We must move quickly. Killer has found the secret way down into to the temple."

A sickly look overcame Antinea's regal features. Her stiffened arm pointed down the tunnel and the burnoosed man whirled, heading into the darkness with Antinea following at his heels. Hareton and N'desi raced after them.

They passed through a warren of crisscrossing, rock-hewn corridors, climbing any number of winding staircases until Hareton lost all sense of the way.

"It's enough to drive one mad!" he said to N'desi.

"We trod the path into madness," the warrior replied, "when we climbed the reaches of the Tibesti. Now we only tread deeper."

Hareton did not argue with the man. The sense that fate had laid a trap for them all nearly smothered him.

Finally the nauseating twists and turns ceased and they entered a large circular chamber, in the center of which a plume of fresh water fountained from a rounded basin. The spurting water glistened redly in the light of twelve massive copper lamps that crowned the chamber's circumference, ensconced in a golden framework that disappeared into the yawning darkness of an impenetrable ceiling. Around the basin curved a number of oversized, deeply cushioned divans, which faced outward in the chamber overlooking a series of low, broad niches set in the highly polished, red marble walls. In front of one of the niches lay three unmoving bodies of the hairy half-men. It was to this alcove which Antinea's large servant led them.

"Your handiwork?" Hareton asked the man.

The fellow seemed not to hear him. Instead, he cast his torch out into the chamber, where it lay smoldering on the marble floor. Then he stepped over the bodies and, crouching on hands and knees, crawled into the niche. Antinea followed suit, sobbing angrily at the sight of a metallic statue toppled from a low-lying pedestal in the alcove. A shallow wooden case lay next to the statue on the ground.

"Ah, my poor Captain, what have they done to you!" Antinea caressed the silvery male face of rigid effigy.

The robed man turned the dark hole of his burnoose toward Antinea. "Nothing worse than what you have done to him."

"I cared for him! As I have cared for all of my lovers!"

"I am not sure the Captain's family will be so grateful when I describe to them the manner of your loving attentions." Then Antinea's defiant servant crawled onto the pedestal and dropped into a square hole in its center, disappearing from sight.

"What lies below?" Hareton asked Antinea, whose face still flushed with an anger not hidden by the room's long shadows.

"Eternity!" she hissed, and with no further explanation slipped onto the pedestal and vanished.

Hareton shrugged. Hefting the Reaver of Worlds, he looked to N'desi with a wry smile. "To eternity!" he cried, and entered the hole.

Hareton dropped two meters down to land on a stone floor. Ahead, faint light cast upward from yet another tunneled, winding staircase. He began descending, hearing N'desi's feet clap the cold stone behind as he jumped into the passage.

The stairway corkscrewed for perhaps thirty meters before passing through a nine-sided doorway, which opened upon the first of three connected antechambers. Shadows obscured the exact size and shape of the rooms, although the dim, pulsating light cast from the doorway at the end of the farthest one gave Hareton the impression that each successive antechamber was of greater size than the previous.

Seeing Antinea about to enter the room from which the light emanated, Hareton raced ahead, gripping his ax tightly. Though a relic of a bygone age, it seemed sturdy enough to do the trick in a fight. Besides, it was the only weapon he had.

He slowed as he reached the last doorway. Then, bracing himself for whatever he might find, he passed through.

Though he had prepared himself, he gasped. But it was not the strangeness of what loomed before him that surprised him–although it was indeed strange–but rather its familiarity. For the breathtaking sight that rose from the center of the enormous oval chamber he had seen before. Or at least something like it. No, it was not humanoid in form like in his dreams. But its rippling, plantlike skin did indeed glisten with the same crystalline mica deposits, which seemed to glow with an inner light. There could be no mistaking the monstrous plant-being from his *taduki*-inspired dreams.

The thick, towering trunk of the plant grew tree-like from the cracked mosaic-tiled floor in the center of the subterranean temple, rising into the darkness of the cavernous ceiling, its many green-leafed branches fanning out over the room and rustling as if blown by a wind that was not there. Great copper lamps like those in the Hall of Red Marble circled the temple, their thin red flames catching in the plant's crystal-mottled exterior. Did the plant glow with its own light? He could not say, although if he looked closely enough he thought he could make out dark forms moving beneath the translucency of the silica.

Hareton and N'desi walked forward to join Antinea and her giant servant as they stood looking up, mesmerized by the colossal tree.

Then, from behind the massive trunk of glittering cellulose, walked a man. Harry Killer. With him came a half dozen of his fierce beast-men. But this was not the same feeble man who had been carried about on a litter by his half-human entourage. No, this man did not stoop or shuffle, or need assistance of any kind to move about. He did sway as he walked forth, but certainly it was with arrogant swagger, not frailty.

"How?" Hareton whispered.

"It is the Tree of Dreams," Antinea said at his side. "I know only that it is, and the youth and vitality it brings, not by what magic it operates."

"I cannot explain it either." Killer stopped a half dozen paces before Hareton, his grin uneven and sneering. "But I do know one thing. Now that I have explained to my friends that the *ilhinen* that killed their fellows is nothing more than a robed native, they have gotten over their love affair with you, my Queen.

"Now!"

With his last word, Killer's beast-men surged forward, their large wooden-knobbed clubs raised high and swinging.

As Hareton raised his own ax, Antinea's giant servant moved like lightning. Already he was amid the howling mass, somehow jujitsuing two of the hairy half-men at once, knocking the club of one attacker to the ground, while snatching up that of the other for himself. N'desi and Hareton advanced together, the former dispatching one of their fallen opponents with a cruel slash of his sword. But Hareton felt no pity for the enemy. It was kill or be killed.

With a savage yell, he swung the Reaver of Worlds, cleaving in two the thick skull of a beast-man.

For a moment, the chaos of battle consumed Hareton. Now he was the feral beast-man, fighting as his kind had done for eons before civilization's futile attempts to weed out the strain of violence from the species.

But savage fury could blind one to danger as quickly and surely as the somnolence of civilization. And so it was that

Hareton Ironcastle failed to notice that Harry Killer had slipped behind him in the furious bedlam.

Killer spun around behind Hareton and grabbed the Reaver of Worlds out of his hands.

In a last burst of energy, he had Antinea by the neck and, trembling, held the ax blade to her throat.

Antinea's servant, no longer hooded, moved toward him.

"Just stop," Killer hissed.

Antinea uttered a small cry as the ax made a thin cut at her throat. A small trickle of blood ran from her neck and down between her breasts.

"You won't make it out. You're trembling. You're at the end of your rope," Antinea's man said.

Killer saw, now that the man's burnoose was drawn back, that he was no Arab, despite the sun-bronzed skin. The man's hair was reddish-bronze and fit his head like a skullcap. His face was expressionless, although the odd gold flecks in his eyes seemed to swirl with energy.

"Who are you?"

The man ignored his question. "Killer, you'd better look behind you."

"Haw, the oldest trick! How stupid–"

"Fairly stupid, I'd say," Hareton broke in. "He's not lying. That…'Tree of Dreams,' whatever it is, is moving toward you."

"You're mad, you're both mad." Killer pressed the ax blade deeper into Antinea's neck, and she squealed. "Any closer, any more of that, and Hoggar's going to have one headless Queen!"

"Killer–" the bronze man tried once more.

"Quiet! Not one more word. Now, the Queen and I here, we're just going to walk out, and you two are going to stand right here in this temple or whatever it is, and not move an inch. Or I'll kill her, I promise you. Understand?" The bronze man stood unmoving. Hareton shrugged in apparent acknowledgement.

"Good, then we all agree. Come on my Queen, you're my safe passage out of here."

Killer took a step forward. There was a problem, though. His feet didn't move.

Something was coiled about his ankles. It wasn't entirely smooth. Rather, it was slightly bumpy and asymmetrical, like a tree branch.

Unlike the branch Antinea had shown him under the throne room, though, this was more root-like, in that it protruded from the ground. Crystalline speckles glowed upon the root's membrane, as if powered by some eldritch source of energy within.

The root moved.

It snaked up Killer's legs, around his torso, and wound in a spiral down the length of the arm which held the ax to Antinea's pale throat. The tip of the root covered the ax and exuded an acid. Killer's eyes widened as he saw the root's digestive juices begin to melt and consume the ax. He grasped it as long as he was able, then released it with a cry.

He watched, held immobile, as the Reaver of Worlds dissolved and was absorbed into the translucent root. Then the root began to withdraw, slowly back into the Earth from which it obtruded, dragging him along with it.

Harry Killer screamed and clawed at the ground.

"Antinea, get away," Hareton called, but the Queen was already pulling herself free. She stumbled over to the explorer, while the bronze man headed in the other direction, toward Killer.

"Help me!" Killer called, and then the erstwhile Arab was next to him, one huge hand gripping Killer's arm, the other on the glowing root. Massive thews tugged and strained.

The bronze man's eyes went from gold to glassy, and his efforts ceased.

"What are you doing? Don't stop–help me!" Killer yelled.

But the colossal man, who had once posed as one of Antinea's servants, did nothing.

The bronze man's vision dimmed. All was dark around him.

Then a strange crystalline light pierced through, and within it a slender dark shape appeared. His sight cleared, and the dark shape was revealed as a massively tall building, towering over the New York skyline. A dirigible was moored to a mast atop the skyscraper. The picture shifted, and he saw Doctor Natas, from whose secret city in Asia he had recently escaped. The image blurred again, and he held a baby in his arms. The infant had his own reddish-bronze hair color. The vision snapped; he was flying an airplane over the Arctic, a beautiful, dark-haired woman beside him in the copilot's seat. Then he was in a cavern, much deeper, down toward Earth's center. He was surrounded by a circle of stone symbols lit by gas jets, and was facing a mirror. He was making handgestures, trying to sign, to the reflection in the mirror. Except it wasn't a reflection. It was him, but the other in the mirror moved of its own volition.

Then the bronze man was lying prone on the ground in the depths of the Mountain of Evil Spirits, still immobilized, and he saw Harry Killer's hand being sucked into the ground, along with the last bit of glittering root.

"It was a dendroid," Doc Ardan was saying, "a semi-intelligent tree being–doubtless an offshoot of the same vegetable life forms your expedition encountered a nearly decade ago in Gondokoro."

The four of them–Hareton, along with Ardan, Antinea, and N'desi–stood round the ten-meter hole in the broken mosaic tiles of the ancient Atlantean temple.

"Of course, I suspected as soon as I saw it," Hareton said, his voice rasping with astonishment, "but to think–the distance the roots must have traveled beneath the soil! And what of the Reaver of Worlds? What drew the dendroid to it and sealed Killer's fate?"

"The roots were hungry," Ardan said matter-of-factly. "I suspect there was a sort of sympathy between the two, the dendroid and the material that composed the ax-head. Perhaps even a symbiosis."

"How can that be?"

"I'm not sure. But I have seen that same composition of glittering iron once before, in a collection at my family's ancestral estate in Derbyshire. At the time, I did not have time to examine the rock fragments closely, although like the Reaver of Worlds, they had all the telltales of meteoritic origin, as well as a provenience of Africa. Zu-Vendis to be precise. And the fragments I saw in Derbyshire were laid out in the shape of a shattered ax-head, perhaps a chunk of the larger ax from which the Reaver of Worlds was reputedly crafted. While I'm hesitant to speculate on such little data, a hypothesis might be formed that a microbe fell to earth in a hollowed out cavity in the stone. Perhaps the composition of the meteorite is what attracted the microbes to it in the first place. It was food for the organism, although the latter had for some reason gone dormant while it traveled through the void of space."

Hareton shook his head, unbelieving. "And the *taduki* that gave me the vision which led to the ax?"

"The herb has peculiar properties which I am fairly certain may serve to connect it with the vegetable life forms which originated in Gondokoro. Perhaps the *taduki* somehow communicates with the dendroid, possessing its human hosts– that is, those who inhale the herb's smoke–and orders them to transport the metal food directly into the maw, so to speak, of the dendroid. Think of the *taduki* as a kind of hallucinogenic spore–a third member of a symbiotic chain: two from the plant kingdom, and another belonging to a very peculiar class of metal. Life beyond this world would likely take on much different forms than we are accustomed to, and possibly the metal is actually in some sense a life form as well. That's one hypothesis. Or..."

For a moment Ardan's gold-shot irises seemed to swirl with excitement. Then he said calmly, "Or perhaps the ax was composed of the metal of an interplanetary vessel under the direct guidance of the dendroid. The vessel might have broken up upon impact with the Earth's upper atmosphere, perhaps as it was consciously intended to do, scattering its contents in a broad swath over Africa, in order to seed our world. After all, the legends of the ax state that it was a gift of the Sky People."

N'desi shook his head. "Not a gift. No, the legends say it is *xanigew*–a curse."

Ardan broke a smile. "More data for our hypotheses, good. It will bear looking into." Then Ardan's smile vanished and he regarded Antinea.

"Is our business finished?"

Anger boiled up in Hareton. "You can't possibly mean to let her go. Haven't you seen her exhibition of death in the chamber above? She's a cold-blooded murderer! What would your father say?"

Antinea laughed coldly. "He would say let me go, wouldn't he, Docteur Ardan? Unless you think he'd like me to reveal to your enemies the source of your family's wealth?"

Now Hareton understood Antinea's pull over Ardan–the woman had somehow blackmailed him into assisting her. How she had managed to spin her web as far as the Ardans' mysterious fortune, Hareton did not know, but he resolved to suss out the details when he returned to America.

"Your punishment will come soon enough," Ardan said coolly, turning away. "And perhaps it already has."

The haughty bearing left Antinea's frame, her shoulders slouching as she gazed down into the blackness of the great opening in the floor before them. The dendroid might truly have slowed her aging as she had inferred, but now it was gone, hopefully forever.

Hareton shuddered. He would gladly forgo immortality if he never saw the dendroid again–in his dreams or in waking reality...

"I can take you in my plane as far as Tangiers," Ardan called over his shoulder as he left behind the gaping hole and headed for the staircase that led above. "Then we must part company."

Hareton and N'desi sprinted to catch up, leaving Antinea to meditate upon her mortal future in the gloom of her subterranean temple.

"You've no doubt heard of the financial crisis which has struck not only America but the very foundations of the civilized world." If Ardan's breathing grew any heavier as he began climbing the steep steps, Hareton could not discern it.

"Indeed," he said, now just behind Ardan. "That's why your father was unable to lead the search for you in the Hoggar in person." Though in excellent health for his 50-some odd years, Hareton struggled to hide his own panting.

"We spoke just a moment ago of hypotheses," Ardan said mysteriously. "I will not go into details, for I don't wish to jeopardize your safety, but I've developed a singular hypothesis about the crisis on Wall Street. And I intend to test it."

But the importance of Ardan's words faded as Hareton's mind–without the aid of that infernal herb, he hoped– transported him back to his home in Baltimore, with Muriel and Phillippe and Aunt Rebecca waiting in the parlor, anxious to hear the story of his latest adventure. Hareton Ironcastle, just this once, would sit this one out and let the younger generation step up to the plate.

He reached forward and clapped the climbing Ardan on his back.

"Go get 'em, old boy!"

Harry Killer was not dead.

He was underground, enveloped, suffocating, wrapped in solid crystal light.

He saw himself strong again, rejuvenated, gathering his criminal empire in America, from the Pacific Northwest to Denver, New York to San Francisco, commanding a secret army of mobsmen, scientists, and beast-men. He saw a figure cloaked in black, face obscured by a large slouch hat, eyes alight, laughing an eerie laugh, twin .45s blazing in the night.

The desert sands spat out Harry Killer, far from the Mountain of Evil Spirits. He lay there a while, catching his breath and orienting himself.

Xanigew. The native word throbbed in his brain.

He stood up and started walking.

The historical Beast of Gévaudan was made popular by the 2001 action-packed movie The Brotherhood of the Wolf. *It seems fitting that Doc Ardan would one day fight this legendary French monster...*

Matthew Dennion: *A Scientist First and Foremost*

The Gévaudan, The 1930s

The moon light lit the forest near the Langogne section of the Eastern Part of Gévaudan. Doc Ardan stalked quietly through the hot foliage as he searched for both his prey and its lair. Ardan was fully aware that in order to put an end to the horror that was occurring once more near Gévaudan that he would not only have to stop the creature that was committing the atrocities, but that he would also have to prove to the people that the beast was only an animal and not some supernatural threat.

The summer was the hottest that it had been in years, which was causing all of the animals in the forest to behave in an excited manner. Ardan knew that he would have to take a moment to compose himself if he was to sort through the noises and smells of the humid forest in order to find what he was looking for.

He stopped and closed his eyes for a moment as he let the acute sensitivity of his ears and nostrils take in the information that the forest provided. All of Ardan's senses would need to function in unison if he was to find the creature's lair, for only there could he put an end to the panic. Additionally, he was also fully aware that finding the beast's lair would either confirm or put to rest his fears that the monster was only the first in a succession of vicious creatures that would plague the Gévaudan.

Ardan could hear birds and frogs chirping and ribbiting around him. He could hear countless crickets singing to each other in the dark of the night. These sounds gave him a small sense of comfort, because he knew that, as long as heard them, the beast was not yet stalking him.

Ardan took a deep breath and, as he inhaled the brisk air of the forest, he noticed the faint smell of water and mud to his left; the scientist began walking cautiously in that direction. As he walked, he pulled the short spear that was slung around his back into his right hand and, with his left hand, he removed the large hunting knife that was strapped to his belt. With the spear in his hand, he tapped the sticks of dynamite and the thick rope that were in the sack attached to his belt. The dynamite was both Ardan's greatest option to end the threat posed to the people of Gévaudan, as well as the greatest threat to his life should the beast stalking the woods catch him by surprise.

Ardan walked slowly in the direction of the scent of the muddy water and, as he did so, his sharp mind reviewed the information in his possession regarding the murders that had taken place in Gévaudan.

Three weeks ago, a young couple by the names of Marie Leclair and Paul Sterguen had been walking home from a late dinner. The couple had opted to take some of the back roads through the fields, as it was a faster route than going through the heart of Gévaudan. When they had reached a deserted path, Paul had grabbed Maire and began to kiss her passionately. Suddenly, the couple heard a loud growl coming from the dark end of the field. They turned to see two blood-red eyes staring at them through the darkness.

Paul pushed Marie behind him and he began yelling at what he thought was a stray dog. Marie screamed in terror when a monster, far larger than any dog she had ever seen, stepped into the light. Paul pushed her Marie out of the way and yelled for her to run.

Marie had only made it three steps before she heard Paul fall to the ground behind her as the monster had jumped onto her lover's back and forced him to the ground.

Marie turned around and saw Paul with a look or terror in his eyes as the creature opened his massive jaws and then closed them around the man's head. With one twist, the monster snapped his neck. Marie only looked on long enough to see the beast tear a chunk out of Paul's back before she ran until she reached the village.

The girl's report was met with skepticism and the gendarme attributed the attack to a stray dog that, in her panicked state, the girl mistook for a monster.

They changed their minds, however, when, an hour later, they saw the remains of Paul's body. There was hardly an ounce of flesh left on the young man's skeleton. His very bones had been bitten open and their marrow sucked out. The gendarmes were well aware that no dog possessed the bite strength or the size to inflict the kind of damage that they saw before them.

Two nights later, a second attack had occurred. The Brier family had opted to host a dinner party in their garden behind their farm. With the weather being far hotter than normal, they were concerned that the house would be too uncomfortable for their guests. The Briers felt that they would enjoy strolling around the garden and the pond after dinner. Their property ended at the edge of the forest, allowing their guests to enjoy the sights and sounds of the woods as well.

The Breir's party was a highly attended with nearly thirty of their friends and neighbors enjoying themselves. Mr. Jean de Saint-Claire was enjoying a conversation with his wife near the back end of the property when he heard a strange growling noise coming from the forest. Saint-Claire's wife urged him to run back toward the house, but her husband did not heed her warning and opted to walk closer to the woods to see what the cause of the sound was.

His wife watched in horror when a huge hairy monster sprang out of the tree line and pinned her husband to the ground. Several other party guests ran over to see the creature raise its paw into the air and tear open Saint-Claire's chest with a single strike. The monster growled, then sprang at the other guests.

The beast had slain two more men before they were able to flee. The Brier's immediately contacted the police but when the gendarmes arrived, the monster and the bodies had disappeared.

Between the guests and the newspapers, the story of the monster spread like wildfire and, with it, so did a panic. The legend of the Beast of Gévaudan was well known. A series of similar events had taken place nearly two hundred years prior. The people of the town formed mobs that went into the woods, looking to shoot any canine that they came across.

The people of Gévaudan were in such a state of mass hysteria that they began turning on their own community, or at least those who were not a part of the region.

The members of the Caillet family lived on the outskirts of Gévaudan and kept to themselves. Nearly three dozen villagers stormed the gendarmerie and demanded that the Caillets be arrested and detained, based on fanciful reports that one of their family had once been a werewolf, and that they may be stricken with the same curse.

Fearing what the mob might do, the gendarmes were forced to arrest the Caillets for their own safety.

A circus from India was in the region, and one of its featured attractions was Felifax the Tiger-Man. The man was said to not only train tigers, but to actually be half tiger himself. Given the story, and that he was of Indian descent, he, too, became a target for the town's fear and anger. The people of Gévaudan soon surrounded the circus and demanded that it left town at once, with its murderous Tiger-Man.

Deep in the woods outside of Gévaudan, there was an ancient castle where, legend had it, a prince had once been cursed and turned in to a hideous beast. The castle was now an archeological site of great interest for the study of Medieval France, but the locals feared that the monster had returned. In an attempt to ward off the Beast-Prince, they burned the ancient castle to the ground and, in the process, destroyed a treasure of architecture and knowledge.

When Ardan saw that, not only was a creature terrorizing the region, but that its people had entered into a state of mass panic, he decided to act to put an end to the beast and to the panic that was tearing Gévaudan apart.

While the locals approached the problem with fear and impulsive behavior, Ardan approached it from the point of view of a scientist. He examined the reports of other scientists and adventurers who had documented encounters with similar creatures, and, when he cross-referenced that information with both weather patterns and geological activity, he felt confident that he knew not only what the beast was, but where it came from, and the true threat it represented.

Ardan's mind suddenly snapped back to his surroundings when he noticed that the birds, frogs, and crickets had gone silent. He opened his eyes and focused them, as well as his other senses, on forest around him. He heard the sound of padded paws stepping gently across the thicket to his right. He slowly turned in that direction and saw the top of the brush, roughly fifteen feet in front of him, lean in his direction.

A wave of adrenaline shot through the adventurer's body raising both his senses and reflexes. He quickly pulled the deadly dynamite off his belt and threw it into a nearby tree.

In a flash of fur and teeth, a canine that stood nearly six foot-tall at the shoulder leapt out of the brush toward Ardan. Its body was covered in a thick red fur. It had teeth that were nearly two inches long, and at least an inch wide, and claws that held the same dimensions.

In less than a second, the beast had reached Ardan, but the super-man's reflexes allowed him to sidestep it and use his spear to quickly strike the monster on its side as it went by. The beast skidded to a stop a few feet past Ardan. The massive canine growled and tensed his legs to charge once again. Again, Ardan's amazing body moved faster than the creature's and he launched his hunting knife at the canine before it was able to spring at him. The knife buried itself in the beast's shoulder, sending a spray of blood into the air.

After Ardan had thrown the knife, he's taken two steps back into a thicket. The beast roared in a mixture of pain and hunger and then sprang again. As it reached mid-air, the doctor was crouching low so that both he and his spear were hidden by the vegetation.

Ardan drove the back end of his spear into the ground and positioned the tip at the edge of the bushes. As the beast came in, Ardan quickly lifted the tip so that it was pointed at its mouth. He held the spear in place as the beast's own weight drove it into its mouth and through the back of its skull, ending its existence.

The beast's body twitched as Ardan shifted his spear, causing the dead animal to slump to the ground.

The scientist bent down to examine the slain creature. He looked at it carefully, taking mental notes on its attributes, in particular its height and weight. After his survey was complete, he spoke aloud to himself:

"A Dire Wolf—just as I suspected. Now, to confirm if my hypothesis about where you come from is correct or not."

Ardan scooped up the dead Dire Wolf in his powerful arms and carried it over to the tree where he had tossed the dynamite.

Ardan lifted the Dire Wolf over his head and placed it upon a branch of the tree. He felt that he needed to return to Gévaudan with the carcass in order to prove to the townspeople that the beast was not some supernatural monster sent to slay them, but rather simply a large animal. Securing the carcass of the Dire Wolf to the tree branch would ensure that none of the local animals would try to eat it and distort its appearance.

Once the remains were secure, Ardan closed his eyes, took a deep breath, and refocused his mind and body. After he had calmed down, he again inhaled deeply. The night time air had no sooner entered his nose than he was able to detect the odor of water and soil mixing to form mud.

Ardan tightened his grip on the dynamite and began moving quickly in the direction of the mud.

Doctor Francis Ardan was an extremely intelligent human being and he was well aware that the success of most of his adventures rested not on the implementation of his unique physical skills, but rather the work and time that his mind put into a quest before he embarked on it. He had spent hours not only researching the original Beast of Gévaudan, but also the atmospheric conditions present at the time of the first beast's attacks. He had also researched the accounts of other people who had reported encounters with strange beasts in the past, and all of the information pointed to what he thought was an inescapable conclusion.

Ardan stopped moving forward when he not only came to a spot where the scent of the newly-formed mud was the strongest, but also to a large fissure torn into the ground. He estimated it to be over thirty feet long and twenty feet wide. He looked into the fissure and all that he could see was pitch black darkness. He quickly walked to the nearest tree and tore one of its branches off. He then pulled a small piece of cloth from his pocket and tied it to the end of the branch. Next, he lit a match and held it to the cloth, creating a makeshift torch. With it blazing above his head, he walked over to the crevice and dropped the torch into it.

It flickered as it fell; the light from the burning branch reflected off of a smooth surface and further lit up the cave. When it hit the bottom, roughly thirty feet below him, Ardan heard a small splash which quickly extinguished the torch. From the way the light had reflected, he was now certain that his hypothesis regarding the origins of both beasts was correct.

Ardan quickly broke another branch off of a tree and tied his rope around the trunk of the oak. Next, he tied the other end of the rope around his waist and then made and lit another torch before walking over to the fissure.

He took one look down into the darkness below him before jumping into the cave below. He had only given himself about ten feet of rope from the opening so he ended up being suspended well above the cave floor. He held the torch above his head as its light reflected off the smooth ice that lined the walls of the cavern. He then shook his head in disbelief at what he saw trapped within the ice.

The slowly melting walls of the cave held prehistoric animals of all kinds trapped within an icy prison. Ardan saw several other Dire Wolves frozen, as well as Woolly Mammoths and Saber-Toothed Cats. Intermixed with these were several dinosaurs. At a quick glance, he was able to identify a stegosaurus, a triceratops, and even a terrifying tyrannosaurus. He looked farther down the cave and saw a tunnel that ran deep into the ground, with ice lining its walls as far as he could see. The sight of these creatures and the descending tunnel confirmed several hypotheses that his keen mind had been working on.

Aside from the attacks of the original Beast of Gévaudan, there was one other well-documented instance where Ardan found a verified report of prehistoric animals appearing on the surface. At the turn of the century, Paris had been attacked by several species of dinosaurs and other prehistoric mammals in an event that the press had dubbed the "Panic in Paris." The animals had rampaged through the city before suddenly dying off. The attack was later reported to have been caused by an underground cave that had held all of these animals frozen in ice in suspended animation. The year of the attack was a particularly hot year, as was this one, and the year of the original Beast of Gévaudan attacks.

Scientists at the time of the Panic in Paris believed that the cave these animals were frozen in must have been opened and exposed to heat from the surface, which had melted the ice and freed the animals. Ardan had come to believe that, based on reports of hot weather during the attacks of the historical Beast, that it had been a prehistoric animal frozen below ground and freed in the same fashion as those from the Panic in Paris. He also believed that, given another hot summer, history would repeat itself and once more free a prehistoric animal from an underground cavern.

When Ardan looked almost directly below him, he could see two gaping holes in the ice. He looked up briefly and determined that the spots where the holes were located were the ones likely to be exposed to the most sunlight. That was the reason why the two Dire Wolves trapped there had thawed out faster than the other animals.

The excessively hot temperatures around the times of both attacks would also have affected the people of Gévaudan, making them more prone to abnormal behavior and mass hysteria. The heat didn't only free the Dire Wolves, but it created situations where the people of the region were most likely to panic and prove unable to deal with the threat. Ardan shook his head as he considered how the heat might have literally inflamed imaginations, creating werewolves, cursed princes, and tiger-men. Had the people of Gévaudan simply remained calm and tackled the beast as just another animal, they most likely would have been able to stop it.

Ardan was also convinced that, given a little more time, the Dire Wolf would have simply died off. The animals who had emerged from the underground during the Panic in Paris had all perished, because, it was thought, that the air had changed dramatically from the ancient times when they had been frozen. Ardan surmised that most of these changes had been brought on by the onset of the Industrial Revolution. The burning of coal and oil on a mass scale was unquestionably changing the quality of the air. His research was also beginning to suggest that the burning of these substances was having a global effect on the planet, which was causing these hotter temperatures to occur more frequently. He was confident that this latest incarnation of the Beast of Gévaudan would have succumbed to the changes in the air just like the creatures from the Panic in Paris had.

This hypothesis was confirmed by the lengthy reign of the first Dire Wolf to be referred to as the Beast of Gévaudan. It had emerged from the ice prior to the Industrial Revolution and, as such, encountered an atmosphere the quality of which was closer to the air that its body had been accustomed to; he was therefore able to survive for a much longer period.

The last mystery that Ardan was confident that his research in the field and in the library had solved was the exact period when which the animals had been frozen in the cave, and where they had originally come from. The idea had long been held that the creatures responsible for the Panic in Paris were an isolated group that had had been frozen together in the prehistoric times. Ardan had long thought that this notion was wrong, because at no time did creatures like dinosaurs and Woolly Mammoths live together on the surface of the Earth.

His research had led him to accounts of people like Professor Lindenbrock and David Innes. Lindenbrock had been the first man to delve deep into the interior of the Earth and had reported seeing several species of prehistoric beasts living there. His discovery was later confirmed and expanded upon by David Innes, who had reported the existence of entire underground world called Pellucidar. Innes claimed that Pellucidar was inhabited by both dinosaurs and prehistoric beasts. After reading these reports, Ardan began to suspect that the Beasts of Gévaudan and the creatures from the Panic in Paris all came from underground tunnels which led to Pellucidar. He guessed that the creatures here in Gévaudan and under Paris had attempted to make their way to the surface during an ice age and had become literally frozen in their tracks.

Ardan looked down at the slowly growing pool of water beneath him and he knew that, with the slowly increasing temperatures of the planet, these creatures would eventually thaw out and wreak havoc on the region. He also suspected that there were other places near the surface of the earth where creatures from Pellucidar might someday thaw out. With the knowledge that his conjectures were correct, and that he had a good deal of research and work ahead of him, if he were to prevent more deaths like those here in Gévaudan, Ardan pulled himself back up his rope.

He then carefully planted the dynamite he had brought around the edge of the crevice, lit it, and caused an explosion that sealed the cave, and the creatures frozen within it, forever.

With this threat addressed, Ardan walked over to the carcass of the Dire Wolf he had slain. His next task was to take the dead beast to Gévaudan and show the people that it was nothing more than an "exotic" animal. After he had quelled their fears, his would return home and start conducting research on other caves which could be holding frozen monsters from the center of the earth. Francis Ardan was determined to find these caves and seal them before their inhabitants could come out and threaten the surface of the Earth.

Peter Gabbani offers us a "slice of life" in the very adventurous existence of Doc Ardan, conveying the notion of what it is like to be confronted time and time again with an unending series of megalomaniacs with their grandiose death machines...

Peter Gabbani: *Small Dreams of a Floating City*

The frozen rain had begun to solidify into blocks of ice on the rear of the floats of the seaplane. This was pitching the plane nose up, and Rodrigo had to lean into the stick to keep the plane level as it sputtered above the dislodged ice chunks that rolled and toppled over in the crests and troughs of the waves. The horizon was gone. He peered out at the propellers on either side, each a blur of gray, but the noises rang true. The engines were holding. The seaplane lurched forward, dipped, and then pitched nose up once more, only to have Rodrigo thrust the stick forward to go level again.

"The ice shelf can't be much farther."

Doctor Francis Ardan was stretched out on the floor behind the pilot, resting to the extent that he could, with his head propped up on a crate covered by a canvas tarp. With a wool blanket for warmth, he was half asleep, the collar of his sheepskin jacket pulled tight, his goggles snug atop his leather flying helmet. A while back, perhaps when a wind burst swept the plane laterally and Rodrigo threw his hands up in a gesture that could only be called hopeless, Ardan had given himself over to a mild fatalism. All he could do was wait. The seaplane rocked, was pushed back, sank, and leapt, and Ardan adjusted his blanket. He had been pressed into accompanying Doctor Yarteb, who sat beside him staring at his compass, on this two-man expedition to the Antarctic. The details were fuzzy, but asking his employer for explanations, especially now, seemed counter to the adventurous spirit. And he had been in more harrowing situations than this. Ardan rolled on his side and looked at the outlines of the other crates stuffed into the back of the plane, as he sensed something shift under the tarp, and then glanced over at Yarteb.

Seeing Ardan, Yarteb announced, "Nature doesn't care, does she?"

"What?"

Here, speaking meant yelling.

"Nature," Yarteb said, leaning forward, "who are we to Nature?"

Ardan detected the tone of a complaint, which marked a measure of defiance different from his brand of resignation.

"How are we going to find San Remo in all this?" Ardan asked as the top of his voice.

The front windscreen of the plane was being blasted by an angular headwind, and thick streaming rivulets of water on the sides of the screen had long since turned to opaque chunks of pearl-colored ice.

"We'll touch down where we can," Yarteb said, still looking at his compass, "and then make our way inland. We'll follow my compass." He struggled to find the words. "At San Remo, there'll be a team there that can get us to where the comet fragment landed."

"Comet fragment?" Rodrigo blared from the pilot seat.

Yarteb sat quietly, while Ardan waited for his response. Rodrigo leaned back to anticipate a reply. But no explanation was forthcoming, and then Rodrigo had to once more jerk the stick forward to level the plane. Ardan looked away. He tensed every muscle in his body once and then twice to generate a little internal warmth. His feet inside his boots pulsed. Leaning on his elbow, he pressed his leather cap to the side window to steady his gaze. Below, beneath the twists of the sea smashing into the ice bergs, beneath the floating ice blocks merging, breaking apart, and then crashing together again, he knew the colors of the Antarctic: the lapis lazuli atop the submerged ice and how it gave way to the indigos of the deep, all fractures of blue and the translucent blue imprisoned in the ice. Here, though, he couldn't see them, with the frozen rain whipping sideways and swirling, but he knew they were there. Ardan closed his eyes and rocked his head on the window before returning it to the crate. The drone of the engines remained. Yarteb looked over and then looked back.

"The ice shelf, there it is," Rodrigo shouted.

The two passengers each looked out their respective windows and saw merely the vague darkness of the sea being overtaken by a motionless white mass. The plane was high enough not to have to negotiate the imposing vertical launch of the ice wall. And soon, once the blueness was behind them, the passengers felt the plane descend.

"No," Yarteb said. "Don't land here." He sat up and reached forward to grab Rodrigo by the shoulder. "We cannot…we cannot navigate the fissures and chasms on foot. This is not the place."

"Ah, the crevasses!" Rodrigo said in a moment of clarity.

"Yes, the crevasses. The crevasses! We haven't time."

The frozen rain continued to beat down on the rattling plane.

"The floats, they've become unstable," Rodrigo explained. "We have to land, chip the ice off, and then we can continue on."

They were screaming at each other. They had to. Ardan sat calmly, squeezing his feet in his boots.

"No, we'll never take off again! The plane won't be able to get off the ground."

"It's not safe to go on like this. We are stopping."

When Rodrigo continued the descent, Yarteb, looking at Ardan resting on his elbow, worked himself into a frenzy. Ardan saw this and came to attention. Yarteb, his eyes aglow, his face wincing with some kind of internal disgust, his chest swelling to monstrous proportions, turned sideways and kicked at the door, bursting the icy seals.

With the door open, swinging on its hinges, Yarteb took out his knife, cut through Rodrigo's seat belt, and then with two hands yanked him from his chair and tumbled him out into the frozen rain. Ardan, as the plane dipped, dove forward, both arm extended. Rodrigo had hooked his arm at the elbow around the rigging of one of the floats, and Ardan had caught the door with one hand, while plunging his other hand out into the rain. He knew his grip would not hold, and the glove on his exposed hand was already soaked and half frozen. The plane plummeted, and Rodrigo slid down the supports.

"Ardan," Yarteb called out with delight, making no movement toward the plane's controls, "will you save him before the plane crashes?"

Ardan looked at the empty pilot chair and then back to Rodrigo, still hooked at the elbow around the rear of the supports while his legs were twisting off the float's extensions. Rodrigo's eyes blazed with fear. Ardan peered through the storm. Perhaps this could be timed.

"Let go!" Ardan yelled. "Let go, and the snow will break your fall! We are low enough! And I can save the plane and come back for you!"

His words disappeared in the rain, and though Yarteb was beyond earshot, he could not be sure Rodrigo pieced the shouts together. But then Rodrigo closed his eyes, gave a slow nod, and unclasped his arms. Ardan pushed himself back into the cabin and scrambled to grab the stick to keep the plane from diving into the ice shelf. He steadied himself in the pilot's chair, while Yarteb jerked the door closed and latched it.

"We are not landing."

"And we are not going to any downed comet are we?" Ardan slammed his palm into the instruments. "When were you going to tell me what this is about?"

Ardan then realized he had to keep both hands on the stick, which occupied him physically and kept him from leaping at Yarteb. Yarteb looked at his compass once again.

"Yes, we are close. Ardan, you see what the compass is doing?"

The rain battered the tiny plane, clattering the windows. Ardan, through the mechanisms of the throttle, could feel the machine struggling. When the plane dipped and pitched, when the weight of the ice on the floats tugged downward at what seemed now like a ridged contraption, his hands sensed the smallest sensations, the subtlest tendencies of the ice box suspended by, and Ardan could now see this, two pounding engines each cranking a propeller.

"My compass, I said. Look at it." Ardan took his eyes from the sheet of gray icy mist and saw in Yarteb's palm one side of the needle starting to point vertically, off the plane of the rose imprint. "Yes, you see that? The needle is pointing not north or south, but upward toward pure magnetic south and the other side downward to magnetic north."

"What does that matter?" Ardan said, the muscles of his arms on fire from the strain of the throttle. "And Rodrigo was right. We have to land this plane. We can't take any more of this. We have to ground it."

"Oh, we aren't going to land this plane on the ground."

"What?"

Looking at his compass even closer now, "Yes, we are almost there."

"Where, Yarteb? Look outside. What can you see? There is nothing there."

"No, not below. Look here."

Yarteb thrust his compass forward where Ardan could see the reading. The needle at the southern marking was pointing nearly straight up, almost against the glass casing.

"Magnetic south. So what," Ardan yelled.

"True magnetic south, indeed. A little farther."

The frozen rain continued to slam against the windscreen as the plane pushed on through the gray mist, and despite wrestling with the throttle, the engines were holding. Ardan's shoulders were lodged against the wall of the cockpit. He shrugged to find some space to reach beneath his left arm to tap his pistol in its holster.

"Save it," Yarteb said. "There will be time later."

"No, the pistol is not for you. I was going to fire at the floats below, hit the welding, and release the weight. The ice there is pulling us down."

"Ah, Ardan. We need those, for they are filled with hydrochloric acid."

"Acid?"

"Yes, each contained in plastic-coated glass containers."

"If they puncture or leak…."

"Yes, yes, gas."

"And we will be engulfed in a fireball."

These precautions, addressing them, were irritating Yarteb.

"I weighed the risk!"

Ardan found this perplexing.

"What kind of madman weighs risk?"

"Madman?"

"A madman who throws men from planes."

"Rodrigo was an unfortunate expense. But he was the only man with an aluminum plane."

"What does aluminum have to do with anything?"

"It's not magnetic."

Just then the plane jolted back from the impact of the something hitting the nose just in front of the cockpit. Ardan instinctively tugged left on the stick and angled the plane away from the barrage, for another object slid off the right wing and corkscrewed into the downpour behind the plane.

"What are those?" Ardan called out, as what looked like a flying animal was chopped by one of the propellers, which chugged and then regained its pace.

"Yes, the propellers are holding," Yarteb proclaimed. "I reinforced them and strengthened the engines before we left.

"But what is attacking us?"

"Unfortunately, my creations: zombie bats."

"Zombie bats?"

"Yes, I created them all: zombie rats, spiders, and other animals of infestation."

A bat crashed into the windscreen, and Ardan could see, as the plane's speed held it pinned against the glass, its distended fangs, its red eyes, how it mindlessly struggled to regain its bearings.

"Yes, I made them, bred them," Yarteb said, and in his voice Ardan detected both pride and regret. "I bred them at the Saint Ambrose."

"And now…"

"Ah, the purest devotees always become the most vehement heretics. I know my standing."

"A change of heart?" Ardan added, and pulled hard on the stick to right the plane. Another bat flew by, missing the fuselage.

"But these bats are merely a nuisance. If we destroy Saint Ambrose, the bats will go with it."

"What is Saint Ambrose?"

"That, there."

In front of the trembling seaplane, above the storm, was what appeared to be a suspended disk hovering in mid air. Only, the disk was the size of several, perhaps a dozen city blocks, and on top were what seemed to resemble buildings, certainly structures, structures that could be inhabited, though the approach angle obscured more details. But it was certain that lights atop the disk gave the surface a glow.

"Isn't it beautiful?" Yarteb murmured to himself, "But as Bacon said, there is no excellent beauty that does not have some strangeness in proportion."

"How does it float? What suspends it?" Ardan eked out slowly, as the bats fluttered about.

"It is above true magnetic south, and as it is made of treated iron and other magnetized metals, the fundamental principles of magnetism keep it aloft." Yarteb spoke as if to himself: "And they want merely to colonize the region, to set up their own city."

"Who does?"

Yarteb barked out, "Who, yes! Who are they, my former employers? Tinkering with this and that is what they are doing. Such small dreams, and me with such abilities. To keep me in the lab, they fail at all aspects of grandeur. They fail to see in the world what even Kant knew. Man is an animal that needs a master!"

"And so you will destroy it?"

"Ah, a wrong step but in the right direction, or is it a right step in the wrong direction? Either way, this is a failure, and as Nietzsche knew, if you are going to fall, learn to fall faster. And I will help them fall faster."

The seaplane, splitting the contours of opposing clouds, rose above the rain, or rather the rain seemed to move past the plane, and the ice shelf below became obscured by the trailing mists. Saint Ambrose sat balanced in the palest blue air there at the bottom of the world. And the plane was ascending now with ease because of how the ice on the floats pitched the nose up. But in the clear air, the two men could no longer hide. The zombie bats swarmed and battered the plane, rattling the door, shredding through the propellers.

"The propellers will sustain, I think," Ardan yelled, "but they'll clog the engines."

"Yes, I am prepared for this."

Yarteb went to the back of the cabin, stumbling as the plane jerked and swayed. He threw off the tarp and unlocked a wooden crate, went to the door, elbowed open the flap, tucked the crate opening into the breach, and slowly released what Ardan determined were finches, birds. Another crate was readied, opened, and more finches fluttered and spun out into the pale blue air. Ardan turned, and in quick motion, surveyed the situation. One crate was left, and Yarteb had refastened the door and returned to the seat just behind and diagonal from Ardan. The swarm of zombie bats flooded the cluster of finches as they scattered in shock and paranoia.

"Zombie vampire bats?" Ardan asked, recalling the fangs on the bat that had stuck to the windscreen.

"Almost. Not zombie vampire bats; vampire zombie bats," Yarteb said with a shrug. For Ardan, that distinction, to be intentional like that, made the whole enterprise even more devious. "Look," Yarteb continued, as he kicked open the door, reached out, caught the wing of a bat with his hands, and yanked it into the cabin before closing the door. He then pinned the bat down with one boot on each wing, and then, oddly, but to Ardan this was becoming increasingly understandable, however horrific, he stood over it like a proud parent. "You see the vacant look in its eye? You see how the saliva suspended between its teeth seems more viscous? And I was able to engineer it to stave off lactic acid build-up, thereby allowing it to maintain its strength, its endurance." Yarteb lorded over his beast, proud, yes, but also in a way that Ardan saw reveled in a monstrous domination. Then, Yarteb, with a tinge of remorse, took out his knife and dragged it across the floor of the fuselage, severing the bat's head from its body. And then in one motion, he flung open the door and kicked the lifeless carcass out.

"The hydrochloric acid is to dissolve Saint Ambrose, I understand now," Ardan began. "And our plane is aluminum, because it won't be subject to magnetic influences." When Yarteb nodded, he asked his next question. "What's in that last crate?"

Yarteb went over, unlatched the clasp, and the wooden sides fell away, revealing a Gatling gun.

"What's that for?" Ardan asked, already accepting whatever the answer might be, as it seemed he had no choice.

"For them," Yarteb said, pointing toward the hovering city.

Two specks in the sky fell away from the disk and were on the approach. Yarteb set the tripod in front of the side door and then boosted the Gatling up to latch it into position.

"Aluminum planes also?"

"Yes."

"We're are going to fire at them from the side of our plane and somehow not hit our engine and wing on that side?"

"Not quite." Yarteb continued to ready the gun. "I am going to fire these rounds—they are capsules of hydrogen, and the propulsion, when it fires, works to dissolve the casing, releasing the hydrogen gas. So, we will be creating pockets of hydrogen, hydrogen clouds, that, and with some other accelerants, will lead to the corrosion cracking of their planes."

"But not our plane? And why not use regular rounds?"

"No," Yarteb said without looking over. "We must erase the trace. Put your goggles down; put them on. I treated your lenses so you'd see the hydrogen clouds as purple. Just don't run into them."

Ardan pulled his goggles down, trying to remember when they were out of his possession. Yarteb, meanwhile, ran the hand crank to rotate the barrels, and once he saw the mechanism was working, fed the cartridge belt through the intake. Ardan, though, began to struggle with the plane's controls even more than before. Though they were out of the rain, the ice on the floats had solidified to the point where the plane's equilibrium was compromised. And, in this thin air, the higher they went, the less responsive the rudder and flaps were.

"The ice on the floats, it's making us unstable."

"Then climb out and chip it off. We have a few minutes until they intercept us."

"You want me to chip it off of those acid missiles?"

"If you can't control the plane…"

Ardan wasn't going anywhere. The Gatling was ready, and Yarteb was eyeing the line of sight. The seaplane was still climbing, and Saint Ambrose was well within view. Ardan slammed hard on the throttle and maneuvered the little plane to an angle that would bring the two approaching aircraft into the Gatling's view. Ardan's goggles were pulled down over his eyes. He was ready for the purple clouds. But still, the seaplane was slow to adjust. When Ardan expected to make a sharp turn, the plane merely started to affect a rounded loop, and when he yanked hard to the left, the plane could only make a subtle bank. Surely, in the open blue sky, these maneuvers seemed amateurish, and without any cloud cover, or even the frozen rain for which Ardan was feeling some slight nostalgia, he felt like a sitting duck for his adversaries. And what if their rounds pierced the, what did Yarteb say the acid containers where made of, glass? The whole plane would be engulfed in a flash of fire that would incinerate the two of them before they had to worry about choking on their own vomit from the escaping gas.

This is not what Ardan signed on for. And he was not about to climb out onto the frozen rigging that held up the acid floats. Then he saw a peculiar switch on the controls, one that seemed to have been added recently, for it was clean, without scrapes or gouges.

"What's this switch do?"

Yarteb leaned around him to see.

"No, not that one. That releases the acid tanks, and we need to be on top of Saint Ambrose. There is no propulsion system. They just fall and explode on contact."

"You mean we could have shed this dead weight long ago?" When Ardan saw his passenger, the look startled him. Yarteb was now wearing a gas mask, fully enclosed around a helmet and attached to thin brown fabric that extended to beneath the collar of his coat.

"Where's mine?" Ardan shouted.

"I had to make sure you did as you were told."

Ardan straightened up.

"Fine. Then we're doing this my way."

He adjusted course directly for Saint Ambrose. The two planes pursuing them had turned to chase at an oblique angle, but now that the course had been reset, their pursuit was established. The seaplane was arcing to the top of the city, with the two planes gaining behind. Ardan yanked the stick to the left, and once the plane had fixed to that direction, he pulled back to bring the Gatling around to face the planes. Yarteb fired. Purple clouds burst into the blue behind them, in front of their pursuers. Ardan swerved again, set the tack, and then brought the Gatling around. More volleys were launched. The spent casings pinged off the back wall of the fuselage and rolled around under the seats. Behind the plane a sharper purple, as seen through Ardan's goggles in the mirrors, bloomed in the foreground. The enemy pierced the clouds without deterring. And again the serpentine maneuver, and again purple sunbursts exploded in the sky, forming an expanding chain of hydrogen gas.

"Any time now, their planes should start to corrode and fall back. Once more, and I'll set a wall of clouds that will do them in."

The seaplane, high above Saint Ambrose, was over the lip of the disk, and Ardan could make out what looked like factories with funnels puffing smoke higher into the atmosphere, in fact so high that the smoke had not time to dissipate before it hit the ceiling of the atmosphere and billowed out in an umbrella. Below, he saw roads and cars, or vehicles of some kind, gliding along. There was even some greenery, maybe a park, and he thought he saw, and perhaps he was right, people who stopped to look upward at this ridiculous plane climbing toward the blackening atmosphere. And Ardan started to breath more heavily. The air was thinning? He looked back at Yarteb, straddling the Gatling's tripod, firing out with a ferocious energy. The man was laughing. Yarteb, in his mask and suit, could breath all he wanted, while Ardan started to labor, as he did all he could to keep the plane on course, bracing with his legs as if he were going to push his boots through the floor of the cabin. When he brought the plane around, he tucked his shoulder into the controls to leverage his weight behind the maneuver. Still, he puffed and mixed short and long breaths.

"We're over the city! When do we drop?"

"Higher!"

"The engines, their combustion will give out!"

"Forced induction. They're fine."

In the diminishing air, the plane began to steady itself, though Ardan was uncertain how his speed was being affected. And Yarteb, anchored by his grip on the Gatling, stood, laughing, sending purple clouds back down in the seaplane's wake. Ardan wrenched himself between his seat and the sidewall to see that the two planes had fallen away. And what a feeble attempt it was. The zombie bats had been repelled with an ease that made this whole adventure somewhat ridiculous.

And only two planes for the defense of a floating city? Perhaps they had thought no one would ever advance on them, not at the bottom of the word and not at this altitude. Ardan could see the curvature of the Earth. He could see the black heavens above. He tugged on his dangling seat belt to find the latch, only to see where the cord had been sliced earlier by Yarteb's knife. Ardan looked back over his shoulder and then, with one hand, unclasped the belt to his pants, removed it, threaded it through the seat supports, wrapped it around his right thigh, yanked it tight, and then buckled it. He was secure.

"Now!" Yarteb yelled. "Release the floats! Flip the switch!"

Ardan, seeing Yarteb bracing for the weight shift and jolt, knocked his hand against the panel below the switch.

"It's jammed!"

"What! Flip the switch!"

Yarteb turned and pumped his fists. Ardan quickly released the floats. Yarteb couldn't see this with his head turned. And once the floats were gone, the plane's maneuverability was regained, and Ardan jerked the plane hard right, toward the open door. First went the Gatling gun. Then, with Yarteb's hands in the air, he too fell toward the door, and through it, only to hold onto the outer rigging that once suspended the floats.

"Ardan, you fool, the mission is over!"

Even in the proper revenge there is no redemption, for Yarteb's larger ambitions were a fantasy that persisted, that lived on successfully and dangerously, parallel to this momentary setback.

Ardan, held well enough in place by his belt, reached inside his coat for his pistol, thought better of it, and then tipped the plane even more until Doctor Yarteb's cries fell away.

The first bomb detonated atop one of the structures, then the other a short ways away on some low-rise barracks. The flashes were too distant to notice, though Ardan would not have seen them, for he had long since turned the plane back around.

This series of interlinked stories by Win Eckert first appeared in the earlier volumes of Tales of the Shadowmen—*this one, in* TOTS 2. *For the uninitiated, the character of "Shrinking" Violet Holmes, who stars in this tale, was created by Matthew Baugh and Win Scott Eckert in order to explain Clive Reston's genealogy. Reston was featured in Marvel Comics'* The Hands of Shang Chi: Master of Kung Fu *series. Violet helps connect the Sherlock Holmes and Fu Manchu novels. Baugh established her as Mycroft's daughter, while Eckert provided her name. Violet's aunt is Sherlock Holmes' wife, Mary Russell, from the novels by Laurie King. Philip José Farmer's* Tarzan Alive *identified Sir Denis Nayland Smith as a nephew of both Sherlock and Mycroft Holmes, thus making him Violet's cousin.*

Win Scott Eckert: *The Eye of Oran*

Oran, Algeria, 1946

No one will ever be free so long as there are pestilences.
The Plague, Albert Camus

FROM: A.L.
TO: Lieutenant Aristide, Section Afrique du Nord, Service National d'Information Fonctionnelle, Paris.
DATE: June 16, 1946
SUBJECT: Oran situation.
    Object, Eye of Oran, reputed to have arcane power. True or false, the gem still has great pecuniary value. Secured object from Natas and have secured it in a temporary but protected location. Am at large in Oran. Natas seeks to recover Eye and utilize as means to control masses who believe in its occult properties.

British agent Reston missing in mêlée while procuring object; presumed dead, but arranged for delivery of object to me before going missing.

Oran under strict quarantine due to outbreak of bubonic plague. Plague bacillus has unusual features, according to medical personnel on scene (Doctors Rieux) and is proving difficult to treat with standard serum. Escape from Oran more problematic than anticipated.

Will report again at designated weekly interval.

FROM: SNIF.
TO: Lieutenant Aristide, Section Afrique du Nord, Service National d'Information Fonctionnelle, Paris.
DATE: June 17, 1946
SUBJECT: Your report re: Oran.

Frankly am concerned that you have chosen to engage services of known criminal A.L. in this affair. A.L.'s skills as a thief and ability to escape from precarious situations are as well known as dedication to own self-interests. Furthermore, is not A. L. rather elderly for involvement in this business?

Against better judgment will grant slight latitude in this matter. If no positive results forthcoming, will be forced to ask SDECE to send FX-18 to Oran.

The city was yellow and dry. The heavy rains at the end of June had given way to the oppressive and unstinting heat. The sand and dirt whipped through the streets, and the people of Oran, already quarantined by the plague–*la peste*–secluded themselves even further in the ostensible safety of their homes and cafés.

In the *Kasbah* was one such haven, the *Café Diable*. Behind the Café, a series of tunnels and warrens led underground to a set of interconnected chambers. The Asian opulence of the lair, accented in jade and gold, would have surprised the listless patrons. They would have been even more surprised to learn that the Café and its hidden lair were built over a temple of uncountable age.

Thousands of years earlier, before recorded history, this had been the site of a Temple of Dagon. When the god's right eye–the Silver Eye of Dagon–had been stolen, a great warrior princess named Bêlit had ventured into the dark realm of the mound-dwellers to retrieve it. She had succeeded where all others failed and became a queen. In the intervening centuries, it was passed down that only a great woman would be capable of ultimately liberating the silver gem from its homeland.

As the years passed, the exact location of the temple faded into obscurity. But the legends of the Silver Eye of Oran, as it came to be known, persisted.

And Doctor Natas knew that there was more to the Eye than its mere financial value. The legend that only a woman could remove the gem from the vicinity of Oran was preposterous, of course. But the other tales of the Eye… To one who had already accomplished impossible wonders, such as the transmutation of base matter to gold, the other stories were a lure impossible to ignore.

Hordes of monstrous fish-men rising out of the sea, bulging eyes and webbed feet, implacable and inexorable, would be his to command. Others had come close to controlling this power. The ancient *Méne* cult. The more recent Esoteric Order of Dagon. With the Eye in his possession, Natas would create and control whole armies of the unstoppable amphibians and succeed where the others had failed.

"Huan Tsung Chao," he called from the shadows. Only cat-green eyes glittered out of the darkness, the rest of his figure draped in black silks.

"I am here, Master," his chief of staff replied.

"Lupin is still in Oran. I can feel it."

"Yes, Master. I agree he cannot have escaped. The city walls are too well-guarded, even for him."

"We have spent too much time and effort here, recovering the Silver Eye. I cannot allow Lupin to make away with it."

"The only way he could escape is with help, and he has had none from the criminal element in this city. If he had, we would know. Smuggling operations in Oran are controlled by Signor Ferrari's gang and we are paying him quite well to keep us informed."

"Summon Pao Tcheou."

"Yes, Master."

When the new arrival entered, he bowed deeply. "I come to serve you, O Li Chang Yen, my cousin."

"I will have the Silver Eye back, Pao Tcheou. Since we cannot locate Monsieur Lupin, find the English spy's wife. If she does not know where the Eye is, then at least Lupin will come for her. He will not ignore a 'damsel in distress.' "

"As you wish."

"Once she is located, bring her here. Send the Korean."

"It will be done."

"Fen-Chu," Natas called next.

Another shape emerged from the dank shadows and asked: "Hanoi Shan?"

"Notify the Council that we shall be arriving soon. And alert Doctor Ariosto to accelerate his timetable. With the Eye at my command, spawning the armies of Dagon will take considerably less time than previously thought."

"By your leave." Fen-Chu bowed and left.

Adélaïde Johnston jumped up as Doctor Rieux came out of the back bedroom of his small apartment.

"Doctor, how is Violet? It's not... *la peste*, is it?"

"No, no. Mademoiselle Holmes shows none of the telltale signs, no buboes at the joints. She is, however, suffering from grief and exhaustion. She needs rest."

"May I go in to see her?"

"Of course, but please do not tax her."

Adélaïde went in to the nondescript bedroom and closed the door. Violet, sprawled on the small bed, looked up without energy at her friend. "Hullo, Adélaïde," she said with affection.

"Vi, are you all right?"

"Yes, just a touch of... exhaustion, the doctor says." Violet smiled wanly. "I'll be fine."

"Vi, I have to tell you, you're looking a little green around the gills, so to say. Are you sure it isn't that... thing?

"The gem?" Violet laughed, sharply. "Don't be silly, dear. You can't tell me you actually believe those stories."

"Well, Charles put some stock in them."

"It was Charles' job to believe. That doesn't mean I do." This was true. Her late husband, Charles Reston, had been an agent for the Diogenes Club, the least known and most eccentric instrument of the British Government, which dealt with matters more unfathomable and *outré*. Reston was a protégé of Beauregard, who had stepped down as the head of the Club's Ruling Cabal several years previous. That the current Cabal had loaned him to S.N.I.F. indicated a state of affairs that touched on both the political and the unknowable. Violet, on the other hand, had been known to refer to the Club and the cases they dealt with as "a bunch of superstitious rot," which had caused some friction between the young couple, but there it was.

"But Vi," Adélaïde continued, "you have to admit, it is awfully odd that you've become sick since Charles died and you started carrying the Eye around with you. You could let me hold it for you for a while."

"It is not awfully odd that I'm all done in. And it has everything to do with my husband being killed by some madman, and us being stuck in this god-forsaken city surrounded by the sick and dying, with a very good chance of becoming sick and dying ourselves," Violet retorted with the trademark Holmes acerbity. "Now, stop mother-henning me and let's get down to cases. This Eye was the responsibility of my husband and his French partner. They're both gone now–not that I ever did lay eyes on the mysterious 'A.L.'–so it's up to us. Those devils must know that Charles arranged to have the Eye delivered to me following his death, and that we now have it. I'll hold on to it, but we've got to figure a way to get the hell out of here with it, and we can't wait for this damnable plague to end. They'll find us long before it runs its course and the city re-opens."

Adélaïde wasn't offended by her friend's tone. In fact, she was long accustomed to it. The two women had first met years ago in finishing school and had become fast friends. When Reston had been loaned to S.N.I.F. and assigned to Algiers, Violet had been left at loose ends in a strange city with no friends. He had suggested that she ask Adélaïde down for an extended visit and all had agreed. After all, when Adélaïde wasn't around, Violet had a tendency to get herself into trouble.

Not that Adélaïde's presence had saved them this time. She was here, having accompanied Violet back to Oran from her recent sojourn in London, and now they were in the deepest trouble of their lives. Through the kindness of Doctor Rieux, they had a place to hide, but it couldn't last long.

"All right," Adélaïde agreed. "There's a man who comes around sometimes to visit Doctor Rieux. It's the reporter, Rambert. He's a journalist for my favorite Parisian paper, *L'Echo de France*. He's trapped here like we are and is desperate to get back to his wife. I'll see if he can help."

Raymond Rambert had readily agreed to include the two young women in his escape plans, and now the three sat together at the Spanish restaurant near the docks waiting for their contact. They had waited the better part of a week for the meet, during which time Violet's condition neither bettered nor worsened.

"The man we're waiting for is called Gonzales," Rambert explained. "It took me weeks to get to him, first through the smuggler Cottard, then through what seemed like an endless series of middlemen. The plan is to hook me up with two of the city guards. When they have sentry duty together and none of the regular soldiers are on duty, that's the time, we'll sail through the gates as if no one was there at all."

"And this man Gonzales won't be upset that you've added the two of us into the mix?" Violet asked.

"Maybe, but he's too close to getting paid. This is to be our final meeting, where he'll introduce us to the two sentries, go over the schedule, and agree on the exact date we go. It's costing me 10,000 francs. I don't think they'll be too upset at the prospect of an extra 20."

Adélaïde nodded, a Red Apple cigarette dangling elegantly from her full red lips. "Ten thousand each is a lot, but we're good for it."

"Yes, especially when the alternative is a hail of bullets," Rambert agreed. Escape attempts and the resounding echoes of gunfire from the city walls had been a nightly occurrence.

Their food arrived; Rambert and Adélaïde dug in, while Violet picked at her own fare.

"Monsieur Rambert," Adélaïde said, "my mother was also a journalist and I find it fascinating. I simply must know–what brought you to Oran? It seems a bit off the beaten path for a Parisian reporter."

"A combination of professional and personal interest, Mademoiselle. I read the reports at the start of the plague, how it spread so quickly throughout the city. I asked to cover the case and arrived a few weeks ago, just before the quarantine was imposed. The accounts intrigued me. They bear certain similarities to a horrendous plague my father witnessed and reported on years ago in Paris."

"Your father? Surely you don't mean–ah, but I see you do! Your father is Charles Rambert, the noted journalist who wrote for *La Capitale* under the byline 'Jerôme Fandor!' "

"Yes, that is so. My father crusaded against a terrorist called Fantômas, who once released plague-infested rats on an ocean liner. If Fantômas has returned…" Rambert paused to light his own cigarette, a Morley. "Well, as I said, there are certain similarities."

"Monsieur, forgive me if I overstep, but didn't I hear once that your father might have actually been related to Fantômas?"

"Yes," Rambert responded quietly. "Some believed he was his son... No one has heard from Fantômas in years, but if he is behind this plague as well... I'm convinced it is unnatural but the information is too dangerous for telephone or telegraph. I must personally bring my report back to Paris and contact the authorities there. In fact–" He broke off as three men approached. "Ah, if it isn't Magistrate Othon! What brings you here this fine day, Monsieur?"

"Won't you introduce us to these two lovely ladies, Rambert?"

"Of course, where are my manners?" Rambert stood up. "May I present Mesdemoiselles Johnston and Holmes, acquaintances of Doctor Rieux. But I am sorry, I have not had the pleasure?" Rambert inquired.

"Indeed," Othon said, "these are my colleagues, Inspectors Fabre and Fauchet of the Sûreté."

The three newcomers seated themselves, and Fauchet, a squat Corsican, spoke first. "Mesdemoiselles, Monsieur, let us come straight to the point. We have reason to believe that you intend to leave Oran by less than legal means."

"I'm sorry, Inspector, I may have been misinformed," said Violet innocently. "Are there legal means of leaving Oran?"

"Ah, well, Mademoiselle, this is the crux of it, is it not? You see, no one is free to leave Oran right now–Fabre. Fabre! Stop staring, it is impolite!"

Without a doubt, Inspector Fabre was unabashedly staring at Adélaïde, at her dark eyes and even darker hair bound up in its French roll. "I'm sorry Fauchet, but... Mademoiselle Johnston, you seem very familiar to me. Perhaps we have met somewhere before?"

Adélaïde laughed, a soft tinkling sound. "No, I'm sorry, it is quite impossible–Violet, dear, are you quite all right?"

The blood seemed to have drained from Violet's face. Her eyes bulged. She looked a little green. Cupping her hands over her mouth, she made a bee-line for the back of the restaurant. Dammit, this was no time to be sick, like some weak-kneed ninny! But autonomic reflexes took over and she retched violently as she reached the bathroom. She turned on the water full-blast. The sounds of her sickness and the gushing of the water pulsated in her eardrums, as she heaved and heaved.

What seemed like hours passed, but it must have been only minutes. Nevertheless, when she emerged from the washroom, the scene had changed dramatically. All the other patrons had departed. Many of the wooden tables and chairs were destroyed, caved in and splintered as if they had been chopped in two. Wooden pillars which formerly supported the ramshackle roof lay on the floor, broken in half. Adélaïde and Rambert lay on the floor, unconscious. Fauchet, Fabre and Othon were in no better condition.

And in the middle of the room stood an enormous Korean clad in a black three-piece suit as if he was off for a day at the track. He was almost as wide as he was tall. He removed his black bowler hat and the next thing Violet knew, its steel brim was embedded in the wood pillar next to her, almost severing it in half. He slammed the side of his right hand into the last remaining pillar. His hands must have been as hard as teak wood.

The roof started to come down. The Korean advanced on her. She never had a chance.

"Miss Holmes?"

Her eyes opened and vision blurred, then cleared.

She was lying on a settee of Chinese design, comfortably propped upon pillows of the finest yellow and red silks. She tried to sit up, but a new discharge of pain in her skull effectively dissuaded any further movement.

"Please, Miss Holmes," the voice continued solicitously, "do not make any further sudden movements and I assure you that you shall feel better in short order."

Violet looked in the direction of the voice; as her vision continued to clear, a tall, lean Asian man came into focus. He was dressed in black silk robes and a black cap was settled upon his skull. He sat, surrounded by flickering candles, upon a dais across the room, which she now saw to be some sort of underground cave decorated with silks and tapestries. Water came down various sections of the cavern walls in tiny rivulets. She didn't know enough about the local geography to know whether the moisture was unusual or not. Certainly it contrasted sharply with the current dry dustiness above ground in Oran. At least, she assumed she was still near, or under, Oran.

She refocused on the man who was leaning toward her, an expression of concern written across his high brow. His hands, clasped together in front of him in a pyramid–a gesture that evoked memories of her uncle–were adorned with long, sharp nails which seemed to be lacquered in black varnish. His eyes were green. Just like the cavern walls.

"Where am I?"

"You are my guest." The man gestured at the cavern. "I must apologize for the accommodations. One makes do with what one has at hand."

Once more, ignoring the blinding pain, Violet moved to sit up. As she did so, her hands moved down her sides and what she felt was discomfiting. The familiar lump that the Eye made in her pocket was gone. In fact, her clothing–khakis and jodhpurs–was gone, replaced by a calf-length, formfitting silk gown in the style of the Chinese. And nothing else. Her eyes widened, and she snapped a glare at the man on the dais.

"Yes, yes. I do have much to apologize for. It was necessary to search you. Your clothing was also searched. There is an object I seek, Miss Holmes. I did not think that you had it. In fact, I was almost positive that you did not. But why take chances?" He leaned back and sighed, somewhat dramatically, she thought. "But I was right, you did not have it, which means that damnable Frenchman still does."

Now her mind raced. She *did* have the Eye. Or at least, she had had it the last time she had checked for its reassuring lump in her pocket. That had been back at the Spanish restaurant.

Where the hell was it? her mind screamed, but she kept her composure. Which was all the more remarkable, given what else she had just realized. Or perhaps it was not that remarkable; she was a Holmes, after all.

"You killed my husband," she said calmly.

"Yes, as I said, I have much to apologize for. To you, dear lady, if not to him." His eyes narrowed, taking on a cruel cast. "Fortunes of war, and all that, as you British would say."

"May I at least know the name of my husband's murderer?"

"Murderer? It was a battle. We were opponents. He lost. I won." He drew himself up regally. "You may call me Doctor Natas."

"I see."

"You do not appear to be surprised."

"I suppose I'm not, at that. This is all too surreal for anything else. And it all fits. Of course, I've heard tales of 'Fu Manchu' before... Your jousts with my uncle, your ongoing battle of wits with my cousin..."

"I would hardly call it a 'battle of wits,' my dear."

"Ah yes, and the fabled charm, too... Is that how you populate your harems, Doctor, on charm alone? Or do you resort to kidnapping the women you desire, drugging them, dressing them as you wish"–she looked pointedly down at her gown-clad form which provocatively revealed every contour and curve–"and keeping them captive for years on end?"

Natas' eyes burned a brighter green, as he replied, "I assure you, Miss Holmes, that I wish you no harm. If you had had the Silver Eye of Dagon, you would be free by now. As it is, you are merely a lure. Once the damnable Frenchman knows you are here, he will return for you and your companions. He will give me the Eye, you will all go free and the matter will be concluded."

Dammit, Violet thought, *we're never getting out of here. The Frenchman doesn't have the Eye, I do. Or did,* she amended.

"Furthermore," Natas continued, "I have too much respect for your vaunted family to treat you with anything other than the utmost deference which you deserve. Neither you, nor your companions, shall come to harm while in my care."

"Adélaïde and Rambert, where are they? And what do you want with this Eye anyway? Surely no mere gem, no matter how exquisite, can be worth all this."

"Your friends are being held safely close by. They have also been searched, as a precaution. Of course, neither of them had the Eye either. As for it, it is merely a key–a key to a deep and unfathomable power. With it, uncounted masses will bend to my will, or else be swept away in the current of history."

Violet was beginning to suspect that Natas was a tiny bit mad, although neither her uncle nor her cousin had ever hinted at that. She decided it would be prudent to get off the subject. "All right, then. If you had already searched us all and didn't find what you wanted, why bring me here for this elaborate audience? Why not just let us go?"

"I can't, Miss Holmes… Not until Lupin comes."

"Lupin? *He's* the mysterious Frenchman? You *are* insane! He'd be, what, in his seventies by now? Besides, I doubt the great Arsène Lupin would ever work as mere agent of French Intelligence. It wouldn't be his style."

"You are mistaken. I know for a fact that Lupin was your husband's partner. And now, he has the Eye."

"Fine then, whatever you say. But how the hell do you know he's coming at all? He could be thousands of miles away!"

"No, Miss Holmes, he is still trapped here, in Oran. He is not free. My little plague has ensured that."

"Your… little… plague? My God, you monster!"

"I created this particular strain in payment for a service the admirable Fantômas rendered me some years ago. I always pay my debts. I held some in reserve for my own use at the appropriate moment. I would say the present situation qualifies, wouldn't you agree?"

"No."

"Ah, of course not. But, Miss Holmes, are you quite all right? It may be the peculiar phosphorescence in these caverns, but you're looking a little green."

Doctor Natas rose, walked over and crouched down to examine her. Was it really the grotto's phosphorescence, or… No. Natas lost consciousness, hitting the cavern floor with a rather ignominious *thud*.

Violet quickly rose, thinking to take advantage of this amazing stroke of luck. Her thoughts of escape, however, were short-lived. She felt a faint odor of mushrooms. Then the cavern spun and swirled and she, too, passed out, falling back on the settee.

FROM: A.L.
TO: Lieutenant Aristide, Section Afrique du Nord, Service National d'Information Fonctionnelle, Paris.
DATE: July 10, 1946
SUBJECT: Oran situation.

Conditions here deteriorating. Tell Champignac his sleeping gas works perfectly, but bag of tricks running out. Plague initiated by Natas in order to prevent escape from Oran and delivery of object. Doctor Rieux highly dedicated but overwhelmed. Plague same as strain used in 1911 by Fantômas aboard British Queen *en route from Southampton to Durban. Suggest American medical expert, if available.*

Object is still safe. Request extraction support. Route response through Parisian reporter Raymond Rambert. If necessary, will report again at designated weekly interval.

It had been almost a week since Violet, Adélaïde and Rambert had been mysteriously rescued from Natas' clutches. They had come to outside of Doctor Rieux's laboratory near the Place d'Armes, and now were in hiding there. It was very kind of him to provide them shelter, without asking too many questions, and he wasn't there much anyway, spending upward of 18 hours a day tending to plague victims.

What was more, the Eye of Dagon was back in Violet's possession, safe and sound, at least for the time being. It was all very strange, but apparently the "damnable Frenchman," Lupin, *had* come for them, just as Natas had predicted. In fact, he must have been in Natas' lair before they even arrived, although that seemed impossible on its face. But how else to explain the mystifying transference of the Eye from Violet's pocket to where it was ultimately found when they awoke outside Rieux's? For it had been found in Adélaïde's generous, raven-colored hair, tucked in her French roll.

Adélaïde had laughed it off with her natural good humor. "After all, Vi," she said, "Monsieur Lupin chose the perfect hiding place. Not even those terrible men thought to look there. And you must admit, dear, that while your hair is quite lovely, it is not quite as abundant as mine, yes?"

Violet had been forced to admit that this was true.

Now, with little else to do but wonder if Natas and his minions would find them again, the days passed slowly, until finally there was a break in the monotony. Since the quarantine, various airlines–TWA, Pan Am, Oceanic, Air France and so on–had generously donated planes. Now, relief cargo flights made regular passes over the city, dropping the usual cartons of supplies and foodstuffs for the trapped citizens. This time, among the usual containers, Rieux received a new drop of plague serum, as well as extensive notes on this strain of the plague.

The new serum came from an unnamed American doctor who had set up an encampment outside Oran to consult on the crisis. Along with it was an unsigned message addressed to Rambert:

M. Rambert:
Tell Lupin to follow the Boulevard du Front de Mer to where it meets the city walls at midnight tomorrow night. There he will find escape.

Rambert, not understanding why he had been identified as a contact for Lupin, or how to contact him, naturally shared the note with Violet and Adélaïde. Though they commiserated about it–after all, Lupin had rescued them from Natas, and what kind of gratitude was it showing to just strand him here?–the three finally agreed that, in the absence of any way of contacting him, they may as well exploit this new escape plan themselves.

As they arrived at the appointed place and time, an airplane flew over the city. The craft's engines must have been muffled, because only Adélaïde's extremely sensitive hearing picked up the noise. Even after she pointed it out to the others, they couldn't see the plane, which was flying without running lights.

Shortly afterwards, a black spot appeared above them, blotting out the stars as it became larger and larger. Eventually the dark spot resolved itself into a black-painted crate, approximately a cubic meter, which was attached to a parachute and a small, absolutely silent engine, both of which were also pitch black to blend in with the night. The engine guided the gently falling crate to a perfect and silent landing next to the three astonished watchers.

The crate had apparently been designed to open upon landing, for the top flopped open and then the four sides of the box separated at the corners and fell to the ground. Violet, Adélaïde and Rambert approached cautiously.

"What is that?" Rambert asked.

As they came closer, they realized that the shapeless object within was encased in packing material, which came away easily and quickly. What lay revealed within took their breath away, at least momentarily.

It was cylindrical and made of metal, glinting in the sparse moonlight. It stood on four fins which were attached to the bottom of the cylinder at 90-degree angles. The cylinder came to a conical point, which was topped by three horizontal rings. In between each fin was a nozzle which pointed at the ground. It looked like nothing so much as a miniature-sized rocket ship from a Saturday-matinee movie serial. Six straps of leather, with buckles at the ends, were attached to the assembly at various points.

Next to the cylinder sat a helmet.

"Um. A rocket pack." Violet paused. "I think I've seen one like it before."

"Well?" asked Rambert.

"You see, this leather belt buckles around the waist, and the other ones go about the shoulders, like so."

"You can't be serious!" Adélaïde said.

"I am." Violet looked at Adélaïde. "I'm getting out of here. Are you coming?"

"Mesdemoiselles, this thing. That thing might carry two, but surely not three," Rambert said. "Your need is greater than mine."

"Are you sure, Raymond?" Violet asked.

"Yes, now that we know that Fantômas is not behind this plague, and that matters will be resolved when you and Mademoiselle Johnston escape with the Eye, I am content to stay and help Doctor Rieux fight this plague in whatever small way I can. Now quickly–you must go!"

"Thank you for all your help." Violet took his hand and held it for a moment, warmly. Then she continued to heft the cylinder onto her back and secure it with the leather bindings.

"Well?" she asked Adélaïde, expectantly.

Adélaïde just shook her head unenthusiastically, as if to say, what madness! She slipped her arms around Violet's waist and tightly through the leather straps, clasping her hands firmly.

"Go," she murmured, "before I change my mind."

Violet nodded and before anyone could say another word, she hit the ignition button.

Flames erupted from the four nozzles, and without further adieu, the two women soared into the air. The flames backlight their airborne figures. Violet, in her jodhpurs and boots, looked the perfect picture of a daring aviatrix test-flying an innovative new device. Adélaïde presented a different picture, holding on to Violet for dear life, her dress fluttering about in the wind, exposing her thighs above black stockings and garters. Rambert didn't even have time to chide himself for impure thoughts, as gunfire from the sentries erupted a second later.

The rocket pack discharged even more flames and noise, and the two women accelerated over the sea. Although the rifle fire continued, the bright dot of the rocket quickly became smaller and smaller, and eventually winked out.

Rambert wished both women a silent *bonne chance* and turned to make his way back to Rieux's laboratory before the guards came to investigate.

Doctor Francis Ardan, as he was known to the French, continued to listen, his bronzed face immobile as he patiently took in the remainder of the fantastic tale. A young, dark-haired man with a thin, white vertical scar down his right cheek sat in the background, representing the British Secret Service. They were aboard a schooner, the *Orion II*, now headed for France. Violet and Adélaïde were wrapped in warm blankets, nursing mugs of strong, black coffee. However, they continued to shiver as much from fatigue as from the dunking in the cold water.

"We were out over the water, still flying. We didn't know how to land the thing. You didn't exactly include an instruction manual, Doc," Violet said, a note of accusation in her voice.

The scientist shrugged. "The rocket pack was meant for Lupin. He knows how to fly it."

"Hmm. Well. We were flying, Adélaïde was barely hanging on, we didn't know how much fuel was left–"

"More than enough," Ardan said.

Violet glared at him and continued, "–and since it was pitch black and we couldn't tell where we were, or what direction we were going, we decided it was better to try to descend. Next thing we knew, we hit the water. Of course, your rocket pack made us sink like a stone, and I didn't think we would make it, but thank God you found us and fished us out in time."

"I followed the tracking signal," the scientist said. "We were following you the whole way and you could have come down at any time."

"Yes, well, no way of knowing that, right?"

"As I said, the pack was intended for Lupin. He would have understood." Violet suspected that Ardan was beginning to become irritated, although he didn't show it. "Do you know what became of him?"

Violet stood up and slammed down her mug. "No, I don't bloody know what happened to Lupin! I never saw the man once the whole time I was there. Now excuse me, I've had quite enough of this."

She stomped off and down the narrow gangway. Stopping, she turned back. "I am grateful, Francis. But this has just all been a bit much."

Ardan nodded, and she continued down the gangway, the young man from British Intelligence following her.

"Violet," he called, and she turned around.

"What is it, James?" she asked, as he moved to take her in his arms.

"Thank God, you're safe now."

"Safe," Violet said.

"Yes, safe. Look, I'm sorry about Charles."

"Yes, well, so am I. I treated him pretty shabbily. Obviously, we wouldn't have lasted. At least now he'll never know."

"Yes. I *am* sorry." He paused. "But you've escaped that devilish place. I'm here to take you back to London, get you well again. You're free now."

"Free? *Free*?" She slapped him hard, once, across the cheek. "I'm *pregnant*, you bastard. I'm not feeling terribly free right now." She stalked off, slamming the cabin door behind her.

Upstairs on deck, Doctor Ardan approached Adélaïde. Remarkably, now that she had cleaned up and dried off, he could see that she was quite beautiful. Remarkable, not because he was immune to feminine beauty (he wasn't), but because he rarely allowed himself to take note of it. She was tall, six feet, and her dress clung to her perfectly proportioned curves in all the right places. Dark, lustrous hair fell about her shoulders. She was, in a word, stunning.

Ardan got ahold of himself and held out a bronzed, cabled hand. "Mademoiselle? We weren't really properly introduced. I'm Doctor Francis Ardan."

Adélaïde sized him up, rather boldly. "Yes, Doctor, it is a pleasure to meet you. I've heard so much about you. The newspapers paint you as an adventurer. How do you say it… a wild man?" she asked provocatively.

"I see." Ardan cleared his throat, choosing to ignore her question. "Yes, well. Mademoiselle, I still have some more questions, and Miss Holmes doesn't seem up to it right now."

"Of course," she said. "What about?"

"About the Silver Eye of Dagon."

"The Eye? We gave it to you."

"Yes, thank you. But how did you come to have it?"

"I don't understand?" Adélaïde looked at him quizzically. "We've given it to you. Isn't that enough?"

"Yes, but, no… I…." Ardan felt out of his element. He was never very at ease with women, but for some reason was even more out of his depth with Adélaïde Johnston.

He took a deep breath and started over. "I am not a representative of the French government, but I have agreed to work with them in this case."

"Yes?"

The scientist started to gain momentum. "They very much appreciate the recovery of this object. But we–they–wish to know. How did it come into your possession? They sent a man here, Lupin, who was supposed to help recover the Eye for them. I expected to find Lupin. Instead, I find you and

Miss Holmes, and you have the Eye in your possession. I still don't understand how that happened."

"Well, it was all very strange." Adélaïde made eye contact and held Ardan's gold-flecked eyes. "Violet and I were hiding at Doctor Rieux's laboratory near the Place d'Armes after we escaped from Natas, when Rambert came to us with a message." She wandered over near the rocket pack and sat down heavily on the deck.

"Go on, please."

"He had received that message in the last medical drop of plague serum. I assume that serum came from you?"

Ardan nodded. "Yes, after Lupin sent his information, I obtained samples of the plague strain Fantômas used over 30 years ago, and was able to develop a serum to combat it. The *peste* in Oran should start to abate shortly."

Adélaïde continued. "The note was anonymous, but it instructed that this Lupin go to a place near the city walls at midnight last night. There he would find a way out of the city."

"Mademoiselle Johnston, that note was supposed to go to Lupin. I arranged to remote-parachute the rocket pack and I don't blame you for using it, but what happened to Lupin then?"

"I don't know, I tell you!" Adélaïde started to sob, slumping further down on the deck next to the rocket pack.

"Mademoiselle Johnston–" Ardan crouched down, close to her.

"Please, Doctor, no more, I am spent!" She hugged herself closer to the pack. "Just hold me, please, a little, and then I'll try to be strong, and answer all your questions."

This was mostly uncharted territory for Ardan. If there were women involved in his adventures (and often there were), he usually left it to the wolves among his five aides to deal with them. *No such luck, this time*, he thought uncomfortably. He leaned down further to console her, and held her as she cried it all out.

Finally, her sobs dwindled, and she nestled further into his arms.

"Mademoiselle–Adélaïde, please," Doc began tentatively. "I need to know."

"Yes?" she murmured, distantly.

"What about Lupin? Do you know anything about him, or what happened to him?"

"Lupin, Lupin, Lupin! Always this man Lupin!" She pushed him away, sharply. "All right, I'll tell you!"

That was when Ardan noticed. Her right arm was now tightly looped through the two leather straps of the rocket pack. Her left hand was also near the pack, fingers poised above the ignition button.

"What–?"

"So you want to know about Lupin, do you? All right, I'll tell you!" The fingers of her right hand flicked, and as if by magic, the Silver Eye of Dagon appeared, held tightly between them.

If Doc Ardan was at all capable of shock, this was certainly the time for it. She had actually managed to lift it from his inner vest pocket without him noticing, quite a feat.

Adélaïde leapt up, left hand descending toward the ignition button, propelling herself toward Ardan. Her lips brushed his cheek at the same time she hit the button. As she launched into the air, accelerating away, she yelled down at him over the blast of the rockets. "You dear, silly man! You want to know where Lupin is? She is right here! You think *my father* is the only one capable of pulling this off? *I* am Lupin!"

She waved at Ardan as she receded into the distance. "*Au revoir, mon cher Francis, au revoir!* We shall meet again! Thank you for the Eye, it's lovely!"

Ardan stared up at her as she receded into the distance, her dress billowing about her shapely stockinged legs. Some of the same impure thoughts that Rambert had had also crossed his mind, and he also chided himself, not for his lack of purity, but for his lack of focus on the matters at hand. A lack of focus directly attributable to Adélaïde Lupin. A.L.

And then she was gone.

She was right. They *would* meet again. He'd make sure of it.

FROM: SNIF.
TO: Sous-Lieutenant Aristide, Service National d'Information Fonctionnelle, Paris.
DATE: July 19, 1946
SUBJECT: Your report re: A.L.

Am more than disappointed with your performance, to wit:

Poor decision-making: You either engaged A.L.'s services sight-unseen, or else knew A.L. was actually Lupin's daughter and failed to inform me. Either alternative is unacceptable. Dealing with Lupin (or a member of his family, obviously), is always a risky business. You should have foreseen that she would double-cross us and keep the Eye. Her acquisition of Doctor Ardan's rocket pack only compounds your missteps.

Using S.N.I.F. funds and resources unwisely: You paid A.L. in advance for services not fully rendered. S.N.I.F. must now dedicate further resources to recovering the Eye from A.L.

You are hereby demoted to the rank of Sous-Lieutenant. Had ultimate objective of securing Eye from Natas not been met, you would be facing immediate termination. Report directly to Montferrand for reassignment

The heroine of this story, Adelaïde Lupin, introduced in the previous tale, is the daughter of Arsène Lupin and American journalist Patricia Johnston, whom the notorious Gentleman-Burglar met in Maurice Leblanc's penultimate novel, Les Milliards d'Arsène Lupin. *Adelaïde was retroactively created and introduced by Win Eckert in our previous tale. In this story (previously published in* Tales of the Shadowmen 3*), he paints a fascinating picture of a post-World War II France that is further beset by the ever-encroaching powers of darkness...*

Win Scott Eckert: *Les Lèvres Rouges*

Paris, 1946

Ilona Harczy hung naked in the damp dungeon, her arms spread and chained at the wrist to the stone wall. She was unconscious. Her wrists and fingers were scabbed over with dozens of small cuts. A brown and withered vine snaked under her dangling feet.

When Ilona next awoke, the blonde woman was there.

Somehow, even in the darkness, the woman glowed, an icy bluish light emanating from a jewel hung at her throat. Her skin was pale, almost translucent, showing blue veins beneath. In a flowing white gown, she floated ethereally above the cobblestone floor. Her lips were painted bright red.

The woman gently took Ilona's wrist and made another small cut. Ilona moaned as blood welled. The pale woman kissed and licked Ilona's wrist. Only a few stray drops of blood escaped her lips, falling upon the floor and the almost-dead plant.

The blonde woman continued to kiss Ilona's wrist, and the bleeding stopped. Then she cupped Ilona's breast in her hand, and softly kissed Ilona's neck and short dark hair.

"Now my love, it is complete," she whispered. "You do love me, don't you? You must, you know."

The blonde woman moved away into a shadowy corner. Two humanoid forms were illuminated as the woman approached them, the light from the jewel glowing brighter and brighter. The woman embraced each in turn, pulling thick necks to her waiting mouth. She intoned nonsense words that Ilona didn't understand.

"*Iä-R'lyeh! Cthulhu fhtagn! Méne! Iä! Iä!*"

The jewel shone even brighter, its soft bluish light filling the room.

Then the three were gone, and Ilona lapsed once more into oblivion.

Nestor Burma looked up at the statuesque figure silhouetted in the doorway of the *Fiat Lux* Detective Agency's inner office. "How may I help you, Mademoiselle…?"

"D'Andresy. Monique d'Andresy." She stood in front of him, raven hair spilling over the shoulders of the London Fog raincoat belted at the waist with a loose knot. "You are working on a case with an American doctor? Francis Ardan?"

Burma leaned back in his creaky office chair and put his feet on the desk. The room's only light was a feeble cone emanating from a small desk lamp. He puffed at his bull's head pipe, red light from the coals illuminating his tired face.

"Mademoiselle d'Andresy, I may be an anarchist, but I wouldn't last long as a private detective if I made a habit of breaking my clients' confidentiality."

"But, Monsieur," she breathed, "my need is great."

She slowly walked around to the client chair beside Burma's desk. Instead of sitting, she stepped one leg up on the chair and propped an elbow on her upper thigh, leaning her chin on her hand. Long nails were done in a perfect French manicure. Facing him, took a drag of her cigarette.

"Perhaps we could come to an… understanding?"

Burma's eyes followed the curve of her leg from the four-inch pump to the lacy black top of a gartered silk stocking–and further. The folds of her raincoat fell away, the belt hanging loosely. Apart from the stockings and garters, she wore nothing else, intimate or otherwise.

"I am sorry, truly, but I don't think such an understanding will be possible."

Monique d'Andresy bent farther over him, providing a clear view of her rather ample charms. She was splendid, in every way.

"Mademoiselle, please…"

"What is it Burma, are you *une pédale*?"

"No, Mademoiselle, in fact you present quite a persuasive argument. But as tempted as I am, it is quite impossible." He puffed at his pipe again. "I believe incest is illegal in France. Now, perhaps I can help you with your coat? It appears you're catching a chill."

"What–?"

Two hands thrust out from darkness behind and gripped her upper arms. The hands were large and bronzed, tendons and muscles stretching across them like small cables. It was no use trying to struggle free.

She sighed.

"Doctor Ardan, I presume?"

"Adélaïde Lupin," Ardan replied.

She glared at Burma. "So Arsène Lupin is your father as well?"

"Not the man who raised me as his own son," Burma said. "But yes, I am Lupin's child from one of his many affairs."

"Clearly blood is not thicker than water." Adélaïde glanced meaningfully at the strong hands holding her solidly in place.

"Please, Mademoiselle d'Andresy–er–Lupin, I am not the one who slunk in here attempting a licentious seduction."

"Perhaps, but you obviously helped set me up. You knew we're siblings–"

"Half-siblings," Burma said.

"*Oui.* You could have said so earlier."

He shrugged. "We've never met before. I don't owe you anything. Besides, I wanted to see what angle you'd take. Quite inventive."

Another voice came from a dark corner as a third man stepped forward. "Your family reunion is very touching, but we have business."

"Yes, time is of the essence," a fourth added in a slight Germanic accent.

Adélaïde sighed. "Gentlemen, on the one hand, I'm not so immodest that I think you need reminding of my current state of *deshabillé*. On the other hand, as Burma said, it is somewhat chilly in here. Is this some bizarre burlesque, or might I be permitted to cover myself?"

Ardan freed one slender arm, and she awkwardly cinched up her coat. He applied gentle but firm pressure to her shoulders, forcing her to sit. She crossed her legs, one elegant and distracting thigh still exposed at the fold of her coat, and lit a fresh *Red Apple*.

"So, Francis, I said we'd see each other again, and here we are. I can think of better circumstances, though. Something along the lines of a snowbound cabin, roaring fire, a bearskin rug and a bottle of *Veuve Clicquot* '32 would do nicely," Adélaïde said playfully.

Ardan's bronzed skin, even under cover of the darkened office, turned ten shades of red.

"No reply, *mon chéri*? Pity. Well, what's it all about? I suppose the story of the Eye of Oran being a fake, and you working with Burma to track down the real Eye–that was all a charade to lure me here?"

Last month, Adélaïde Lupin had tricked Doctor Francis Ardan and the French Intelligence agency S.N.I.F., making off with a precious gem, the Eye of Oran–also known as the Silver Eye of Dagon–using Ardan's experimental Cirrus X-9 rocket pack.

Doc Ardan nodded. "Yes, the story was a plant to draw you out. This man is a representative of the French government. If you turn over the Eye to me, they are prepared to drop all charges. You'll go free, no questions asked."

"All true, Mademoiselle Lupin." The third man said, stepping forward, limping slightly. He had grey haircut military style, and wore round-rimmed glasses. "Return the Eye and the matter will be dropped."

"I suppose you're S.N.I.F.'s Aristide? Sorry if I caused you some difficulties." A slight quirk at the corner of her mouth said she wasn't overly sorry.

"I'm not Aristide, and yes, your actions caused him no little trouble. You can call me Roger Noël. This is Jens Rolf, a mystic and expert on the Eye's occult nature."

The short German nodded curtly.

Noël continued, "Now, what do you say?"

"I say… I cannot."

"Mademoiselle," Noël replied, "if you don't return the Eye, you'll be locked up with the key thrown away."

"Don't you threaten me, you little bureaucrat. If you think any jail cell can hold Lupin's daughter for long, you'd better–"

"Enough," Ardan interrupted. "Gentlemen, would you excuse us please. I'd like a moment alone with Mademoiselle Lupin."

Burma looked at Noël and Rolf, shrugged, and got up. They all stepped into the outer office.

Adélaïde looked at Ardan, red lips parted expectantly. "Well, it's about time, *mon cher* Francis, I've practically been throwing myself at you."

"Drop the act, Adélaïde. I studied with your father when I was a boy. He was a thief and a scoundrel, but when push came to shove, he would do the right thing. I think you will too."

"Don't be so sure."

"I am. Do you have the faintest idea what Doctor Natas was planning to do with the Eye, before you conned us all and stole it? I've seen a lot and most can be explained without resorting to mysticism, but in this case, even I support the

French in recruiting an occult expert to properly study and contain it."

"You, the medical man?" she scoffed. "The 'science detective'?"

"I grant you, almost all of the strange adventures my associates and I have had around the world have ended with rational explanations. But a few have not. When I was a young man, during the Great War, I saw a long whitish worm crawling over the skeleton of an infant, a victim of a satanic ritualistic sacrifice. Even today, I cannot classify that worm; it is unknown to science. In 1925, I encountered an entity which slaughtered many members of an Antarctic expedition. I have no explanation. Two years later, I observed our own Doctor Natas transmute lead into gold; I have not been able to reproduce this with any scientific means. In 1929, my colleague Doctor Littlejohn also traveled to the Antarctic, and had strange experiences which he, also a rational man of science, cannot explain. Three years ago, I was involved in a case in which an herbal concoction allowed its taker to see into the future. A specific prophecy came to pass. And now, the Eye."

" '*There are more things in Heaven and Earth, Horatio…*' "

"Precisely. Why won't you help?"

She shook her head. "Francis, first you must help me with a problem I've run into. If you can do that, I'll gladly abandon all claims to the gem."

The gold-flecks in Ardan's eyes seemed to swirl. "Adélaïde, I promise we'll help you with whatever trouble you're in," he said solemnly.

"All right, then."

"Good. Herr Rolf will secure the Eye while the rest of us tackle your problem. Once that's handled," he said, "I want you to return the rocket pack as well."

"Deal. But, Francis, you see, the quandary is… I no longer have the Eye."

FROM: Lieutenant Montferrand, Division Protection, Service National d'Information Fonctionnelle, Paris.
TO: SNIF.
DATE: August 21, 1946
SUBJECT: Silver Eye of Dagon

The Eye of Dagon is a large silver gem reputed to have occult properties. It is now in possession of a "Madame Elisabeth" who operates a series of brothels in Normandy and Brittany, with headquarters in Paris.

After absconding with the Eye outside Oran last month, Adélaïde Lupin (A.L.) was contacted by Madame Elisabeth. Elisabeth was holding a friend of A.L.'s, one Ilona Harczy, prisoner under the threat of forced labor in one of her bordellos. A.L. was instructed to turn the Eye over to Elisabeth as a ransom payment. To date, A.L.'s friend has not been released. Ardan and Burma's scheme to bait A.L. with a story that the stolen Eye was a fake unwittingly played into A.L.'s concerns about Madame Elisabeth's failure to release her friend. A.L. appeared in Burma's offices with startling alacrity.

It's unknown how Madame Elisabeth knew of the Eye in the first place. It's possible we have a leak, or perhaps she was in league with Doctor Natas, who also sought the Eye.

We have no prior intelligence on Madame Elisabeth, and are relying on A.L. for the following information. Elisabeth and a partner purchased the network of brothels known as the Cordon Jaune, *in January of this year. It is unclear where the money for this purchase originated, but the purchase was apparently intended as an investment. The venture went bad with the passage of the Marthe Richard Law last April, banning all such houses of ill-repute. We can guess that Elisabeth needs the Eye to mitigate her bad investment.*

Madame Elisabeth's partner in this venture is called "Le Chiffre," ostensibly a paymaster for the Syndicat des Ouvriers d'Alsace, *a Communist-controlled trade union. Le Chiffre is otherwise unidentifiable, having come out of the camp at Dachau last year with a case of incurable amnesia. He is always accompanied by two bodyguards highly skilled at personal defense and close range combat. He is described as small, with coarse reddish-brown hair and a voracious sexual appetite.*

Madame Elisabeth, too, is described as insatiable, but it is unlikely she satisfies her needs with Le Chiffre; during their one face-to-face meeting, she made a pass at A.L. which was "exceptionally forceful." Although A.L. portrays Madame Elisabeth as exceedingly charming and charismatic, she declined Elisabeth's offer. Doubtless Madame Elisabeth and Le Chiffre sample their wares on a regular basis. Madame Elisabeth's proclivities may also account for her failure to keep her bargain and release Mademoiselle Harczy, who is reported to be quite beautiful.

There should be no doubt: Madame Elisabeth and Le Chiffre are a deadly combination.

Under my "Roger Noël" cover, I have assembled a team dedicated to recovering the Eye of Dagon: Doctor Francis Ardan, Nestor Burma, the mystic Jens Rolf and Adélaïde Lupin. Unfortunately, we must again rely on A.L. At least, this time, we are dealing with a known quantity, but she is still a Lupin and I will proceed with care.

As an aside, A.L. learned–to her chagrin and my amusement–that Burma is also a Lupin, if only by an accident of birth. The so-called Gentleman Thief had nothing to do with Burma's upbringing, and despite Burma's leftist views I believe he will prove a reliable companion on this venture.

Recommendation: I suggest the establishment of a formal division dedicated to handling unknowable matters. The skills of those I have assembled are without peer, but they are not properly integrated as a team and have not trained together. We are far behind the British Diogenes Club and the American FBI's Unnameables Section in this regard.

"What are you doing here, Burma, slumming again?" Commissioner Faroux asked tiredly. "What brings you to the humble office of the *Police Judiciaire*?"

Burma pulled up a chair and made himself at home. "I want to know all you can tell me about a brothel run by a woman called Madame Elisabeth."

"Well, well, well. Don't your shady friends keep you updated on the latest houses of ill repute? What would Hélène say? She pines for you so–"

"Not for me, you dolt. I'm on a case, obviously."

"How are you involved? There have been three murders in the neighborhood of her establishment in the last two months! If you've been holding out on me…"

"Three murders? I came to you for information, remember? What's the scoop? And why is Madame Elisabeth still open for business?"

"Fine, fine. Her associate greases the right palms to keep it open. An unexpected expense since the Marthe Richard Law, eh?" Faroux chuckled. "Now there are three girls, all beautiful, all found dead in that neighborhood, their throats cut. We suspect they worked at Elisabeth's, no proof, no witnesses willing to say they saw any of the victims there."

"Of course not," Burma rolled his eyes. "None of this made the papers. You're holding out on me, Florimond. What else?"

"All right, all right. We've clamped down on the press, don't want to start a panic, you know. So here it is. All the girls? Not a drop of blood to be found, anywhere. Completely drained."

Burma whistled and exhaled. "Where's her place?"

"Not so fast, your turn now. If I can connect the murders to the *Cordon Jaune*, I can shut it down, bribes or no."

Burma puffed at his pipe. "Look, you're wasting my time and yours. Far be it from me to invoke government powers, but S.N.I.F. is involved. Cough it up, or don't. Either way's fine by me, I don't give a shit. Don't and the spooks'll be down here next. What'll it be?"

"S.N.I.F.? Jesus Christ, what're you into now? All right, she set up shop in the old Benet mansion. Place has been empty, gathering dust, since Doctor Benet kicked off back in '35. You know where it is?"

Burma nodded and got up to leave.

"Goddamn it, Burma!" Faroux shouted at his departing back. "You have 48 hours to fill me in, or I'll have you back in here for withholding evidence, S.N.I.F. or no goddamn S.N.I.F.!"

Burma gave a friendly wave.

In the parlor of the Benet mansion, the shades were tightly drawn against the afternoon Sun. Le Chiffre paced nervously back-and-forth in front of Elisabeth and took a loud snort from his Benzedrine inhaler.

"You can't continue disposing of the merchandise! This is the fourth one! We're practically insolvent as it is."

Elisabeth bestowed a serene smile upon him and stretched her feline body on the chaise. A clingy black gown set off blond curls. Wrists and plunging neckline were ringed in purple feathers, a silver-blue gem resting between her pale breasts. She looked like a Hollywood starlet.

A young, white-haired girl in a *negligé* lay curled on the floor, her head and one slender arm resting in Elisabeth's lap. The girl's eyes were open, but vacant. "Shhh. You'll wake her up." She caressed the girl's hair, but stared steadily at Le Chiffre. As always, her gaze had a tranquilizing effect.

"And why should I not use the 'merchandise,' as you so artfully call it, as I please?" She continued. "I own half of this venture."

Le Chiffre sat down and smoothed his dark suit. He put a *Caporal* in a cigarette holder and lit it.

Continuing more calmly, he said, "You cannot continue to kill these girls. Our financial situation is precarious and you're making it worse by killing off our only source of income. Not to mention the police are sure to become suspicious!"

"Ah, yes, isn't that always how it is," Elisabeth sighed, a faraway look in her eyes. "Always the peasants hound us, chase us on to the next village. Don't we have a right to peace and quiet, like everyone else?"

"Just promise me you'll stop. Eventually I may be able to sell off the *Cordon Jaune*'s assets, recoup our losses, but not if we're both in gaol, Elisabeth... Elisabeth!"

"Hmm? Oh yes, of course I promise, of course."

A discreet knock came to the parlor door, and one of Le Chiffre's bodyguards entered. The man was tall, with wide lips and slightly bulging, glassy eyes. He came over and whispered in Elisabeth's ear.

"Oh, by all means, do show her in, Denis, bring her to me!" Elisabeth clapped gleefully. At the noise, the white-haired girl awoke. "Plaster, we have a visitor. Go help Denis bring her to me."

The girl obeyed, and in a moment they escorted a tall, well-built redhead into the parlor.

Elisabeth looked at the newcomer and cocked her head in seeming puzzlement for a moment; then a smile spread across her face and she clapped her hands again in approval at Le Chiffre. "Beautiful! Splendid! What a find. All legs and curves and breasts. She'll do magnificently for us."

Speaking to the girl, Elisabeth said, "You understand our working arrangements, my dear?"

The redhead nodded.

Back at Le Chiffre: "Bravo, she's wonderful, quiet and shy as well. Herr Ziffre, you've outdone yourself. Denis, escort our newcomer–what is her name again?–yes, escort Jeannette to her room. No. 13 will do, I think. Yes, take her there straightaway, let's get her settled in, and rested. She starts tonight!" She blew a kiss at the retreating figures.

Le Chiffre looked at her warily. "You promised…"

"Oh, don't be tiresome, Ziffre. We've nothing more to discuss. You may leave me now."

Le Chiffre frowned once more, then shook his head and left.

A little while after he exited, Plaster returned the parlor and came to kneel before her mistress. Elisabeth took her hand. "Did you and Denis make our newcomer… comfortable?"

The girl nodded eagerly. "*Oui, Madame.*"

"Excellent."

Half a block down the street from the *Cordon Jaune*'s Parisian headquarters, a nondescript 1932 Citroën C6G pulled up at the corner. Roger Noël was at the wheel. Doctor Ardan sat next to him in the front, while Nestor Burma and Jens Rolf sat in the back.

Noël looked at his watch and ticked off the time. Adélaïde Lupin had gone in 20 minutes ago. Ardan didn't need the watch; his internal clock was as accurate as the atomic chronometer in his New York headquarters. His only response was a slight twitch of an index finger.

Burma noticed.

"Aren't you at all worried, Doctor?" Burma inquired. "Such a beautiful girl… Might she end up in a compromising position this evening?"

"Why should I worry, Monsieur Burma? She knows the risks. Besides, according to the plan, she'll be out of there long before evening falls."

"*Tu parles*. I've seen the way you look at her." He tapped the side of his head. "I'm a trained detective."

Doc turned away without responding. Was he flushed again?

"Do you mind?" the usually quiescent German asked Burma. "If I am allowed to concentrate, I may be able to sense the Eye from here and pinpoint its location."

Properly chastised, Burma settled deeper into the back seat and lit his pipe.

Adélaïde followed Denis and the white-haired girl through the corridors of the *Cordon Jaune*. She reflected smugly on her disguise's success. She had only met Elisabeth once, briefly, and had correctly predicted she would not be recognized. Ardan had objected, but Noël had wisely overruled him.

When these two left her alone in her quarters, she'd be free to explore and locate Ilona. Then back to the parlor to rip the Eye of Dagon from where it hung around Elisabeth's translucent neck.

The whole place had a freakish ambiance to it. Noël had briefed them all before sending her in. The mansion used to be the clinic of Doctor Felix Benet. Benet had used a new source of radiation–Radium-X–to cure blindness and other illnesses, and had been brutally murdered here. It still stank of death.

Add in the mansion's current occupants: Trollish Le Chiffre snorting his amphetamines. Languid Elisabeth... fascinating in a menacing sort of way, like a flame drawing in the moth that cannot resist. Did she have a slight Hungarian accent? And her two escorts, they were quite a pair. Denis with his bulging eyes and bluish-green, almost oily skin emanating a squalid fish smell; he was in serious need of a shower. And silent Plaster, a girl of no more than 20 with a shock of white hair. Was it the fear permeating this place that robbed her hair of color?

As they passed a large mirror hanging in the hallway, Adélaïde caught a quick glance in it and could have sworn... Had she really seen only her own and Plaster's reflections? No, she must have missed foul Denis' reflection because he was lumbering a few steps ahead of them.

No matter, she'd be in and out of here quickly. Free Ilona, snatch the jewel and disappear. It was a bit of a trek to Room 13, though, and they seemed to be headed toward the basement...

As they approached a heavy wooden door, Plaster's hand clamped over her mouth and nose with a chloroform-soaked rag. The last thing she saw was her friend, Ilona, shackled and hanging in the dank cellar.

When the Sun declined, the ladies of the *Cordon Jaune* were brought down for their evening lineup before Le Chiffre and Elisabeth. Counting the new girl–had anyone met her yet?–there were ten women currently working at this establishment. Last night, before Jeannette had come on board, so to speak, there had also been ten, but Claudette had left.

People came and went in this line of work, and the ladies weren't concerned. They might have been if Madame Elisabeth allowed them newspapers or radios–Claudette's body had been discovered nearby just that afternoon. Her corpse was completely depleted of blood, and the police, as usual, were baffled.

Le Chiffre, conversely, was concerned. Of the ten, only nine appeared at the lineup.

"Elisabeth!" he shouted, then turned back the women. "Back to your rooms, all of you! Now!"

Several of the girls, lead by the waif Cabiria, protested but complied on further threats from Le Chiffre.

After the ladies dispersed, he beckoned to his two looming bodyguards, and faced Elisabeth.

"Where is the new girl? Where is Jeannette!"

Elisabeth smiled at him lazily. "Ziffre, you really must learn to control your temper."

"Woman, you'll be the end of us all. Denis, Karl–" He snapped his fingers at the bodyguards "–take Madame Elisabeth to her room and lock her there."

Elisabeth began to giggle softly. She raised one elegant arm and pointed behind him, urging him to look.

Le Chiffre slowly turned and almost fainted. Denis and Karl's dark tailored suits were splitting at the seams. Eyes swelled in their sockets. Snouts elongated. Webs formed between fingers and toes of feet which no longer fit in discarded shoes. Oil seeped from bluish skin showing through the splits in once stylish clothing.

Thick red lips opened, showing row upon row of razor-sharp fangs. The incisors were particularly lengthy.

The jewel at Elisabeth's throat glowed momentarily with ice-blue intensity, and then softened.

"Gentlemen, Herr Ziffre is becoming a nuisance. Take him to the cellar. No, no! Don't hurt him–yet. He may still have his uses."

Karl punched Le Chiffre in the face, and the two fish-men started to drag him away, gibbering quietly to themselves.

"Oh, and gentlemen?"

The two creatures paused.

"Better stay out of sight. We wouldn't want to frighten the girls, would we, darlings? I'll call them down for this evening's lineup."

The two fish-men gesticulated in parody of a human nod, and continued to shamble away, dragging Le Chiffre and leaving a faint trail of fish-slime in their wake.

It had been too long. Adélaïde should have been out over an hour ago. Time for Plan B.

Doc Ardan and Jens Rolf had come into the *Cordon Jaune* with the evening's first round of customers. They had both noted the Eye of Dagon hanging from the Madame's neck, but the first order of business was to locate and liberate Adélaïde and Ilona. The Madame had made cooing noises over Doc, murmuring over the handsome bronze giant and making a point to caress his shoulders and biceps.

Elisabeth was undeniably mesmerizing, but Ardan could sense something vile and repellent at her core. He stoically bore the indignity of her touch, but when Elisabeth prattled on about what a lucky girl Plaster would be that night, Rolf kept things in motion, playing his part perfectly.

"Fraulein Elisabeth," the German snapped, consulting his watch, "if we could proceed, our time is limited."

"Of course, Mein Herr, forgive me. This girl's name is Manon. I presume she is acceptable?

"Quite, thank you."

Now both men were in separate rooms with the girls. Doc had broken a small glass tranquilizer under Plaster's nose and eased her into a comfortable position on the bed. As he exited, Jens Rolf silently came from the room across the hall.

Through the open doorway, Doc could see the girl Manon sitting straight up in a chair, eyes open and yet vacant.

"A slight trance, she'll come out of it shortly," Rolf whispered.

Doc nodded, and scanned the corridor in both directions.

"That woman, Elisabeth," Rolf continued. "Something evil and depraved owns her soul."

Doc nodded again, and raised a hand for silence. After a moment, he pointed and the two men made their way toward a butler's staircase at the back of the house.

Nestor Burma was stationed out back of the Benet mansion at a basement window. His associate, a reformed burglar called Zavatter, worked at the lock.

"*Voila*," said the cracksman as the lock came loose. Burma paid him off, sent him on his way, and held his position.

After 30 minutes, Ardan and Rolf had still not appeared with the women and the Eye. Burma emptied out his pipe on the pavement. He sauntered casually from the back alley and down the block to the idling Citroën.

He said a few words to Noël, then retraced his steps, crouched, and went in the open window.

Adélaïde's wrists were shackled to chains hanging from the cellar ceiling. The room was featureless save for the tendrils of greenery which snaked the ground around her feet.

Adélaïde had been stripped down to undergarments and pumps. Her red wig was gone. She yelled at Ilona to wake up, but her friend was unresponsive. Adélaïde quieted when she heard the click of footsteps on the wooden stairs descending from the cellar door.

Elisabeth appeared, wearing black riding pants tucked neatly into black patent leather riding boots, and a white blouse cut low at the neckline. She held a riding crop behind her in both hands. Out for a day at the races.

"Welcome my dear, welcome!" She smiled broadly at Adélaïde, then whispered conspiratorially in her ear. "I knew it was you earlier today, as soon as you came into the parlor. I have an unusually strong sense of smell, and I could never forget your alluring scent."

"What do you want?"

"What? What do I want?" Elisabeth asked innocently. "Why my dear, shouldn't it be obvious? I want you."

Adélaïde shook her head in confusion.

"Oh, I admit, I probably should have left Paris long before now, but once I met you when you delivered the Eye– isn't it just exquisite, by the way?" She gestured at the luminescent jewel hanging between her pale breasts. "In any event, once I saw you, I knew it would be worth the risk of remaining a while longer. And I was right! Here you are, pretty as a package."

"I still don't understand. This was all a trap? For me?"

"But of course! When I met you, I could tell right away if I kept the Eye, you'd come here looking for Ilona. I'm a very good judge of character, you know."

"Why me?"

"Do I have to explain everything? Dear Adélaïde." Elisabeth pouted, puffing out her lower lip, then caressed Adélaïde's cheek with the end of the crop. Adélaïde stiffened.

"Oh, don't worry, this is just for show." She pointed at the cuts on Ilona's neck and wrists. "You see, no crop made those cuts."

Adélaïde shook her head.

"Oh, very well, I'll explain, though it doesn't matter in the end. Soon you'll be pleading to join me. So. Your friend, Doctor Natas. Remember him? Once you had escaped from Oran with the Silver Eye of Dagon, he was able to piece together what really happened. He discovered the true thief of his prize. And–surprise! He put a price out on your head and a reward for the Eye's return!" Elisabeth's smile illuminated the room.

"Word spread–I am somewhat well-connected in that area," she said modestly. "Natas' head of intelligence, Pao Tcheou, also sent out a personal dossier on you. Information on your parents, your friends, anything that might be of use. You can imagine my astonishment to find Ilona Harczy listed as one of your closest friends."

Adélaïde stared at her blankly.

"No? You are still confused?" Elisabeth sighed. "I once knew another Ilona Harczy. I was forced to kill her in Vienna, long ago. I counted it a stroke of good fortune to learn my late nemesis had a distant namesake! Out of curiosity, I sought her out, and discovered she was a chanteuse at the Calyx Bar–yes, the very place I took delivery of the Eye from you! I must say, the latter Ilona is much more beautiful than her predecessor, and once I saw her, I decided to keep her.

"Killing two birds, as the saying goes, I contacted you and arranged to exchange her for the Eye. After all, why not still collect on Natas' reward? When we met, I knew I'd have you as well. I was smitten, I confess. It's extended my Parisian stay a bit, and I probably should've moved on by now, but adding you and the lovely Mademoiselle Harczy to my stable will be well worth the risk and undue attention."

"Undue attention?" Adélaïde asked. "It's you. You've been killing those girls."

"Well, one needs to replenish, after all. I think I've been pacing myself quite nicely, but you're right, it is time we leave this place before the day breaks."

"I'm not going anywhere with you."

"Oh, you will," Elisabeth said softly, and kissed her cheek gently. "You'll beg to come with me."

In the upper cellar, Burma had discovered and released Le Chiffre from his cell. The small man was volubly cursing Elisabeth and Denis and Karl.

"Where is Madame Elisabeth, Monsieur? I must locate her."

"I have no idea," the other man growled, "and I don't aim to find out."

"Not so fast. You know your way around this chamber of horrors. You're going to help me find her, and the new girl–a redhead–who came here earlier today." Burma began to reach inside his trenchcoat, then stopped, slowly withdrawing his hand.

Le Chiffre had anticipated Burma, producing a gleaming Eversharp razor blade from the heel of his left shoe. "I'll flick this blade in your eyeball. Don't twitch, don't sneeze, you understand? Nod slowly if you agree."

Burma nodded, and Le Chiffre took off.

Ardan and Rolf approached the late Benet's laboratory. The scientist held up a hand, tapped his nose and raised two fingers. His sense of smell, akin to an ape's, far exceeded that of a normal human.

There were two… somethings… waiting in the laboratory.

Rolf understood Ardan's signal, and the two went in.

Nevertheless, neither was prepared for the ferocity of the attack. Sharp claws extending from rubbery webbed hands embedded in the wall inches from Ardan's head. Razor sharp teeth with exceedingly long canines snapped at his face. The scientist dove past the creature, and the creature's other set of claws raked across his chest, drawing blood. Doc jabbed a strong elbow into the creature's back.

The other fish-man backhanded Jens Rolf across the room, knocking him almost senseless. The second creature then leapt for Ardan, who rolled to the side and bounced up lightly on his feet.

The first creature freed its claws from the wall, and now both approached the scientist, backing him into a corner.

Four sets of claws came flying at Ardan.

"Never," said Adélaïde, "never will I willingly accompany you."

"You will, darling, but let us not argue. Soon you will love me."

"You're delusional. What you've said makes no sense. You decided to collect on Natas' reward, and yet you still have the gem and I'm hanging in your dungeon."

"As for you, I thought I had made myself clear. I have decided to keep you for myself. As for the Eye… I quickly discovered its special properties, and how to tap into them. One as well-traveled as I picks up quite a bit, you know. Human servitors are tedious; with the Eye I have created two completely loyal, relentless servants."

Her expression became wistful. "As the years have passed, it has become increasingly difficult to stay ahead of the forces of so-called 'justice,' moving from town to town, city to city, stopping only long enough to rejuvenate once or twice and then moving on. Now I can stop running, return home to Čachtice Castle. The Carpathians are particularly beautiful this time of year, as autumn approaches. As you'll see.

"These servants will go forth and gather the sustenance I require. All they'll need is the lake nearby the castle in which to replenish themselves. No more vagabond lifestyle. Home.

"So you see, I too have reason to keep the Eye for myself, and fully intend to do so. I am tired of running."

She went over to Ilona and began releasing her chains. "By tomorrow, we–the three of us–will be home."

Ilona slumped to the cold floor, senseless. Elisabeth left her there and returned to Adélaïde, made a swift cut above her left breast, and began to sup. As the blood flowed into Elisabeth's mouth, Adélaïde began to go into another world; it was pleasurable, but another part of her mind screamed silently in resistance.

Uncounted minutes passed, and Adélaïde came back into focus. She saw Ilona approaching Elisabeth from behind. Her approach seemed somewhat stealthy, and Adélaïde surged with hope. Elisabeth had made a tactical mistake in releasing the other girl. But she was weakened and pale… Would she be able to immobilize Elisabeth?

Ilona crept closer and closer, reaching in toward Elisabeth, who still was bent over Adélaïde, draining her life-blood. Adélaïde faded out and in once more again, and now Ilona was impossibly closer, about to grab the Madame and thrust her away from Adélaïde. Ilona took her shoulders, and Elisabeth reached back an arm, slipping it around her waist and pulling her in toward her victim.

Elisabeth kissed Ilona, covering her lips in Adélaïde's blood, then made another cut above the girl's right breast. The blood started to pour out, and she pushed Ilona's mouth down to the wound.

Ilona drank greedily of Adélaïde's blood.

The now-healthy and budding greenery which snaked around her feet seemed to be moving slightly, as if intercepting any stray falling droplets of blood.

Elisabeth returned to her victim's breast and joined Ilona in the feast.

Doc Ardan's superfirer pistols hummed busily, shooting hundreds of rounds of anesthetic "mercy bullets" at the two misshapen amphibians.

To no avail. The creatures advanced upon him. And advanced. Then stopped.

Rolf had regained his senses. He chanted words in an ancient and arcane language.

"*Ph'nglui mglw'nafh Cthulhu R'lyeh wgah-nagl fhtagn. Iä!*"

The two monsters who had been Karl and Denis strained. Their eyes swelled in their sockets but they were otherwise immobilized.

"Hurry!" the German mystic yelled at Doc. "This hex will not hold them long!"

Doc nodded once and went for the opposite corner of the laboratory, an area he had not been able to reach during the pitched battle.

Moving faster than most humans could conceive, the bronze man began to gather and piece together large pieces of old, dusty equipment.

"Faster!" Rolf yelled.

"I am," came Ardan's curt reply. Finishing the assembly, he hefted it under his massive, cabled arm. The object was black and conical, the tip coming to a rounded point of glass or some other transparent substance.

Doc reached inside his equipment vest and pulled out a small rectangular box. He wired the box to the cone, which came to life with a high pitched whine. The transparent emitter at the tip illuminated. He pulled out two pairs of goggles, put one on and tossed the other to the German.

Ardan nodded at Rolf, who released the spell and collapsed.

The two fish-men came toward them, moving faster than their deformed shapes gave them any right to.

Doc flipped a switch on the black cone, and the light of a thousand suns, powered by Radium-X, burst out from the emitter.

The beam hit Denis, then Karl, and both fish-men shrieked and burst into flames. Within moments, both had dissolved. All that remained was two piles of ashes on the floor, and a stench.

Burma came running into the room, pistol in hand, and stopped short at the sight and smell. "Mmm. Burnt rancid fish. My favorite."

Elisabeth and Ilona were still bent over Adélaïde. She became more and more pale, but paradoxically felt a strange warm sensation exploding out from the center of her body.

Mercifully, she had almost passed from consciousness when Ardan, Rolf and Burma burst into the dungeon.

"She's almost there! Don't stop!" Elisabeth ordered Ilona, and turned to face the men.

Ardan held the Radium-X projector under his left arm, a superfirer in his right hand. He sprayed Adélaïde's attackers with mercy bullets, but Elisabeth laughed it off, while Ilona continued to draw the remainder of Adélaïde's blood.

Ardan tossed the spent superfirer away and hefted the projector into position.

Simultaneously, Rolf uttered incantations–"Iä*! Iä! Ph'nglui mglw'nafh Cthulhu fhtagn! Méne!*"–and the Eye of Dagon exploded off of Elisabeth's graceful white neck in a detonation of blood and bluish light.

The gem bounced on the stone floor and rolled toward Ardan. Before he could seize it, the energy released from the Eye crackled and struck the Radium-X projector, frying and fusing circuits.

The projector began to heat up and blaze white hot in an uncontrolled reaction. Ardan dropped the projector before it could burn his hands. It bathed the room with sun-like light. Burma, *sans* goggles, was blinded.

Elisabeth and Ilona screamed and collapsed, writhing on the floor. "The light! The Sun!"

"The projector is going to blow. It'll take out the whole cellar, maybe more. I can't stop it!" Doc yelled at Rolf. He gestured to Burma. "Help him out of here. I'll follow you with Adélaïde and these two."

Ardan turned toward Adélaïde, but paused at Rolf's hand on his arm.

"These women," Rolf said. "I understand and respect your policy of humane rehabilitation. But these women are gone. You cannot help them."

Doc paused a moment further, then nodded and went toward Adélaïde.

Minutes later, he burst from the front of the Benet mansion. Adélaïde looked like a small child cradled in his massive arms, broken chains trailing from her wrists. He placed her gently in the back seat of the Citroën.

Roger Noël gunned the engine and floored it, Ardan mounted on the running board, as a violent explosion rocked the *Cordon Jaune* headquarters.

Just before sunrise, large boulders shifted and rolled down the piles of rubble in the debris of the Benet mansion. A large vine, now the circumference of a man's torso, pushed the rocks away. At one tip of the vine was a pod which vaguely resembled a Venus Fly Trap. The vine slithered free, and glided down the Paris streets.

Anyone who may have observed this singular phenomenon could also have heard, just at the edge of audible range, a tiny whispering voice, barely distinguishable from the slight breeze.

"*Nourrissez-moi ! Nourrissez-moi!*"

The murmurs gradually faded into the morning dawn.

FROM: Lieutenant Montferrand, Division Protection, Service National d'Information Fonctionnelle, Paris.
TO: SNIF.
DATE: August 26, 1946
SUBJECT: Silver Eye of Dagon

The Eye of Dagon has been secured and turned over to Doctor Ardan. Jens Rolf has provided Ardan with detailed and specific instructions for its safekeeping.

There was no sign of Le Chiffre anywhere in the Cordon Jaune *headquarters, nor of any of the other women employed in his house of ill-fame. It is presumed they all escaped in the confusion prior to the explosion.*

Burma's blindness was temporary, and Ardan has given him a clean bill of health. According to Ardan and Rolf, A.L. will suffer no lasting ill effects from her experience.

When the rubble was cleared from the lower cellar of the Benet mansion, Elisabeth and Ilona Harczy's bodies were recovered and taken to the morgue. However, the next day, the bodies were inexplicably gone.

Recommendation: The International Police Commission should be on the lookout for two women matching their descriptions.

Deep in the Arctic, in a solitary fortress, Doctor Francis Ardan checked on the Eye of Dagon. It was stored safely away from those who would use it for ill purposes. Likewise Doctor Benet's Radium-X projector.

He moved silently into the next chamber, a warm room decorated in the fashion of an Adirondack hunting lodge. Then, through the fortress' insulated walls, he heard the mechanical whine of rocket engines.

In a huge stone fireplace, embers from a once-crackling fire still glowed. A large bearskin rug in front of the fireplace was askew. A note was pinned on the mantle, near a half-empty bottle of *Veuve Clicquot* and one champagne flute (Ardan did not drink):

My Dearest Francis (the note began),
What a wonderful storehouse of treasures your little hideaway is! I left you the gem this time, although you know, of course, I easily could have taken it. Thank you for refueling the Cirrus X-9 for me. I know you'll be cross with me for making off with it again, but really, how else can I make certain we'll see each other once more?
Au revoir, mon sauvage.
Mon amour,

Adélaïde

He shook his head ruefully and smiled faintly. He just couldn't seem to hang on to those damn rocket packs.

But he didn't really care.

Finally, in this story, previously published in Tales of the Shadowmen 1, *Win Eckert depicts what might have happened twenty years after the events of* City of Gold and Lepers. *...*

Win Scott Eckert: *The Vanishing Devil*

Prologue: New York, 1949

In an empty penthouse suite on the 86th floor of the grandest skyscraper in New York, the telephone rang five times before the line clicked over. Inside a cherry-paneled box in the telephone alcove, a mechanical arm lifted the receiver. A pre-recorded vinyl disk was inserted against one needle, while a fresh wax cylinder was inserted and aligned with another.

A voice began reciting, "This is the Doctor. Please speak–"

"Doctor Ardan! This is Louise–"

"–into the receiver loudly and clearly enunciate your words. State the nature of your business and how we may contact you. Your message will be recorded and immediately conveyed to the Doctor or one of his associates. Thank you. Begin speaking now."

"Doctor Ardan–Francis! This is Louise Ducharme. My daughter, Justine, has disappeared!"

Sussex, 1949

Doctor Francis Ardan reflected that the Great Detective was quite spry for a man of 95 years. The tall, lean, grey-eyed man moved freely about the cottage, filling leather-bound footlockers with books, clothing and other personal items.

Ardan had been in London for a scientific conference and had taken the opportunity to visit his old mentor. Or rather, one of his former mentors who had participated in the strange training program devised for him by his father. The program had been instituted from Doc's birth and was designed to create a superman capable of tracking down and defeating evil all over the world.

There had been many others involved in his preparation for the fight against the criminal element. Professor Kennedy, who had instructed him in scientific detection. The sallow Frenchman, M. Senak, who had taught him the trick of temporarily paralyzing an attacker by pinching the nerves where neck met shoulder. Wentworth, who, along with Indian fakirs, had coached him in adding or subtracting six inches from his height. The list went on. Of all, though, Ardan reserved his highest admiration for the hawk-nosed man bounding about the Sussex cottage.

Now, observing the elderly Detective, and considering his mastery of disguise, Ardan wondered if the excessive wrinkles and liver spots weren't a sham. However, by unspoken agreement, Ardan had never pried into the Detective's beekeeping activities, even when he was a boy brimming with curiosity. In turn, his former instructor in the fine art of detection and deduction had never inquired into Ardan's synthesis of the African Kavuru elixir received from their mutual cousin.

As the Detective packed the trunks, Ardan finished relating details how he and a masked vigilante called the Yellow Jacket had disrupted the annual assassin's auction being held in the French Quarter of New Orleans.

"And you?" the bronze man asked, finishing his story. "Where are you off to this time, sir?"

"Tibet, Ardan." The Detective tossed a copy of *The British Bee Journal* in a bag and sat down on the divan, curling his legs under him like a cat. "An extended stay. I'm afraid you arrived just on the eve of our departure. Russell is up in the City, finalizing our legal and financial arrangements with M."

"I'm sorry for dropping in unannounced, sir. The neuroscience conference in London ended earlier than expected."

"Not at all, not at all. You know you are always welcome here, my dear Francis." The older man's grey eyes twinkled.

"It's been a long time since I went by 'Francis Ardan.' " In fact, it was the name he had used a boy, when he had spent summers being coached by various experts on the Continent while living with his great aunt Michelle Ardan; here in England learning the fine art of detection from the Master, as well as Thorndyke and Blake; and later still when adventuring in Asia in the 1920s. "The only ones who still call me that are you and Lupin."

The Great Detective's eyebrow arched at the mention of the notorious thief, with whom he had finally made his peace some years before, but the ringing telephone cut off his retort.

"Hallo? Yes? Yes, Violet, tonight will be fine. Yes, we depart at first light tomorrow. Very well. Yes, goodbye." He wrapped his mouse-colored dressing gown around him, curled up again, and started to fill his clay pipe with a foul smelling shag. "My niece, Violet, you know. Recently widowed, she was married to one of M's men. She's letting the cottage in our absence with her son, Clive. Dickson will keep an eye on them for M while we're gone."

The Great Detective lit the pipe, inhaled deeply and continued to speak when the telephone rang again.

"Confound it," he said, borrowing a phrase, "what does she want now?"

On the other end of the line, a mechanical voice intoned, "*Important message for the Doctor. Important message for the Doctor. Important message–*"

Bemused, he handed the receiver to Ardan. "Apparently this is for you."

Ardan took the telephone. "This is the Doctor."

As Ardan spoke, an audible click indicated that his voice had been recognized, and over a trans-Atlantic hiss, a tinny message recorded on a wax cylinder in New York began to play back.

"Doctor Ardan–Francis! This is Louise Ducharme. My daughter, Justine, has disappeared from her laboratory above Le Chateau Mireille club! All the doors and windows were locked from the inside, and there's no trace of her! If you get this message, please come to Paris immediately. I've been instructed not to contact the authorities, but I am desperate. I've tried your friend, Captain Morane, but he's away on a case. You're my last hope. Please help me. I'm staying at– wait. That smell. Like ozone… What is that blue light–?" There was a sound of a high-pitched whine, followed by the dull thud of the phone hitting the carpeted floor, after which the message ended abruptly and the line clicked off.

"That's quite ingenious," the Detective said as Ardan hung up the telephone. "How did the machine know to ring you here?"

But Doc didn't answer the question. Instead, he asked, "Would you contact M, or his successor if necessary? I need a favor."

Doc Ardan was not sure he would ever become accustomed to jet travel. His first supersonic flight over a year ago was marked by the eerie silence associated with faster-than-sound flight. This craft was not supersonic, but was close enough.

The RAF pilot, Major Roger Gunn, had shown him around the two-seater plane, a de Havilland DH 113 *Vampire* NF Mark 10, before takeoff. The British military were testing this prototype, which had a maximum speed of 545 mph at 30,000 feet, and a range of 1,200 miles. Although the dual tail craft was a night fighter, Doc's reputation and years of fighting wrongs across the globe had led the British government– and it had been said occasionally that M was the British government–to place the *Vampire* and her pilot at Ardan's disposal for the hop to Paris.

Periodically through the short flight, Major Gunn had attempted to break the monotony by drawing Doc into conversation, regaling him with anecdotes of his recent holiday at the estate of the 14th Earl of Marnock.

"The Lord of the Manor is a real gentleman, that he is. And of course the estate, Greensleeves, is kept up impeccably. But that boy of his, Brett, is a bit of a wild one. Oxford lad. Turn in the Service would do him good. Do you know the family, sir?"

"No," Doc replied.

Gunn was quiet for a bit, and then tried again, telling Doc about his plans to eventually retire and move his family to Kenya.

"Even at three months old, I can already tell that my boy James is going to be a real strapper. Do you have any children, Doctor?"

This time, Doc didn't even reply, but Gunn wasn't offended. Doc's mind was clearly elsewhere and the two lapsed into a companionable silence.

As they entered French airspace, Major Gunn reduced thrust to the DH Goblin 3 turbojet engine, and the *Vampire* began to descend. Nearing Villacoublay airfield, Ardan and Gunn simultaneously noticed several dark blobs materialize in the sky above them. The plane descended, and the blobs tumbled down along with them, finally coalescing into what appeared to be large chunks of dirt, rock and pavement flying through the sky.

"Taking evasive action!" the RAF man said as he swung the fighter around in a tight arc. The hunks of rock missed the jet by an uncomfortable margin and continued speeding downward to rain on the ground.

"Damn. What the hell was that? They came out of nowhere!"

"Yes," Ardan agreed. "They certainly did."

As the plane approached the military airfield, both occupants noticed what appeared to be giant gaping holes in the runway. The plane pulled up and began to circle for a new landing approach.

"I'm being directed to a different runway," Gunn explained to Doc. "Seems there's construction or some such on our original landing strip."

As the plane began its second approach, several large dark spots appeared in the new runway. From this distance, they looked like small potholes on an upcoming stretch of highway, but both men knew that the dark spots would prove significantly more dangerous to their small craft if they tried to land.

"Aborting," Gunn said as the thrust increased once more and the *Vampire* pulled up–right into the path of more tumbling chunks of concrete and debris. Swinging violently aside, Gunn and Ardan's plane barely avoided being pummeled as the pavement flew past them.

However, one large mass of rock remained directly in their flight path. Gunn reacted instantly, firing the *Vampire*'s four 20mm nose cannon and blasting the chunk into tiny fragments though which the plane blazed.

"I suggest landing as soon as possible," Ardan said. "We're not going to be able to avoid this flying debris forever, and if the intakes get clogged..."

"I'm way ahead of you, sir." Gunn brought the plane around fast and headed for the nearest undamaged runway, this time landing at Villacoublay without incident.

As the fighter slowed and taxied toward a cluster of outbuildings, an official French police vehicle came alongside. The plane stopped and Gunn popped the canopy. Ardan exited the plane at the same time that a middle-aged man in an overcoat and fedora exited the car.

"Doctor Francis Ardan?" the policeman inquired.

"Yes."

"I am Inspector Maigret of the Sûreté." Maigret displayed his identification to the bronze man. "I must speak with you immediately. In private. Will you come with me, please?"

Doc dryly thanked Major Gunn for the interesting flight and entered the Inspector's vehicle. Maigret promptly sped away, dodging the gaping fissures in the pavement which looked as if they had been smoothly dug out of the ground, as if with an ice cream scoop.

"Doctor, do you have any idea how these giant craters in the runway came to be?" the Inspector asked.

"It appears that the rubble we were dodging as we tried to land came from the holes," Doc replied.

"But how is this possible?" asked Maigret with disbelief.

Instead, Doc responded with questions of his own. "What is this about, Inspector? Why did you meet me at the airfield?"

In reply, Maigret handed Ardan a slip of paper. "I received this very strange note this morning. It did not come by normal post. I had momentarily turned away, studying a case file, and when I turned back, the note was spiraling down through the air to land upon my desk. When I noticed this, I went to my office door and checked the hall, but there was no one. My office is situated such that I surely would have seen a messenger, and yet as I say there was nobody. This would have been extraordinary enough, but the contents of the note were even more peculiar, especially given what we both have just witnessed." He gestured that Ardan should read the note, and drove on.

My dear Inspector Maigret [the note began]–

Please excuse the unusual nature of this missive's delivery, but I implore you to treat it with the utmost seriousness. You will note the impending arrival this a.m. at Villacoublay airfield of Doctor Francis Ardan of New York City. He will arrive via RAF jet, and though he shall encounter some small difficulties upon landing, I trust he shall arrive intact. It is not my intent to discourage the good Doctor's advent in Paris. Far from it. Rather, this morning's unique exhibition should demonstrate to you both my utter power over this situation, and the futility of any opposition.

You shall meet the Doctor's plane immediately upon his arrival. You shall not notify your colleagues or anyone else of the contents of this message, with the exception of Doctor

Ardan. You shall immediately escort Doctor Ardan to the clinic on the Rue Mouffetard–you know the clinic to which I refer–and leave him there.

Do not deviate from these instructions in the slightest. The fate of two brilliant women depends on it. I would very much regret depriving the world of their future scientific contributions. Ardan understands.

Doctor Natas

The stone-walled chamber was smoke-filled, scented with a hint of jasmine incense. The lavish Oriental decor reminded Louise Ducharme of her time in Shanghai, China, when she was a researcher at the School of Medicine.

"Welcome to my humble clinic, Doctors." A man with the face of a devil, resplendent in his silk robes, emerged and ensconced himself in what was essentially a small throne. He fixed his diabolical gaze on mother and daughter, Louise and Justine Ducharme.

Louise visibly blanched.

"Yes, Doctor Ducharme, it is I," came the sibilant reply. "It has been a long time. But not so long, I see, that you forget your former opponent. I am honored." He turned to the younger woman.

"Doctor Ducharme–I shall call you Justine, in order to distinguish from your honored mother–Justine, I will come straight to the point. You are a recognized expert in theoretical physics, specifically the disassembly, transmission and reassembly of solid objects. Your experiments with Professor Rushton are legendary among my scientists, and I expect great things from him. But you are in Paris, and he is not. Thus, your presence here."

"Professor Rushton!" Justine exclaimed. "But that research is classified!"

"My dear, nothing is hidden, nor remains hidden, if I wish it to be revealed. You, Mademoiselle, have knowledge which I require, expertise in the area of accurately directing and controlling the integrity of the matter transmission over large distances. You shall be escorted to my laboratory, where you will consult with several other professionals in my service. They will brief you on the precise information which we require from you. Your mother is here to ensure your cooperation. That is all."

"Who are you?" Justine demanded. "How dare you?"

"Your mother knows me as Doctor Natas, and I dare much, my child." There was no flicker of recognition in Justine's gold-flecked eyes. "I see you are not familiar with the name."

Natas directed an inquiring glance at Louise. "So you never told her the tale? The story of our adventure together in Tibet? Never told her of Doctor Ard– "

"That's enough," Louise interjected. "We are here. You have us. Get on with it."

Natas' cat-like green eyes blazed briefly, but his visage quickly calmed. "You are right, of course. Time is of the essence." He clapped once, and two lascars emerged from behind the throne. Natas pointed to Justine. "Escort the doctor to the laboratory."

The two burly men took Justine by each arm and directed her to a wall of bookcases, one of which slide aside to reveal a hidden elevator. As the three entered the elevator cage, Justine turned and looked imploringly at her mother, but Louise merely nodded reassuringly. Then the elevator's folding door closed and they were gone.

Louise looked at the satanic visage of Doctor Natas. Twenty-two years ago, he had held her and Doctor Francis Ardan captive in his "City of Gold and Lepers," hidden deep in the wasteland of the Koko Nor desert of Tibet. Then, Natas had mastered the alchemy of converting base matter to gold. He had captured dozens of eminent scientists–including Doctors Francis Ardan and Louise Ducharme–as well as thousands more menial workers. All the prisoners had been held as slaves, hostage to an especially virulent form of leprosy. Only the City's Z-Rays, another of Doctor Natas' discoveries, held the sickness in check. And thus had held Natas' slaves captive to toil in the City, for to flee was to die.

Natas had aspired to world domination, and would have achieved it, if not for Francis Ardan and Louise Ducharme.

Now, Louise's face took on an expression of profound disgust. "What do you really want from her?"

"Information, Doctor Ducharme, merely information."

"You won't get it."

"By hook or by crook, I will."

"She is but a girl!"

"She is of age. And she is genius... Just like her father. She will share her secrets. They will be safe with me."

Two more lascars appeared. "Take Doctor Ducharme to her room." The three entered the hidden elevator and disappeared from sight.

Another Asian man came forward from the shadows behind the throne. "You play a dangerous game, Master."

"Perhaps, Pao Tcheou, perhaps. I have been patient, have waited 22 years. I am close. The danger is necessary."

"But to lead Ardan here. It is hazardous," Pao Tcheou said.

"I decide what is necessary or not. Remember that, honorable cousin. When you lead the Council, you may decide."

"Master, you have my allegiance. But the other Council members do not have your foresight. They do not understand your plans. Fen-Chu, in particular, grows restless."

"Pao Tcheou, all is unraveling as I planned. I brought Doctor Ardan and Doctor Ducharme together all those years ago. I set them in the perilous circumstances that drew them to each other. Though they destroyed my City of Gold, it was I who won in the end. All is as it should be. You will reassure the Council," Natas said.

"Very well, Master."

"Excellent. And now, go to check in the laboratory. Ensure that Doctor Caresco is obtaining what he needs."

Pao Tcheou bowed deeply and withdrew.

"It is time," the villain Natas said to himself. Turning to a large apparatus in the corner of the throne room, he activated several switches. A screen came to life, and focused on the outside of the clinic, just around the corner from the nearby dairy. A police vehicle pulled up to the corner.

Arriving at the clinic on the Rue Mouffetard, Doc Ardan instructed Maigret to wait outside, but to bring police backup if he did not appear after four hours. Maigret agreed and turned to enter his vehicle. At the faint sound of a high-pitched whine, he looked up and saw a slight shimmer in the air, almost as if he were looking through waves of heat on the desert, although the waves were tinged with blue light.

And nothing else.

Ardan was gone, leaving nothing but the faint hint of ozone in the air, although he couldn't possibly have rounded the corner so quickly in the time Maigret had been turned away.

Doc Ardan materialized in Natas' throne room, appearing in mid-air and dropping to the floor. Cat-like, Ardan landed on his feet. He stared for long seconds at the Asian man standing by the apparatus in the corner, an assemblage of electrodes, antennae and globes topping a control panel of knobs, switches and sliding levers.

"Congratulations, Doctor Ardan," Natas said, assuming his seat in the room's center. "You are as agile as ever. The perfect physical and mental specimen."

"That's an interesting trick," Doc said.

"Oh, that. Merely a refinement of a technology developed by another of your many foes, which was in turn based upon Nemor's Disintegrator."

"Yes, I know, the teleporter. That's how you abducted the women. Delivered the note to Maigret. And cast debris into the air at my plane."

Doctor Natas was only momentarily nonplussed. "Very clever, Doctor. I will not underestimate you again. Since you are familiar with the technology, you also know that the teleporter as originally designed only worked in a straight line, limiting its range. We have strengthened the integrity of the transmission stream considerably, but the device's range is still not to my satisfaction. Perhaps you would care to 'take a crack' at it?"

"I don't think so," Doc replied.

"Come now, Doctor. You and I are giants, supermen. Immortals, even! Does not the science of this device intrigue you? I fail to understand how you could let this technology languish these 14 years."

"I'm not surprised," Doc said wryly.

"Nevertheless, you will assist in the completion of the teleporter," Doctor Natas said. Six more brawny dacoits appeared from the shadows and took positions circling Doc.

"On no less than three separate occasions you have interfered with my plans," Natas continued, raising three long, clawed fingers.

"Tibet, 1927. The destruction of the City of Gold and Lepers. The dispersal of my labor force. That was a considerable inconvenience, Doctor." One finger curled inward.

"Limehouse, December 1931. You and Allard interfered with my plans and those of my colleague, Yu'An Hee See." The second finger closed, leaving one long forefinger pointing at Ardan.

"Haiti, April 1940. The complete destruction of my arsenal, including various advanced aircraft and submersibles." Natas closed his last finger into a fist.

Throughout this recitation, Doc had remained standing as motionless as a Greek statue, evincing no sign of emotion.

"You are a worthy adversary, Doctor Ardan, deserving of my respect." Natas paused. "But the scales must be balanced. Debts must be repaid. You will assist me with the teleporter."

"Enough of this charade, Natas," Doc said. "You've already kidnapped Justine Ducharme, and she's the expert in this area. Louise Ducharme is a medical doctor, so if you're only seeking to perfect your teleporter, then you have no reason to capture her, except to force Justine's cooperation. You don't need me at all."

"Au contraire, Doctor. You were present when the teleporter was first used. Doubtless you analyzed its secrets. You are a scientific genius in numerous fields of study, a genius perhaps only second to my own. Do this thing for me, and in consideration of our distant… familial relationship, I will release you unharmed."

Ardan's silence was his answer.

Natas gestured for the dacoits to close in on Ardan. "Take the Doctor to the laboratory," instructed Natas, but before the men could act upon that order, Ardan was a blur of bronze motion.

Two solid punches sent the first two men immediately to the floor.

As two more adversaries approached, Doc tore hanging shreds away from his already ripped shirt, took a classic Baritsu stance and waited for the men to press their attack. They coordinated their assault, and faster than thought, the men were flying through the air in different directions, hitting opposite walls and collapsing insensate on the ground.

The final two lascars appraised Ardan with more caution.

Ardan leaped, and before they could react, he was behind them, with each cabled bronze hand gripping them at the base of their necks and working at the junctures of neck and shoulder. Both attackers slumped to the floor, unconscious.

By this time, however, Doctor Natas had made it to the apparatus in the corner, manipulating several switches and dials. The granite ceiling above Doc's head was already enveloped in the shimmering blue light. Before even Ardan could react, chunks of stone were raining down upon his head, knocking him unconscious. Only the skullcap resembling his natural bronze-colored hair protected Ardan from suffering a concussion.

Natas pressed another button, and shortly thereafter Pao Tcheou appeared from the elevator hidden behind the bookcases.

"Put him with the others. We are almost done here," Natas said.

Pao Tcheou bowed deeply.

Ardan, Louise and Justine sat in a dank cell deep below Natas' throne room.

"Louise…" Doc had just awakened from the blow to his head.

"Francis," Louise asked with concern, "are you all right?"

"Yes, there does not appear to be any permanent damage."

"I gave you a quick once-over while you were still out, and I agree. Although I have to say this is obviously not the first time you've taken such a blow to the head. Or elsewhere, given all those scars."

Doc looked uncomfortable, and shrugged slightly, but didn't say anything.

"Thank you for coming."

Doc finally looked up and took in Louise's milky complexion and raven hair. Memories and emotions buried for 20 years came swirling back unbidden, but he quickly suppressed them. "Thus far, my presence here has been unproductive," Doc said ruefully.

"But you came. So thank you."

"You're welcome." Ardan looked over at Justine. Her eyes, swirling with gold-flecks, stared blankly into nothingness. "Is that…?"

"Yes. That is Justine. She appears to be hypnotized. They brought her back half an hour ago in this state, and she hasn't come out if it. I've examined her, and she appears to be unharmed, but nothing I do or say elicits a response."

There was an awkward silence, broken only by the incessant sound of water dripping outside the cell door.

Finally, Doc said, "I respected your wishes. I stayed away from you after Tibet. I didn't realize it was because we had a daughter." There was a hint of anger in his voice, although his face remained a bronze mask.

"I had hoped to spare Justine from incidents just like this one by raising Justine alone. You were prepared, trained in that strange program your father arranged, to fight evil all over the world. That is no life for a wife and daughter, and who was I to try to dissuade you from what you had spent your whole life preparing for?"

"Perhaps if I had known, I would have made a different decision."

"That is easy to say," Louise flared, "but it is rather less easy to overcome a lifelong program of indoctrination. Your path was set. It didn't include me. I missed you, and occasionally wondered… But I have not pined away for how it could have been. Justine and I have a good life, happy, safe and healthy. And from all the news accounts, and all the stories I've heard over the years of the people you've helped, I think things turned out the way they were supposed to."

Doc was quiet for a bit. Then, he ventured, "Many of those accounts are drastically exaggerated."

"Nevertheless." Louise was firm.

"Yes. Nevertheless." Ardan inhaled, exhaled deeply. "I had another child once, a son. Before we met."

"You never told me."

"No… It didn't turn out well."

"I'm sorry."

"You needn't be." Ardan looked over at Justine, noting her coppery blonde hair and bronzed skin. "She is a beautiful young woman. And intelligent. Her scientific reputation precedes her."

He paused, and then looking back to Louise, told her, "You've done a wonderful job raising her. You made the right decision."

Louise took Ardan's hand in hers and squeezed it, smiling. Then she took him in her arms. "Thank you, Francis," she whispered.

At a slight moan, they both looked over at Justine, who started to come out of her trance.

"Justine, Justine. Are you all right?" As the girl nodded, Louise went over to her. "This is my… colleague, Doctor Ardan."

"How do you do, Doctor Ducharme," Doc said formally. "How do you feel?"

"I feel very well, thank you. As if I have slept for hours…." She stretched.

"What happened in the laboratory?" Louise asked.

"I don't remember… We went to the lab. There were several men there, all in white coats. One gave me a brief physical exam, and took a tissue sample, which I thought was odd. Then he gave me an injection. The next thing I remember, I woke up here with you."

"Clearly," Ardan interjected, "Natas' men have managed to extract the information they wanted while you were under. Why else return you here so quickly? He must be stopped. Now that Justine is awake, we can leave."

"How do you suggest we do that?" Louise asked. "Shall we just ring for the porter and tell him we're ready to check out?

Without answering her directly, Doc unloosed his belt, aimed the buckle at the heavy cell door, and depressed a tiny switch. After about 30 seconds of this, while the two women stared at Ardan and began to doubt his sanity, the door latch started to glow with heat. Doc aimed a massive kick at the latch and the door flew open. He glanced at Louise expectantly, with one eyebrow raised ever-so-slightly–a habit he had also picked up from his old master M. Senak–and gestured for the two women to follow.

"I withdraw the question," Louise said.

Unhindered, the three traversed several maze-like corridors of the abandoned dairy underneath the clinic before they finally found the elevator's lower entrance. When they emerged on the top level from behind the hidden bookcase, Natas' throne room was deserted, save for the telltale hint of ozone.

Doc went over to the teleporter apparatus in the corner and examined it. Looking closely at the rematerialization settings, he noted that they were set for latitude and longitude coordinates which were across the globe. In China.

Doc, Louise and Justine emerged from clinic onto the Rue Mouffetard, and introductions were exchanged with Inspector Maigret. Ardan was quiet, reflecting that their escape was too simple. However, before Ardan could bring Maigret up to speed with the details of their ordeal, the call box outside the erstwhile clinic rang.

Ardan exchanged glances with the other three, and then walked over and picked up the receiver.

"*Oui?*"

A familiar mechanical voice recited, "*Important message for the Doctor. Important message for the Doctor. Important message–*"

"This is the Doctor."

Once again, a click indicated recognition of Doc's voice, and another wax cylinder in his New York headquarters carried its message over the Atlantic.

"Greetings, Doctor Ardan! I wished to set your mind at rest that, despite your interference in my affairs, I have extracted the information I needed from Mademoiselle Ducharme. The teleporter can now be aimed much more accurately and at much longer distances, as you no doubt saw when you examined my equipment. No, do not bother attempting to follow me, the apparatus has already self-destructed in the time it has taken you to evacuate the clinic and receive this message. And to further ensure that you do not attempt to follow me, I have arranged a further distraction for you, which, I assure you, you will ignore at your peril.

"I also pledge to you that Mademoiselle Ducharme will remain unmolested by me in the future. Please convey to Justine, and to her mother, my deepest regrets at inconveniencing them, and my warmest regards. They are both the finest examples of their gender, and come from excellent stock, as you well know. I have nothing but the highest admiration for them both. And for you, my dear Doctor. Goodbye."

The line clicked off and Doc hung up the telephone. He conveyed the gist of Natas' message to the two women and the Inspector. Natas' statement about Ardan interfering in his affairs struck him as strange, in this instance. Ardan had really done nothing substantial in terms interfering with Natas' plans and rescuing the two women, and yet Natas clearly wanted him to think he had. Why?

Nonetheless, Ardan kept his lingering doubts to himself. Instead, he told the two women that he had been considering a semi-retirement from his life of adventuring, in order to focus more of his energies on scientific research. He concluded by cautiously suggesting that he visit Louise and Justine when they had more time to become better acquainted. Louise looked skeptical, but Justine was enthusiastic.

"Yes, Doctor, I would like that. In fact, I would very much appreciate your input on a new area of research I've been contemplating with my British colleague, Dr. Rushton. It may be that in addition to teleporting objects from place to place, we can actually dematerialize them at one end of the process, and rematerialize them at a different size."

"The laws of physics—"

"Yes, yes, and just a few years ago conventional wisdom dictated that we would never exceed the speed of sound. The laws of physics state that objects cannot travel faster than light, and yet I firmly believe that as we learn more about the universe, the laws of physics will be rewritten to account for practical interstellar travel. Given your own inventions and scientific discoveries, and what we have seen today with that fiend Natas' teleporter, how can you disagree?" Justine challenged.

"In truth, I cannot," Ardan admitted.

"Very good. Now, if we can attain a practical means of rematerializing objects wholly intact, but at a much smaller size, why the possibilities for surgery, engineering–"

"Doctors, Doctors, please!" interjected Maigret. "There will be plenty of time later for these discussions. Right now I must insist that you all accompany me to headquarters, where I must take your statements and file a report on the kidnappings."

Ruefully, the three scientists agreed, and started to move toward Maigret's vehicle.

The call box on the Rue Mouffetard jangled again.

Doc raced back and picked up the phone.

"Doc, Doc, is that you?" a high-pitched male voice squeaked.

"Yes, you've tracked me down."

"Well," the squeaky voice continued, "it wasn't tough with that phone-tracker thing you invented. Lissen, anyway, Doc, you've got to get back here, quick! Somethin's up in Port City, just up the coast from Innsmouth. Some kinda creature washed ashore, complete with gills and scales and webbed feet and bulging eyes. Johnny's up there now, and even he can't identify it for sure. Best he can say is it's some kinda amphibian frog-thing."

"All right, Mo–"

"Hang on, Doc, there's more! There's some nutjob up there, calling himself Doctor Ariosto! He's stirring up the local Chinese immigrants with stories about this frog-boy, and it ain't helpin' that some of them are starting to disappear without a trace. Me and the boys are heading up there now! Lissen, Doc, where are you, anyway?"

"Go up to Port City to check it out. I'll meet you there as soon as I can," Doc said, and he hung up.

The distraction, Doc thought. He turned to Maigret. "I need to get back to Villacoublay airfield right away. Can you drive me, Inspector?"

Epilogue: Honan, 1951

Doctor Natas' eyes were heavy-lidded and opaque in the darkness of his reception chamber, which was only dimly lit by a few inadequate flickering sconces. The room was redolent with the fragrance of jasmine from a single cone of incense burning in a jade brazier.

Pao Tcheou's light footsteps padded quietly across the stone-tiled floor and stopped in front of Natas. He waited patiently for Natas to acknowledge his presence.

Natas' green-flecked eyes glistened as their nictitating membranes slid back. "Well?"

"Success, Master. As you know, after instigating the growth of a clone from the cultures and samples we took from Mademoiselle Ducharme in Paris, that madman Caresco was able to stimulate the clone's rapid growth to child-bearing age."

"Yes," Doctor Natas reflected, "Doctor Caresco may be mad, and his resistance is growing, but he remains under my control, for the time being. We shall dispense with him shortly. And the clone... That magnificent example of the female of the species has been scientifically selected from all the women of the world. And not only selected, but bred, by me. These Westerners are so charmingly predictable. It was frightfully easy to place her parents together in a situation which caused them to gravitate toward each other, so many years ago. Going back generations, Justine Ducharme had better breeding than one could have hoped for, even through a purposeful eugenics program. Justine Ducharme is among the most perfect women, both intellectually and physically, in the entire world. And so is her clone."

"It was a stroke of genius to cause Ardan to believe that once he had rescued the two women the matter was concluded," Pao Tcheou said.

"Yes," Natas agreed, "despite the vast resources at my disposal, I had no wish to suffer the ongoing distraction of making a permanent enemy of Ardan by kidnapping his daughter. His daughter's clone is more than sufficient, and Ardan need never know the truth."

Doctor Caresco entered the far end of the chamber and approached Doctor Natas and Pao Tcheou.

"Speak!" Natas commanded.

Doctor Caresco's face gleamed with dementia and the strain of continually trying to fend off Natas' controlling drugs. "As you know, Pao Tcheou successfully impregnated the clone of Mademoiselle Ducharme. The pregnancy has come to term successfully. The baby girl is strong and healthy."

"I am pleased," said Natas. "The girl will be called Ducharme, in honor of her 'mother' and 'grandmother.' She shall be prepared for a life in my service."

"Yes," replied Caresco, his voice thick with resistance, "the experiment has been a complete success. Justine's clone will be ready for you after she has recovered."

"How long?"

"Most likely, in a few weeks."

"Excellent. For 24 years, ever since I brought together Ardan and Louise Ducharme, two of the finest physical and mental examples of humanity who have ever lived, I have worked toward this moment. The result of their breeding, combined with my own mental perfection, shall culminate in the greatest living weapon ever created! The finest genetic background, combined with my eugenics expertise… My son will be a great avenger, whose spirit shall rise and advance over the West, striking without warning, and executing my will and vengeance wherever and whenever I see fit.

"And then…" Doctor Natas smiled diabolically, "the world shall hear from me again!"

Credits

The Midas Menace

Also Starring: **Created by:**

Also Starring	Created by
Francis Ardan Sr.	Guy d'Armen & Lester Dent
Josephine Balsamo	Maurice Leblanc
The Minions of Midas	Jack London
Grace Dunbar Gibson	Arthur Conan Doyle
Iverton	Arthur Conan Doyle
Jack Smith	Arthur Machen
J. Neil Gibson	Arthur Conan Doyle
Victor Savage	Arthur Conan Doyle
Culverton Smith	Arthur Conan Doyle
James Moriarty	Arthur Conan Doyle
The Black Coats	Paul Féval
Black Gulf Canyon Gang	Arthur Machen
Aloysius Doran	Arthur Conan Doyle
Count of Monte-Cristo	Alexandre Dumas
Francis Ardan Sr.	Guy d'Armen & Lester Dent
Mrs. Ardan	Guy d'Armen & Lester Dent
Long Island Cave	Arthur Conan Doyle & Robert J. Hogan
Palais-Metropole Hotel	Frank L. Packard
Ahaggar	Pierre Benoit

The Biggest Guns

Also Starring	Created by
Hans Von Hammer	Robert Kanigher & Joe Kubert
J.T. Maston	Jules Verne
Lord John Roxton	Arthur Conan Doyle
Pamela Thibault	Lester Dent & Pierre Saurel
Biggles	W.E. Johns

Andrew Blodgett Mayfair	Lester Dent
Theodore Marley Brooks	Lester Dent

The Star Prince

Also Starring: **Created by:**

The Little Prince	Antoine de Saint-Exupery

The Dreadful Conspiracy

Also Starring: **Created by:**

Inspector Ménardier	Arthur Bernède
Berthelaux	Vincent Jounieaux
Andrew Blodgett Mayfair	Lester Dent
Theodore Marley Brooks	Lester Dent
Monsieur Ferval	Arthur Bernède
Jules de Grandin	Seabury Quinn
Judex	A. Bernède & L. Feuillade
Leclerc	based on Dennis E. Power
Ivana Orloff	based on Henri Vernes
M. Ming (The Yellow Shadow)	Henri Vernes
The Shin Tan	Henri Vernes
Inspector Pujol	Claude Desailly
Inspector Terrasson	Claude Desailly
William Harper Littlejohn	Lester Dent
John Renwick	Lester Dent
Thomas J. Roberts	Lester Dent
Judge Coméliau	Georges Simenon
Doctor Lyndon Parker	August Derleth
The Si Fan	Sax Rohmer
Anton Zarnak	Lin Carter
Chantecoq	Arthur Bernède
Chevalier Auguste Dupin	Edgar Allan Poe
Comtes de Boehm-Orloff	Paul Féval
Commissaire Valentin	Claude Desailly
Doctor Septimus	Edgar P. Jacobs
The Mega Wave	Edgar P. Jacobs

The Depository Bank of Zurich	Dan Brown

Ardan at the Pole

Also Starring:	**Created by:**
Hareton Ironcastle	J.-H. Rosny Aîné
The Inutos	H.P. Lovecraft
The Lomarians	H.P. Lovecraft
Jean-Louis de Venasque	Charles Derennes
The People of the Pole	Charles Derennes
Michel Ardan	Jules Verne
Louis Valenton	Charles Derennes
Jacques Ceintras	Charles Derennes
Tsathoggua	Clark Ashton Smith
The Gun Club	Jules Verne
The God Slayer	Robert E. Howard

Family Reunion

Also Starring:	**Created by:**
Michel Ardan	Jules Verne
The Steam Dog	based on Jules Verne
The Gun Glub	Jules Verne
The People from the Pole	Charles Derennes
Antinea	Pierre Benoît
Dale Ardan	Alex Raymond
Dr. Zarkov	Alex Raymond
Flash Gordon	Alex Raymond
Psi Cassiopeia	C.I. Defontenay
John Savage	Agatha Christie
Henri "Monocard" de Lanselles	T. Varlet & A. Blandin
Professor Helvetius	Arnould Galopin
Button Bright Ardan	L. Frank Baum
The Morlocks	H.G. Wells
The Time Gem	Jim Starlin
Chronovores	Barry Letts

Iron and Bronze

Also Starring:
Hareton Ironcastle
N'desi
Harry Killer / Zanigew
Antinea
The Wandarobo
The Reaver of Worlds
Blackland
Gondokoro

Created by:
J.-H. Rosny Aîné
based on H. Rider Haggard
Jules Verne & Walter Gibson
Pierre Benoît
John Peter Drummond
based on H. Rider Haggard
Jules Verne
J.-H. Rosny Aîné

A Scientist First and Foremost

Also Starring:
The Beast of Gévaudan
The Werewolf of Paris
Félifax
The Beast

Prof. Lindenbrock
David Innes
Panic in Paris
Pellucidar

Created by:
Historical
Guy Endore
Paul Féval, fils
Gabrielle-Suzanne Barbot de Villeneuve
Jules Verne
Edgar Rice Burroughs
Jules Lermina
Edgar Rice Burroughs

Small Dreams of a Floating City

Also Starring:
Yarteb

Created by:
Peter Gabbani

The Eye of Oran

Also Starring:
Lieutenant Aristide
S.N.I.F.

Created by:
Vladimir Volkoff
Vladimir Volkoff

Doctor Natas / Li Chang Yen,	Guy d'Armen
	& Agatha Christie
Hanoi Shan / Fu Manchu	H. Ashton Wolfe
	& Sax Rohmer
Huan Tsung Chao	Sax Rohmer
Pao Tcheou	Edward Brooker
Fen-Chu	George Fronval
The Korean (OddJob)	Ian Fleming
Doctor Rieux	Albert Camus
The Diogenes Club	Arthur Conan Doyle
Raymond Rambert	Albert Camus,
	& Marcel Allain
	& Pierre Souvestre
Magistrate Othon	Albert Camus
Inspector Fabre	Leo Malet
Inspector Fauchet	John Pearson
James Bond	Ian Fleming
Adelaïde Johnston	Win Scott Eckert
	based on Maurice Leblanc
Violet Holmes	M. Baugh & Win Scott Eckert
The Silver Eye of Dagon	Roy Thomas
	based on Robert E. Howard
	& H.P. Lovecraft

Les Lèvres Rouges

Also Starring:	**Created by:**
Ilona Harczy	Pierre Drouot, Jean Ferry,
	Manfred R. Köhler
	& Harry Kümel
Countess Elisabeth Bathory	Pierre Drouot, Jean Ferry,
	Manfred R. Köhler
	& Harry Kümel
Nestor Burma	Léo Malet
Lt. Montferrand (Roger Noël)	Vladimir Volkoff
Jens Rolf	Anonymous
S.N.I.F.	Vladimir Volkoff

Florimond Faroux	Léo Malet
Le Chiffre	Ian Fleming
Plaster	Will Eisner
Cabiria	Federico Fellini, Ennio Flaiano & Tullio Pinelli
Manon Lescaut	Henri-Georges Clouzot & Jean Ferry based on Abbé Prévost
Zavatter	Léo Malet
The Fish-men	H. P. Lovecraft
Audrey (The Vine)	Charles B. Griffith
Adélaïde Lupin (Monique d'Andresy)	Win Scott Eckert based on Maurice Leblanc
The Silver Eye of Dagon	Roy Thomas based on Robert E. Howard & H.P. Lovecraft
Le *Cordon Jaune*	Ian Fleming
Radium-X	John Colton, Howard Higgin & Douglas Hodges

The Vanishing Devil

Also Starring:	**Created by:**
Louise Ducharme	Guy d'Armen
Sherlock Holmes	Arthur Conan Doyle
Roger Gunn	J.T. Edson
Jules Maigret	Georges Simenon
Doctor Natas	Guy d'Armen & Sax Rohmer
Pao Tcheou	Edward Brooker
Doctor Caresco	André Couvreur

www.ingramcontent.com/pod-product-compliance
Ingram Content Group UK Ltd.
Pitfield, Milton Keynes, MK11 3LW, UK
UKHW041410180426
11947UKWH00007B/33